Monday's CHILD

LINDA CHAIKIN

HARVEST HOUSE PUBLISHERS
Eugene, Oregon 97402

Cover by Koechel Peterson & Associates, Minneapolis, Minnesota

MONDAY'S CHILD
Copyright © 1999 by Linda Chaikin
Published by Harvest House Publishers
Eugene, Oregon 97402

Library of Congress Cataloging-in-Publication Data
Chaikin, L. L.,
    Monday's Child / Linda Chaikin.
        p. cm. — (A Day to Remember Series)
    ISBN 0-7369-0067-5
    1. Title. II. Series: Chaikin, L. L., A Day to Remember Series.
PS3553.H2427M66   1999
813' .54—dc21   99-20926
                                                                                          CIP

Printed in the United States of America.

                99 00 01 02 03 04 05 06 / BC / 10 9 8 7 6 5 4 3 2 1

FAMILY TREES

KLOSSNER FAMILY, ST. MORITZ AND DAVOS, SWITZERLAND:

Gerhart Klossner: doctor
Inger Grendelmier Klossner: Gerhart's wife
Franz Klossner: Gerhart and Inger's son
Anna Klossner: Gerhart and Inger's daughter
Peter Grendelmier: Anna's husband
Krista Grendelmier: Peter and Anna's daughter
Elsa Klossner von Buren: Gerhart's cousin and Wilhelm's wife
Henrich Klossner: Franz's cousin
Veena Klossner: Henrich's wife
Vonda Klossner Gotthard: Franz's cousin and Georg's wife

GOTTHARD FAMILY, ZURICH:

Josef Gotthard: owner of Gotthard Enterprises
Georg Gotthard: Josef's brother
Paul Gotthard: Georg and Vonda's son

VON BUREN FAMILY, ZURICH:

Wilhelm von Buren: retired banker
Ehrlich von Buren: Wilhelm and Elsa's son

COHEN FAMILY, AUSTRIA:

Benjamin Cohen: tailor
Sarah Cohen: Benjamin's wife
Judith Cohen: Benjamin and Sarah's daughter
Reuben Harman: Judith's husband
Tirzah Cohen: Benjamin and Sarah's daughter
Fritz Cohen: Benjamin and Sarah's son
Stella Cohen: Fritz's granddaughter

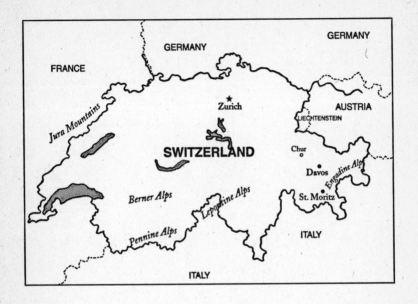

1

ZURICH

Krista walked uphill from the von Buren mansion near Bergstrasse 19. If she were under surveillance her mid-morning stroll appeared ordinary enough: between modeling assignments for Gotthard Enterprises she always came home to Switzerland, often to Zurich in particular, for a warm, loving visit with her bachelor uncle, Franz Klossner. Nothing surprising there. She was very devoted to Uncle Franz. He had taken her under his wing when she was twelve and raised her after the tragic death of her parents in a climbing accident near the St. Moritz ski lodge, now run by her cousin, Henrich Klossner.

Yes, she thought as she walked along the Zurich street. Anyone who cared to notice could see that she and Uncle Franz were close. There would be no reason to question her visit. And she also shared a strong interest in his work as head professor of Swiss and German history at the University in Zurich's Old Town. Why, she might even have followed his steps and opted for a teaching career in history herself, except for her appearance. The tweed and oxford society of the conservative academic world would not take a beautiful woman seriously.

Her mouth tightened as she trudged uphill against the bone-chilling wind. At least Interpol found her appearance an asset for their cause in Europe; she was above suspicion. Her face might adorn Europe's esteemed fashion magazines, but it was also useful for the underground work that secretly linked Gotthard Enterprises with international espionage.

What would Uncle Franz do when Paul broke that news to him this morning? Paul would be waiting at her uncle's apartment when she arrived. It was Franz's birthday and the best excuse she had to bring him the small, rare copy of an early history of Roman rule in Zurich. She'd stumbled upon the book during her last modeling job in Venice while roaming the little used bookshops with Paul.

Her thoughts turned again to her concerns about working with Interpol. What is the new job all about this time? she wondered. Paul had told her so little in last night's late telephone call at the von Buren mansion. Her mission was simple, he had told her. While on her way this morning to see Uncle Franz she was to visit B. Rhinefelden's out-of-print bookshop and purchase another book—this one of old World War II photography, taken by Elsa Klossner von Buren. The book would be on display in the window. Everything had been arranged beforehand and should go smoothly. She was not to worry.

Krista's supple black leather boots echoed across the damp cobbles as she began the climb up the street that circled the University. Wherever she looked there were Gothic buildings, some with stone spires and what she considered ugly little demons—gargoyles grinning at her in stone.

The chill wind blew against her and she pushed her gloved hands deeper inside the pockets of her ankle-length black coat. The weak February sunlight failed to warm the stone where frost lingered, glistening on venerable old buildings. The two- and three-story cloistered houses, occasionally interspersed with small town squares, lined the hilly, twisting streets that stretched from the University's heights down to the shores of the blue-gray River Limmat that eventually flowed into the German Rhine.

She paused to look back in the direction from which she had come, studying the shore of the lake below as if seeing it for the first time. Her eyes were busy, making sure she hadn't been followed by a man she had first noticed in Rome.

This morning she thought the river looked sullen and secretive. She knew that the river was concealing an age-old past, like many of the Swiss who, for the first time that she could remember, were being asked probing questions about their neutrality during the war across their northern border. Had Swiss Banks cooperated with Nazi Germany by laundering looted gold reserves from the occupied countries of Belgium, France, and Poland in order to finance Hitler's Third Reich and its atrocities?

The scandal grew, for it was also common knowledge that Europe's Jewry, faced with growing anti-Semitism under Hitler's dictatorship, had tried to preserve their family wealth from confiscation by sending it into neutral Switzerland before being sent to the death camps. But now, many of those same banks were under scrutiny for continuing to hold onto perhaps billions in secret numbered accounts, while refusing to disclose information to the families of the holocaust victims. Jewish groups wanted the matter looked into with restitution made to the rightful heirs. Meanwhile, the bankers were accused of delay tactics. In response, some Swiss bankers and political leaders in Switzerland had made what Jews considered anti-Semitic remarks. Apologies were demanded, resignations were on the brink. It was an ugly time, and even more disturbing to her, Paul seemed to think the family might somehow be involved. For Krista, the thought was revolting.

"At all costs we must save our good name," he had told her.

"Our good name?" she had countered. "What is that when our nation may have turned its back upon thousands of desperate people trying to reach our neutral border, leaving them no alternative but to return to Adolph Eichmann's gas chambers?"

"That has yet to be proven," he had said stiffly.

As she stood looking down at the Limmat, Krista felt unduly cold. Perhaps it came from the unpleasantness brooding on the horizon and the thought that her future was changing more rapidly than she could handle in her own strength. The months and years flew by and subtle changes were occurring in her faith. Franz had given her a new Bible for Christmas. She renewed the decision to begin reading it again in earnest.

The shoreline of the lake was packed with turn-of-the-century houses and small private boats. Paul kept his luxurious yacht anchored on the left shore of the lake. The two of them had once gone sailing on a pleasant Sunday afternoon. After attending the church service at the historical Grossmunster where Zwingli had preached the Reformation, she and Paul had enjoyed a leisurely luncheon at one of the popular cafes on the Uto Quai—the wide promenade connecting the small harbors—then they enjoyed the view on the lake until late afternoon when the sun set. They had walked back uphill to the University where her uncle was waiting for them in his comfortable apartment with coffee and Swiss chocolate. Such pleasant Sundays would eventually draw to a close after an evening discussing history and literature. Yes…those had been better days, and it felt to her that the time for them was also drawing to a close.

Krista watched the wind beat the lake into silvery ripples as a few clouds gathered near the lower hills overlooking the water. In the distance, behind the hills, monumental snow-clad Swiss peaks gazed down on Zurich as though undisturbed by the modern rush of civilization. She cooled her emotions by taking a moment to dismiss the tension from her mind. The Alps dwarfed and humbled everything. The grandeur and stability declared the Creator's sovereignty over men and nations as well as the diabolical forces that ruled unregenerate political leaders. Natural man's tainted history might flow onward like the Limmat, but his final journey would always lead to a righteous accounting.

Krista turned away casually, as though in no hurry, and continued her trek uphill toward the University. She had gone a third of the way up the street when she neared the bookseller's shop. She paused as she had done at some other store windows and looked at the items on display. Her gaze fell to the narrow window space and studied the copies of rare books. Yes, it was there, the book Paul had telephoned her about last night. A 1938 edition of photographs taken in Austria and Berlin by an inexperienced photographer named Elsa Klossner who had been hardly out of her teens. Paul had told her the family didn't realize there were any surviving copies and it was important to visit the bookstore and purchase it. He hadn't explained more on the telephone, and she knew enough of Paul's ways not to ask. At least not now. She needn't worry about the price, he had told her. All the cumbersome details had been previously arranged with the owner. She was to merely buy the book and bring it with her. Paul would be discreetly visiting Uncle Franz at the University. He would arrive unnoticed and leave in the same way. She was not to worry, he had repeated.

She did worry. Her heart beat faster. The other books in the display were on history, with title pages open to scrutiny and yellowing with age. Elsa's collection of old black and white photography might show her early ama-teurish style, but the photograph on the book's open page was graphic, evoking memories of dark and violent history. She looked at it more carefully. It was the Austrian Prime Minister Englebert Dollfuss, a somewhat handsome looking man, arms swinging at his side as he strolled in uniform before Austrian troops. The caption below the photograph read: "Dollfuss before his assassination."

In the summer of 1934, a year after Hitler came to power, the Nazi Party had been outlawed in Austria and had gone underground, infiltrating the government. In order to bring Hitler's birthplace under German control, Nazi thugs had staged a plot to storm the Austrian palace. They brutally murdered Prime Minister Dollfuss and other officials in the palace who had been opposed to Hitler's young Nazi party, and afterward placed a Nazi stooge over Austria, thus establishing the first Nazi government. The stunned populace had no organized response.

Why did it seem that those committed to evil were able to conquer with methods that the righteous could never use, Krista wondered. She remembered that Uncle Franz always pointed her back to his favorite Psalm, 37. "Fret not because of evildoers...for they shall soon be cut down like the grass, and wither as the green herb…do not fret because of him who prospers in his way, because of the man who brings wicked schemes to pass. Cease from anger, and forsake wrath; Do not fret—it only causes harm. For evildoers shall be cut off; But those who wait on the Lord, they shall inherit the earth. For yet a little while and the wicked shall be no more…"

Krista glanced up and caught her reflection in the shop window. Whenever she talked about the Bible, Paul was amused. "You just don't look the serious sort." That remark always disturbed her. The striking image frowning back was that of one of Europe's top-paid models who, though usually draped in sleek black velvet when displaying glittering Gotthard diamonds, presently appeared as a somber twenty-four-year-old woman with flaxen hair, eyes now as hard as turquoise, flawless pale skin, and a mouth drawn tight.

At least I won't be recognized, she thought.

She entered the bookshop, the tinkling bell chiming. She whiffed heating oil, old paper, and morning coffee from a small crowded room in the back. A heavy white-haired man with rimless glasses came out and looked at her with keen pale eyes.

"Guten Tag, fräulein," he murmured softly.

"Yes, good morning," she repeated casually, glancing about. Someone else was in the bookstore. He wore a nondescript gray raincoat and Homburg hat. His shoulder was toward her as he leaned by a shelf reading an old book. Something about him troubled her, but she couldn't decide what it was. She walked up beside him, pretending to look on the shelf where he lounged. "Excuse me," she said in German. He moved to the side, but continued to read. She was aware of his height and a muscular build. A skier? Climber?

"Excuse me again, have we not met before?" It was a bold thing to do, perhaps foolish, but she could not walk out with Elsa's book if there were any chance she was being watched. Paul had told her the shop would be empty, but he couldn't manage everything. Why hadn't the owner kept the store closed until he saw her at the window? She had worn a green scarf around her neck as Paul had requested. The shopkeeper, she noticed, hovered in the background looking nervous.

She had forced the patron to look at her, always dangerous but now, necessary. He did so without apparent concern, adjusting a pair of tortoiseshell-rimmed glasses. He removed them and looked at her squarely. Krista peered into a pair of dull gray eyes with a glassy expression. "Nein," came the brisk German. "Are you a friend of my wife?" He removed his Homburg, revealing tight curly auburn hair.

She murmured her apologies and he waved them aside and turned back to his book. She had noted the title, *The Reformer Zwingli.*

Mr. Rhinefelden spoke from behind her. "Professor Zimmer, I have found the other book on Zwingli you wanted. Shall I wrap it?"

"Yes, please. Include this one as well." He handed it to the little round man and excusing himself again, stepped around her and walked up to the counter to pay.

When he had gone, the door chimes still pleasantly ringing, Mr. Rhinefelden removed his glasses and shined the lenses on a long white handkerchief.

"You have met Professor Zimmer before, at the University perhaps? A friend of your uncle?"

He was too curious. "No, my mistake," she said.

"Professor Zimmer comes here every week."

Was it her own uncertainties or was Mr. Rhinefelden a little too anxious to explain Professor Zimmer's presence? She showed no interest—she had already shown too much. Paul would reprimand her for it if he knew.

"The book?" she asked simply, glancing toward the store window. The sun had disappeared and it was becoming gray and windy. "Looks as if it is going to rain soon. I must hurry."

"Yes, yes, it is here on the counter waiting for you, Fräulein von Buren. Will there be anything else I can help you with?"

He had already brought the book from the front window and wrapped it in brown paper. "That will be all," she told him, walking up.

He handed it to her, watching the door. Krista placed the package in her leather satchel, thanked him, and walked to the front.

"Auf Wiedersehen," she said as she left the warm enclosure.

"Auf Wiedersehen," he called as the chimes again tinkled.

On the narrow street again, Krista braced herself against the wind. Before walking on she glanced at the display in the front window. Yes, the book was gone. She turned and resumed the climb uphill toward the University district. She half expected to see Professor Zimmer a block ahead of her on his way to class, but he was nowhere in view on the street. Perhaps he had stepped inside one of the other shops, or had made better speed than she. There was a bakery ahead that was often crowded with professors and students. Perhaps he had stepped inside.

Once more her nerves were pricked by the obvious: if he had been planted there to watch her, her little tactic to force eye contact may have been a mistake. She had gotten a clear look at him. That was always dangerous.

With the tense moment in the bookshop over, Krista was soon her optimistic self again. She hurried on energetically into the opposing wind. It would be good to see Uncle Franz's smiling face after being gone for two months. She always looked forward to returning to her roots, forgetting the flashing cameras, the fashion reporters, and the dozens of wealthy, powerful men trying to make lavish dinner appointments with her. Her automatic refusal was smiling but perfunctory. "Thank you, but I have another engagement."

Yes, it would be stimulating and spiritually edifying to talk with dear Uncle Franz in his comfortable apartment, all pretense of bright glamour far removed. She held the satchel closely against her side, her boot heels clicking.

2

The rolling green lawn in front of the graystone University was immaculately trimmed. The trees were well-rounded and the rosebushes were protected from cold temperatures, both waiting for the first new buds that would appear in early May. Krista followed the stone walkway toward the lodge behind the classrooms. The college porter greeted her and opened the private gate.

"Professor Klossner sent word he would be in his apartment. Shall I ring him you're coming?"

"Yes, please." She smiled her thanks and as he went inside his bungalow, she quickened her pace through the stone quadrangle.

The two-story lodge stood in the back of the campus before a thick wall of fir trees, the branches casting shadows on the slanting roof. Krista walked to the last apartment on the ground floor and thumped on the double-thick pine door.

Franz Klossner opened it quickly. Her friends were usually surprised when they saw her "old professor uncle."

"The way you talk about him conjures up visions of a sprightly old man with white hair." They would always look at her surprised and whisper: "Why, he's handsome. And he doesn't seem old at all."

Franz always laughed at that. "Well I hope I'm not decrepit yet," he would say. He habitually took long nightly walks about the campus or Zurich's Old Town and refused to own an automobile. Each summer he went off alone to climb the Swiss mountains he loved, using his Cousin Henrich's lodge, situated between the two famous ski resorts of ritzy St. Moritz and popular Davos, as his headquarters. He was of sturdy height and frame, with brown hair, just beginning to gray at the temples, and pleasantly handsome features. He looked relaxed in a comfortable rust-colored corduroy jacket and darker brown turtleneck sweater.

Although he had never married there were rumors that he might consider changing all that. He was continuing to correspond with Trudy, the Christian woman that Cousin Henrich had hired to run the ski school connected with St. Moritz. Usually in a mellow mood, he had a passion for Swiss chocolate, coffee, old books, and French street paintings in oils. "I love the smell of old books," he had told her when she was thirteen. "There is a wonder in musty white pages filled with black words. But the best Book of all is the Bible. His words never grow old. They offer hope and life to every new generation."

Yes, that was her Uncle Franz. A sometime cynic, but more often than not, an optimist. A man who loved to lounge in an overstuffed chair with old books and a pipe, but who had the physique of an out-of-doors-man. However, this morning Franz was not smiling.

"Come in, Krista." He kissed her forehead and drew her inside the warm room. "You look frozen. Warm yourself by the fireplace. Paul made coffee and Ursula dropped off a chocolate cake. Cake! This early!" he chuckled. "Leave it to my housekeeper, bless her heart. Too bad she won't be here to clean up after us."

"Happy Birthday, Uncle Franz!"

The modest living quarters were full of rich brown leather and heavy wood. It was a man's world, a bachelor's room, but one she felt welcome in and at home. A fire invited from the hearth. There were ponderous chairs on either side and tables stacked with newspapers and prestigious literary journals. The middle of the room was open for pacing, a habit both Franz and Paul appeared to enjoy. Recently, Krista had begun to cultivate the annoying habit. A large front window with heavy forest-green drapes drawn back faced outward onto the side campus lawn. About a hundred feet away stood an old oak tree with expansive overspreading branches.

There was a wrapped birthday present from Paul sitting on the low table and a pot of coffee by the milk chocolate frosted cake.

As she entered, Paul Gotthard came forward from the fireplace in a brown tweed jacket and wool trousers. His sandy-colored hair was waved, and his light olive-green eyes were cautiously veiled as he smiled but glanced momentarily at her satchel. He could have passed as a fellow instructor with Uncle Franz at the University instead of the wealthy heir of his own bachelor uncle, Josef Gotthard of Gotthard Enterprises.

"Hello darling," Paul said, taking her shoulders and barely brushing a greeting on her cheek. "You managed?"

She knew what he meant, but Uncle Franz did not. She smiled cheerfully while pulling off her gloves and removing her hat. "It wasn't difficult at all. I enjoyed the brisk walk."

Paul assisted her with her coat, checking his Swiss gold watch. *You're late*, his glance suggested. *A cause for worry.*

Uncle Franz did not appear to notice the wordless exchange. He handed her a steaming mug of coffee and refilled Paul's, then removed her satchel from the chair, placing it on the end table. "Heavy...dear girl, did you carry this uphill from von Buren's place? Feels like an encyclopedia. Did you buy me a book?"

"Uncle Franz! You're not suppose to ask that," Krista teased.

Paul shot a glance toward him.

"I don't suppose anyone is ready for breakfast," Franz said wryly, looking at the chocolate cake.

Krista sank into the comfortable chair. "Home sweet home, Uncle Franz." She sipped her coffee. Then she noticed that Paul's square jaw had tightened. What was wrong? Had she missed some exchange?

Franz set the cake aside. He picked up the wrapped birthday present that Paul had brought and untied the ribbon. "Ah, a new Homburg. Just what I needed, Paul." He tried the brown hat on.

Paul looked down at Krista. "You have a present for Franz?"

Krista set her cup down and picked up her satchel. She unbuckled the leather strap and her fingers brushed against both books. Her conscience was pricked by the thought of misleading her uncle, but she convinced herself that she wasn't actually deceiving him. Since his Cousin Elsa's book wasn't meant for him, storing it in his collection was merely a safeguard, though she knew her excuse was a lame one. She felt a sudden irritation toward Paul for putting her in this situation, but knew the choice had been hers to make.

She dug out the book she had bought in Venice, still wrapped in brown paper. "Not exactly birthday bright, and it has a small tear on the dust jacket, but I knew you were searching for this one so I bought it when Paul and I were working in Venice."

Krista stood and handed the small volume to Franz.

His eyes twinkled as he removed the brown paper and tossed it into the fire. He then inspected it with pleasure. "A rare find, Krista! I didn't think there were any left of this first edition."

"That's probably the only one left," Paul said. "Krista and I were lucky to run across it."

"Interesting." Franz put on his glasses and carefully leafed through it. "It is in excellent condition. The collector I do business with in Vienna would pay handsomely for this, but it's a gift I could not part with."

"So it's best he never knows," Paul said with a friendly laugh. "Some of those collectors are like bloodhounds. Once they pick up a scent they never give up."

"You're right. This volume shall be our little secret—at least until Krista wishes to sell my collection when I leave it to her in my will."

"Don't even talk of such things," she scolded, looping her arm through his. "You're more important to me than any book collection, even if it is worth thousands of francs."

"She's right," Paul said. "Nevertheless, Franz, I hope you took my advice and had the collection insured. Anything could happen besides burglary. Even a fire."

"No need to worry. Everything is taken care of. Krista, why not go ahead and cut the cake? I'll put this book away until I can enjoy it."

She and Paul watched Franz take it to the little antechamber off from his drawing room. It was there that his rare collection was kept, some of them behind a glass book shelf under lock and key. Paul turned to her. Krista removed Elsa's book from her satchel. Paul murmured in frustration about the wrapping paper. It took a moment to remove it. He handed it to her. She watched him go to the common bookcase where he slipped it unobtrusively into the lower shelf behind several others.

"I don't like deception," she whispered.

"Neither do I. It's only for a short time. We'll explain everything to him eventually."

"Why not now? What's the secret? He can be trusted."

"Of course he can, but the less he knows the safer he'll be."

"Safe? From what?" she glanced worriedly behind her toward the anteroom. Franz was still busy.

"I intend to explain to him this morning about Interpol. But Elsa's book is best kept a secret until this matter of Swiss cooperation with the Nazis has died down."

Mention of the Nazis sent a cold ripple along her nerves. So that was it. Cousin Elsa's work in Berlin during the war. "You're not suggesting that Elsa was a willing Nazi..."

"No, but we cannot permit a rush to judgment. Any breath of scandal, though unfounded, will hurt Gotthard Enterprises. It will do us all harm." He looked at her, his olive-green eyes chilled. "Even you."

"Me!" she breathed, shocked, then unbelieving: "But..."

He laid a firm grip on her arm, glancing toward the anteroom. "Not now!"

Franz's footsteps were heard returning. She moved quickly away from Paul toward the birthday cake. Paul was swiftly beside the fireplace warming himself when Franz walked into the drawing room. He looked cheerful. "There. The book is safe. A wonderful gift, Krista."

Any joy she would have felt over his pleasure was now gone. She avoided his eyes and cut the cake. She felt two warm spots in her cheeks. "Breakfast or not, we must taste it," she managed brightly. "Ursula went to a lot of trouble."

"I'll try a slice," Paul said congenially, coming toward the table. "I'll have a little more of that coffee too."

Krista noticed the morning paper that sat on an ottoman, along with the *New York Times*. The ominous black headlines stared at her, adding strength to Paul's warning about scandal: SWISS BANKS ACCUSED OF HOLDING BILLIONS IN JEWISH ASSETS, "ZURICH MUST OWN UP," JEWISH GROUPS ANNOUNCE, and SWISS BANKERS— HITLER'S WILLING PARTNERS?

Krista handed the dessert plate with a slice of cake to Franz. The headlines' probing questions made her uncomfortable. She had always been proud of being Swiss. Her ancestry conjured up thoughts of neutrality and humanitarianism. A white cross on a red banner was the emblem on the Swiss flag. And now—

Perhaps she should have taken a few minutes to look at Elsa's book before turning it over to Paul.

With each tick of Franz's heirloom clock on the mantle the mood in the drawing room grew more tense, or was it her imagination? By the time they had finished their cake, the birthday celebration was far from anyone's mind. Uncle Franz surprised her with his statement: "Paul finds himself in an uncomfortable position. He appears to have gotten Gotthard Enterprises into a cloak and dagger espionage situation. Of course you wouldn't know anything about that would you, Krista dear?"

She glanced at her uncle and saw a rueful smile. She looked quickly toward Paul. Then he had already explained some of her ventures in Rome?

"How much are you involved in this, Krista?" Franz asked gravely.

"Espionage?" she repeated innocently, gaining time as she glanced again toward Paul.

"She's not involved," Paul said. "And more correctly, Gotthard Enterprises stepped into trouble and Krista has supported me."

Krista was no longer resorting to innocence as she looked at Franz. "Anything I've done to cooperate has been quite small, Uncle."

Franz appeared to want to draw the curtain of secrecy aside. "Out with it, Paul. It's no good trying to pad things by keeping me in the dark. Not if you expect our cooperation."

Our cooperation. What did he mean?

Paul walked to the window, then back again as though he couldn't keep still. He sat down in the nearest chair facing Franz at the fireplace. As he looked from him to Krista, she guessed he was making up his mind about how much he could explain. She realized suddenly that he had changed since their return from Venice two weeks ago. She had noticed yesterday on the phone, but only now fully grasped the impact. More than ever, Elsa von Buren's little book of photography began to worry her.

Paul appeared thoughtful. Perhaps worried too. Naturally he would be since he was managing the jewelry fashion business for Josef Gotthard. Paul was the heir of his elderly bachelor uncle who was related to Wilhelm von Buren through marriage. Both she and Paul had been raised by their respective uncles after their parents' deaths. As for Josef, no one, so it seemed, had heard from him since he had departed for the diamond mine in South Africa five months ago, and Paul was carrying on as liaison.

"You're right, Franz," Paul was saying. "The reason for my visit this morning has more to it than your birthday."

Franz retrieved his old pipe from among some others on the mantle. He reached for his tobacco can and filled it. "Does this trouble Gotthard Enterprises finds itself in have a connection with the banking scandal?"

"No, why should it? Gotthard is completely separate from the Swiss banks. Uncle Josef would never approve. The banks are Wilhelm's concern."

"I suppose you're right. I sometimes get Josef confused with Wilhelm von Buren."

Paul looked at him. He laughed. "I don't see why. They look nothing alike. There's no blood between them at all."

"No argument there. Didn't Wilhelm von Buren retire from the Bank of Zurich Corporation a few years ago?"

Paul lifted his cup and drank. "Three years ago to be exact. Ehrlich has taken his place," he said of Wilhelm's son. "What made you think this might have a connection with the bank?"

Franz struck a match and held the flame to his pipe. "No secret there. Everyone is talking about the scandal. It's in the morning papers. Ehrlich will be meeting with Jewish representatives tomorrow."

"Yes," Paul said crisply. He began to pace.

Although Krista was not related by blood to the von Burens or the Gotthards, she did have distant connections through marriage: Elsa was a cousin of her uncle, Franz Klossner. She sat stiffly, looking from one to the other, trying to guess what really lay beneath the surface of their questions and answers.

"And this situation you mentioned before Krista arrived," Franz said, "of what connection, if any, does it have with this scandal?"

Paul shrugged carelessly. "Oh, none, since Gotthard Enterprises is separate from the von Burens. The client is interested in a diamond showing, which Krista is often assigned to."

Krista raised her brows. "This is the first mention to me of a new client, Paul. Is there to be a showing here in Zurich?"

Paul looked at her. "Yes, I haven't had time to inform you, darling. I just explained it to Franz earlier. Our newest customer is a very wealthy woman named Ava St. John. She claims to be an actress and the heiress of an American movie producer. Her lawyer called me yesterday. He's one of those brash Americans, almost humorous. He fills in "double duty," as he put it. He's also her theatrical agent. His name is Jorden Keller."

There was a moment of silence. Krista looked over at her uncle. His pipe had gone out and he struck another match. He was staring at the clear, bright flame.

"Are you suggesting Mr. Keller is not what he claims?" Krista asked.

"We have only our suspicions to go on, but perhaps neither of them are what they claim."

"Oh? What makes you think so?" Franz asked, biting the end of his pipe.

"A hunch I suppose. For one thing Ava St. John insists on speaking with Krista alone. We might wonder why."

"Yes, we might," Krista said surprised. "What possible cause would she have?"

"That is what we hope to discover," Paul said.

Franz was thoughtful. "Then you don't know if their names are genuine, or who they might represent other than themselves?"

"No. It's important we find out. If she is who she claims, then Ava St. John is a tremendously important client. She's interested in buying the South African diamond collection, the one you modeled in Venice that Prince Ahmed wants to see in Monaco this April aboard his yacht."

Krista stood from her chair and moved restlessly about the drawing room. She did not care for the Saudi Arabian prince. She had first met him for a showing in Venice. Prince Ahmed had sent his bodyguard afterward to ask her to join a number of rich European guests in his suite of luxurious rooms. She had not cared to go, but she had, only to regret the decision soon after arriving since neither Paul nor anyone else was there. Krista had been able to escape the prince's attentions when a clumsy waiter had dropped a tray of caviar and champagne all over the prince. Before that incident had occurred, Ahmed had gone so far as to request her presence on a private cruise to the Mediterranean.

Paul was saying: "We're inclined to think Ava St. John's interest in seeing the collection is merely a front."

"For what?" Krista asked, frowning. Her thoughts swerved back to Elsa von Buren's book. "Thievery? A diamond heist?"

"No, seeking information, most likely," Franz offered.

Paul looked over at him curiously, but Franz was looking at his pipe.

"Interesting you would think so, Franz," Paul said. "What information and why?"

Paul shoved his free hand into his trouser pocket. He looked at Franz as though expecting an answer. Franz offered no explanation. He tapped the stem of his pipe against his teeth and leaned against the mantle. "Curious, all right," he agreed. "What cause do you have to suspect her and this lawyer agent beside a hunch?"

"It's not what I suspect, but what certain esteemed friends think."

Interpol, Krista thought.

"Do these 'friends' have any idea what kind of information Ava St. John may want from Krista?"

Paul waited a moment. "No. Nor do I. That is what we want to find out. It can be accomplished best by going through with the meeting. And so we need you once again, Krista," he said, looking at her worriedly.

"Do I dare be so bold as to ask who these friends may be?" Franz asked.

Paul turned his full attention on him. "That's why I'm here. These friends have agreed to let you and Krista know something more of what Gotthard Enterprises is really all about."

Krista already knew: espionage for the West. Gotthard Enterprises served a list of clientele from throughout the European and the Arab world that included both members of royalty and politics. The important clientele were not above passing on information to Paul and others in Gotthard when it was in their individual interest, or in their nation's interest, to do so. Gotthard Enterprises, in turn, passed that information on to the "friends" working with Interpol. So, at least, Paul had told her. She was surprised that he would tell Uncle Franz. Not that her uncle wasn't a stalwart, trustworthy man. But if he could explain his working with Interpol to Franz, why was it deemed precautionary to conceal Elsa's simple book of old World War II photographs she had taken? Why couldn't Franz be trusted with a family secret, if that's what it was?

Paul sat down and leaned forward in his chair, looking at Franz. "We are, shall I say, very friendly with Interpol."

Krista simply looked at him, but Franz held his pipe still.

Interpol, the International Police Organization, as Krista knew, was headquartered in Paris, and had in the past dealt mainly with tracking criminals who thought crossing a frontier would protect them. Paul told her they had more recently established their own counter-terrorism department.

"Are you suggesting Gotthard jewelry is a front for cooperation with Interpol?" Franz asked, mild astonishment in his voice.

"Gotthard deals in jewelry and gold," Paul stated. "The business also offers us a wide range of travel throughout Europe and sensitive locations, including the Middle East. We have many diverse and interesting clients."

"And contacts," Franz concluded for him with a meager smile.

"Yes."

Krista wondered if Uncle Franz would take Paul seriously, but the gravity of his gaze convinced her that he did. She wondered at the tense moment of silence that seemed to hang suspended between them, as though both men were waiting for something more from the other.

Finally Franz stirred, breaking the silence. "Well, Paul! I did not think you had it in you."

When Paul shot him a look that showed he was not altogether pleased with the remark, her uncle smiled and walked over to the window puffing on his pipe. "I thought you were a compromiser when it came to sacrificing personal gain for principles of good and evil."

"Thank you, Franz," came the barbed retort.

"No offense. I'm pleased to discover I was wrong."

"Really, Uncle," Krista scolded, "you need not be so condescending," and she glanced at Paul, hoping he wasn't too offended. Paul seemed more ironically amused than upset, as though he'd already known what Franz thought.

"It delights me to prove you wrong," he said, grinning.

"I'm sure it does. But using Krista? I don't like the notion of her being involved with Interpol. Are you telling me she has been in the past?"

Krista began to protest but Paul interrupted: "Only on inconsequential matters. So far, I have seen that she's been kept out of anything dangerous. But we'll need her more active involvement now. Ava St. John asked for her. We cannot do this next job without Krista. She'll need to meet with Miss St. John at the next showing."

Krista simply raised a shapely brow.

"Your greatest asset to us lies in your being kept in the dark. That way you'll behave normally when you meet with her to answer whatever questions she will ask." He turned to Franz. "For Krista, it will be just another showing. Like the hundreds of others she's participated in across Europe."

Uncle Franz had walked up and was watching them both. "What does Interpol expect them to try to learn from Krista?"

"All we know is that Ava and Keller want to meet with her alone. And they're going to a lot of trouble to arrange it. You add it up, Franz."

"It could be they want very little. They may be exactly who they say they are."

"They could be," Paul agreed. "If that's true, I'll be a happy man. I'd give almost anything to sell those diamonds before Josef returns."

Franz turned and studied Krista's face gravely. "What do you think could be their reason to meet with you?"

"I'm totally baffled by it. But…" she glanced from Franz to Paul. "There was someone following me in Venice. I first noticed him when we were sightseeing in Rome. You remember, Paul I mentioned it to you."

He frowned and opened his cigarette case, taking one. "You did? I don't recall. You must not have made much of an issue of it. I would have been very upset. Are you sure?"

"Certain." She looked at Franz but he was watching Paul. "Don't worry, Uncle," she hastened, "it couldn't have been very important. I'm up to another diamond showing. After traveling throughout Italy, Zurich will be easy. Afterward you and I can get in some skiing and a visit with Cousin Henrich at St. Moritz. It will be good for the family to be together again. And," she said, trying to ease his slight frown, "there is someone else at St. Moritz who is wondering why you haven't been skiing since before Christmas." Her hint about Trudy appeared to have not penetrated his armor.

"I wouldn't mind some skiing and climbing myself," Paul put in. "You see, Franz, stop worrying. Krista will be perfectly safe. If I didn't think she could pull this off I wouldn't have agreed to have her go through with it. As for your being informed about it—it's because you're her uncle. I couldn't bring myself to ask her to keep the modeling appointment without you knowing."

"My approval, though reluctant, is valuable, is that it?" Franz watched him over his pipe and a small haze of gray smoke.

"Without doubt."

"Well that's something," and he looked over at Krista. "Nevertheless, I don't like it."

She stood, and said in a low voice, "Come, Uncle, you must come to see it for what it is. There simply isn't any way I wouldn't help Interpol if they asked me."

"Yes. Clever of them to know that's how you feel about it."

From his tone it was clear he knew that Paul realized it as well.

Paul walked away and picked up his coffee cup from the table.

"I'll be talking with Jorden Keller soon. He'll let me know when Ava would like the showing. Once it's arranged I'll let you know, Krista."

Krista frowned. "I don't see how this will harvest any information, either for them or us."

"Only after you meet with them will we know. We want you to carry a small listening device. Everything discussed will be recorded for Interpol."

Franz poured coffee into his cup. "So what you really want to know is why Miss St. John is interested in Krista."

"I suppose you could put it that way. They must feel something important can be gained by all the trouble they're going through."

"Mostly to talk privately with Krista—and we haven't the foggiest notion what it is they are after?" Franz mused.

"No," Paul said. "No idea at all. Baffling, isn't it?"

Am I privy to some knowledge that even I don't understand? she wondered. Perhaps the answer was before her very eyes and she didn't see it. If she allowed it, the notion was rather unnerving.

With one hand in his corduroy jacket pocket, and the other holding his pipe, Franz walked about, concentrating on the pattern of interconnecting squares in the carpet.

When neither she nor Franz offered any further protests, Paul began to relax, as if he believed things were progressing after all. Franz stopped at the front window and stared out, hardly responding when Paul said he must be going.

Krista brought him his hat and raincoat and walked arm in arm with him to the front door. It was drizzling rain and the once pretty morning was gray and cold.

He took her hand into his and squeezed it, smiling grimly, his voice low. "Sorry darling. We wouldn't ask this of you if we didn't think it were important. I'll be in touch as soon as the final plans are ready." He turned and looked back at Franz. He was still looking out the front window as though unaware of them. "Good-bye Franz. I've asked permission to keep you posted. Your career here at the University is highly respected."

"Yes," he said over his shoulder, his voice preoccupied with his thoughts. "Good-bye, Paul."

Paul smiled. "I may stop by again to see you on Friday night. We still have that game of chess to work out."

Franz turned as he went out and watched the heavy door close behind him.

He remained by the window when Krista came back into the room.

"When did you first notice the man following you?"

"Rome, then Venice."

"You haven't noticed him in Zurich?"

"No..." she walked up beside him, watching the rain falling more heavily now, dripping from the fir branches. Her gaze skimmed the lawn, the shrubs. "I don't think we'll find our rabbit hiding anywhere about on a wet day like this, or should I say skunk?"

Their eyes met, then she turned, keeping her gaze from wandering to the bookshelf where Paul had concealed Elsa von Buren's book. More than ever she was curious. She turned her back on the shelf, as if by doing so she could end the nagging questions.

"Uncle Franz—do you know a Professor Zimmer?"

"Why yes, he's a fine historian on the Reformation."

She shrugged, relieved. "Well that accounts for his interest on a book on Zwingli."

"Why did you ask?"

"Oh, no reason, really. I think I embarrassed him, and myself as well."

"I doubt Zimmer could be embarrassed. He's conditioned to responding to his own world. It would take quite a jar to affect him."

Krista carried the dishes toward the kitchen.

"Besides, he's retired," Franz said.

She turned and looked back at him. "Retired? So soon?"

He arched a brow. "My dear, when I am eighty I shall retire too."

Krista stood there for a long silent moment. Franz had walked back to the chair near the fireplace. He picked up a piece of brown wrapping paper. "I thought I burned this." He turned it over, looking at it several times. Krista held her breath. What if the name of Rhinefelden's bookstore was stamped on it somewhere? She couldn't go on and lie further to her uncle.

She said quickly: "Were you surprised about Paul cooperating with Interpol?"

"Astonished is a better word for it. Paul and Interpol!"

"Yes, who would have guessed?"

Franz walked to the fireplace and tossed the paper into the flames. Her breath released. He stood fussing with his heavy tobacco tin. "I would not have guessed, certainly," he said. "It makes one wonder if that weren't his reason for telling me."

She looked at him strangely. "Whatever do you mean?"

"Oh, I don't know myself, exactly. Except it does appear curious to me why he felt he needed to confide in me today. I don't think his explanation was adequate."

His doubt surprised and worried her. "Well—it's obvious that he was showing concern. Respecting the brilliant professor who took me under his wing a number of lonely years ago and raised me. He wanted you to know I would be operating with him on this latest venture only if you honored that relationship."

"Do you think so?"

"Yes, it is so, Uncle. Paul thinks so much of you."

"I'd like to think so. But you'll admit, my dear Krista, that he never so concerned himself before. You've been modeling Gotthard jewels for five years. I never really approved of your travels. I trust you implicitly, but I had hoped you would go into teaching. I've always thought you looked better in a dirndl dress," he said of the native costume of the peasant girl.

"You're making me feel badly, Uncle Franz. I want to take some pride in my work. I don't want to apologize for what I do."

He looked at her gently. "And you can take pride. You've elevated the position you hold in Gotthard's. Don't pay any mind to my rumblings. What do you expect from an old professor?"

She smiled ruefully. "I don't think Trudy will agree with your explanation of yourself. And neither do I."

He grew serious again. "I don't know on how many occasions you've cooperated with Interpol, but this is the first I've heard about it. Would you mind telling me about the last time?"

Krista felt uncomfortable. "There were only a few times. Nothing important. Once in Paris when I was a carrier."

"A carrier of what?" he asked quietly.

"They wouldn't tell me. An envelope. I brought it to a jewelry shop."

"Where? Do you remember?"

"Boyers, on Francois Street. Another time I wore a listening device at a dinner table. For the life of me I still can't
understand why it was important, or what was garnered. It
was all simple dinner talk if you ask me." She set the tray
down and walked toward him.

"I should have told you sooner, Uncle Franz, but he
asked me not to."

"Which was wise." His blue eyes were sober. "If either
of you are going to play espionage you'd better cover your
tracks well so neither uncle nor enemy suspects you."

Though his eyes crinkled at the corners with intended
wry amusement, Krista picked up the underlying sobriety
in his warning.

"Now you know very well Interpol would never use me
for anything as important as espionage. I've no credentials.
I'm a complete amateur."

"Sometimes an amateur is what is needed. But you're
missing my point."

"Which is?"

"That in the past, Paul asked you to keep the matter
quiet. A healthy thing to do. Now, he went out of his way to
inform me of this cooperation with Interpol. All, so I
wouldn't worry about something I didn't know anything
about anyway."

He laughed unexpectedly when she frowned. "You do
get my point?"

She did. And had no satisfying answer.

"Oh well," he said. "I suppose I'm inclined to judge
Paul a little too harshly at times."

"You admit it!"

"Of course I do." He grinned. "I'm particular about the
man my girl is going to marry." He put an arm around her
shoulder and walked her toward the kitchen and the dirty

dishes. "I'm even going to show you my concern by washing up our mess this time. You can dry."

She laughed. "You won't find me arguing. But about Paul. I would think that you'd find my marriage to the heir of Gotthard Enterprises a satisfying match."

He looked at her doubtfully. "Financially, at least." Then, his eyes twinkled. "Why, you'd even be able to afford a dishwasher."

She glanced at him, shaking her head ruefully. He looked innocent as he opened the kitchen door for her to pass through.

Krista began to discuss other things. He had forgotten the brown wrapping paper, and she had nearly forgotten Professor Zimmer. Perhaps it was a fair exchange.

3

Krista's modeling career with the family-operated Gotthard Enterprises had taken several mountainous twists recently and Paul's phone call this morning was just the caboose at the end of a fast-moving train of events. Krista's fingers tightened about the telephone. "Today? But Paul—"

Paul's voice reflected his own brand of anxiety: "Look, darling, I'm almost helpless to stop things. This is just one of the daily fires demanding my attention now that I'm reporting directly to Uncle Josef. It's got to go forward as soon as possible. The woman and her agent are due to arrive in Zurich after lunch. She wants the jewelry showing *tonight*. She's going to be staying with friends in town and wants no publicity. That tells me they may be worried that we're on to them. You need to meet me in two hours at the Hauptbahnhof," he said of the Main Railway.

"Paul, I haven't a trace of makeup—" she turned in desperation toward the floor-length mirror. "And my hair is in braids—"

"Don't worry. You'd look beautiful parading about in a burlap sack."

She resented that. Parading about?

"Look Krista, I know this short notice changes your plans. I'm sorry, very."

She wondered.

"I'll try to make it up to you. Once this assignment is over you can take a week off."

"A week?" she repeated cautiously, not knowing if she could take his generosity seriously.

"Yes, a week," he said decisively. "And I'll even give you the gown you wore in Venice. The one with the red rose."

"Really, Paul, that isn't necessary," she began, beginning to feel guilty. The man she intended to marry was in a difficult situation, and he evidently felt he must offer her a bribe to get her to come to his aid.

"After this is over we can go home to St. Moritz and get in some skiing. Maybe we can talk Uncle Franz into meeting us at Cousin Henrich's lodge."

"Oh Paul, do you think we could?" The very thought of going home drew her like a frosty night to the fire.

"Of course we can, darling. How long has it been since either you or Franz saw Henrich? It would be good for the family to be together again. And," he went on, as if trying to ease her worry, "as you mentioned to Franz at his apartment, there is someone else wondering why he hasn't been back to ski since before Christmas."

Trudy, of course. Krista had received a letter from her only last week discreetly inquiring about how Franz was doing with his busy schedule at the University.

"Franz coming with us might be a good idea," she agreed. "And I wouldn't mind some skiing and climbing. It's been months, and I'm restless."

"That's my girl," he said congenially. "You've still got a lot of countryside in you despite your sophisticated European audiences."

"But, Paul, why must this Miss St. John have the jewelry showing tonight?"

"Her lawyer didn't explain. But it's our opportunity, don't you agree?"

How could she agree when she knew so little about it?

"This arrangement is what our friends have been anxious for."

The "friends," she knew, hinted of his working with Interpol.

"I'll have everything set up. Knowing you, you'll slide through without a glitch."

It was sometimes like Paul to flatter to get his way. "I doubt that," she said wearily, "but I'll do what it takes."

"Good girl. Look, I've got to ring off now. I've a lot to do and I'm still at the bank—there's a Jewish delegation of lawyers meeting here with Ehrlich. Things are rather uncomfortable. I'll meet you at the train station. And Krista—" his voice lowered by habit, "do not mention meeting Ava St. John to Wilhelm. Leave the house without being seen."

Again, her fingers tightened on the phone. That seemed a rather strange request. "Just leave? Really, Paul, you ask things of me my conscience won't permit. I'm a guest in his house. I cannot simply walk out without a thank you or a good-bye. What about telling Elsa?"

"Forget Elsa. You know what old age is doing to her. She's getting odd about things. And she can't keep a secret.

Anyway," he rushed on as though afraid she might protest, "she won't miss you. She's busy preparing for a possible showing of her later World War II work at the museum in Vienna."

"Is she?" This was the first time Krista had heard about it.

"If you simply must, then leave a note, but don't explain where you've gone."

"That would be rude. Why not at least tell Herr Wilhelm about your client? Won't he be delighted about an interest in the diamonds? If she is so important..."

"Krista, Krista, do use your lovely head. St. John is not her real name. She's *Jewish*."

Krista tensed slightly. There was a pause. "So?" she asked in a small, tight voice.

"Must I spell it out? You know what Wilhelm thinks of Jews."

A tense, almost painful silence pinched her throat. As the pause lengthened, Paul sounded out, "Krista!"

"Yes...I'm here..."

His voice softened as if he knew he had upset her. "That's his flaw of course, not ours. But we must be aware of it and work around it if we want his financial support."

"Do we?" she asked flatly. "Why?"

"Krista," he breathed in a low frustrated voice. "Not now." He added more gently: "I'll be waiting for you, darling." He hung up.

She did not feel like anyone's darling, and at the moment she was far from caring. Her heart felt as heavy as a stone. She replaced the receiver in its gilded cradle, and stared down at it distastefully as if it bore some disease. She felt her heart pulsating in her temples. She rubbed the tension from the back of her neck. Her thoughts were passing through a whirlwind, and Paul's voice seemed to echo in the wind: *You know what Wilhelm thinks of Jews...meet me at the Hauptbahnhof...*The Swiss Banking scandal and looting of the assets of victims of Dachau, and Auschwitz-Birkenau was also heavy on her mind.

Krista walked briskly from the phone, as though by doing so she would cut off the whirring onslaught of things dark and diabolical. She considered the Jews beloved for the Father's sake. Why should one loathe the family from which Jesus had been born? But many did, accusing them of the crucifixion of Christ. In blindness, the Jewish religious rulers had rejected Him, but it was the Romans who had executed Him, who had pounded the nails and thrust the Roman spear. And, thought Krista, He had claimed about this life that "No one takes it from Me, but I lay it down of myself."

She came awake and looked in the mirror. *Esther was beautiful*, she encouraged herself. *And God used her to serve Him. Maybe God can use me in spite of my beauty.*

She scrutinized herself with harsh eye and almost laughed in derision. This morning she looked anything but the discreet, high-paid Swiss model of a South African diamond and gold enterprise. Her fair hair was wrapped into two thick braids and pinned up at the back of her neck. Her face, with contours that many women would envy, was scrubbed clean of every vestige of makeup, and her turquoise blue eyes, appearing too large for her face, stared back suspiciously. *You don't trust anyone*, she thought. *Not even Paul. Admit it.* But she wouldn't. She needed Paul. She needed and wanted her glamorous job. Even if it meant added problems in keeping untrustworthy male admirers at a distance. Even when Uncle Franz did not completely approve. She insisted that if God had other plans for her besides modeling for Gotthard, then He was quite capable of making a career change clear to her heart. Besides, she was also an amateur spy for Interpol, wasn't she? She was serving the West.

She walked to the wardrobe. Paul was right about one thing. Returning home to the St. Moritz lodge might be the emotional reprieve she needed. At least it would remove her from all that had been storming about her recently.

She pulled open the wardrobes's folding doors and was accosted by the rich texture and color of designer gowns and furs used in her work—all belonging to the von Burens.

As she continued to mull over the idea of going home to St. Moritz where she'd been born and raised, her longing grew suddenly fierce. She could envision the homey back kitchen where Cousin Veena baked her apple strudel from scratch using an old family recipe, which seemed to invite Krista with strong open arms and a friendly face. She could almost whiff the fragrance of the fresh cinnamon and crisp mountain apples. She could imagine Cousin Henrich entering the back kitchen door thumping the snow from his boots. He would reach for the urn of dark, rich coffee on the back of an old ceramic stove and chuckle over the world-famous guests who came to St. Moritz. "Though rich and powerful, the snow and mountains of Switzerland defeat them every time," he would say with glee.

"Ever see a prince slip on his skis and sit down hard in a snow drift?" and he would laugh loudly as Veena tried to shame him for gloating. "A prince isn't so much better than we are after all."

Krista smiled reminiscently. She sighed as she held up a very expensive satin dress. Yes...home...and if Paul and Uncle Franz joined her it would be like a holiday! A good climb, a race through the hills, and a snowball fight with

Uncle Franz and she would be ready for Interpol again—maybe even Prince Ahmed.

She leafed through the fabulous gowns. This was one of the reasons she stayed at the mansion when in Zurich; the wardrobe belonged to Herr Wilhelm and Frau Elsa. She would merely check-out the gowns she needed for each new job. Elsa was especially careful in her inventory of the jewelry, using a magnifier to see that the stone mountings were secure and the clasps tight. If Paul was serious about giving her one of the gowns Elsa would certainly have a say in the matter. Krista wouldn't accept it anyway.

Sapphires, diamonds, gold, and jewels in abundance. The Gotthard diamond and gold business was owned not just by Paul's uncle Josef, but also Wilhelm. She wasn't supposed to know this. It was a guarded secret not to be discussed by anyone outside the tight inner family circle. Krista knew there was even more jewelry in the safe in Wilhelm's rooms; jewelry she had never seen.

"Why doesn't the family sell it along with the rest?" she had asked Paul one day. His face had gone into a mask.

"Maybe in another generation," he had said, and wouldn't explain.

Krista had only learned about the von Buren's share in Gotthard by chance when Paul had let it slip in a conversation in Paris last year. He had caught his mistake at once and asked her not to ever mention it. "If you do, Uncle Josef will disinherit me from ever owning the business. That will effect your future as well as mine. We may never have the opportunity to marry."

She had wanted to ask why, but it had been clear from Paul's mood that he would not explain further.

Jewelry...Her eyes dropped to the unusual ring on her right hand. Krista had found it among her mother's possessions soon after her death in a climbing accident, and it had remained one of Krista's most precious possessions since Anna had prized it. Her mother, Anna Klossner Grendelmeier, hadn't been the type of woman to wear lots of jewelry or expensive, trendy clothes. She had been a hardworker at the family lodge, a recreational skier and mountain climber. She would often join Krista's father, Peter, in leading a group of climbers on a mountain hike. It had been on one of those excursions that Anna had lost her life. Peter had tried to reach her on the ledge, but there'd been a snow storm and he too had slipped. Krista remembered waiting for their return to the lodge as the weekend drew to a close, how she had sat at the kitchen table while the hot soup grew steadily colder. There had eventually come the dreaded knock on the door and Uncle Franz had walked in from the search to tell her that her mother, his sister, and her father were dead.

Thinking about it now brought a lump to her throat. Even after twelve years she continued to miss them. Sometimes dreadfully. If it hadn't been for God, and Uncle Franz—

She looked at the gold ring with its ruby encircled with smaller diamonds in the shape of stars. She had only worn it once on a modeling job where, unfortunately, a photograph of her was taken which had appeared in *Europa* magazine. Someone had complained about it to Paul. It was too tawdry for a Gotthard model to display while on an assignment for diamonds. "The caption reads: 'Diamonds are eternal.' Why have her wear a ruby ring?" He'd had his point, of course, and she was careful after that to slip it off before modeling sessions. But she always put it back on immediately afterward. She rubbed her finger over the ruby. In her heart the ring brought her close to her parents.

Krista stirred from her memories. She shut the wardrobe door with finality as if to lock away the past, and turned to glance at the porcelain clock on the bedroom bureau with its diamond numerals. Eleven o'clock, She would need to hurry to meet Paul in time.

She crossed the thick braided rug in the austere bedroom and swiftly removed a brown leather traveling bag from the cupboard. It was a room that was always waiting for her when she returned to Zurich, which happened several times a year. The last six months had been extremely busy. She had not been home to St. Moritz since the fall. She had arrived in Zurich a week ago after showings in Monaco, Paris, Rome, and Venice. Her job brought her into contact with many of the world's most wealthy and influential, both private citizens and royalty. She thought again of the Saudi Arabian Prince Ahmed.

She had learned on her first modeling trip to Europe some years earlier that to be born fair of face and figure was not all blessing. Hindrances, testings, and snares waited at every hand, and could trap the unsuspecting heart. There was also the temptation to rely on appearance to gain her goals rather than leaning on the Lord.

But it wasn't just the secular world of high-profile modeling and wealth that had its allurements and hidden traps. Even her Christian acquaintances could be distracted by her looks. Rather than approval, she might receive aloofness. Some may have assumed that because she was attractive enough to have her face on a fashion magazine, she was naturally spiritually shallow, with little interest in the deeper life of knowing Christ and growing in her faith.

No. Physical beauty was not always something to be desired. Except for Paul, it seemed as though the men she met were only drawn by her appearance. She was kept on guard wondering if their interest was in the real Krista, or only in the shapely body with blue eyes and fair hair.

Some of her friends had jested that they could only dream of having such a trial. But Krista knew what it was like to endure a lustful stare when you wanted to be pure in your fellowship with the Lord.

There must be satisfaction when a woman is sought out by a man because he enjoys and desires her company, when compliments are not always centered on her appearance, she thought. It was no wonder that beautiful entertainers, who based their worth on a temporary God-given gift, often turned to alcohol and drugs as they aged. When spring fades into summer, and from summer to fall, then what? When they can no longer dazzle men, they feel that their lives are over and they are doomed to boredom. How pitiable! Especially when the love of the Lord remains steadfast forever.

"Even to your old age, I am He, and even to gray hairs I will carry you! I have made, and I will bear; Even I will carry, and will deliver you," she quoted from Isaiah, chapter 46.

Krista opened the bag and laid it across the eyelet cover with authentic embroidery from the famous Canton Appenzell, Switzerland's "Ozarks." Carefully she packed the one dress she would need tonight. The slim black velvet dress was ankle-length, designed for her by Andre of Paris. She gathered necessary accessories that she kept in readiness in a small satin bag and buckled the strap.

Her casual navy wool slacks and Angora sweater would do for meeting Miss St. John and her lawyer at the Hauptbahnhof. She slipped into a long, hooded coat and caught up the phone receiver to call down to the private garage for Herr Wilhelm's chauffeur. She stopped, phone in hand. No.

She would need to walk. A call from the house to the chauffeur might alert Wilhelm that she was leaving the mansion.

She turned back to the closet and pulled on her stylish boots, remembered her gloves on the bureau at the last moment, then catching her breath, slipped out the heavy bedroom door into the ornate corridor carrying her satchel. She frowned. She felt like a thief. It was troubling to sneak out like this, as though she had something to hide.

She walked silently toward the stairway.

Elsa von Buren's voice, speaking in German, called out from the corridor. "Where do you go, Krista?"

Krista's back stiffened. She turned, feeling caught, as bright spots formed in her cheeks. She faced Elsa standing in the doorway of her photography studio.

With dramatic flare, Elsa von Buren held the slim gold cigarette holder between her fingers as she drew on its end watching Krista evenly. She maintained her blond hair color. "Gray depresses me," she had stated, and her elegant stature remained, despite her age. Her facial skin was tight and too shiny from several cosmetic surgeries through the years to rid herself of wrinkles. The widely-spaced gray-blue eyes looked out like rain-swept pools, now void of the intensity surviving in photos taken of her when she was a smiling blond of eighteen in Hitler's Youth Corps.

A red chiffon dressing gown swirled about Elsa's ankles as she leaned in the doorway of the room she had turned into her photography studio. She had covered its walls with a display of the best of her black and white pictures taken during the war years. Why these were considered safe and the book published in 1938 was not, Krista hadn't discovered. She would rather not think about it.

"Was that Paul on the phone?" Elsa inquired.

So she was being watched after all. Krista set her bag down, answering in soft, fluent German.

"Good morning, Elsa. Yes, it was Paul. He asked me to meet him for another showing. This time it's on very short notice."

Footsteps sounded on the stairway behind her, and Krista turned, hoping it was not Wilhelm.

The tall, black-garbed, grim-faced housekeeper, Mrs. Brandt, paused on the steps. Krista momentarily had an unflattering thought of a thin crow sweeping in through an open window and landing there. Mrs. Brandt carried a silver tray with Frau Elsa's meager breakfast of caraway toast and skim-buttermilk. Several vitamins and pills lay on a napkin. The housekeeper's sharp eyes had already noticed Krista's bag on the landing, but she made no comment as she came past.

Mrs. Brandt and her husband, Willi, were devoted to the von Burens, especially to Elsa. They had come with her to Switzerland from Berlin at the war's end when she had married the respected Swiss banker, Wilhelm. He preferred to keep Elsa's connection with Germany away from public scrutiny and might have succeeded, except for Elsa herself. As she advanced in years, anything connected with her past took on a nostalgic glow and she often discussed her work with boldness.

"I was eighteen and I made some mistakes. I served in Hitler's propaganda department," she had confessed. Then, with that twisted, rueful smile she often displayed, as if in mockery of herself, had added: "Only back then we did not call it 'propaganda.' It was for the Fatherland. Everything was for the glorious Third Reich. I was a fool and believed Hitler's fiery speeches."

"But you are Swiss," Krista had protested.

"Yes, but my loyalty belonged to Germany. Wilhelm does not wish me to speak of the past. He is embarrassed for me. But how can I not talk of it, think of it?" Her innocent eyes opened still wider, as though the idea were an absurdity. "Who in Berlin did not swear loyalty to Hitler? Oh, they say they did not," she scoffed, energetically lighting a cigarette, "but they did. We all did."

Not all, Krista had thought. *There were many individuals who had resisted. Unfortunately most are not alive to tell about it like Elsa.*

Mrs. Brandt neared Elsa with the breakfast tray. "You must eat, Frau Elsa. You grow thin."

"Put it on the table, then stay. We have work to do sorting some old boxes of photos. And several are missing. I want them found."

The tone of her voice appeared to surprise Mrs. Brandt, or was it something else? Krista saw the housekeeper's mouth droop. "More photographs, Frau Elsa?"

What photos were these, Krista wondered. Now that Elsa had turned her attention away from her and Paul's phone call, Krista could see she was visibly upset, or perhaps angry. With Elsa it was sometimes difficult to know the difference. It was her natural demeanor to be cynical and brusque.

"Someone removed two boxes from the storage room. You know that I do not approve of anyone handling or rearranging my work."

"Yes, Frau Elsa, but I was not in the storage room—"

"Never mind. I'll get to the bottom of it later. And don't disturb anything," she ordered, following Mrs. Brandt into the room. "On second thought, ring down to the garage. Tell Willi to come up. I want to question him as well."

Krista heard a scuff of shoe, then a thump and a clatter. The tray, she thought, wincing. She hurried into the studio to see if the housekeeper was hurt. Mrs. Brandt was on her knobby hands and knees trying to push herself up from the rug among boxes, which had evidently caused her tumble, the contents scattered and piled on the floor in precarious places.

"If anything was ruined—" Elsa cried, rushing to see.

Krista held Mrs. Brandt's arm and helped her back on her feet. "Take a seat, Mrs. Brandt. You look shaken."

"Nein, nein, I am well, fräulein," and she limped to pick up the glass, and grimaced painfully at the buttermilk spill on the rose colored rug.

"Call Willi."

"Yes, Frau Elsa." She nervously picked up the telephone and rang down to the garage.

Now that Elsa was distracted from asking further questions about where Krista was going, perhaps she could slip away before Wilhelm himself heard the commotion and came down. She moved slowly toward the doorway. As she did so, she glanced curiously at the wall where Elsa had meticulously arranged numerous photos of people and places of another generation. She couldn't help admiring her work. These were later pictures than the book printed in 1938. Some of the photographs on the wall had appeared in magazines throughout Europe and America in 1940 and '41 before Pearl Harbor.

Krista paused. The expressions on the faces were as vivid as though they might suddenly step out from the stillness of the past.

"You approve," Elsa stated confidently, coming up beside her, a smile on her lips for the first time that morning.

"This is practically like a museum. Your photography is very good, Elsa. This is the first time I've seen your display."

Elsa looked proud. "I have some that no one has seen, not even Wilhelm. Here are my favorites," she said as she led Krista toward a table nearby filled with unsorted pictures. Elsa glanced toward Mrs. Brandt, but her back was toward them, still on the phone. Elsa removed two pictures, apparently hidden behind a large photograph of the building for the Deutsches Reich. She handed one to Krista with an excited glow in her eyes.

"A friend took this one," she said in a low voice. "I was eighteen. I can't bring myself to destroy it."

Krista saw a young smiling Elsa standing with some German SS officers.

She felt an unpleasant chill as she recognized the face of Hermann Goering. She waited to see the second picture, but Elsa had changed her mind. She slipped both back behind their hiding place.

"I should not have showed you." Her mouth drooped. She looked like a child hiding too much candy from her mother. Krista realized that Elsa, despite her face lifts and hair color, was an old and aging woman whose mind was growing weaker with time. Her only remaining pleasure in life was the past and what she believed were its glories.

"I've no reason to mention it," Krista said dully.

"Wilhelm would burn them."

"Did he take the other boxes you're looking for?"

Elsa glanced at her. "There wasn't anything left in them," she said sullenly.

What did she mean? That she had hidden them or that incriminating photographs had disappeared?

"What is Herr Wilhelm afraid of?"

"His reputation. All that scandal about the Swiss Banks cooperating with the Nazis. Anything connecting me to Berlin upsets him."   She sighed. "As well it should. I keep the photographs only because it's my work...what else do I have?" She turned and looked at Krista with vulnerable eyes.

Krista sensed her tragedy and for a moment could not answer. She was thinking of the book hidden in Uncle Franz's collection at the University. What would Paul do if he knew about this picture of Elsa with Goering? And who was in the second picture she hadn't shown her?

"How did you meet Goering?" Krista tried casually, but Elsa blinked, appeared to awaken from a dream. "No, no," she said, waving a veined hand, and walked away to where Mrs. Brandt was gathering the boxes to stack.

"Leave them, Gerta, they are too heavy," she told her.

Krista was still looking at the display on the wall. She was remembering the first time Elsa had come to the lodge at St. Moritz from a skiing vacation at Davos, three years after Krista's parents had died in the accident.

"So this is Peter and Anna's daughter," Elsa had said, as though surprised. "There's not a touch of Anna's dark hair and eyes in her."

Elsa's remark had seemed to anger Cousin Henrich. "There is everything of Franz's sister in her."

"How sad that Anna didn't live to see her duckling turn into the proverbial Nordic swan." Elsa had taken Krista's arm. "Stand up, my lovely, move about full circle."

Krista had done so, embarrassed, but somehow pleased by the attention. Life at the lodge, waiting on tables, had become lonely. After three happy years with Uncle Franz, he had been called away to travel extensively throughout Europe and Krista had come home again to the lodge.

But Cousin Henrich hadn't been pleased when Elsa asked her to stand and turn around.

"Do not do that, Elsa."

"Do not be foolish, Henrich. Krista is beautiful."

During the time Elsa stayed at the lodge she had amused herself, so she intimated, by taking a number of photographs of Krista in various poses. "She is photogenic," she told Henrich. "I will show these to Wilhelm and see if Krista should go to modeling school. Josef Gotthard is looking for just the right appearance for his modeling business."

"Aryan, maybe?" Henrich had slurred.

"You're an old man, Henrich, and you talk too much. When does Franz return from Paris?"

"I don't know," he grumbled. "I haven't heard from Franz. He is still traveling with the Rhode Scholars."

"Don't hold her back, Henrich. She has a gift of beauty. Let her use it. We will pay her well."

"That is all that matters," Henrich quipped.

But Krista had tugged at his arm, her eyes begging. "Oh, Henrich, I want to do this!"

He had looked at her thoughtfully. "Franz will not approve."

Krista remembered her confusion and pain at the time. "If it displeases Uncle Franz..."

"Of course he will not be displeased," Elsa had said. "And you, Henrich, I will pay for the loss of her waiting on your tables." She had turned to him with an unpleasant smile. "You can always hire someone to work at the lodge, can't you, Henrich? And Veena could use some help in the kitchen. Her back aches, she tells me."

Henrich's eyes had dropped to the floor.

"Franz will want the best for your future," Elsa said to Krista. "You won't find that if you remain buried away here in St. Moritz, bringing plates of cabbage soup to the tables. You'll lose her anyway when Franz comes home. Let her meet the rich elite of Europe and Monte Carlo."

Krista had looked at him, eyes shining with excitement, and Cousin Henrich had relented. "I am only a cousin. I can make my wishes known to Franz when he returns to Zurich, but I have no authority to keep Krista here."

"Good. Then it's settled. I'll call on Franz when he returns to the University."

And so Krista's future had changed as simply as that. Later, Uncle Franz had returned to the University and then visited her in Paris at the modeling school. "Are you content, Krista?" he had asked. "Is this what you want?"

"For now, Uncle Franz. Later, I may want to become a professor of history."

He had laughed. "From model to professor!"

"And...Paul is here to keep me company."

"Yes...so I've heard." He had looked at her for a long moment, his eyes grave. "I have been away too long. From now on I intend to stay in Zurich as much as possible."

He had smiled, and Krista had hugged him.

The tight voice of the housekeeper, Mrs. Brandt, cut into Krista's memories. "Willi is here, Frau Elsa."

"Come in, Willi!"

He was a squarely built man with a large head, bulging eyes, and thick gray brows. Those brows drew down above pale eyes that skimmed over his wife's worried face, then came to rest on Elsa.

"Yes, Frau Elsa?"

"That man who called yesterday about my work, what was his name?"

"The gentleman from the Vienna museum?"

"Yes, yes, the one you talked to in the drive. I've misplaced his business card…" She looked about distractedly.

"I do not know his name, Frau Elsa."

"He will call again," Mrs. Brandt urged.

"Find out his name. Call the Vienna museum," Elsa ordered. "And Willi, I want help with these heavy boxes." She nervously used a lighter on another cigarette. "Stack them against the opposite wall. Yes there, but not so high I cannot get into them. There are more boxes in storage. I want them all brought here. If you need help ask Hans."

Willi glanced at Gerta. The housekeeper was rubbing her wrist where she'd fallen, but her darting eyes had come back to him.

Elsa was pacing, her red chiffon billowing about her thin ankles. "Well?" she demanded when Willi stood transfixed.

"All the photographs?"

"All. The museum wants to show my work this spring in Vienna. Maybe in Berlin. I must…I am getting old…"

"Oh no, Frau Elsa," Mrs. Brandt insisted.

"So I may end up giving my photographs to the museum. Make certain everything I need is at my disposal when he comes again. And send the girl up to clean this room. There is dust everywhere."

Krista glanced quickly at her wristwatch. She slipped out unnoticed and went to the stairway, picked up her traveling bag and hurried down. The entrance hall waited below, chilly and silent, the great cuckoo clock ticking there like a time bomb.

Krista lifted the hood of her coat over her head as the cold morning welcomed her. She went down the front porch steps. It would be a long, brisk walk but it would help her to wear off her nervous energy.

Frost glittered like diamonds on the needles of evergreens, catching the sunlight as she walked along the edge of the cobbled drive.

Paul's phone call had begun the day with doubts, and now her questions were expanding like concentric ripples on a pool after a stone toss. Paul's knowledge of what was going on could alleviate some concerns when she saw him at the Hauptbahnhof if he would just share his thoughts. He too, had seemed worried. The book hidden at Uncle Franz's apartment and the photograph she had seen of Elsa with SS officers added to her concerns.

Her pace quickened over the little bridge that brought her to a street meandering down toward the Limmat. Going home to St. Moritz for a visit had been the furthest thing from her mind that morning when she had wakened. She had assumed she would remain in Zurich until flying with Paul to Monaco for another showing of Gotthard jewelry. Now her bedroom at the ski lodge beckoned like warm arms. She was suddenly anxious to greet Paul at the Hauptbahnhof. The sooner she met Ava St. John and her American lawyer, the sooner she could board the train home to peace.

4

When Krista left the von Buren mansion, which overlooked the Uto Quai, there were sailboats braving the lake below, tacking and veering, as energetic businessmen took advantage of lunch-time sailing before returning to work.

The left shore of the lake was crowded with hotels, offices, and two- and three-story turn-of-the-century houses scattered amid twisting medieval streets. She could envision the 16th century Swiss Protestant Reformer Zwingli stepping out from among one of those Gothic structures. *Perhaps,* she thought, her imagination running rife, *he would be on his way for a secret meeting with Martin Luther.*

The message of Zwingli and the truths of the Reformation had settled generations ago into lukewarmness, into mere church ritual. Zurich was no longer the bastion for biblical truths recovered at the price of the death of martyrs. Rather than guarding the great doctrines that had been recovered, and contending for the faith once for all delivered to the saints, Zurich had become the world's banker with secret numbered and nameless accounts that protected not only the honest, but also the world's dictators, drug cartel lords, and the mafia.

But on this windy morning it was not the Reformer Zwingli who stepped out from among the stone structures: it was the stranger who had been following her. It had begun that night in Rome when he had followed her back to the hotel after she had dined with Paul. Then again in Venice. She and Paul had gone out to dinner and afterward taken a charming moonlit voyage on a rented gondola. The man had been in the cafe and afterward was standing on the street as the boatman rowed away. She could have mentioned it again to Paul at the time, but she hadn't wanted to add to his concerns. There'd been so much to trouble him on their recent showing in Italy.

Who was this stranger? What did he want? Was his presence now just a coincidence? She wasn't sure. Somehow her instincts told her he wasn't from Interpol. The man was unfriendly. What did he hope to learn?

He behaved as though he didn't notice her. He paused on the hilly street, bent his head beneath a dark Homburg hat, and opened a map. He then strolled on, crossing the narrow street to the other side.

Krista turned away, her hurried steps echoing over the stones. Why follow her? She didn't slow her pace until she came down from the narrow street to the swift-moving Limmat.

The river bisected the historic Old Town from the newer section of Zurich, and a number of attractive low bridges criss-crossed it, connecting the two sections of town. She had reached the bridge at the juncture of the river and lake, and waited for the traffic lights to change. She resisted the temptation to turn around to see if he had followed. She must avoid revealing that she knew. She need not look. She sensed he was there, walking behind the group of pedestrians crossing the bridge, keeping out of her view.

The signal turned green and she kept pace with a group of businessmen in sedate dark coats and polished leather shoes carrying bulging briefcases. There was a short stretch of heavy traffic, a few more streets to maneuver, then a busy square with rattling trolleys.

She began walking briskly on toward the Hauptbahnhof. The railway station had undergone a lengthy renovation the last few years and its impressive 19th-century structure boasted various splashing fountains, immense halls, and waiting rooms with sparkling light fixtures. Krista passed heavily upholstered European seats, gilded mirrors, numerous flower bouquets, and buffets. But where was Paul? Would he have the diamonds with him, or would they be delivered as usual by his select group of security guards?

The throng in business suits hurried to and fro. Krista glanced at the time. She was fifteen minutes late. But Paul, always perfunctory and even early when worried, was nowhere in sight. She turned and walked back. Something had come up. He must still be at the bank with Ehrlich. She'd call and tell him she would meet him at the Bank of Zurich Corporation.

Krista's arm bumped against something solid, jarring her. "Oh—Entschuldigen Sie," she murmured her apology, and for a moment confronted the man's surprised gaze. Blond, Nordic features, intelligent but hard gray eyes, broad shoulders under a navy raincoat. He brushed past as though he hadn't heard her.

She recovered, heart pounding, and hurried on. *The man following her!* She had taken him by surprise. Did he think it was deliberate? That she had pulled off that collision just to get a look at his face? It was the worst thing she could have done. She had already made that error in Rhinefelden's bookshop with the other man pretending he was Professor Zimmer. She could identify both men now. And they knew it. This couldn't have turned out more badly.

But maybe he hadn't noticed her alarm when she recognized him. She prayed he had not.

She found the open phone cubicle near a splashing fountain. Her hands shook as she dug into her handbag for a coin.

Dear God! she prayed reverently. *What do I do now?* She was certain he was the same man she had noticed in Venice.

"Hello, Paul? Yes, yes, it's Krista...I'm at the station..."

"Krista, I'm sorry, there's been an unexpected change. Her agent's already arrived." His voice dropped. "He's here at the bank...a mistake on his part. He looks as if he makes a lot of them. The man is pure Hollywood—a dunce. I don't think we have a thing to worry about. This whole matter looks genuine after all. Franz and the rest of us can take a deep breath."

"I'm glad to hear that. After what's just happened to me I don't need more problems."

His voice tensed. "What is that, darling?"

"Paul, the man I told you and Franz about? He's here. He's following me. I collided with him by mistake."

"What! You are sure?"

"Certain."

"You're all right?"

"Yes, but..."

"Darling, I'll be right there. Stay in a crowded area."

"Paul, *no*, don't come here. It's better if he doesn't think I've alerted you. I'll...I'll come to the bank. I can be there in ten minutes."

"Be careful! If you're not here in exactly ten minutes I'm coming after you."

"I'm on my way now."

Krista hung up, steadying her nerves. She drew her shoulder bag closely beside her, left the booth, pretending to straighten her hood as she glanced in either direction to see if the man were nearby. He was sitting near the splashing water display facing the phone booth. His head was bent as though watching the pigeons he was tossing bread crumbs to.

Krista walked across the square looking straight ahead. He stood and followed, keeping his distance.

She took the escalators down to the underpass that would bring her beneath the square to the Bahnhofstrasse, Zurich's world-famous shopping street.

Distances here were short; they only seemed complicated to the tourists. But for Krista the way felt long today. Her nervous energy served to quicken her steps.

Halfway through the underpass, she resisted the fatal urge to turn around. *Keep walking. Do not think about him.*

She slipped her way past a group of slow-moving tourists, and within a short time emerged onto the street where she met a gray mizzling rain. Having no umbrella, she tightened her coat hood.

The shops on the Bahnhofstrasse offered the most luxurious goods with prices that grew progressively more extravagant as the street headed south.

Krista came to the top stores where the gowns and accessories for her modeling were usually purchased. Further down Bahnhofstrasse she came to the banks. Most of Zurich's international financial business took place here discreetly behind upstairs windows. Her only clue to the banks was the digital trail of market data flicking silently above her on the walls. Zurich had an international precious-metals market that was rivaled only by London. And much of the gold and silver lay heaped beneath Krista's feet under Zurich's most glamorous boulevard. Here, beneath the sidewalk and street, there were tremendous vaults of gold.

She entered the Bank of Zurich Corporation. Immediately the atmosphere changed to one of sedate gray and navy suits. A group of conservative Swiss bankers with unsmiling faces and reserved voices had just emerged from a cloistered conference. Their faces appeared even more somber than usual. Elsa's son, Ehrlich, was among them. Though his father, Wilhelm, was retired, Ehrlich continued the family banking tradition and was esteemed in high financial echelons as a member of the SBA, the Swiss Bankers Association. Paul had said that Ehrlich was meeting today with a Jewish organization about accounts opened in the late 1930s. Krista was experiencing quiet fears behind shuttered windows as the voices of six and half million Jews echoed from the flaming past. Yes, foreboding shadows were gathering over the von Buren mansion, but would they stretch all the way to St. Moritz?

Pausing in the foyer, she noticed Ehrlich, who was in his fifties, with a slight paunch and a thinning blond hairline, making stiff excuses to two men in dark suits. One of them, stalwart in looks, appeared determined, but his colleague looked reticent, even offended. She could just catch some of Ehrlich's words—

"I am sorry about this, Mr. Morgenthau. They might at least have offered you a chair to sit down."

"I never expected one, Herr von Buren." He offered his hand.

Ehrlich hesitated, then shook it limply.

Mr. Morgenthau's mouth curved. "Auf Wiedersehen."

"Yes, yes, Auf Wiedersehen, Mr. Morgenthau."

The two men strode across the bank floor toward the exit, one of them glancing toward the waiting room, then looking quickly away.

Krista saw them pass through glass doors and out onto the rainy street.

Paul Gotthard came from the conference room the two men had just left and joined Ehrlich. They stood in a huddle, talking in low German. Apparently neither of them had yet noticed her. Paul also looked distracted by the meeting. Whatever it had been about, it had not gone well, she decided. She turned toward the waiting room just behind her. There were some leather chairs, potted palms, and the inevitable stack of newspapers. Her eyes stumbled over a man lounging in a chair whose choice of clothing sent shivers of distaste along her fashion sensitive nerves. He wore a glittering gold cloth shirt embroidered with, of all things, black bucking broncos and Stetson cowboy hats. His own cowboy hat was tipped low over his eyes, as though he were snoozing. One arm was behind his head, and his long muscled legs in designer jeans were crossed at his shiny boots. *Good grief,* she thought.

He had left his sunglasses on, and his expensive-looking western jacket lay beside him. His tanned hand sported several big gold rings and a thick gold watch. Several fancy cameras were piled indifferently on the chair next to him, along with a bulging black leather satchel.

Maybe money, she thought with irony. Could this possibly be our great Hollywood agent sporting Miss Ava St. John around Switzerland?

Krista felt an unexplained sense of irritation. He looked so oblivious to the tension commanding the bankers. *No one has the right to look so relaxed when everything for us is going so wrong*, she thought. She almost had the notion he was watching her from behind those sunglasses, though he looked as if he were asleep.

Krista turned away as Paul walked up, brisk and tense, checking his watch. "Terribly sorry, Krista. Were you followed?" he whispered.

"Yes. I don't know where he is now. Maybe looking into one of the shop windows until I leave again."

"I'll look into it. Let's hope it means nothing."

He towered above her in a sophisticated Italian-cut suit. He looked over at the cowboy, amused contempt in his olive-green eyes. "Our American is able to sleep anywhere." He changed the subject, his amusement turning to concern. "The bank has encountered some unpleasantries. Ehrlich needed me in the meeting with the Jewish delegation."

So that explained the two men she had seen leaving.

"What happened?" she whispered, her expectations already geared for disappointment.

"Our troubles have just begun."

"Then the bankers are not cooperating?" She had been afraid of Swiss intransigence all along.

"They will delay as long as they can."

The matter was disturbing. She had hoped the Swiss would do what was just and right, getting the ugly past behind them. Evidently this bank, at least, was not willing to own up to any guilt of cooperation with Nazi Germany.

Was the chilliness that the Jewish delegation group experienced a harbinger of more to come?

"This could end up costing Switzerland billions," he commented in a low voice.

"It shouldn't cost them anything since it's not their money," she said. "It belongs to the families of Jews sent to the—"

"Krista, sometimes your mind is too simplistic," but he softened the rebuke with a smile that said he still found her beautiful. There it was again—that little innuendo that suggested that if one were beautiful it could make up for almost anything else.

"They are returning to London then?" she asked shortly.

"Tel Aviv. This group came from Israel. They say they did not come for money, they want justice."

"But will they get it?"

Paul looked again at the dozing cowboy agent. He had stirred from his siesta and was stretching like a panther.

"I'm told by Ehrlich the SBA has agreed to conduct its own preliminary search for dormant World War II accounts. They'll create a set of guidelines by which the Jewish families can make claims to conduct searches. This was done previously at the request of the London Jewish organization. They've discovered perhaps $32 million worth of assets that could belong to Jewish survivors. At least that's what they've offered to pay."

"I assume those representing the Jewish families don't trust the SBA," Krista said. "I can't say I blame them. After all, they held the assets all along and made no move to find the owners. They're cooperating now only because they're being forced to."

"Whose side are you on?" he asked with a hint of irritated amusement.

Krista raised her brows. "The side of justice."

"Well—I know that the London group also did not trust the SBA. They've asked for an independent accounting by a third-party commission."

"I'm sure the SBA will be against that."

"Naturally. They insist no one is allowed to meddle in their system of secret banking laws."

"It's my opinion the SBA asked for trouble by the way they treated the Jewish organization when they arrived from London," she said. "I read a newspaper account that said they deliberately kept the Jews waiting in a cold bare room. They wouldn't even offer them chairs to sit on. And when the SBA chairman entered, he merely read from a prepared statement in a cold monotone, then asked if they had any questions. The treatment angered the Jewish organization. It was a deliberate affront. So they demanded the independent accounting, letting the SBA know they didn't trust them." She shrugged. "So the SBA has been forced to go along with their request."

"You'll be happy to know Ehrlich just told me there will be an independent audit of their accounting procedures. The Jews won round one."

"No. They got what was fair. Really, Paul, I'm shocked at your response, as well as that of the Swiss bankers. For a nation that claims we're out front for human rights, we're behaving as if this were 1939 all over again."

"Don't be absurd, Krista. The Jews come here demanding! Demanding! They're offensive!"

She smiled stiffly. "It is your manner that is offensive. You and the entire Swiss Banking association..."

Suddenly he laughed and caught her hand in his, squeezing it tightly. "You're right. And this banking mess isn't even mine to worry about. We have our own particular problems to handle right now."

She did not return the smile and took her hand away as soon as she could. "And the delegation from Israel? What did they come here about?" she asked, refusing to retreat.

"That was something entirely different," he said with concern in his lowered voice. "They're from a group of independent lawyers in Tel Aviv. They're asking for information about a Jewish family from Vienna—Benjamin Cohen, who supposedly opened an account here in 1938. His great-granddaughter is being represented by the Tel Aviv group."

"The two men who just left?"

"Yes. But Ehrlich insists he can't grant any information because of Swiss secrecy laws. The granddaughter, Miss Cohen, is trying to discover the account number."

"Well, I hope she gets it," Krista said cheerfully, and saw a spark of irritation warm his eyes.

He squeezed her arm. "Excuse me. Our cowboy from Dallas is stirring from hibernation." He left her standing there inwardly fuming, and walked over to the man in the waiting room, greeting him politely.

The cowboy stood and was offering a friendly hand to Paul. Krista discreetly examined him. He had the build of an athlete. He pumped Paul's hand good naturedly and talked too loudly. She was embarrassed for him. *Americans are forward and brash,* she thought.

"Well now, it's a pleasure, Herr Gotthard—did I pronounce your name right? I'm not too good on German—but I got a little book here I can leaf through and find things." He reached inside his shirt pocket and whipped out a pronunciation guide. He began to read phrases so badly that Krista turned her head away to hide a smile. The man was harmless. And to think Paul and his contacts in Interpol had been suspicious! Well, good. She could get this diamond showing over for Miss St. John and catch a train home to St. Moritz in time for a wonderful weekend of skiing.

Paul returned and drew her aside. He too, looked amused.

"I don't think either of them know what they are really doing. They have the brains of a weather vane, but she has money, and he claims he's a lawyer, though he doesn't seem smart enough to me. Ava has more money than she knows what to do with. She's very interested in those diamonds and wants a showing this afternoon."

"Why such a hurry?" she complained. "I'm not prepared to model."

"You needn't worry about that. He says she has everything you need—hairstylist, makeup artist. She's staying with wealthy Zurich friends and we're to have dinner there tonight. He'll bring you there now, and I'll join you later. I've got to get the diamonds and security guards."

She glanced toward the American. As she did, he replaced his sunglasses, adjusted them twice, then removed them. He cast her a silky smile that could have passed for Ava St. John's leading man in some romantic movie. Krista did not return the smile. She turned back to Paul, looping her arm through his. That gesture should show the American he was out of line.

"Are you sure he's not an actor? What better way to set us off guard than show up in a gold cowboy shirt? Is any American lawyer as naive as he appears to be?"

"I thought of that. We're taking nothing for granted. We're already checking into him. So far, he's who he claims. Jorden Keller, one of four below-average lawyers from a Dallas firm representing some fading Hollywood stars in the entertainment world. He was previously engaged to some movie starlet until she balked and ran off with her leading man. Believe me, he doesn't have a clue as to what life is about in Zurich. He's so unsophisticated it's amusing."

Krista wondered. She glanced at Jorden Keller again. He was a little too "amusing" if he asked her. She'd know soon enough. She'd catch him at his masquerade if that's what it was.

"All right. I'll go through with it."

Paul led her toward the waiting room. Krista schooled her expression into a modeling pose that would conceal her own thoughts. Two could play games, if it came to it, she decided as Paul brought her to Ava St. John's cowboy agent. She would pretend to be little more than a pretty model with few brains.

"May I introduce Gotthard Enterprises' world famous model, Miss Krista von Buren? Krista, this is Miss St. John's lawyer and agent from America, Jorden Keller."

5

Jorden flashed a wholesome grin. "Originally, I'm from Oklahoma. A place called Corn. Ever been there on your modeling sprees, Miss von Buren?"

What a tease! She studied his eyes. They were innocent, but she didn't fall for it. She turned just as innocently and dumbly to Paul. "Oh Paul, let's do it! Let's set up a jewelry showing in Corn!"

Paul's lip twitched as he smiled at her.

"How do you do, Mr. Keller," she said, smiling sweetly. "Why, you're the first real cowboy I've ever met!"

"Jorden," he said with a slight smirk. "Just plain old Jorden will do it every time."

For a moment Krista saw a flicker of something like irony in his earthy dark eyes. It was gone so quickly she wondered if it had been there at all. He stood grinning down at her, rocking back on his heel boots.

"You look just like your picture in the magazines."

"Oh! Do I? I'm so pleased."

"I've got quite few tacked on my office wall—black velvet dress and loads of diamonds. Real nice."

If this is an act, he's not embarrassed by it at all, she thought, *but I'm not as comfortable as he seems to be*. "Oh. Why, that is very nice," she repeated for lack of anything else to say.

Their eyes held briefly before she lost the battle and glanced away, feeling the warmth creep into her cheeks. Did he see through her dumbness?

He pushed his tanned hand toward her. "In Oklahoma friends shake over a business deal. I'm sure this one with Gotthard is going to turn out swell."

The suggestion came robed with a smile. She was on the verge of quipping that in Zurich they did things differently than in Corn, but caught herself. She smiled and held out her hand. "Far be it from Zurich to not measure up to the friendliness of the Americans, Mr. Keller."

"Say, I like your style!" he said with grin, and took her hand.

Surprisingly she found his touch brief, contradicting the impression of boldness and confidence. The ring on her finger flickered in the light coming from the window.

She looked at Paul, silently pleading. Be kind, be brave, his gaze assured her. She looked back at Jorden Keller. He was looking at her ring. Was she mistaken again, or was that a thorough but brief study? She could almost think he had asked to shake hands just to see the ring.

"Oh dear, I'm not prepared to represent Gotthard Enterprises. You see, I was expecting a train trip to St. Moritz, so I've dressed casually."

"Don't worry about a thing," he assured her breezily, slinging his western jacket over his shoulder. "I know just what to do. Ava's had hundreds of sudden appointments, and she's anxious to see the diamonds. Her own makeup artist and hairstylist are at the mansion. No reason why you can't use them, is there?" He smiled easily, showing nice white teeth against his California tan, and glanced at his watch. "Ava's an impatient woman. We best get moving along. I wouldn't want to get fired. Shall we go?"

Paul glanced over his shoulder at Ehrlich, and Krista followed his glance. He gestured casually to Paul that he wished to speak with him.

"Yes, do go on without me," Paul told them. "I'll need to get the diamonds. I'll call you at Miss St. John's house," he told Jorden Keller. "Do I have the right number?"

"Sure. Right here." His rings flashed as he reached into his pocket, took out a card, and handed it to Paul.

"When can Ava expect you tonight? She wants to discuss the transaction over dinner." He didn't wait for an answer: "How's seven sound?"

Paul was looking at the address on the card.

"That will give me time to get ready, Paul," Krista added. This was the strangest modeling appointment she had ever been involved in.

"All right. Seven. Lars will bring the diamonds."

Krista sensed an internal response from Jorden, however slight, but Paul seemed taken up with Ehrlich. "I must go now. I've some other business to attend to."

She wondered about Jorden's response. He must be concerned for the safety of the diamonds. There was no need to worry. Paul was an expert at moving jewels all around Europe.

"Just as long as I know who to expect," Jorden was saying casually. "Is Lars your security man?"

"One of them."

"He supervises Paul's special security guard," Krista offered. "You don't need to worry about Lars. He's trustworthy. He's been with us on all our travels throughout Europe."

Paul was looking toward Ehrlich again. Krista followed his glance. A man had walked up and was talking to him. Again Ehrlich von Buren glanced in their direction.

Jorden was smiling at Paul. "How many on your security staff? I want to make sure everything is mighty safe." Krista looked at Jorden, studying him more closely now that he was not watching her. For a moment the cowboy friendliness and naivete had left his face. She saw an alertness, a different kind of boldness. More like calm confidence.

"Five guards," Krista told him.

"That include the driver?"

Paul smiled. "You're very astute about these things, Mr. Keller. Yes, five, which includes the driver."

"Just want to make sure who to expect. All armed to the teeth, I hope?"

"Oh yes," Paul said smoothly. "Expert marksman."

The American raised his brows as though impressed. "Must be hard getting trusty men like that. Sure wish I could find a bodyguard for Ava."

Paul scanned him. "You look well-qualified yourself."

"Oh no." He waved both hands. "I've no stomach for violence. Hey, I marched against the death penalty in college," he said proudly. "And I've paid all my dues in the No-Nukes Club of Dallas. Totally against violence of any sort, including nuclear energy. Bad for the environment and all that. That's why I respect Switzerland so much, and Germany. The Green and White Party. Neutrality. No borders between nations and people. Caring. Sharing. One religion, all that sort of thing."

Krista glanced at him again. She was almost convinced he did not mean a word of his smooth sarcasm.

"Well—that is very nice," Paul said, his boredom barely veiled. Evidently he had accepted the speech. "I'm afraid my source of guards can't help Miss St. John, however. My resource pool are ex-military men who have served their tour of duty."

"Wow. I've heard of the crack Swiss Army."

Krista's glance shot to his smiling dark eyes.

Paul smiled. "Yes, but my guards are from Austria."

"Ah! Well! That accounts for their superior qualities then. I'm sure the diamonds will arrive safely."

Krista watched the exchange, wondering. Paul rarely discussed the background or past careers of the elite guard used in Gotthard Enterprise. Even she had not known they were from Austria. She had thought Lars came from Bern.

"Just want to make sure who I'm dealing with," Jorden explained again. "I see you have a very tight operation. Ava has nothing to worry about at her friend's house. I'd hate to have some thugs follow your men and rob them. Embarrassing, you know?"

Paul laughed. "I'm not quite as naive as all that, Mr. Keller. Rest assured there will be no robbery."

"Well, that makes me feel a whole lot better."

Paul turned to Krista, gave a squeeze to her hand and turning on his heel, nodded briefly to Jorden Keller, then walked sharply away to meet with Ehrlich and the man with him.

Jorden whistled as he slipped into his jacket and replaced his sun glasses. "Sharp guy."

Krista smiled coolly.

Keller turned and looked off toward Paul, Ehrlich, and the other man. He adjusted his glasses several times before he turned to her. "I have a car waiting."

"You come prepared," she said smoothly. "All except those sunglasses. They seem to be troubling you."

"Uh—yeah, so you noticed." He took them off and dropped them into his pocket with a frown, then smiled at her. "I lost my other pair at the lodge, so I bought these this morning. The fit's all wrong." He grabbed up his string of cameras. "Shall we go? I'll take that bag for you."

But when she hesitated for no particular reason, he grinned. He leaned toward her and said in a low voice, "Are the diamonds already stashed inside? I thought so."

She giggled dumbly. "Oh, you're so funny. No, my employer has told you the truth. I've some modeling things inside, is all. And I prefer to carry it myself, thank you."

"We aim to please."

Yes, a tad too much. Why?

At the front door of the bank he opened it wide and let her pass into the noontime rush.

"Golly, look at that traffic," he breathed.

"Don't you have traffic in Dallas?"

"And still raining too," he said as if he hadn't caught her quip. He pulled his Stetson low. "Wouldn't you know it? Clouds and rain. We'd better put a stampede on."

She almost had to walk double time to keep up as he steered her along the Bahnhofstrasse. Her irritation at him was growing as he whistled cheerfully. They had walked a block when he stopped suddenly to look in a store window at some cameras.

"You must like cameras," she stated flatly, glancing at the three slung over his muscled shoulder.

"They're like women." He grinned. "The more the merrier."

No, she didn't like him. But she dimpled. She walked on leaving him to shift for himself. By the time he stopped gaping in the window she'd be half way down the Bahnhofstrasse. She hadn't gone far when she felt a twinge of pity and stopped to look back and wait. Mr. Keller was fussing with his sunglasses again, this time staring behind him at some approaching sightseers. He soon caught up with her.

"I think I've finally adjusted these things. They fit comfortably now," he said, as though he had noticed her irritation.

"Let's hope so."

He propelled her in and out of the foot traffic. A few minutes later he surprised her by changing directions and leading her off the sidewalk and across the street, dodging a honking Volvo.

"Must see this Swiss clock shop," he said. "You don't mind?"

"Oh, not at all!"

He led her through the doorway and down a narrow isle filled with ticking clocks. He wound the spring on one from the Black Forest. A Swiss maid and wood-chopper came out and bowed. "Say, now, isn't that cute?"

The proprietor came forward offended, and Jorden shook hands with him. "Sorry, sir, he said. "I mean—" he whipped out his phrase book: "Entschuldigen Sie!"

The proprietor muttered something in German and pulled his hand away.

"What did he say?" Jorden asked her as he propelled her toward the back of the store.

She shrugged.

Krista hastened her steps. He didn't let her down. As expected, he steered her out the back door and down a narrow stone alleyway. Who was he trying to lose?

"If this is a kidnapping-for-ransom game, Mr. Keller, you're very good at it," she said breathlessly as they almost ran.

"Believe me, I'm not having any fun," came the low mutter.

"I didn't think you were," she challenged. "Just who are you, really?"

He frowned.

"My," she gasped as they ran. "The cowboy is frowning. How different you look. Why, you're almost another person, Mr. Keller," she pressed. "Do you frown often? I've seen nothing but flashing smiles since I first saw you in the bank—"

"Believe me, my moods change like a summer thunderstorm. In here. Move!"

"What—" she began angrily.

He propelled her through the back door of a dress shop. Then into a corner behind some fluttering gowns. "Silence."

She stared up at him. His face was that of a stranger, his gaze cool and alert, his movements calm and disciplined. His hand rested in the pocket of his jacket as he watched the door they had darted in. She tensed, trying to silence her breathing, her thumping heart. Her mind raced in one direction, then another.

He appeared satisfied when no one followed them, and moved her down the aisle and toward the front entrance back onto Bahnhofstrasse. He was no longer smiling.

"Who are you?" she whispered finally.

"Jorden Keller," he said, when she thought he would never get around to answering. "Just trying to avoid a particular journalist. He's a torment to Ava. Tried to black-mail her once. I don't want him tailing us to the house."

He did seem his normal self again, not that she had much to judge his "normalcy" by. "Somehow you do not remind me of a man from Dallas."

He smiled. "I doubt you're much of a judge. What do you know about cowboys from Dallas?"

"Very little. Maybe you don't either."

He looked at her, relaxed again, amused. "Well, honey, that just shows you how wrong you are. I rode horses in Dallas down yonder on my father's ranch."

"And then became a flashy Hollywood agent escorting Miss St. John about Europe?"

"Not at first. I went to Yale. I've a list of clients in my briefcase back home that would set you swooning."

She deliberately giggled again. "Really? Well, I just love to swoon over American stars."

"And conservative Swiss bankers? Well, follow the money they say."

She gave him a cool side glance but he didn't see it. "You don't look so poor yourself, Mr. Keller. Flashy gold shirts, silver spurs, two hundred dollar sunglasses—I didn't know cowboys liked gold shirts. I thought they liked old Levis with tears in them."

He laughed. "Cowboys aren't supposed to dislike guns either. But I'm one of those harmless types."

"Sounds to me like something made you afraid of guns?"

"My grandfather shot himself in the foot once with a .22."

"How dreadful. And that made a pacifist out of you. Very wise indeed. So what's that in your pocket?"

He looked at her, amused, then grinned. He pulled out a gold writing pen and held it up. "Fooled you didn't I? I'll bet you thought I carried a revolver." He handed her his jacket. "Go ahead. See for yourself."

He probably expected her to believe him, but she called his bluff. She took the Western jacket with its gold trim, checked both pockets and even the inside lining. She handed it back.

"All right, you're afraid of guns. How is your grandfather's foot?"

"Gramps has a hole in his big toe. I used to call all the neighbor kids over to show it to them. I was quite popular until I got older. I soon found out pretty girls weren't interested in that sort of thing. It was then I decided to make money. So I became a lawyer." He smiled. "And behold. Here I am, smart, rich, but—still afraid of guns."

Well, maybe, she thought, relenting.

"This way—" and he steered her through a bakery smelling of strudel and hot cocoa. "Too bad we don't have time."

They went out the front door and back onto the busy street walking in the opposite direction. "You mean we haven't lost your journalist yet?"

"Just playing it safe. He's persistent. My car is just ahead. It's that white Fiat." He gestured. "Cheer up, fräulein. You'll soon get to relax."

A Fiat? "It's not exactly the kind of automobile I would have expected the flamboyant Jorden Keller to drive."

He smiled and made no reply. Then she remembered the journalist and the man who had been following her ever since she had left Rome. Yes, an unobtrusive white Fiat was a wise choice.

He had unlocked the door for her by the time she came around to the passenger side and helped her in. He glanced back down the street from where they had come. In another moment he was behind the wheel inching out of a too-tight parking spot and merging with traffic. He was watching the rearview mirror.

"Very smooth operation, Mr. Keller."

"Thanks."

He accelerated and turned several corners before heading in his desired direction. "Well, we ditched Donaldson."

Apparently he was satisfied for he slowed down and relaxed a little.

Krista glanced at him as he tossed his Stetson in the back. Dark hair, very nice...Dark eyes, just as nice, that changed quickly from laughter to veiled cynicism, as though he was secretly laughing at her. Almost too good looking for her tastes. She remembered his flippant remark about "the more the merrier." He was certainly rugged enough to be one of those American cowboys she had read about in Uncle Franz's books. And she had seen a few John Wayne movies. In fact, he'd also make an excellent cross country skier, a mountain climber...Suspicious, she tensed a little. That Dallas accent had disappeared in the clothing store. What accent had it been?

He fussed with his thick gold watch, removed it, tapped it, held it to his ear, frowned, and shook his head impatiently. He laid it in the clean ashtray facing them.

"Battery's dead. All gold and no brains." He smiled. "Guess I need a Swiss watch."

She looked away.

"I was knocked for a loop when Gotthard told me your name isn't von Buren."

Krista looked at him, surprised by the sudden switch in conversation. Was that a deliberate tactic, to evoke a quick, unguarded response? "Paul told you that?"

"Why, wasn't he supposed to?"

"No."

"Oh well. Your secret's safe with me. He was showing me your portfolio. Nice pictures, with you wearing jewels and furs. All those fancy jewels come from the Gotthard mines in South Africa?"

Caution. "I suppose so. He's never said."

"I said how much you looked like him and Ehrlich. He had a fit."

She smiled. "It's no wonder, since I'm not related by blood." She could imagine Paul's mild offense at another man linking them together as brother and sister, with Ehrlich as father.

"Sure could have fooled me, though," he repeated. Then, his dark brows came together. "You looked surprised that Paul told me who you were. Is it something you want to keep under wraps?"

"Under wraps?"

"A secret. I didn't want to spoil things for you. I was thinking maybe Paul Gotthard wanted his friends in Zurich to think you're a blood relative to keep the men away. If that's the case, don't worry. I've no reason to blow the whistle."

Krista looked at him for a long moment. His smile came off as sincere, his eyes invited congeniality. She looked for a deeper meaning behind his question but didn't find it. Why mention Paul? Why not the von Burens? After all, it was their name. Unless it was the von Burens he wanted to discuss but was approaching the subject cautiously? But maybe Paul was right after all. There was nothing clandestine about him or Ava St. John. Maybe there really had been a nosy journalist harassing his client and he had wanted to lose him.

"Say, maybe I'm not too smart, but I don't get it. What's the big dark secret?"

"I don't know of any secrets, Mr. Keller. Should I? Just because my name isn't von Buren?"

He merely looked at her, his smile warm and almost guileless.

"My name is Grendelmier," she confessed.

"Well I don't see anything unattractive about the name," he said testily. "Maybe von Buren has a little more Nordic class to it, but hey, Grendelmier is good. It's better than Gotthard. I don't get Paul."

He was wrongly assuming. Deliberately, maybe? Well there was no secret there to hide. She corrected him politely. "Paul didn't change my career name because he was prejudiced against Grendelmier or Gotthard. It wasn't even his idea."

"Oh, well, I'm way out on a limb, aren't I? Sorry about that. I misunderstood him then. He implied..." he stopped.

Krista waited. What had Paul implied? But Jorden said no more. "I'm surprised Paul would even discuss it with you," she said. "It was someone else who thought the von Buren name would benefit my career."

He was quiet, glancing at her now and then as he drove the crowded street. That glance, though friendly, was like a yapping little dog nipping at her heels, steadily pushing her forward. Was he really this interested? Then she remembered with a flash; wasn't she supposed to be the topic that interested his client, Miss St. John? Still, she saw no harm in a few brief details. "I am related to the von Buren's in a small way, though not by blood. Through Elsa von Buren."

"Ah, Elsa. She'd be the wife of the respected banker Wilhelm von Buren," he said, as though proud that he'd been able to put it together.

"Yes, and Elsa is a Klossner. She was my grandfather's cousin."

"I can understand why she'd want you to use her married name. Family pride and all that. Sure, I can see how that makes sense. The von Burens and Klossners all intermarried, so why not?"

She hesitated. There was no blood shared between the two families, but what did it matter? After Ava St. John bought Paul's diamonds, Jorden would be returning with Ava to America anyway. His curiosity would soon evaporate. "There aren't any more von Burens. Just their son, Ehrlich."

"No aunt, uncles, and second-cousins?" he jested.

"I've never heard any mentioned."

"Then it's not like Texas. What about Paul?" he asked. "No von Buren blood?"

"Hardly. He's all Gotthard and proud of it. His uncle Josef is a bachelor and the owner of the fashion enterprise. Actually, I work for Josef. Paul is his only heir."

He gave a low whistle. "Rich, huh? Whoever marries him will be floating on Swiss Francs—and maybe some Jewish gold too." He laughed, as though they shared a tainted little secret, one he did not particularly find too offensive.

Krista flushed. "I don't find that remark amusing, Mr. Keller. Not with all the scandal about the Swiss Banks. I can assure you that neither the Gotthards nor the von Burens— or the Klossners or Grendelmiers for that matter—have one ounce of looted Jewish gold." But was that true? She hastened: "In fact, I find your jest crude and offensive!"

He held up a hand with a low whistle. "Hey, all right, I'm sorry." He sobered. "You're right, it was a low remark."

She jerked her head away and stared out the window. She wouldn't answer any more of his nosy questions. No, she didn't like this American at all. They were all like that—pushy.

After a minute of silence she began to think he knew it too, and perhaps regretted his words. She gave him a discreet glance and saw that same expression he had worn in the shop when they had ducked inside. He looked quite cool and collected, and deep in thought. Her eyes narrowed as she studied him thoughtfully. He must have sensed her cautious stare, for he turned his head and caught her gaze. For a brief second there was none of the exaggerated Texas cowboy. This time he looked away, as if he knew it too.

She snatched up his gold watch and put it to her ear. "The battery must have come to life," she said stiffly. "It's making a humming sound. Do batteries hum?"

He grabbed it from her and put it to his ear. "Well I'll be, the crazy thing is running again." He grinned and shook his head, as though the oddities of life were beyond his ability to fathom. He whistled a tune and slipped it back on his wrist. "Say, here we are! Safe and sound." He parked the Fiat next to the curb, left the keys under the floor mat—"Hate these things jangling in my pocket," he explained when she raised a brow—and sliding out from behind the steering wheel, he got out and came around to open her door.

Krista sat there pondering, arms folded. There was something odd about that watch—and his sunglasses. She recalled the cigarette case Paul had used in Rome to record a conversation at dinner one night. Later, he'd told her what it was. Agents used all sorts of unusual gadgets to take pictures and record—and to kill.

He opened the car door and Krista found him watching her, an alert glimmer in his eyes as though he read her thoughts. She avoided his gaze and stepped out, looking up at a house set back among some thick trees and shrubs.

"That's not the one," he said with dismissal. "We need to walk a few blocks."

She looked at him for an explanation but he didn't offer one. He hauled out her bag, followed by his cameras.

Fallen leaves muffled their footsteps as they walked in silence.

"Who owns the house?" she inquired.

"Some sleek guy named Hans Fischer. A friend of Ava's. They met at Monte Carlo once and became instant friends."

She watched the side of his face. "Do you know him?"

"I've met him," was all he said.

He had grown quiet and she glanced at him again. She had a notion to turn around and march back to the automobile. Something was very wrong. She ought not to trust this man, yet he appeared so easy going, almost innocent in his bungling ways. Was she a fool?

"You said you lost your sunglasses at the lodge—"

"Oh did I? Can't remember exactly. We've been sightseeing at so many places."

"Did you and Miss St. John ski at St. Moritz lodge? I was born and raised there."

"Don't tell me you're related to that friendly dude who ran the place?"

"Dude?" she wrinkled her brows.

"The manager...what was his name? Henrich?"

"That 'dude' as you Americans say, is my cousin Henrich Klossner."

Was his show of surprise genuine?

"Well, I'll be! So the family runs the St. Moritz lodge too. Brave, I'll say that for him."

She had never thought of Cousin Henrich as particularly brave. "Why so? Don't tell me he showed you his gun collection?" she asked glibly.

Jorden winced. "So that's how he hurt his knee. He shot himself? Just like my Gramps."

"Oh, Jorden!" she stopped, and smiled ruefully. "My cousin hurt his leg in a fall. He was a very good mountain climber at one time, just like my parents. It's been hard on him to stay at the lodge. My parents' death hasn't helped either. He took over running the lodge after them. He's been depressed for years now. He blames himself. He tried to rescue them but failed."

Now why had she unburdened herself by telling him all that? He seemed so easy to talk to, though handsome, yet safe and unintimidating compared to a Prince Ahmed or even Paul.

I'm being foolish. He could even be more dangerous.

"I'm sorry about your parents."

She actually believed him. It was one of the few times he appeared serious.

"How did the accident happen?"

"No one seems to know exactly. There was a snow storm blowing in and the local gendarmen think my mother became separated from the climbers trying to get back to the lodge. She must have slipped. My father was an expert mountain climber, though. Somehow he found her, went to rescue her, and also fell."

"So that's what the police told you?"

Why had he put it that way? She also realized suddenly that he hadn't asked what a gendarman was. He had known they were police. Fairly smart for a cowboy who an hour ago had stumbled over pronunciations in his little tourist book of phrases. She caught herself talking too much and changed the subject. "What of you, do you ski?"

He looked off toward the mountains. "Me? No way. Getting on those mountainous slopes could prove dangerous."

She covered a smile. "In fair weather it's safe. One gets used to heights. I've been skiing since I was five."

He looked horrified. "I hate to admit this, but I am, well, afraid of heights."

"Oh. I'm sorry." She glanced him over. For being so masculine he was afraid of a lot of things. *Remind me never to get in a situation where I need to depend on you to help me*, she thought dryly.

"But there are, um...well, children's ski courses at the lodge," she suggested kindly. "You might try one sometime."

"Maybe...if it isn't too steep." He looked at her and smiled, then put on his sunglasses.

"When are you going back to St. Moritz?" he asked.

"Just as soon as I've finished this job for Paul." More than ever she was anxious to go home.

"A kiddie's run, huh?" He settled his hat. "Maybe I'll stop by for a weekend sometime. Would you teach me? You know...go along and encourage me?"

On the children's course. She briefly scanned his height and solid muscled frame and held back a laugh. "I suppose you could learn." She couldn't resist: "That is, Mr. Keller, if you're not afraid of the snow."

"Afraid of the snow? Why? Is it very deep?"

She drew in a breath and walked ahead, hands shoved in her coat pockets.

They approached a large, gray stone house sitting back from the cobbled street on a mound. A flight of short stone steps led up to a porch with sturdy gray pillars—and more ugly little gargoyles grinning at her.

There were a few other cars parked along the curb, all small, non-descript, hunched under a line of trees. No one else was in sight as he opened a gate and allowed her to pass through. They walked along the brick path and up to the front porch in silence.

"Ava will be a little disappointed you're not a von Buren." He took out a key and turned the lock. The door swung open.

She looked at him. "Why disappointed?"

"Oh, she's heard all about Elsa von Buren, about her award-winning photography."

Photography. Her spine tightened. She kept her expression non-committal. "Oh?"

He went on: "To Ava, Frau Elsa is as much a celebrity as she is. Ava's collected her published works through the years. She may have a few with her now to show you."

She felt a chill as the silence of the house enclosed her. Caution...

"Elsa would be pleased to know her work is appreciated," she managed flawlessly.

"Ava would give anything to meet her, to see her work. So would I. Do you think you could arrange a little meeting?"

He closed the front door, and Krista found herself in the square hall looking up into his dark eyes.

"You're in luck," she breathed. "At least about seeing her work. The Vienna museum is going to show her photography. Someone from there is coming to talk with her soon. She mentioned it to me this morning."

Was it her imagination or did his jaw flex. "I'm disappointed. I'd like to see it while Ava and I are in Zurich. I don't think we'll be stopping in Vienna on the way back to America. We thought you might manage it."

"I'm so sorry," she said with a smile. "I wish I could oblige you both, but I haven't that sort of liberty with the von Burens."

"Paul Gotthard said you lived at the mansion."

He didn't need Paul to tell him, she thought. Somehow she suspected he already knew. "Only as a guest, and only when I'm in Zurich between modeling jobs. It's more of a business arrangement than family. You see, all the gowns and some of the jewelry I model are kept at the mansion."

"Ah well then…"

She had foiled him. She felt pleased. She stood there as he walked to the stairway.

"No housekeeper," he called back cheerfully. "She has the day off."

"With a dinner party planned for Miss St. John?" Her brows arched.

He smiled. "She plans to cater. If you need anything in the meantime, you can ring me. Your room is up here. Second one to the left. I'll tell Ava you've arrived."

She looked around bewildered. The house appeared empty. "What of the hairstylist? When Paul arrives tonight I want to be at my professional best."

He looked at his watch and frowned. "She should have been here by now. I'll ask Ava."

He allowed her to pass him on the stairway, then escorted her down the hall. He opened the door of a bedroom and extended his arm wide. "I hope you'll be comfortable." His eyes showed humor.

"I'm sure I will be, Mr. Keller." She entered. Setting her bag down and removing her coat, she laid it on the dark wood chair. It was a handsome room with expensive furnishings and a window that looked onto the front gate. She turned about, taking in everything, and saw that he was still there watching her. She caught him off guard and was shocked by what she saw in his face when he hadn't expected her to see: anger and outright dislike.

She was so taken aback by the discovery that she stood staring at him. *Why, he doesn't like me. He doesn't even find me pretty. All those words at the bank had been pretense.*

He looked back, brows raised, pretending he didn't know he had given himself away. She flushed. His jaw set. *He knows I saw what was really in his heart*, she thought, dismayed.

He turned almost abruptly, pulling the door shut behind him in the hall. She heard his footsteps die away.

Her eyes narrowed slightly. She was still standing there a minute later trying to recover.

She had been suspicious of him, and yet, strangely, she had rather liked him and thought the feeling was mutual. She had accepted his smiles and smooth, innocent cowboy remarks as playful. But that stark look of dislike could not be denied. She felt a strange sensation in her stomach. He wasn't real at all. Just as she had feared, he'd been playing a role. For whatever reason, he disliked her and everything about her.

The realization was startling and painful. For a blind moment she almost grabbed her bag and walked to the door. She wasn't about to stay in this strange house with a man that was most likely dangerous. And if not that, at least sinister.

But what about Paul? She had promised him she'd go through with this. And there was Interpol. What was it about her that Jorden Keller and Ava St. John wanted to find out?

Yes, she was sure of it now. The sun glasses, the watch, they were most likely a camera and recorder. And Paul had been deceived into thinking Jorden Keller was harmless. Keller had tricked him. But he hadn't completely deceived her. She would be on guard. And that talk of the von Burens just now in the hall, and of Elsa's photography—there was something to all that, but what?

She suddenly remembered something; Paul had mentioned planting a recording device on her for her meeting with Ava. Interpol would be disappointed. It appeared as if Paul had failed this time. The lack of a recording device for Interpol would be a loss. If Jorden and Ava intended to record their interview with her—as most likely they were—he could have played that game too and gotten down their questions. That would have told Paul everything on their mind.

In frustration she walked over to the door and bolted it. As she turned away, her face strained, her eyes fell on some magazines on the table. *Mademoiselle* and *Europa*. She picked them up and leafed through them, knowing she would find her photo in the advertisement for Gotthard diamonds and gold. Had Jorden placed them here?

She found the page that had a marker. There she was, a beautiful fantasy dressed in black velvet and draped with white diamonds. "Diamonds are Eternal," read the simple caption. She looked at the flawless face, a trick of the cameras. She saw herself as a stranger. A beautiful stranger. She dropped the magazine with distaste. She thought of Jorden. For the first time she felt the sting of rejection. He had not been impressed with her. It cut deeply. For the first time in many years her emotions bled.

Little fool, she thought. *You meet a total stranger and find yourself strangely attracted. Despite the risk, you enjoyed your foolish rush through the streets with him. And after all that, he turns out to be the one man that rejects you with scorn and dislike written all over his handsome face!*

She walked to the mirror and looked at her flustered expression, and was surprised to see the look of vulnerability and pain in her eyes. Rejection. He did not like Krista von Buren. He did not even think her pretty, she thought again, amazed. Or maybe he did, but he still rejected her. Although she had decried the fact that her appearance had been the one thing men were attracted to, she felt frightened when she discovered that she had failed where Jorden Keller was concerned.

She turned her back on the mirror. *The Lord won't reject me, no, not even when I'm old and decrepit*, she told herself.

The moment was a point of self-realization. Despite all of her boasts that she hadn't trusted in her appearance, she found, to her dismay, that she had. At least to a certain extent. Her beauty was her strength, even though she had told herself time and again that it was the Lord she depended on. That the Lord looked on the heart, not the body.

Slowly she opened her bag and removed the velvet dress, laying it out carefully on the oversized bed, followed by the black strappy heels, and all the delectable little things she wore with it. She wouldn't admit it, but she had looked forward to looking nice to see Jorden's response. She looked toward the door, where she had bolted it. How wrong she had been. And how unnerving to know she could be that wrong. Who could she trust in life? The skin on the back of her neck crawled. She looked over at the telephone. Yes, she must call Paul and warn him. There was danger here after all. Perhaps for both of them—even Elsa?

6

Jorden Keller shut the bedroom door behind him and discarded his smile. A cool, formidable calm was reflected in his features. "Sweet Little Heidi" was lying. She was a von Buren by blood. Working with Gotthard Enterprises to protect the few remaining Nazi war criminals in disguise across Europe. The respectable "Swiss" banker Wilhelm von Buren was an old SS officer from the Auschwitz-Birkenau death camps. The Mossad, the Israeli secret police, of which he was a member, was determined to get him. Wilhelm would stand trial in Israel, just like Eichmann had been tried there and hung.

He must act swiftly, waste no time, count each second. Paul Gotthard had temporarily fallen for the absurd masquerade of the easygoing cowboy agent, but Jorden knew Gotthard. Beneath his own facade of diamond entrepreneur there lay a man of cold, shark-like abilities. The charade Jorden was now involuntarily enmeshed in had too many discrepancies to hold up.

His jaw tightened as he strode down the corridor to Stella's room. Ava St. John! This entire fiasco, planned by Stella, could cost him his position with the Mossad if they found out. If it hadn't been that she was in danger, that they had once thought themselves in love, he would never have come, never involved himself. He had known from the beginning that the plan had its risks. If his superior found out he was working with her again...

This house, for instance, he thought with frustration, too many windows, too many doors, too many terraces—a security agent's nightmare. And all flanked with shrubs and a high fence lined with trees. The perfect set-up for surveillance by the enemy. No wonder Stella had been dismissed a year ago from cooperating with the Mossad. She had blown a job through taking unnecessary action and an ally had been killed. His death at the hands of the Moslem extremist group, the Hizbullah, in the terrorist camps in Lebanon had not been a pleasant one.

First lesson, Keller, never go against your own instincts. They've saved your neck in some tight places so far.

All right wise guy, be fair with her. You know why you came, why you listened.

Stella had first contacted him when he was in Rome watching the beautiful but deadly Nordic model in black velvet, Krista Von Buren. His eyes narrowed. How guileless she behaved! A man could end up dead by trusting her. She was Paul Gotthard's little sweetheart, all right, but his partner in espionage as well.

As for Stella Cohen, she had been on her own since he'd been forced to suspend her from the Israeli secret security at the decision by his superior, Avi Herschel. Stella was now living in Vienna and trying to track down her Jewish roots through her grandparents, the Cohens, who had died with six million other Jews. She had found something, she told him, that might also benefit him in his plan to get Wilhelm von Buren. Could she fly to Rome to meet him there? He had told her no. It was better to meet her. Stella might trip his cover in Rome.

Stella had found something all right. And now she had Gotthard Enterprises' secret terrorist group on her trail. Jorden had flown to Vienna and met her in a cozy little cafe where members of the "superior race" had once sat and calmly devised ways to send the earthly seed of Abraham to the gas chambers.

Stella was too risky to keep in highly sensitive locations, but it was equally true that when she did stumble across something important, it turned out to be dynamite. And what she had told him, if it could be proven, was the first big break he had obtained on unmasking von Buren as a Nazi war criminal. If only he could nail him. It wouldn't be easy. He was now a respected conservative Swiss banker. Jorden didn't even have Wilhelm von Buren's real Nazi name. His secret cover-up had proven nearly flawless—except for Elsa—who talked too much about her photography. He smiled coolly. There was always a weak link somewhere if you could just find it.

Jorden paused in the hallway and tapped twice on Stella Cohen's door.

She opened quickly and stepped back. By habit Jorden's alert gaze swept the bedroom before he entered.

She closed and locked it behind him. "Well? What do you think of her?" She anxiously searched his face for vindication of her story.

Stella was smart and likable with raven-hair and big brown eyes. He'd discovered two years ago that his attraction to her was not lasting. Instead of love, he had discovered the relationship had turned into friendship. She had become almost like a sister. It had been a disappointment to him. He had wanted it to last. He had tried. Perhaps he had tried too hard to fall in love. In the end he learned that love wasn't something he could arrange. More often than not, it came at an inconvenient time and in unexpected ways. He could do without it.

"What do I think?" he said evasively. "My dear girl, I still think you ought to go home to Queens." He smiled, but his eyes were sober. "Find some stable, respectable guy and get married. Raise those half dozen kosher kids you always talked about."

She offered him a Mona Lisa smile. "I gave that dream up a long time ago. Say—you're not making any bids are you? You'd be surprised at how forgiving I am."

Out of affection for her he maintained a rather harsh indifference. She still blamed him for the end of the perfect romance. He had hated hurting her.

"The only bids I'm making is on getting you home to your Aunt Tirzah. Maybe we'll both be in Queens by August—but who'd want to be with such a nice view!" He walked casually onto the terrace, scanning the layout of the back yard where the blue water in the pool ruffled in the breeze. "You're slipping, Stel. I asked you to keep these terrace doors shut and bolted, drapes drawn—like so." And he slid the bolt into place and drew the blinds shut, darkening the room. He switched on the overhead light.

He walked over to the table and poured himself a cup of coffee. She followed, watching his face. "Evidently Paul Gotthard fell for your theatrics? It fit well, did it?"

He noticed she looked pleased over her success. He gave her a wry look and placed the Stetson hat on her head. "Just barely. Like these boots. Next time get them a size larger. On second thought, don't plan any more masquerades. I'll manage on my own. A cowboy lawyer-agent!"

"It worked, didn't it? I delivered, didn't I? She came with you? Did you see the ring?"

He looked at the sandwiches she'd made. "Come on, Stella, sauerkraut? Has it actually come to this?"

She shrugged, looking downcast at his mood. He relented and picked one up. The rye bread was soggy and smelled vinegary. "This is revolting, you know that, don't you?"

"That's all there was," she said. "It was either that or ham. Look, Jorden, I appreciate your help. I really do. How can I thank you?"

"Don't try. And your ham joke wasn't funny."

"I'm serious."

"So am I. You want to thank me? Then call this off and catch the first plane out of Kloten airport. Go home to New York like I begged you. You're through with espionage, sweetie."

"Oh, yeah? We'll see. You can't make me return to Queens. I know too much."

"Blackmail?"

She grinned. "Come clean. I know why you came running to Zurich to help me."

He looked wearily at the ceiling. "Wrong. I didn't come running to Zurich to help you. I'm here on a job of my own. The two happened to supplement each other nicely." He looked at her evenly. "For a time, and only that." He tapped his watch. "Our time ends tonight. At the stroke of midnight. I've work to do in Liechtenstein."

He could see she pretended not to hear him. He bit into the sauerkraut sandwich. He was right. It was disgusting.

What men put up with when they're hungry and the woman is helpless and at risk.

"What's Krista doing now?" she asked.

"Heidi is dressing to impress."

"Stop calling her that. She may be my cousin."

"You're dreaming. She's a full-blooded German." He dropped the soggy sauerkraut bread back to the paper plate, wiped his hands on a napkin, and shook his dark head. "I'm out of my mind to have come here."

"Jorden, that ring proves she's related."

"It proves nothing. The Nazis stole everything they could get their bony fingers on. Where do you think Gotthard got all that jewelry for his early years of business? You don't mine rubies and emeralds from South African diamond mines."

Stella turned away, her expression sickened. Jorden was past feeling emotionally sick over the holocaust. He finished his coffee with cool determination. Stella never got over it. She could still cry when she looked at the old nightmarish photographs of the death camps. As far as he was concerned matters at this date in history revolved around one thing: keeping Israel strong. Never again must the Jews permit themselves to be vulnerable. They must be militarily strong. And the Mossad must remain a secret police that was free to act as it saw fit whenever and wherever it was needed.

"The ring didn't come from the death camp victims," she insisted. "Not from the train of jewelry and watches leaving Auschwitz's gas chambers. I'll get the answer today."

She turned, smiled a peace offering, and planted a quick kiss on his cheek before he could resist. "You were good to come and help me, Jorden. Just like a brother." She glanced at him with a smile, but he pretended not to notice the deliberate emphasis. She swept over to the mirror, turning herself about. "Well, how do I look? Like a Hollywood star?"

He laughed softly.

"Brute," she said good naturedly.

"Not bad," was his casual comment. "Little Heidi has swallowed your role like a trout. With no credit due to either of us, I hasten to add. All I go through, dear, for brotherly love. To make sure your neck is delivered from the Gentile chopping block."

"Thanks. But you're not fooling me. I've given you useful information and you know it. You're just afraid Avi will find out about it and reinstate me with honors."

He poured himself a second cup. She was wrong. Only three out of a thousand candidates were chosen to serve in the Mossad. Stella had served in the inner circle of friends of the agency; those who helped the regular agents in an emergency. They were world wide. "I'm sentimental about losing old friends whom I've worked with in tight spots," was all he said.

Her face sobered and he guessed she was remembering Finney. Finney was the agent's code name of course. He'd been killed tracking a terrorist who had blown up a bus in Tel Aviv. Stella had liked Finney. There had been a small chance the two of them might have gotten together romantically.

She walked over to the chair beside the table and sat down.

Jorden had taken no pleasure in reminding her of Finney. By doing so, he also reminded himself. It was too easy to forget those who were dying in the line of duty. He'd knowingly settled for a short life. A wife and children belonged to those who didn't meet terrorists on crowded busses. He wouldn't leave behind a wife and baby. He did his job because he believed in it, not because it promised longevity. Stella was another matter. He had hopes for her to settle down and tell stories to her great-grandchildren.

"I'm smart enough to understand I'm out of the agency for good," she admitted. "If I hadn't stumbled onto this information in Vienna, I'd still be there researching my book." She leaned forward, growing intense. "I'm not going back to Queens, Jorden. I'm staying in Austria."

He shook his head, displeased. The Nazi past was dead, or it was supposed to be. He wasn't convinced. Anti-Semitism was like a latent disease always ready to crop up under the right circumstances. There was no love for Jews in Austria. Not that there were many Jews left. Most of them were new emigrants from Iran, Iraq, or from the north in the old Soviet Union. Why any Jew would wish to emigrate to Austria or Germany baffled him. Perhaps they had no other place to go. This was another ongoing problem facing the state of Israel. There weren't enough jobs, not enough land. And the UN wanted them to give up still more to their sea of Arab neighbors, most of whom were sworn to Israel's destruction.

"You're sure it isn't a mistake to stay there? It's one rough place for a lone Jewish girl to settle down, isn't it? No family, friends, a nearly empty Jewish neighborhood full of haunting memories and old houses? In my mind it's like adopting a hair shirt. You can pursue a writing career anywhere. Someplace where you're safe." *So I won't need to worry about you*, he could have added.

"Living there does have its moments," she admitted. "I wouldn't be honest if I pretended otherwise. But, Jorden," and her eyes moistened. "You can't imagine what it's like to have actually walked into your grandparents' old flat. I found things that belonged to them—yes, still there. It was all like another world. I couldn't believe it. Imagine, the same worn rug after all these years. But there it was, just as Great-Aunt Tirzah described it to me. Even the sagging bed. It was incredible. And emotional enough to give me a migraine."

He couldn't imagine himself wanting to go back. He wanted to remember the past because there were lessons for future survival in remembering, in keeping alive the holocaust for new generations, but his ambitions didn't drive him the way Stella's did to rekindle live memories from dead ashes. Maybe it was different for a woman. They were sentimental about family trees, about cultivating emotional roots.

"Stella," he warned softly. "You're asking for raw pain. Like deliberately playing old love songs and looking at photographs from some forgotten summer. Why set yourself up for hurt? Throw all that aside. Get on with a life of your own. That marriage I mentioned, those kids..."

She stood and shook her head. "You think that's an answer for everything don't you? Yet you run from those things. Oh I know." She tossed a hand airily. "You're different from them. Well I'm different too. The things you talk about for me don't exist and probably never will. I'm not going to cry about it. Nor am I going to play old love songs and weep into my chicken soup. I'm going to write that book on my grandparents and what happened to them." She smiled crookedly. "Right now my heart is in touch. It will make all the difference when I write."

Jorden scowled, pretending strong disapproval, but loving her for her bravery. He'd need to work on Avi to get someone to keep an eye on Stella.

She pulled her sleeves up as she paced, watching the floor. "That Swiss bank account number is there somewhere. Great-Aunt Tirzah was sure her father wrote it down on something permanent. Something that wouldn't get lost."

Jorden's lawyer friends Morgenthau and Hammerstein were pursuing information from the Bank of Zurich Corporation, Wilhelm von Buren's old workplace from where he'd retired a few years ago, but he knew from a brief meeting with them last night that they were far from getting anything important out of Ehrlich. He smiled to himself. They hadn't even recognized him this morning as the cowboy, although Hammerstein had glanced his way. He didn't want them to know he was working secretly with their client, Stella. Word might drift to his Mossad superior. Mistakes happened that way. Avi Herschel would be furious.

"Grandfather Benjamin was ill the first time he returned to the flat after the Gestapo called him for interrogation," Stella told him in a low voice. "His head was injured, Tirzah said. Her father was afraid he'd lose his memory. So he wrote it down." She stopped pacing and looked at him. "It's got to be somewhere in that Vienna flat."

Jorden was looking at his coffee cup with distaste. He set it down. Could the number be there still? So far, luck had not been on their side. If the elder Mr. Cohen had written it down, where would he write it for permanence, for safety? A ledger would be confiscated by Nazis or lost through the years. Maybe Stella was right. Somewhere inside the flat itself.

"I want his account," she continued, twisting her hands as she paced. "Oh, not for money, that's what the Swiss think, but they've always misunderstood us. I want it for the sake of justice." Her eyes flashed. "He earned every reichsmark from his business. Why should the Swiss banks have it? Drawing interest all these years? That number must be there somewhere," she repeated, "and I'll find it. The Swiss have no right to intimidate me, to stall, to behave the offended party before the world's newspapers! The neutral Swiss, my foot! Nazi collaborators, Hitler's bankers. The Swiss border guards turned back the Jewish refugees—turned them back straight to the Gestapo—and my great-grandparents and their son and daughters were among them."

"Easy, dear, you don't need to convince me. I understand."

She turned away, drawing in a breath. "Yes, of course you do. Sorry, Jorden." She looked at him sheepishly. "I didn't mean to launch off like that. I get overly emotional sometimes."

"Don't worry about it," he soothed. "I also know what they now say: 'Forget what they did, it was our grandparents' generation. How long will you keep throwing this in our faces?' It's a symptom of this generation," he told her. "Today nobody wants to face responsibility. Don't trouble us with unpleasant things. It's just one more..." he stopped, catching himself. "Now I'm soapboxing," he admitted, impatient with himself. He had thought he was past all that, able to just do his job.

Stella shook her head and walked back to the chair. She looked exhausted, he thought as she slumped into the cushions. He refilled her cup and brought it to her. "Hold on, kid, you'll be all right one of these days. Israel will survive, and so will we."

His own family had gotten out of France before the Germans marched in. His grandfather had seen the betrayal coming and through contacts inside Switzerland and bribes, managed to make it into England, then after the war to New York, and eventually in 1949 to Texas. His grandfather had money and hated city life. He'd bought a ranch and hired one of the best ranchers to manage it while Jorden's grandfather learned, and then he had passed it on in turn to Jorden's father. His father had cultivated hopes of also passing it on to him. In high school, however, Jorden had made a break to become himself. Injustice angered him. It had seemed right to become a lawyer. His father, a mellow, loving man, had released him from his expectations and encouraged him to enter Yale. Later, after graduation he had opened up his practice in Dallas and became successful, eventually working for the state prosecuting attorney. After his father died, Jorden sold the ranch and emigrated to Israel. He'd met Stella Cohen, who was a New York college student working for a summer on a kibbutz farm on the Golan Heights. They'd become friends, then a mild romance had struck up. Jorden then went into the army, fought in Lebanon against the Hizbullah, and served as an agent helping American troops in the war against Iraq. Because of his record he had been recruited by the Mossad. The training had been tough, with hardships, and finally even an unexpected capture by the Mossad itself, with ruthless interrogations and beatings. He had passed their stringent, brutal test, proving to them and himself that he would die before talking. So he had become one of them. Their rule was that there were few if any rules. Almost anything was allowed. They were on their own once given an assignment. If an innocent got in the way when catching a terrorist, that was to be lamented. Once a member of the Mossad shot an enemy, he was taught to fire a second shot to the head to ensure death. No, the Mossad was not for the squeamish. But the Mossad needed to exist. And Jorden believed in it without apology. The Mossad was so secret, its very existence, at times, was denied by the Israeli government. No member of this elite, highly patriotic group could even speak its name, on threat of removal, except at their special meetings.

Meanwhile, it was made possible by those higher up in government circles, CIA included, to allow Jorden to also keep his position at the Dallas firm as a cover. For all practical purposes he was an American. Because the firm handled international cases he had legitimate reason to spend a good deal of time in Europe. From Europe he secretly went into Israel, the Middle East, and often came here to neutral Switzerland. Zurich crawled with spies, international agents, and informants. He had secret friends here and several enemies.

"What happened at the meeting this morning between Morgenthau and Ehrlich von Buren?" Stella asked. "Were they able to gain any cooperation about my grandfather's account?"

"No. But Ehrlich looked worried. So did Paul Gotthard. They'll report to Wilhelm. You've stirred up a den of snakes. Be sure you watch your step. After this meeting with von Buren's granddaughter, I want you out of Zurich—not that Vienna is going to be much safer. You're sure you won't reconsider and let us handle all this?"

She shook her head firmly. "I need to be in Vienna to follow through on my research."

He wondered if Vienna would satisfy her. "St. Moritz is likely to prove a dangerous place to be. Don't go there. Get what you can from Miss von Buren, then catch the next flight out of Zurich for Austria."

She smiled. "Yes, sir."

He returned the grin. "All right, what's this new tidbit you have on Wilhelm?" He rummaged through the small bag of lunch goods she had brought. There was a package of Swiss cookies, tiny lacy things dribbled with chocolate. He munched on them while she settled back to tell him her story.

She looked self-satisfied as she glanced at him. "I have something important."

"Do you?" He watched her. Stella could be frustrating. "Out with it." He pointed to his watch.

"My grandfather may have written down something more besides the numbered account in the Bank of Zurich Corporation." She hesitated and said in a low voice: "The name of his Nazi interrogator who wanted his account number, perhaps before he crossed the borders into neutral Switzerland to change his name?"

Von Buren. Jorden's hand with the cookie stopped dead. His heart raced. Could it be? He dropped the package on the table, walked up to her chair, took hold of her hands and pulled her on her feet, holding her arms tightly. "How do you know this? Is this just your brain child or have you any proof?"

"Proof. How does Aunt Tirzah sound for someone stable and dependable? She was the one who told me. She's beginning to discuss details she wouldn't speak about before." Her eyes gleamed. "It's there, Jorden. In the flat. It's got to be. It's somewhere with the account number. Some place that grandfather believed was permanent. He knew he'd lose it at Auschwitz, so he took a chance and did the one thing that was feasible at the time: he must have written both the account number and the name of the Nazi agent in the flat."

Yes, yes, unless the flat was bombed or torn down, it offered a chance of survival to a desperate man like Benjamin Cohen. Yes, he might do something like that himself. Where would he put it in the flat that would last until he believed Germany would be defeated?

"Grandfather was right. The flat," she said in a low voice, "is still there. Vienna, in most respects, looks just the way it did back then. Just like Zurich's Old Town."

"If I can find the Gestapo's real name and trace it to Wilhelm Von Buren, to the account he stole, I've got him."

They stared at each other. She winced, and he realized his grip was too tight. He turned her loose, but only after he'd planted a kiss on her forehead. "You do have your times of brilliance, Stella dear."

She looked pleased.

He paced, restlessly. It was perhaps one chance in a hundred, but all he needed was one fortunate break. "Why didn't you tell me sooner? In Vienna I could have gone straight there."

"I didn't know then. I told you, it was Tirzah who broke the news to me."

"Tirzah," he repeated. "Bless her heart. When did you see her about it?"

"At Chanukah. I was home gathering information from her. One last try before I tackled the book. But you know Tirzah, she doesn't like to talk about it. She knew I was researching and making preparations to return to Vienna, but she found it convenient to blame her aging memory. I felt that she might be using that as an excuse. The big break came after I returned to Vienna in January. I wasn't there a week before I received a letter from her. She suddenly began telling things about her girlhood in Vienna, and about her father, Benjamin. More letters came. Each with more information. She told me about the ring. It was then I contacted you."

"Do you have the letter she sent about the account number and Gestapo?"

"That information was too crucial for a letter, she said. I heard about it straight from her when she arrived. She's in Vienna. In the hospital. I'm due to see her again as soon as I get back."

Jorden turned sharply, troubled. "Tirzah? She's with you in Vienna?" Tirzah had turned 76 on her last birthday and was in weak health. To have made the trip to Vienna would have been painful and emotionally exhausting. Tirzah, who had been unable to deal with the holocaust, had preferred to live with a lapse in memory all these years. Until just this last year she would not even discuss her father, who had died at Auschwitz. Only when the Swiss banking scandal broke and the Republican senator Alfonse D'Amato had begun his publicized hearings into the banks, had Tirzah appeared to awaken from a bad dream. She had taken a sudden, profound interest in the hearings. It was then that she had begun to disclose information.

"Yes, she's here," Stella repeated. "I was waiting for the right opportunity to tell you. She flew in a couple of days ago from New York looking for you."

He walked up to her, frowning. "Looking for me?" Had she first intended to give the information to him instead of Stella? "Did she say why she wanted to see me?"

"No, not yet. It may have been the information about her father writing down the account number and Gestapo's name, or maybe something else. She won't say. She wasn't well...it may have been the trip back to Austria. And— seeing the flat again."

"Are you saying Tirzah entered the flat?" He frowned again, worried.

"Believe me, Jorden, I didn't expect her to do so. I never would have asked her to come there. I thought the dear old sweet would collapse when she walked in. Neither of us could sleep that night."

He breathed his frustration. "You should have told me sooner, Stella."

She looked hurt. "I've just seen you for the first time since our meeting. Did you want me to blurt out everything on the phone?"

He smiled and cupped her chin, soothing her almost as if she were a child. "Relax. It's all right. I'll see Tirzah as soon as I can get away from Zurich. I can't go now, though. I've got to keep this meeting with an agent in Liechtenstein. I want you to go ahead of me to Vienna. We shouldn't be seen together. Lars is on my trail. Maybe a few others as well. As soon as I get back here I'll fly to Vienna and see Tirzah. What's she in the hospital for, anything serious?"

"No, the doctor said she was overly tired. A few days rest and she'll be all right."

"Then let's get this meeting with Krista over with." Jorden walked to the door. "I've got to search that flat."

"I've searched a dozen times and found nothing."

"And Tirzah says she doesn't know anything?"

"She says no. I believe her."

Maybe, he thought. But Benjamin Cohen would have trusted someone in his family with the information. Why had she come to Vienna at this stage in her life, when leaving New York seemed such a risk for her? He worried about the elderly woman in the hospital. If only he didn't need to meet the CIA contact in Liechtenstein! But knowing

Flanders, he had something important. Maybe more important than what even Tirzah may have to give him.

Stella anxiously searched his eyes. "What I want to know is if she has the ring on."

"Yes. I told you. It's exactly as you described it. A ruby, gold, encircled with smaller diamonds in the shape of stars."

Stella removed the folded sheet from *Europa* magazine. Krista stared up at him with a smile. His mouth tipped downward. Delectable morsel, but one that promised certain indigestion. On her hand was the ring Stella described. "Yes, that's it," he admitted. "And she probably got it from Wilhelm or Paul Gotthard. I wouldn't set so much hope by it."

"There, you see?" she said as though vindicated. "It's enough she's wearing the ring. The ring that belonged to my great-aunt. Tirzah said it was the same one."

"Look, I admit it isn't likely there would be two such rings in Europe. It's very unusual." Jorden believed the stars to secretly represent the kingly star of David, but it was unusually done. The stars could also pass for the Christian cross. He knew why a Christian cross might be arranged in the center of the star of King David. There were friends who were trying to prove to him that Jesus was the promised Jewish Messiah. He had to admit that the Old Testament prophecies pointed to Jesus' fulfillment. Since he hadn't been raised Orthodox, considering Jesus as the Messiah didn't disturb him as it apparently did many religious Jews. Also, his mother was a Gentile and about as Texan as one could get.

"It *belonged* to Tirzah's sister," Stella said stubbornly. "My Great-Aunt Judith."

"All right, I'll go along with that," he said gently. "Still, we've got to play this carefully with Krista. If what we suspect about Wilhelm von Buren is correct, then he smuggled enough jewelry across the Swiss border after the war ended to open up ten jewelry shops. That ring *could have* been among the personal items of the death camp victims. I'm not altogether convinced."

It was also true that Stella was walking on thin ice. If Wilhelm suspected he might be unmasked as a former Gestapo agent he would do whatever needed to silence his accusers. That was where he and Avi believed Gotthard Enterprises came in. They had access to clientele who in turn would act to eliminate a perceived enemy if ordered to do so by von Buren.

And Krista was working with Paul. He had information showing she had met with enemy agents on at least two occasions recently to deliver information to a terrorist group.

"Did you get anything out of her about the von Burens?" Stella asked.

Jorden looked at the gold watch. He had recorded their conversation in the Fiat. That had been a mistake. She had suspected he might be recording her. She had also guessed about the sunglasses. All this convinced him further that she was no wide-eyed novice. The watch and sunglasses were rather outdated and clumsy, nothing like the miniature mechanisms now available. In Argentina and Berlin he had used a camera hidden behind a button. And Stella once had a microphone that looked like a sequin. This time he'd been caught unprepared, just like this entire cowboy fiasco. Still, all was not lost. He had gotten what he wanted. Several pictures of Paul Gotthard and Erhlich Von Buren at the bank, along with the third man who had shown up. And hopefully a snapshot of the thug who had been following them when he left the bank with Krista. He had never seen this man before. Did he work for Gotthard or Wilhelm? Time would tell.

Certainly Paul Gotthard was no fool either. As for Krista, there were times when she had watched him with a knowing eye, as though she peered through him, searching for the man beneath that flashing smile. She hadn't offered much information, but there were a few things worth passing on to Avi.

"I didn't learn anything astounding. She denies being a von Buren, but that's expected. She also made quite a show about being outraged over anti-Semitism. It was all an act," he said coolly. "A good one. She almost convinced me. Maybe you'll do better. But be careful with her. She's clever and she may be onto us. We'll need to work everything out with her before nightfall. She'll be wondering why Paul hasn't arrived with the diamonds. You're supposed to have arranged a dinner for him here at seven. His personal guards are to arrive before him with the jewels. I gave them the wrong address. Someone tried to follow me, but I lost him. Don't underestimate them, though. These guys are experts."

Stella nodded. "It shouldn't take me long to talk to her and learn what I need to know. An hour at the most. Maybe not even that."

He looked at the time. "All right. Speed it up if you can. The man following me would have reported in by now that I ditched him. I want us both out of here while she still expects Gotthard."

"Do we just leave her here?"

"She's on her own," he said indifferently. "Zurich's her turf. Once she guesses we've gone and left her, she'll wait for Gotthard. When he doesn't show, she'll call him. As soon as he tells her he had the wrong address she'll figure out something was wrong."

Again, she nodded agreement.

"How do you intend to play this meeting with her now?" he asked. He wanted no slip-ups.

"I'll ask questions about the diamonds first," she said, as if checking off a list. "She and I will talk on the divan while you play Mr. Nice Guy. I'll get a good look at the ring, steer the questions to other forms of Gotthard jewelry and eventually make over to the ring, asking where she got it."

He frowned. "I suppose it's the best we can do."

She frowned. "I thought I was doing pretty well."

He found his revolver in the wardrobe and slipped it inside his belt. It had been uncomfortable walking Zurich's Bahnhofstrasse without it, knowing the East German named Lars was following him, but he couldn't risk the chance of carrying a .38. He had been right about that. He tried not to smile when he recalled Krista's beaten expression when he'd pulled the gold pen out of his jacket instead of a gun. She had been so sure. Little did she know the pen was as dangerous as the revolver. One whiff of its gas, and its victim would be rushed to the Zurich hospital with the diagnosis of heart attack. No further questions asked.

Lars probably had something just as lethal, like a briefcase with a hypodermic needle. Bumped against a leg on a crowded street...the possibilities were endless.

Jorden slipped into the Western jacket to cover his revolver and walked to the door. "If she asks, your makeup artist has been called away. And your hairstylist was caught in traffic."

She nodded. "I'm ready. Let's get Act II over with."

He agreed. He would hate to have Gotthard and his "Gestapo" drive up. They had uncanny ways of showing up even when he didn't expect them.

He left her and walked slowly down the hall toward Krista's room, trying to get his mind back into the role of the easygoing cowboy agent.

Krista von Buren was coming back to mind. After watching her for the last six weeks on her fashion tour to Rome, she was as much a question to him now as she ever had been. He didn't like contradictions. Krista stood out as one woman he didn't understand. He had thought her private life while traveling with Paul Gotthard and the staff of Gotthard Enterprises would afford him with material to know what she was like. If he had formed any premature judgments she had wiped them out almost at once. He knew her from afar of course, since he had kept his distance, but he knew almost as much about her as he did Stella's recent activities. Though he had a file that included everything from her blood type to her favorite perfume, how did one explain a woman who modeled jewels and furs for oil-rich sheiks but who also carried a Bible?

She was engaged to Paul Gotthard and traveled with him and his secretary, but she never saw him alone on a date. They had dinner together, but he left her at the door without a kiss. Now, *that* absolutely amazed him. He could see why she may not be interested in his advances, but he couldn't understand Paul for not trying. Especially since they were supposed to be engaged. Was it a front? Maybe their relationship in espionage was strictly business? That made her more dangerous. She not only appeared a wide-eyed innocent, but she was chilling enough to keep herself from emotional entanglements. Yes, she was intriguing...

and that meant he had better watch himself. It had been a long time since he had found a woman so interesting.

Her light was out by ten in Rome and Venice. She was up by six and jogged for twenty minutes before breakfast. She was beautiful, but always alone.

There were two ways to interpret all this, he told himself again. Either she was totally committed to the espionage work of Gotthard's group or she was deceived. When he'd first found out about her he had hoped it would be the latter. But after her contacts with some of Gotthard's agents, Jorden was convinced otherwise.

He stopped outside her door and leaned there for a moment, his hand shoved in his pocket. She reminded him of that line from a poem his sister had placed on her bedroom wall when growing up: *Monday's child is fair of face...*

What else was Monday's child? he wondered. A nasty little spy with turquoise blue eyes. "Beauty is only skin deep," the old saying went. What was the other one? "Pretty is, as pretty does." He smirked as he raised his hand to tap. Fair Face probably kept a German luger concealed under black velvet.

He had learned three years ago in Argentina to watch his every step if he wanted to stay alive when it came to beautiful enemy agents. He dismissed Krista's looks as coolly as he did his Stetson hat.

He could do without it.

7

Why were there no servants moving about the house? And what was keeping the hairstylist? The rooms were too silent. Too still to be occupied by a busy family that entertained frequently. The Hans Fischer house seemed more like a mausoleum.

Again Krista went to the front bedroom window and peered below onto the wet gray street. There was no sign of either Hans Fischer or the hairstylist. She let the drape fall into place and turned away thoughtfully, glancing at her watch. In less than two hours Paul would arrive with the security team bringing the South African diamonds. She would be wise to be ready, just in case her suspicions were without merit.

There was a bathhouse with sauna connected to her room. She went there, sliding back the glass doors that opened onto a small balcony and stepped out. Below, a large pool with inviting aqua blue water beckoned. A stairwell at the side of the balcony led down two steep flights to a courtyard where pale blue enameled flower pots were filled with geraniums. Beyond the pool was a small tree garden surrounded by a high brick wall. She could just see over its ledge into the backyard of the neighboring house.

Who lived in the neighborhood? University professors? European celebrities from the films? Diplomats? Americans, perhaps? Who was Hans Fischer?

She breathed deeply of the fresh air, shutting out her concerns. *If I'd brought a bathing suit...*She leaned against the terrace railing enjoying the breeze.

A faint sound caused her to look down at the yard just below her balcony. Her eyes—or was it her senses?—must have overreacted to the day's tensions, for she was sure she had seen something pass by at the corner of her eye. She walked to the edge of the terrace for a better view, leaning over the rail. There was a porched-in area below running the full length of the back entrance to the house. Some tall feathery ferns moved silently in the breeze and some bright red primroses stared up at her mutely, as though guarding their secrets. What had she expected to see?

The bedroom phone gave a single short ring. Paul! She rushed from the balcony through the bath and sauna room and into her bedroom. She picked up the receiver, "Hello, Paul?" sounding breathless, a little overwrought. She waited expectantly. An awkward silence commanded her attention. She waited a moment longer, then: "Paul? Is that you?" When the silence deepened she slowly replaced the receiver. Strange. Had the call come from downstairs? Was Jorden Keller checking on her?

Krista became conscious of a disturbing presence. She turned and looked toward the window overlooking the pool. There was a large tree with overspreading leafy branches. If someone climbed into it they could stare right into the room. Her skin crawled. What about the man who'd been following her since Venice? What if he were some weird person who had a crush on her?

You really do need time away from Zurich, she told herself wearily, but nevertheless went and lowered the blinds. Only then did she throw herself into the task of preparing for modeling the diamonds.

It was perhaps a half an hour later when she crossed the room gowned in the simple but exquisite black dress designed especially for her. She turned her attention fully on her hair. She was fortunate that the long smooth waves had some natural curl of their own, so she needn't worry about setting it. She had watched the professional hairdresser long enough to copy the style used in her portfolio. She twisted and twirled the sections and pinned them into the sophisticated upsweep. Then she compared the outcome with her photograph shown in *Europa*. Not bad, she thought, but it wouldn't last without hairspray, and she had none. As for makeup, she used the bare essentials she had brought with her in her handbag. So much for depending on Ava's makeup artist. When she had finished, though she lacked the painted drama of her typical modeling sessions, it would do. As she stared at her reflection she thought again how her face and form affected her future. Would her appearance yield success, happiness? Maybe not...but without it, Krista von Buren would fade away into a forgotten entity. A woman without a future, without security and confidence, without Paul. Without anyone. Wrong! Who was in control of her destiny? The Lord. She had already begun working on her new commitment to develop a closer fellowship with Him. "Do not be conformed to the world," Paul wrote in Romans chapter 12.

"You are not alone. You will never be truly alone. Got that?" she told the woman in the mirror.

The image frowned at her, a stranger. *And I used to think beauty was a blessing*, she thought. *Is it? Perhaps. I suppose that fairness of face is like almost everything else, it depends on what the owner does with it.*

At last she had completed the ordeal, adding the finishing translucent powder. It was then that she heard what sounded like snapping branches outside the window. She froze. There was somebody in those tree branches. Thank goodness she had closed the blinds. Fingers of chilling fear tripped up her back. She told herself to be reasonable. Maybe it was just the wind rising again, disturbing the silence surrounding her and the strange house. No, there was someone out there.

She stood without moving, listening, then laid down her comb and looked toward the window. Maybe Ava or Jorden had gone out for a swim? Her frayed nerves rejected the weak explanation. Poor Jorden would be afraid of the water...

Every sound seemed sinister. Unfriendly. She walked to the blind on tiptoe, making no sound, and lifted one of the slots to peek out. A man stood below, close to the house. Even as Krista looked at him, he stepped back from the wall and stared up at the windows above him on the second floor as if contemplating how to get inside. Yes, it was the man she had bumped into at the Hauptbahnhof earlier that morning. The man she had first noticed in Rome. He could not see her, she knew, and yet his confrontational stare immobilized her. His jacket was unbuttoned and she noticed a flash of shoulder holster as he moved away toward the other side of the house. Was the front door locked? She didn't think so!

She stood without moving as if her feet were stuck to the floor. It was then she saw a second man—this one moved into the shrubs growing close to the house wall—just below the bathhouse terrace.

She rushed to the bedroom door and unbolted it so that she could alert Jorden Keller, then recalled his fear of guns. He would be no help at all. She ran to the telephone. Her cold shaking fingers rattled the phone from the cradle as she picked it up. Yes, Paul would know what to do—what was the bank's number? No, call the police, hurry—

She dialed for the operator, hearing her heart thudding in her ears but no dial tone. What was wrong? The connection was taking too long to get through. "Hello?" her demanding whisper sounded. "Police!" There was no response. Then she understood the reason for the delay, for the still, dark silence. The phone line was dead. He must have cut it. She remembered how the phone had made only a short ring, how she had gone to answer it, only to find no one there. He must have been trying to find out if she was in the room—

"Lord, help! What shall I do?" she prayed.

From outside in the hall there came a tap on the door. Krista whirled, the phone clutched in her hand.

"Jorden!" she called. "Hurry!"

He flung the door open and entered.

She rushed toward him and grabbed him.

"Nice welcome," he quipped silkily, but the slight smile vanished when he looked at her face and read her fear.

Krista saw an immediate change in the friendly cowboy. The handsome Jorden Keller with the easygoing smile had vanished. In his place was a cool and efficient stranger, whose eyes were intelligent and grave.

"What is it, Krista?"

Krista he had called her, for the first time. "Krista."

For a moment the words lodged like stickers in her dry throat.

"A man...below. Trying to get inside. He has a gun."

The dreaded word did not appear to phase him. She had anticipated that he might panic. Instead, he drew her to his side protectively as if trying to encourage a frightened girl. "Just one? You're sure?"

Just one?

"No, two. The other one walked around the house. I was going to call Paul but the line is dead."

"Nice and calm. The man below, what did he look like, did you see him at all? Was he blond-haired?"

"Yes, he looks Swiss."

"German, actually. Would he pass for an athlete, a skier perhaps, a climber?"

"Yes, yes! Does it matter now? What can we do?"

"Lars," he said under his breath, and glanced off thoughtfully. "I was sure I'd lost him."

"No, not Lars," she whispered. "I know Lars, he works for Paul. Lars can be trusted."

Jorden looked at her sharply. She wondered why.

"He travels with us when we are on tour. I told you at the bank. This is someone else. And the other man I've seen him before in Rome."

"Are you sure?"

"Yes, I saw him again today. He followed me when I left the von Buren house for the Hauptbahnhof. I even bumped into him." She hid a shiver. "I think he realizes I recognized him from Rome. That's why he's here..." her voice trailed with meaning.

He caught up the phone by the cord, placed it to his ear and listened. "Someone's cut the line all right," he commented in a low voice. He dropped the receiver silently onto the overstuffed chair.

His grip on her arm tightened. "Why didn't you tell me in the car?"

"Why should I?" she asked in genuine surprise. She could have said she hadn't wanted to frighten him, but checked her tongue.

He hesitated, looking at her thoughtfully, for what seemed to Krista an eternity. He appeared to come to some reluctant decision."

"What is it?" she whispered, her eyes searching his.

"I'll need to trust you won't I? At least for a while. You do look genuinely frightened. Unless you're a good actress as well as a model."

The answer was anything but what she'd expected. It was she who must trust him. "That goes both ways, doesn't it, Mr. Keller! Cowboy!"

He scanned her face, showing no emotion at all. "If this is a trap you've laid..."

Her lips parted. "Why you..."

"Quiet." He took firm hold of her elbow as she glared at him, now more offended by Jorden than the man prowling below. Jorden appeared indifferent to her open dislike of him and glanced from one window to the other. He checked the front, making sure it was locked, then propelled her to the rear window.

Krista tried to pull her elbow away but he held onto her. "Just relax, sweetheart."

"Don't call me that. What can we do?"

"I'll bring you to Ava. Stay with her until I get back. She has a gun—"

"Oh!" she said in a tight, breathless squeak. "You're going to run out on us! You...you coward." She jerked her arm away and turned to run, to find Ava and warn her of intruders, but his hand reached out and snatched her. She could feel the silky embroidery of the Stetson hats and broncos on her palms on his shiny cowboy shirt. He made no explanation, but neither did he seem angry that she had called him a coward.

"Too late. Stay put. I'm afraid this is going to get rather nasty."

He pulled out a small plain looking case from his pocket and extended an antenna.

"It's J," he spoke quietly. "A hyena was spotted. I need help."

"Hey, it's the Oklahoma kid."

"Just get a move on, joker. Get to Stella. Over and out." He replaced the case into his jacket, ignoring her scrutiny.

"Where did you get that?" she whispered.

He didn't answer. In the next moment she sensed that something alerted him from the direction of the bathhouse.

"Oh no…" Her breath tightened as she envisioned herself as she had been earlier, standing out on the terrace, hearing the phone ring, then rushing indoors to answer…and leaving the sliding glass door wide open!

She gripped his arm and pointed toward the door, but he must have already heard the sound. To her stunned surprise, she saw a .38 revolver was already in his hand, complete with silencer. He drew her behind him. "Under the bed," he whispered, but Krista was too frightened to move. She knelt there staring at the bathroom door, a cold hand over her mouth, the name of her God on her tongue.

This was a dark and evil nightmare! This could not be actually happening. With an overwhelming flood of horror she understood that it was, that danger and death were barging into her comfortable, sheltered life.

The man was entering the bath and sauna room, each move almost as stealthy as the silent paws of a mountain cat. Then—something drew her gaze away from the bathroom door and across the room to the bedroom door that led into the corridor. She froze when she saw a dark crack where there hadn't been one moments earlier. It was opening wider.

"Jorden! The bedroom door!"

He had already noticed. In a second he dropped to an automatic crouch raising the heavy revolver. The intruder rushed the room, crouching as he fired. Bullets flew from both silencers making deadly but restrained popping sounds thudding into the wall. Window glass shattered above the bed. Krista felt her face sting. The man was struck and fell.

There followed an unnatural silence. It had happened that quickly. Dazed, Krista wondered if the force of such violence could strike and leave its ruin in so few seconds, three, four at the most?

But it wasn't over.

Jorden was on his feet, moving to one side of the bathroom door. He opened it, kicking it aside. The sound of footsteps were beating a retreat across the terrace, clamoring down the stairwell toward the pool. It took a moment more before Krista realized Jorden had gone after him. Several more shots sounded, muffled. Then someone else neared the hall door. A woman's voice called: "Jorden! You all right?"

Krista turned her head. A woman entered, crouching as she had seen Jordan do. A black pistol in front of her was held steadily with both hands. Krista stirred.

"Halt!" the woman commanded. "On your feet."

"I...I'm Krista. Are you Ava?"

"Back toward me! Hands behind your head!"

Krista did so, wincing, expecting any second to feel searing fire between her shoulders.

The woman was making fumbling noises behind her. Krista guessed she was side-stepping the body sprawled on the floor, checking the man to see if he were dead. She heard Ava kick his revolver into the opposite corner away from Krista.

"All right, come on. Stand in the middle of the room. No, keep your hands behind your head."

"I don't have a gun. I couldn't use it if I had one," Krista said as she obeyed, moving from behind the side of the bed.

The woman was apparently satisfied they were alone. With the revolver still on Krista, she went to the hall door, closed and bolted it, preventing any more surprise entries. She neared the man's body again, crouched to one knee, and with her other hand turned his face toward her. From her response, she didn't recognized him.

Krista glanced at the dead man and then looked away to Ava. The woman was watching her now, her eyes as cool as Jorden's had been. As they sized one another up, Krista heard muffled voices, then a race of footsteps up the stairs onto the terrace. Jorden was not alone. He was saying: "I think it was Lars."

The other man's voice was too low to be distinguishable. Krista remained in the middle of the room, her back toward the bathroom door, hands behind her head. She heard both men enter. The man Jorden had spoken to on the two-way radio?

"How is she?" came Jorden's short question to the woman calling herself Ava.

"Seems all right."

He walked up to Krista, and for a moment was silent, studying her face. Her eyes narrowed slightly. He reached up and brought her arms down, reached into his pocket, drew out a white handkerchief and touched it gently to her throat.

Krista was startled when she saw blood.

"Don't panic. It shouldn't leave any scars. If you're not arrested for spying for the East Germans, sweetheart, your pretty face can still decorate *Europa*."

Krista was shocked by his blatant arrogance. She slapped him harshly, then stared back defiantly.

A low whistle came from the other man behind her. "I guess she told you, Keller."

Jorden's mouth curved and held her gaze as though nothing out of the ordinary had happened. Krista's eyes faltered. Her palm stung.

Ava barged up, her brown eyes sparking, grabbed Krista's right hand and stared at it. Krista tried to pull her hand away. Was Ava looking at her hand because she had slapped Jorden?

Krista saw Jorden's expression change perceptibly. "Later, Stella. Give her a few minutes to pull herself together."

"No, there's no time, that rin…"

"You heard me." He grasped her arm and led her over to a chair, plunking her down. He leaned down and said something that Krista couldn't quite hear, something in another language, but Krista couldn't quite make out what it was. Ava, whom he had now called Stella, dropped her head in her hands and nodded, as if forcing herself to emotional stability.

Krista, now totally confused, angry, and afraid, turned away. She accidentally looked into the face of the dead man and involuntarily gasped.

Jorden must have thought she had lost her nerve and was going to faint, because he left Stella and was swiftly beside her, catching her as though she would fall. "Hans, get a couple of wet washcloths. Stella, get this blood cleaned from her face."

"No...I can handle it myself," Krista said in a steady voice that must have surprised him. She snatched the handkerchief he held and brought it to her face again.

"Easy. There may be glass splinters. You'll cut yourself worse." He took the handkerchief back and looked over at the other man to see if he was moving on his orders.

He was replacing the phone. "Dead. Line's been cut. We couldn't call Doc over if we wanted to. Unless you want me to go for him?"

"No, don't involve him in this. He's too important."

Who was Doc? Some fellow conspirator in Zurich? A physician?

"Bring that lamp closer," Jorden told him, gesturing. "If there's glass in those cuts..."

"No, I don't need a doctor or a nurse, Mr. Keller. Just leave me alone."

He smiled unpleasantly as he scanned her. "Sure. Anything the colonel's granddaughter says."

Colonel's granddaughter? Where had that title come from? She watched him through narrowed eyes, but he accepted her request and turned away from her as if she no longer mattered.

That attitude irked her even more. So he didn't care at all. Well, why should he?

She finally looked at the other man and gasped a second time. Jorden turned, looking down at her. "What is it?"

She pointed at Hans. She recognized the blond hair, the pleasantly rugged face, the hard, intelligent gray eyes.

"That's him. The man I told you about. He's been following me since Rome."

The two men glanced at each other. "You're slipping," was all Jorden told him. Hans walked over to search the dead man's clothing.

Krista was amazed. "Aren't you going to do anything about it?" she demanded of Jorden.

"No. He's the friendly sort. This is..." his voice trailed off, questioning as Hans looked up at him.

The man smiled at her. "Hans Fischer."

Jorden glanced at him. Hans' smile faded and he was all ice again. He stood and stared down at the dead man. He made a clucking sound. "Messy. Very messy, Jorden."

What is all this? Krista thought, and found she was growing terribly exhausted and cold and that her mind didn't want to think any longer. She was shivering as the wind blew in through the shattered window. She wrapped her bare arms around herself and sat glumly, a strand of her hair sticking unpleasantly to her throat—dried with blood?

Jorden turned, saw her and frowned again. She probably looked pathetic, she thought, but she refused to complain about her misery. A dead body lay on her bedroom floor in a strange house, and two impossible men with revolvers were giving orders.

Jorden caught up a fringed throw from the bedroom ottoman and placed it around Krista's shoulders. "Are you going to be all right?"

His keen dark eyes had softened a little, and she relaxed, glancing toward Hans. Maybe he was not as dangerous as she had thought at first. "I'm all right, yes."

Hans had finished searching the stranger sprawled on the floor. "Nothing."

"Maybe he believed in bad luck," came Jorden's cynical crack. He turned to Fischer with an exchanged glance she wasn't supposed to understand. She knew they were in a pretty mess. Who was the man he had shot? Why had he stormed the house and barged into the bedroom firing his weapon? Had he been after her? She shuddered. Or had he been after Jorden Keller? With a start, she looked at him again. Maybe she'd been wrong all along. Those two hadn't been after her, but him.

Hans gestured his head toward the hall as he walked from the room, but before joining him, Jorden spoke quietly to Stella. "Pull yourself together, honey. See to her, will you?"

Stella nodded, smiled wearily up at him, and managed to stand.

Krista busied herself with the fringed throw, as though she hadn't noticed the exchange between them. He looked over at her, then walked into the corridor where Hans waited.

Stella appeared to have regained control of her emotions. "Say, I'm sorry," she managed. "I shouldn't have been so rough on you. You see, at first I'd thought you'd betrayed us. That you'd assisted those two men to get inside. I wasn't sure Jorden was safe."

"Betrayed?" Krista asked pointedly. If anyone had been betrayed, it was herself. "You'll overlook my apparent ignorance, Miss...if I feel confused and the one betrayed. Who are you? Ava St. John or someone named Stella?"

Stella shook her head. "Later. Jorden's orders. We've got to get you cleaned up. Let me help you with those cuts and scrapes before we go. There's some alcohol in the bathroom cabinet."

Krista nodded. She seemed to be a strange woman who seemed to see-saw from one extreme mood to the other. And where was Paul! If only he would show up with his guard!

Stella grimaced at the body on the floor. "Awful, isn't it? Believe me, I'd no idea it would turn out like this. It wasn't Jorden's plan. It was mine. If it had been his…" she stopped, as if catching her rambling tongue. Her eyes came back to Krista.

Krista blinked, behaving as though she'd missed the meaning. So Jorden Keller hadn't planned this debacle. Well, that said something for him, at least where efficiency was concerned, but it did not explain who he was or what he was after.

"I'll get the alcohol and cotton," Stella repeated and went off.

When she left, Krista threw aside the throw and was on her feet. The bedroom door leading into the corridor stood ajar.

Only by straining to hear and concentrating painfully, could she catch something of the exchange between Jorden and Hans.

"Look, don't worry. I'll cover my tracks once I leave here for Liechtenstein. After tonight she won't see me again. There's no way she can trace me."

That sounded like Jorden.

"And Stella? She'll be around. They'll get to you through her."

"I admit I shouldn't have involved myself in this meeting. I was worried about her."

"You don't need me to remind you of mistake number one. Stella's a good kid, but she has tragedy written all over her. Keep risking your cover to save her neck and you'll end up like junior in there, or worse. Trapped, and facing inter-rogation somewhere in Iran."

"Lay off, Fischer, I get the message."

"Just worried for you, Jorden, that's all. Things always get back to Avi. You can't hide anything from that blood-hound. I'd hate to see a good man kicked out of the group."

"Well taken. I plan to get this wrapped up as quickly as possible before the whole thing explodes. One thing—Stella's given me important information. I consider it worth the risk I took today."

"Avi will be delighted to hear about it. When do you contact him again?"

"In a few weeks. After I return from Liechtenstein."

"Give F my regards. As for this mess I'll take care of it. Better get out of here. I don't think those shots were heard, but let's not take chances."

"Especially since the other hyena got away," Jorden said. "You may have some unwanted company soon. Sure you can handle it?"

"Zurich police will be here soon. Lars won't try any-thing with them combing the area."

"If this gets to the wrong people in the Zurich police..."

"It won't," Hans Fischer stated.

"How can I be sure?"

"We have a special friend here connected with Paris. He'll handle it."

"Mind telling me who?"

"He needs to keep his cover. I'll manage. Better get out of here fast. Including Stella."

"I'll get her on a plane to Austria tonight. All right. We'll remember this favor, Hans. Anytime you need help, give me a call."

"I'll do that. Shalom."

Shalom? Krista quickly darted from the doorway as she heard their footsteps. Had the language Jorden spoken to Stella a few minutes earlier been Hebrew?

They were returning. She had flung herself onto the end of the bed just in time. She looked glum, as if too dazed to fully grasp all that was going on around her, therefore posing little threat. She held the throw like a security blanket and stared at her shoes.

Hans Fischer had gone back to the body and was rolling it on the blood-stained rug. She could feel Jorden's eyes on her, measuring her shrewdly. He was too clever, she thought. Was he wondering if she had been listening at the door?

"Where's Stella? She was to keep an eye on you."

She looked up just as Stella came out of the bathhouse. Jorden said something to her and she nodded, then hurried out. Probably to gather her things, thought Krista. They wouldn't want to leave any suspicious evidence. She was beginning to think now that Jorden Keller had never given the right address to Paul on that business card he had passed to him. Where the two men had come from remained unclear to her. She knew they had no relation to Paul. The man Jorden called Lars must be someone else. The Lars she knew who worked for Paul was a family man.

Jorden walked up and drew her to her feet. He led her in silence toward the bathhouse. The light overhead was already switched on. He checked the terrace doors, making sure the bolt was in place, the blinds shut tightly. Stella had already prepared the alcohol and cotton swabbing, and a tube of antibiotic ointment.

Jorden behaved as though he were oblivious to her presence. He found a clean washcloth from the cabinet.

"Don't rub your skin. Just splash your face with cold water first. Then I'll need to take a look at those cuts."

"I told you. I'll do it myself," she said stiffly.

"Look, kid, you're about as spoiled and bratty as I thought you were..." he stopped, eyes narrowing. "Have it your way. Just be quick about it. I'll wait outside the door."

She couldn't resist: "You sound very professional. Do you shoot people for a living?"

He scanned her. Then he turned to leave.

"Look, just take your girlfriend and go, will you? I don't know what you expected to learn from me, but you're not likely to win my cooperation now."

He paused, drew to one side of the door and folded his arms as he leaned there. "Do you want to be here when the police arrive?"

"Why not? I've nothing to hide." That wasn't quite true, and she was afraid, but she knew Paul could get her out of trouble by using his connections with Interpol.

Jorden watched her. "I think you and the rest of the von Burens have plenty to hide. Maybe Paul as well, and his jewelry operation."

"I don't know what you're talking about. I really don't even care. Just go."

"You're quick with orders, aren't you? You must have learned them from your grandfather. You know, fräulein, it won't be easy explaining a dead man on your bedroom floor."

What did he mean to suggest— "learn them from her grandfather?" "My grandfather has been buried at St. Moritz for years. I never knew him, but I don't like your insinuations that he has done something wrong—or that I follow his footsteps."

He actually smiled! He didn't believe her. "I'll take my chances staying here," she said flatly. "You don't like me, and I don't know why. But I assure you, Mr. Keller, I'm not worried about it."

"Hans wants you out of here. So do I. Are you going to deal with those cuts or am I? We're wasting time."

"Oh?" she asked stiffly, "I have nothing to fear from the Swiss police, but you, you just shot a man."

His gaze swerved back, and she could see the flicker in his eyes as he restrained himself. "Yes, while protecting you."

That silenced her. She had momentarily forgotten the man below the terrace. She looked in that direction. But was Jorden's statement completely true? He couldn't have been after her. The only man she knew trailing her had been the one now calling himself Hans Fischer, and he had turned out to be rather nice, at least nicer than the so-called lawyer from Dallas.

"The man lying dead in there isn't the one who followed me in Rome," she said. "I told you it was your friend in the next room getting rid of the body. And you...for an 'innocent cowboy' afraid of guns, you did very well, Mr. Keller," she accused.

A shadow of a smile was the only answer she got. He turned to leave. "Don't be long."

"If you think I'm going to walk out with you, and...and that woman, you're mistaken."

She stood, shakily, still effected by shock, and Jorden reached and steadied her. His eyes were grave and his tone was gentle. "You'll find 'that woman' quite harmless. After a little talk with her, I'm putting you in a taxi for the University. You have an Uncle Franz there, don't you?"

"How did you know about him?" she asked worriedly.

He did not answer. He scanned the cuts on her skin again. "Better let me deal with those."

"No. I'll be all right."

"When you get to your uncle's apartment better have a physician look at them. If there's any bits of glass remaining they could cause swelling and infection."

Her eyes moistened with weariness and growing fear. "You'd like that, wouldn't you? That's why you keep mentioning it. For some reason you dislike me. You'd like to see me scarred, my career ruined!"

His gaze swerved to hers, but the anger had turned to surprise, as if her suggestion left him momentarily vulnerable. He seemed about to deny it, but then the muscle in his jaw tightened and he made no comment.

Krista was emotionally exhausted and withdrew into a moment of self-pity. She whipped about, sniffing back her tears. No man had ever been so unsympathetic to her before. "Please go, Mr. Keller."

"My pleasure," he quipped. "I'm glad I'm not one of your smitten admirers. You can give a man a pretty rough ride emotionally." He shut the door.

Krista twisted the faucet so energetically the water splashed against her thousand dollar dress, adding to her frustration. That wasn't true. What a miserable day it had been thus far! How unfair it all was!

She stopped, surprised by her new, disturbing attitudes. She had never vented her frustrations like this before. Jorden seemed to bring out the worst in her. Perhaps that wasn't all true. Maybe her circumstances had been too comfortable to reveal her weak spots? When the heat got turned up, well—now certainly wasn't the time to analyze her emotions!

She sniffed back her tears as she splashed cool water on her face and throat. She looked in the mirror above the basin for the first time and was startled by the extent of her abrasions. No wonder he had insisted she needed attention. Fear clutched her heart. *Oh Lord, please, please, don't let them leave any scars. And forgive me for my horrible attitude. My job, Lord, my job, it's all I've got...don't take it away from me...*

Her eyes blurred with even more tears, causing the salty stream running down the cuts on her skin to make them sting. She could only hope she had flushed any specks of glass out. He was right; she must see a physician as soon as she got home tonight. Uncle Franz! Oh how she longed for her beloved uncle now. She would go back to the University and spend the night at his apartment. Yes—Uncle Franz—he would comfort her, assure her everything was all right, promise to intervene with Gotthard Enterprises to see her safely kept from any nightmarish scandal that had taken place tonight. Maybe Interpol would explain what had happened.

She felt a little braver. She found the bottle of alcohol and unscrewed the cap, applying it to the cotton. She dabbed each cut, grimacing. Her skin was very fair and sensitive and the alcohol stung terribly. Her once flawless face was turning red and splotchy. Her hair too was mussed, the fair strands falling limply from the once elaborate upsweep.

She thought, dazed: *Well, Krista, your face may no longer be flawless now. And Elsa will dismiss you as the Gotthard Girl!* Her mouth tightened. She could blame Jorden Keller for this. And Stella. Just who was he? Who was she?

Krista dried her hands on the towel and caught a glimpse of the ring on her finger. Had she been mistaken, or had Stella begun to ask about it until Jorden silenced her?

Her stomach churned. She found some chewable tablets in the medicine cabinet and ate a couple of them to settle the feeling.

Jorden Keller was wrong. She wasn't about to leave with him and Stella. Nor was she staying with Hans Fischer.

She turned the tap water on again to cover any sound, removed her shoes, and tiptoed to the terrace door. She pushed back the bolt. The glass door slid open silently. She stepped out onto the dark terrace, shivering from the blast of cold wind that struck her bare arms. Quickly now, she lifted the hem of the black velvet dress and descended the steps into the yard below.

Within seconds she had reached the courtyard surrounding the swimming pool. The black water shone beneath the moonlight, rippling gently in the wind. She ran ahead to the courtyard, intending to go around the house and come out in front at the gate. She could get away easily. There were only two of them, both in the house with Stella.

She reached the front gate and passed through onto the darkened street. She turned and ran, still holding her sandals, and didn't stop until the Fiat came into view some two blocks away. She arrived, gasping for breath. All was quiet and deserted as she reached the automobile. The keys should still be inside under the floor mat...just where Jorden had left them.

8

Moving swiftly, Krista held the door open while she felt with her hand under the floor mat, and with great relief touched the keys. She slid onto the seat, her fingers fumbling. Before she was even able to get the right key into the ignition slot, the door opened on the passenger side. Startled, she looked at a shadowy figure of a man. He got in beside her. A second man stepped up to the driver's side and opened the door wide, snatching the keys from her. He held the door open while still a third man emerged from the shrubs. Seeing her, he looked surprised, and ran up. Relief swelled her heart. *Paul.*

"Krista! I didn't know it was you."

She scrambled out and he enclosed her in his arms. "Paul," she gasped against his shoulder, her voice breaking, as he held her tightly.

"Did we frighten you? I'm sorry. We expected Keller. It's all right Krista," he said gently. He gestured for the man to leave the passenger seat.

Keller! So Paul knew he was here. "We've got to get away before they realize I've gone. By now he would have checked and..."

"Someone is coming," one of the men warned in a low voice.

"Into the shrubs," Paul ordered.

The two men scattered. Paul pushed her into the passenger seat, then scrambled in behind the wheel.

He must have checked the car earlier but not found the keys. Where was the car he had arrived in with the guards? He released the brake and they rolled downhill about a hundred meters before he stopped beside the curb and stared in the rearview mirror, probably watching the approaching figure. For a stark moment, Krista felt alarm for the man, who would undoubtedly encounter the two in the shrubs. What if it were Jorden?

After a minute or two, Paul started the motor and entered the street, driving away into the darkness with the lights out until they had taken the narrow bend. Krista heard no gun shots, but that offered her little solace after her experience tonight with the silencers. She gripped the seat as Paul took a sharp turn. In a few minutes they were nearing a lighted street.

The lights in the town below flickered brightly like diamonds. On the black Limmat River the gleam of the bridges reflected on ripples of the strong-flowing currents. The peaks of the hills rose behind either side of the riverbank, and still further behind the hills, the mountains, encircling Zurich, would be white with snow. Krista leaned her head back against the seat, aware of the tension emanating from Paul.

"They didn't harm you?"

"No—but there's been a shooting. I don't know who the man was, but he's dead."

"He was one of ours, I'm afraid," he said gravely. "Are you all right?"

"Yes." The man worked for Paul? She looked over at him. "I did not recognize him belonging to the security guard. Who was he?"

"His name no longer matters."

She shuddered at the cool resignation in his voice. "But the second man who was with him got away."

His voice and behavior rallied. "Yes, he's a smart one. Don't worry."

"Jorden Keller, if that's his name, and another man are in the house now. Things didn't work out, Paul. I didn't have time to learn what they really wanted from me."

"Yes, I'm afraid the two men misunderstood our orders. They weren't to enter the house. They were just to watch Keller."

"'Our' orders?"

"Wilhelm's," he said, his voice taut.

He looked nervous, she thought, concerned. "The men are hired detectives," he said when he caught her watching him.

She said nothing. She didn't quite believe him. Perhaps he knew she did not but was willing to let the matter go. They passed beneath a lighted street lamp. "Krista! Your face, what happened!"

The turbulence in his voice reflected his inner horror and the sound was blanching to her soul. Rejection. She had gone most of her life without it, tasting only the self-confidence of others' acceptance and approval. Now, in one short day she had sipped twice from the ugly cup of rejection. And from Paul, she had felt the cutting affirmation of what she had feared. The sense of weakness and fear that dropped over her was more frightening than the thought of any minor disfigurement. Makeup, she assured herself, could conceal most flaws and even some scars, but what internal balm could gloss over her sense of loss?

And I thought I was strong in faith, trusting God with my life, she thought, amazed. She was looking into the mirror of her heart and what she found was not pretty.

"I'll take you to Elsa," he said suddenly. "She'll know what to do. She has a number of cosmologists, all experts. Don't worry, darling, we'll get past this."

Her hands tightened in her lap. "No, I don't want to see the von Burens. Not now. Not tonight."

"Don't be foolish, Krista," he said sternly. "If anyone can help you it will be Elsa."

She imagined the look of distaste she would find in Elsa's face as she looked at her, seeing only cuts and puffiness. Krista couldn't take Elsa and Wilhelm von Buren now, and she protested, but Paul made light of her fears and lectured against her frailties as he always did, in the end making her feel silly for her concerns.

"It's the best place for you," he said, turning the Fiat toward Bergstrasse 19. "You'll be more comfortable there than at Franz's cramped apartment at the University. There will be servants to take care of you and solitude."

At the moment she felt too exhausted from the day's jolting experiences to continue her protest. Sometimes Paul's methods seemed to her to be a steamroller, squashing any form of expression. Usually she convinced herself he had her best in mind. Tomorrow, regardless, she would go to see Franz.

"The first thing is to abandon this car," he said.

A few minutes later he pulled to a stop on another darkened, deserted narrow street. She should have been surprised that a Mercedes waited in a quiet, curving drive, but somehow she was past that. Little surprised her now. In a moment they had switched cars and were heading in another direction toward Bergstrasse 19.

Meir waited out of sight across the street until the headlights on the Mercedes disappeared. He had watched Paul Gotthard and Krista von Buren get into the car and drive away. When the night settled back into silence, he looked at his watch, then removed a slim case and pushed a button.

"It worked. Gotthard just pulled out in the Mercedes. He's headed south on Strassbourg 9. The von Buren girl is with him. Over and out."

He looked at his watch, counted the seconds, then keeping to the shadows of the overgrown privet hedge that lined the driveway, he walked across the street to the Fiat. All was quiet and dark. He opened the driver's door, felt beneath the dash for the recording device Keller had mounted earlier, placed it inside his overcoat, and slipped into the shadows of a tree. He waited, making sure no one trailed him. He'd been cautious as always, but he double-checked everything.

When he was reasonably certain, Meir skirted the hedge on the lawn of the stone house he had checked out the day before, making certain there were no watchdogs. Then he cut across the yard and over the fence to the next small side street. From there he walked his planned route three blocks downhill, making several turns on other quiet side streets until he came out at his destination.

Parked ahead he saw the Mossad agent's dark-colored Audi. He paused, and glanced toward the car. He knew Ziv would have seen him. The dome light inside switched on, then off. That was the signal. Meir came alongside the car and slid in. They pulled away. Meir glanced at Ziv who was looking through the rearview mirror. Apparently he was satisfied no one had followed.

Meir settled back, loosening his collar, trying to calm his heart. Men died young in this business, he thought. If a bullet didn't land you, heart disease would. "Keller did his work," he said simply.

"Avi is anxious. Maybe he can make something of Gotthard's conversation with von Buren's granddaughter."

"Let's hope Gotthard talked plenty." He settled back into the plush seat, glancing about casually, touching the rich leather. "Nicest enemy I've seen."

Ziv smiled. "Don't get spoiled, Meir. Your next job may be herding camels." He turned serious. "Heard from Avi. Keller and Fischer made it out. Fischer's on his way with Stella to Vienna."

"Fischer's one German we can trust."

Agent Ziv shrugged as he turned and headed toward the Uto Quai. "Avi should be having a leisurely dinner about now. Leave it to him to enjoy his cuisine even when the heat is on." He drove quietly for a moment, then he said, "Avi is unhappy. With Keller."

Meir was silent. He had been worried about that. "Keller worries about Stella. With good reason. Anyone watching her?" He tried to sound casual, as if his interest in Stella was merely professional.

"Not that I've been told, but we're short-handed as usual. The heat is on, and Avi's turning it up. We bungled the last operation in the Gaza Strip. He hasn't forgiven us yet."

Meir smiled. "He never will." He grew silent. He didn't like it about Stella being left on her own. It seemed to him she was in as much danger as Keller was.

"Keller better be right about von Buren. We'd better end up getting him."

"We will." Meir was certain of that. "Keller wants him bad."

Ziv swerved into a parking spot a block from the Uto Quai. He reached over and switched on the radio, turning it to a station playing classical music. He turned it down low and they sat in silence, waiting.

They didn't wait long. Someone was walking toward them from the direction of the crowded cafes along the lakefront. Meir recognized the hefty form of Avi Hirsch. He opened the car door and got out.

Avi walked up. He was a tall heavy-set man in a rumpled raincoat, carrying a black umbrella. He had a package of some bakery goods that he tossed to Meir, who in turn, tossed to Ziv, who opened it and sighed. "Eclairs! Say, Avi, these kosher?"

"Eat to your heart's desire, my boy." He removed his hat from a balding head with a thick lion-like fringe of black hair tinged in gray. His rough but amiable features broke into a misleading smile. "No," he commented as Meir was about to turn over the front passenger seat to him. "I'll get in back. I want Keller. He's at the airport. Let's go."

Ziv was devouring the eclairs as they drove toward Kloten airport.

"What do you have for me?" Avi asked Meir.

Meir reached inside his jacket and passed him the recording he'd taken from the Fiat.

Avi opened his attaché case. It was perfected with gadgets specially created in Israel to his specifications. He placed the small cassette recording into the player and pushed the button. He settled back, watching the traffic pass as Ziv sped toward Kloten. The first thing Avi heard was Jorden Keller playing the Dallas cowboy with Krista von Buren as they had driven from the Bank of Zurich Corporation. He smiled to himself a few times and saw Meir and Ziv exchange amused glances. Avi learned little more about Krista that he hadn't already known. The recording went silent, then took up again with Paul Gotthard talking to Krista. Avi turned up the volume, listening carefully, as did Meir and Ziv. When it ended, he rewound it and played Gotthard again. The recording was coming to an end for the second time as they entered the parking zone at Kloten. Avi leaned forward. "Keller will be seeing Stella and Hans off at gateway 5. Get him."

Both men exited the Audi and walked briskly in overcoats toward the terminal.

As Avi watched them, he proudly recognized that his men fit well into the scheme of things. Both Meir and Ziv passed for any other European businessmen intent on catching a flight out of Switzerland. They might look ordinary, but they were anything but that.

Within fifteen minutes Avi saw three men returning to the Audi where he waited, Jorden in the middle in a dark coat, hatless, carrying his bag.

The car door opened and Avi gestured Keller into the backseat beside him.

Jorden looked at Avi as he slid in, plopping his bag at his feet.

He's irritated that I would actually haul him in for questioning, Avi thought, amused. *He thinks he can get by with anything because he's good at what he does.*

Jorden was one of his best, but like a father who must chasten a willful firstborn, Avi was not in the mood to be smiling pleasantly. He held Jorden's dark eyes as Ziv and Meir got into the front seat and drove away.

They drove in silence for ten minutes. *He's stubborn*, Avi thought. *It is well that I am more stubborn.* Before he berated him, Avi played the recording for the third time. When it ended, he shut it off. Ziv had driven to a lonely section near the lake. Here it was nearly deserted, just a lone house near the end of the shore. The wind stirred the trees. A pale glow of new moon was blotted from view by clouds.

"Take a walk," he told Meir and Ziv.

They got out, Ziv taking the last eclair with him. Meir shot a restrained look of sympathy toward Jorden, then closed the car door and walked off toward the lake. "It's going to pour in a minute," he told Ziv, turning his collar up and looking at the sky.

"Let's head for those trees."

Inside the Audi, Avi Herschel looked straight ahead. He too saw the dark clouds. A rain drop wet the windshield. His inquiry into Jorden Keller's latest activities began.

The von Buren residence was similar to the other turn-of-the-century graystones on the hilly ridge above the lake. The lights were ablaze in the lower windows as Paul parked the Mercedes in the garage. There were some steps to a side door that entered through the kitchen and dining room, and a discreet knock brought the chauffeur to open it. Perhaps it was the way she felt, but tonight Krista thought Willi looked more secretive and unfriendly than usual. He had been eating his supper at the kitchen table, and he still held his hunk of rye bread stuffed with cabbage and some sort of meat.

Paul ushered her inside. Mrs. Brandt was at the stove cleaning up. She had stopped when they entered, the dishcloth still in hand. Her sharp-featured face looked paler than ever under the bright kitchen light, with her severe black dress buttoned tightly at the neck. One look at Krista and the housekeeper raised her hand against her heart. She breathed something in German and gripped the dishcloth.

"Is Wilhelm home yet?" Paul asked.

Mrs. Brandt nodded briskly, at last finding her voice. "He did not go out tonight. He is in the drawing-room listening to music and smoking."

"And Elsa? Is she awake?"

"Yes. She is happy tonight also. The man from the Vienna museum called and made an appointment for next Thursday." Her small eyes darted back to Krista like a nervous bird. "Fräulein Krista, you are hurt…"

"Never mind, Mrs. Brandt," Paul interrupted briskly. "Do you know how to contact Elsa's doctor?"

She dropped the dishrag and wrung her hands dry on her white apron, nodding that she did. "Ja, I do."

"Good. We need him to come at once. Krista has had an accident. We're afraid of infection."

Self-consciously, Krista put a hand to her face, feeling the pitying eyes of Mrs. Brandt and the curious, almost rude stare of Willi.

Mrs. Brandt hurried off. Paul led Krista out the kitchen, through the dining room and into the hall. He left her at the stairway, smiling encouragingly. "Better lie down and rest until the doctor arrives."

Krista felt a cold draft of wind from somewhere. Before she could turn toward the front door, Paul went on: "I'll go speak to Wilhelm about what's happened…"

"Wilhelm?" came the coldly assured voice from the front door. "Why, Wilhelm?"

Both Krista and Paul turned toward the hall. Paul's surprise turned to a gaunt look of anxiety.

"Josef!"

"Yes, it is I. You are glad to see your beloved uncle, are you?" The smile on the finely-boned face with its scar across the left cheek was lacking warmth.

Paul left her on the bottom stair and walked across the hall to his bachelor uncle.

In looking at Josef Gotthard, Krista did not see an elderly man, stooped and preserved in vinegar. Through the years he had rigorously kept a routine that maintained his body and mind as that of a much younger man.

"I did not expect you back in Zurich until next week."

"So it seems. After tonight, it is good I have come home sooner." Josef looked at Krista and walked across the hall to her. Dressed in a dark suit, he looked especially tall and lean tonight, with smooth silver hair. His fair skin was tautly drawn against his bone structure and seemed somewhat transparent. One would expect him to have pale blue eyes but they were a dark gray, like smoked glass, oftentimes with no expression.

"Guten Tag, Herr Gotthard."

He did not bother to return her hello. "Your face. Did this happen at the Hans Fischer house?"

So he knew. She wondered how. "Yes."

"What happened?"

The wind blew the rain against the window. They looked at each other and Josef took her arm and brought her to the small table beside the stairway where there was a lamp. He picked it up and held it toward her face. The painful glare made her blink.

"Those are lacerations from glass," he stated.

Paul came up beside them, taking her hand comfortingly. "Yes, flying glass."

"Bullets hit the window?"

"Yes," Paul said. "It could have been worse…"

Josef switched the lamp off and shadows embraced her face and his. He turned to Paul. "Whose idea was it to send her with Keller and that woman who hired him?"

"Mine," Paul admitted.

"It was a stupid mistake."

"They requested to meet with her. I thought it worth the chance to see what Krista could learn about them."

"She is no match for liars and spies."

Krista had resented his cool scrutiny beneath the hot bright light. How would Paul handle his questions? Did his uncle know he was friendly with Interpol? Josef, the owner, would surely understand the delicate and dangerous balance between cooperating with the governments of the West and selling jewels to the world's elite buyers.

"Krista did learn something," Paul said, now sounding self-assured. He turned toward her. "You can tell Uncle Josef. He knows everything."

"She is not Ava St. John. Her name is Stella."

"We know that," Josef said indifferently. "She is Stella Cohen from New York. She hired Morgenthau and Hammerstein to represent her to the bank. Keller is friendly with them."

If Krista was surprised, Paul looked more so. "Keller?" Paul repeated.

"The law firm he is affiliated with is in America. Dallas. His true loyalties lie with Israel. They insist Stella's grandfather opened a 1930s account with Wilhelm's bank. It is more Jewish arm twisting. If they can find ways to make Germany and Switzerland feel false guilt over those who died in the war, they will do so."

Krista was confused. "But why would Interpol be interested in Jewish holocaust claims? And why does this mean they are spies? Spies for whom? I see no reason why we should need to fear them."

Josef's jaw flexed with restrained impatience. "I shall talk to you later, Paul. Alone." Josef walked toward the drawing room where German music played softly. He did not bother to knock, but opened the double doors. He stopped, as if vaguely surprised.

"What a pleasant evening," he said.

He walked in, as voices greeted him. Elsa said: "Josef! You're back."

"You two are enjoying each other's company while music plays, I see."

The doors shut behind him.

Krista turned to Paul. "He doesn't like me."

"Nonsense. But I wish you wouldn't go off on a crusade for the Jews every time he mentions them."

"I didn't. I just don't feel comfortable when the family makes anti-Semitic remarks…"

"That's absurd. No one is against the Jews. You look for such remarks. One would think you were one."

Her breath drew in, not so much for what he said, but the sting with which he had meant it—as an insult.

She stared at him for a long silent moment. Something died within her. Paul Gotthard was looking more and more like a stranger, a man she grew more cautious of as a future husband.

He looked stricken, as if he knew his slip of tongue had cost him.

"Krista, I…"

"Never mind."

He shrugged, took out a cigarette and flicked a gold lighter.

"Josef did not ask me many questions about tonight," she said. "Why? Is it because you are to ask the questions for him and report back later?"

"Uncle Josef has always been an impatient man. That is why he never married. Maybe he did not want to upset you. You are obviously distraught." He paced. "I think it was a mistake for me to send you off with Keller today. I didn't know he was Jewish."

"And that makes all the difference?"

"Of course! With the banking scandal in progress? He must be working with Stella Cohen and the two lawyers from Israel. What they are after now is becoming clear. Why they thought they could learn something from you is not." He turned on his heel and studied her. "They must have said something to you about it. What did Stella ask?"

"There was no time to meet with her. It was planned, but then the men arrived. Wilhelm's 'detectives.' "

He cast her a sharp glance.

She had best be careful of glib remarks. "Does Josef know about them?"

"If Josef does, he will not say."

"How does Josef know so much?"

He waved a hand, drawing on his cigarette. "What did Keller tell you on the way to the house?"

"Nothing of interest. Small talk."

"He must have asked questions."

Another interrogation! "He said nothing. I just told you."

"Think again. He must have."

So this was the way it was going to be. Paul would be demanding, because Josef expected information from him. Paul must find vindication for sending her with Keller to meet Stella Cohen. And Josef trusted Paul to come through to keep his position as his heir.

"You must have learned something," Paul insisted again, his eyes pleading as they searched hers.

Krista's head ached. She drew a hand across her forehead. He now switched tactics and looked apologetic. He came toward her. "Darling...You can rest soon."

Yes, as soon as he was certain she had told him everything she knew. So Jorden Keller actually was a lawyer from Dallas. That he was affiliated secretly with the legal firm from Tel Aviv surprised and interested her. Why would he and Stella think she could help them about Stella's grandfather's numbered account?

"If you don't talk to me, Krista, then Wilhelm will be up to see you in your room."

"No, Paul," she took hold of his arm on the stairway. "I don't want to see them tonight."

"Naturally they will want to see you. They are fond of you. You are an important commodity to them. To all of us."

Commodity. She knew what he meant. Especially to Gotthard Enterprises.

He noticed her response. His smile vanished as he drew her toward him. "And very important to me," he said gently.

Jorden wasn't the only good actor about. Krista looked at him, remaining silent, until he released her. She understood why he insisted on bringing her here instead of to Franz's apartment. It wasn't just the reputation of Elsa's doctor. He had wanted her alone to question her. Badger her, if he must.

What was it that Hans Fischer had said to Jorden? That he would cover his tracks for him. That they had a friend in the Swiss secret police? What Paul would give to know that!

Yes…she did have quite a bit to share, didn't she? And all of that suspicious low talk in the corridor as well. What was it about Jorden going to Liechtenstein to meet someone? Josef would like to know that.

Paul took her arm and led her to the small chair in the hall. He sat her down. "Darling, I'm not enjoying this, believe me. Wait here a moment."

Krista watched him enter one of the other rooms.

If only Uncle Franz were here. He could best advise her what to tell them. But why not tell them everything?

Yes, Paul needed her support. Paul's responsibilities were bound up in the family business. She did not particularly like Josef Gotthard. Perhaps Paul was even afraid his uncle might remove him from managing the business. He was sorry he had allowed her to meet with Jorden Keller and Stella.

Still…How much did she want to tell?

What did she owe Jorden Keller? Yet, why would Interpol be against Jorden and the Jewish group of Morgenthau and Hammerstein? They had no cause to be concerned about Stella Cohen. Paul would need to answer that question to her satisfaction before she told him anything more.

Paul came back with two small glasses of sherry. He handed her one. "You know I don't drink," she said.

"You need this. It will help pull you together." She doubted that. If anything it would loosen her tongue. She took the glass but only held it.

"You're certain no one at the house saw you with Keller and Stella Cohen?"

She shook her head. "No."

"No housekeeper, neighbors?"

"The house was empty. Hans Fischer showed up later."

Paul repeated the name as if it jarred his memory. "If it was Hans Fischer."

"What makes you think it wasn't?"

"The Hans Fischer who owns the house lives and works in Berlin. He is friendly with us."

Whatever that meant.

"What did he look like?" Paul asked.

She described him. "Paul, he was the same man who's been following me since we were in Rome and Venice." *Only, he had been much friendlier,* she thought. The hard gray eyes had actually reflected emotion. There were times too when Jorden Keller and Stella had shown feelings, especially Stella, who had appeared rather sorry about what happened. Still, when Stella had entered the bedroom with the revolver, she had been as hard as nails and capable. While Krista had been dazed by the violence, Stella had appeared more accustomed to it.

"The same man?" the first real interest glinted in his eyes. "You are sure?"

"Yes, I'm sure. Jorden Keller also seemed to think so."

"Then Keller and his group have been watching you for weeks." He paced. "Go on. You're doing very well, Krista. Josef will be surprised."

He continued his questioning, asking her dozens of questions: "Do they know who the man was that Keller shot?"

"No," she said. "They searched him. There was nothing to identify him."

"Do they know who the man was that got away?"

"Keller thinks it's Lars that got away. Surely it's not the lead guard who works for you and Josef, but someone else by that name."

Paul looked grim, but said nothing.

It was time for a question of her own. "Who were those two men you left in the shrubs when we escaped in the car?"

"Private guards. Don't worry. They know what to do. They'll follow Keller and the man who called himself Hans Fischer. We'll get someone on to Stella Cohen too. We'll learn more that way. Let the Swiss police handle the shooting."

They would follow Jorden Keller...there would be more violence.

She thought of something; it seemed odd that Jorden had left the keys available. She glanced toward Paul who was deep in thought. Had it all been planned? A way for Keller to follow her and Paul, instead of the other way around? No matter. They would be disappointed. Paul had brought her to the von Burens'. There was nothing suspicious about that. Bringing her home would be the expected thing to do. And Josef's arrival would not bring any suspicion either, since Josef was related to Wilhelm and Elsa by marriage and often came here, though he had his own house in Zurich. Jorden had already known about her staying with Elsa on her visits between modeling jobs. Then, what had he hoped to discover, if anything, by leaving the keys?

Perhaps she was wrong about it all. She was in the dark, while Paul, Josef, and Jorden Keller knew more than she.

She looked up. "Paul, how did you know you could find me at Hans Fischer's house? I was under the impression that Keller had given you the wrong address on the business card at the bank."

He smiled. "Keller isn't as clever as he credits himself. Yes, he gave me the wrong number. He even lost the first man I sent to follow him. What he didn't know was that Cousin Ehrlich made a phone call to a friend while we were still at the bank. Remember the man who showed up to talk to Ehrlich after the lawyers left?"

She did. And the man had looked several times in Jorden's direction.

"He had someone waiting near the Fiat."

She kept doubt out of her voice. "Is Ehrlich involved with Interpol?"

"No," he admitted. "He recognized Keller and alerted me."

"Why did he recognize Keller at the bank? Recognized him from where and what?"

Paul looked secretive, pleased. "From a banking trip he made recently to Vienna." He reached into his pocket and took out a photograph and handed it to her. "This will win Josef's approval over how we've been handling things. Wait until I show it to him. I've been waiting for the right moment when I meet with both him and Wilhelm."

Curiously, Krista looked at the small photograph taken at a sidewalk cafe. "Did Ehrlich take this?"

"No, no," he said with a tinge of impatience. "Someone else. Who it was does not matter to us."

It was Jorden Keller all right, handsome and enigmatic, talking to a heavy-set man in a raincoat. He was balding on top, but had a thick lion-like fringe of black and gray hair. His face was amiable but undoubtedly gruff.

"Who is he?"

"I wish we knew. Ever see him, Krista?"

She shook her head no. By now, faces, names, and unpleasant events were all merging into one confusing blob. She was growing more weary by the moment. "I have a feeling he does not wish to be seen very often," Paul said. "He could be very important."

And he was with Jorden, Krista mused.

The double doors into the drawing-room opened and Josef emerged with Wilhelm, Elsa between them.

Wilhelm appeared older than Josef, though he colored his hair ebony black. The color did him no favors, turning his broad face with iron jaw into wintry white with a ruddy flush. His deep set eyes were small, bright blue, and widely spaced beneath a narrow forehead. He looked worried, but it was Elsa who left the two tall men and swept toward her in her flowing chiffon dressing gown. As always, she carried a cigarette holder and her blond hair was nicely arranged. She smelled strongly of sherry and cigarette smoke and Chanel No. 5.

"Krista, your face! I am devastated. Brutes, all of you! Leaving her here like this! Why is she not in bed, resting until my doctor arrives?"

Paul looked across the room at Josef and Wilhelm. They showed little expression, but Josef appeared more attune to Elsa's complaints.

"She will be all right, Elsa. I looked at the cuts. They will not scar."

"Men, they know nothing," Elsa scoffed, taking Krista's arm. "Come! Gerta," she called, and like a genie from a bottle Mrs. Brandt nervously appeared.

"Yes, Frau Elsa?"

"Help me get Krista to bed. Josef! Is that a car I hear in the drive? Good, that will be Henri. We don't want any infections."

Krista went with Elsa and Mrs. Brandt up the staircase. She wanted nothing more than to escape Wilhelm von Buren and Josef Gotthard. Neither man had ever been particularly warm or friendly toward her. *They remind me of cold fish,* she thought. *So correct and superior. If only I can escape later and find Uncle Franz.*

She thought of Jorden Keller. Darkly handsome, vital, earthy. She paused on the stairs and turned around. She looked down at the three men. Paul smiled encouragingly. His questioning was over, he seemed to say. Now he was on her side again. He was asking her to forgive him.

Wilhelm had gone into the hall to answer the chiming doorbell.

"I overheard Keller telling Hans Fischer he was going to Liechtenstein. It may be important," Krista said.

Paul looked victorious as he turned toward Josef. You see? he seemed to say. I told you she was intelligent. We need her on our side.

Josef smiled. "Excellent, Krista. Excellent." He turned briskly to Paul. "Give her one of the gowns she models." He walked into the drawing room and picked up the phone. Krista recoiled. She felt like a pet dog that had just pleased its master.

She would make certain to refuse the gown when it was brought to her. She had only spoken what she knew about Liechtenstein for Paul's sake.

Exhausted, Krista entered her bedroom and almost fell into the soft, comfortable overstuffed chair. Her head ached and her face was swollen. As Elsa went back to the stairs to meet her private physician, and Mrs. Brandt went to make her a cup of hot chocolate, Krista stared up at the ceiling, looking at the shadows from the lamps.

It was raining again. She heard the tinkle on the windowpane as the wind blew the drops against it. If she could get through tonight, tomorrow, first thing after breakfast, she would leave for Franz's apartment. She thought of calling him, and glanced toward the telephone on the table. He would come at once, she knew that. And if ever she needed his emotional support it was now. But the less he knew of this, the better off he would be. Who knew the path where this ugly debacle might take them? Nor did Franz particularly like the von Burens. Tomorrow must be soon enough.

Her weary eyes closed. I'll rest just this moment, she thought, hearing the doctor's footsteps on the stairs, and Elsa's welcome. As her eyes shut, a memory jarred her to alertness and she sat up.

Krista raised her hand and the ruby ring sparkled beneath the light from the lamp on the table beside her chair.

Stella had shown interest in the ring tonight. She hadn't told Paul that. Stella had barged up, her brown eyes sparking, grabbed Krista's right hand and stared at it. "Give her time, Stella," Jorden had ordered, but Stella had seemed driven. What had she said before Jorden interrupted her, concerned she would give something away before he was ready perhaps? Krista held her aching head between her hands and tried to remember. So much had been happening, including a man shot—

"There's no time, that rin..." Stella had begun.

She hadn't finished. Jorden had made Stella sit down. That ring...

That ring! Yes, that was what Stella had been going to say. That ring....

Krista, alert now, held her hand beneath the lamp and stared at the red glimmer, the gold shining and glittering. Her heart began to beat faster. Stella's interest could not have been in its value, since it couldn't compare with the Gotthard diamonds she was supposed to have purchased from Paul.

Yes, things were making more sense now. It was the ring that Stella was interested in, not diamonds. But why? How did it fit into her quest to gain access to her grandfather's account?

Krista was almost certain she wasn't mistaken. She would ask Franz about the ring tomorrow when she saw him. And she would go home to St. Moritz and ask more questions of Cousin Henrich. She would ask, and keep asking until she got all the answers. If necessary, she would even go to Vienna and find Stella Cohen herself. If anyone could explain what it was all about, it was Stella.

Krista now believed the ring had become all important. Whatever secret may have surrounded its history, that story must be unveiled.

She heard footsteps in the corridor outside the bedroom.

When the foundation beneath my feet begins to crumble, I can reach out to God, Krista told herself. She must not try to hide the ring now, or conceal her hand. If she did so, she would only draw attention to it. So far, neither Paul nor the von Burens had even thought of the ring. She must keep it that way until she could discover the truth for herself. She was now sorry she had told Paul and Josef that Jorden Keller had gone to Liechtenstein. She would have liked to have spoken to him about the matter.

I must begin to learn to rely more on God, she thought. He alone offered a strength that wouldn't fail her. His faithfulness burned clear and bright, even in the midnight darkness. When all she relied on: the gifts of beauty, talent, favor, the confidence of an exciting career based on acceptance, when these pieces of her earthly armor were threatened by the unknown, or even by declared enemies, God loomed large in her thinking. She had a new confidence that He would not forsake her. No matter what.

9

Avi Hirschel knew how to lay it on the line while still retaining his quiet voice and lopsided smile. Jorden was under no illusions about where he stood as Avi expressed his concerns over the contrived meeting with Paul Gotthard and Krista von Buren. Jorden took the five-minute rebuke like a recruit. It ended like a summer thunderstorm, the highly charged sealed environment could only dissipate slowly. He'd been wise enough to not voice a word in either his defense or Stella's. Had he done so, in the heat of battle with his superior, it would have undermined Avi's confidence in him, and he knew Avi well enough to know he would eventually have his chance.

Jorden watched the boat lights winking on the black velvet lake. A drizzle of rain began to dot the windshield, and the wind, growing stronger, tugged at the side of the Audi. Vaguely he wondered how Meir and Zev were keeping dry. By now, Stella should be safely on a flight back to Vienna, though quite dissatisfied that she had not been able to discuss the origin of the ring, even though she had seen it, and was convinced that it had been her great-aunt's.

"Now," said Avi, "I want to know how you got involved in this operation to quiz Krista von Buren, and why you risked your cover to assist Stella."

"She contacted me from Vienna. Said she had something on von Buren I'd be interested in. 'Something important.'"

"And what was that?"

"A small chance for a breakthrough. Stella said she had learned that Grandfather Cohen may have written down his Bank of Zurich account number."

Avi looked interested, but made no comment.

"...along with the name of his Nazi interrogator who wanted that number."

Avi didn't move. Jorden could almost see the skids going on in his mind, and felt vindicated.

"Von Buren?" Avi said.

Jorden kept his emotions under tight leash. "Maybe," he agreed, in the same tone of voice. He explained Stella's reasons for believing her great-grandfather may have written the number down somewhere in the flat in Vienna. It was fortunate Avi already knew about Tirzah Cohen. He had made a trip to New York last year to talk with her, asking if she knew anything about Wilhelm von Buren. Jordan also knew that Avi personally supported the Jewish organizations that were requesting a third-party look into the holocaust accounts.

"In the Vienna flat," Avi repeated in a low, thoughtful voice to himself, awed, "Could it be?"

"Tirzah seems to think so, but she doesn't know where." Jorden began to relax. He could see he had won Avi over to his side. His risky operation with Stella had not been a complete failure. Avi didn't mind reasonable risks, but he worried over foolish ones, especially if they endangered several agents. Playing the "Texas Cowboy" had been dangerous, and even though he had obtained important information from Stella, he had been foiled in his attempt to learn more from Krista about Wilhelm.

"Tirzah has arrived in Vienna. The trip was too much for her. Returning to the flat where she was a girl when the Nazis arrested her parents has been traumatic. She's in the hospital. She wants to see me; it's frustrating! And I've Flanders to meet at Liechtenstein tonight!"

The tension between them had fizzled. "You take a long time to clue me in, Keller."

"Sorry, I didn't expect you to show in Zurich. I've been on my own for two months. I expected it to stay that way. I want to get Wilhelm for Nazi war crimes."

Avi nodded thoughtfully, tapping his finger on his knee. "How long have you known the Gestapo agent that sent Stella's family to Auschwitz could be von Buren?"

"Since about lunchtime at Hans Fischer's house."

"The house is empty and up for sale," Avi told him. "You knew that?"

Jorden nodded. Stella arranged it for the place of meeting. She had checked earlier with a real estate agent, pretending to be a German interested in a vacation house in Zurich. She drove by it and liked the setting. She had stopped and talked to the neighbors and learned it was empty. She had thought it was the perfect place for a rendezvous with Krista von Buren.

Jorden thought of Krista. He'd been pretty rough on her, and he knew a moment of regret. That, as small as it was, surprised him. He hadn't thought himself capable of sympathy for the granddaughter of Wilhelm and Elsa von

Buren. The stirrings didn't last long, like a brief flicker of a comet streaking across the dark sky.

"Fischer contacted our ally in the Swiss secret police. His friend the mortician has covered your trail as well as Hans'," Avi said in passing. "It was rash of both of you to use your real names before the von Buren girl."

Jorden agreed. "I had no choice. I'm a lawyer from Dallas. That's the best cover I have."

Avi hit the eject button on his recorder. He held the cassette in the palm of his big hand. "We think Ehrlich von Buren recognized you and warned Paul Gotthard. You are in a precarious situation." He rubbed his chin, sighing, as if in a dilemma. "I should dismiss you at once and send you home to Dallas."

Jorden looked at him sharply. His emotions were too wrapped-up in getting Wilhelm to Israel to quit now, but he knew it would do no good to try to persuade him. With Avi one was safer to play things down. Too much emotion, too much pleading convinced him you were risky in an explosive situation. A cool head was demanded and steely emotions that, no matter the personal level, must not be allowed to boil the pot. Caring too much, a sudden flash of anger, emotional involvement—especially over a woman—these placed a Mossad agent at deadly risk.

Avi looked out the side window at the rain. "But I can't afford to let you go."

Jorden released a breath.

"The account number is worth searching the flat for," Jorden told him, his tone steady and businesslike.

"You'll be watched now. It's too dangerous. For Stella too. I want her out of there. I'll handle it from here."

"Then you convince her, Avi. I've run out of words."

"She'd listen quickly enough if you promised to see her in New York."

"No. I respect her too much for that. I won't lead her on."

"All right," said Avi, "I'll get her to New York." He opened his palm-top computer and pushed a few keys. "What was the name of her newspaper chief?"

"MacElhenney."

"I'll have Ziv go to Vienna. I want the flat combed— every centimeter."

"Stella says she's searched and found nothing."

"Tirzah can't remember?"

"That's what Stella thinks. It's curious she came to Vienna, though, a place she'd never set foot in again unless something important had driven her."

"The elder Cohen would have trusted someone with the information he considered so crucial."

"My thoughts also," Jorden said quietly. "He was determined enough to write it down and hide it from the Nazis."

Avi rubbed his chin thoughtfully. "You go on to Liechtenstein. See what Flanders has for us. I'll be in touch when it's safe."

"What about Tirzah? I told Stella I'd come by the hospital in a few days. After what happened tonight someone had better talk to her about what she knows."

"I'll visit her. You can see her when you return to Vienna. I'll speak to Stella too and send her back to the bustling newspaper office with MacElhenney in New York."

That was fine with him. Jorden got out of the car with his satchel, into the cold, gray rain when Avi said: "Keller?"

Jorden paused and looked in at him.

"Watch your back, will you? I'd hate to lose you. I mean that."

Jorden was surprised by the brief show of concern.

"Sure," he said casually. He turned up the collar on his raincoat as the cold water dribbled down his neck. "In case I need to contact you, where…"

"Don't try. I'll be around. In the most unsuspecting places, expecting a report, and a harvest. Just come up with what I need to land von Buren's neck in a noose. A good victory over our enemies will play well in Israel. We need more funding. The liberals are squawking about cutting back. It may even help reelect the prime minister."

"For that, I expect to be invited for one of Aryeh's suppers when I get back to Tel Aviv."

Avi smiled. "We'll take you up on that."

"Shalom."

10

Krista woke, tension filling her body. The heavy drapes were drawn aside and the rain had ceased. Clouds were passing, occasionally uncovering the moon and revealing sweeping sections of clear black sky. She distinctly recalled Mrs. Brandt drawing the drapes before she left the bedroom and turned out Krista's lamp. It had been after eleven, long after Elsa's physician left the house. The lacerations were not deep, he had told her. He couldn't promise, but he believed there would be few if any scars, and if there were, they would be small enough to be hardly noticeable. His one concern was a deeper cut beneath the left eye. It was serious enough to warrant watching during the healing process, he told her. "You were most fortunate. An inch higher and the flying glass may have left you blinded."

Yes, by spring there would be no reason why she could not be back to traveling with Paul. In the meantime, some Swedish skin remedies, some of his own making, and an antibiotic cream would prevent infection and reduce risk of scarring. Soon the redness and swelling would disappear. The right makeup and lighting would secure her modeling career as Gotthard's golden girl.

Krista was surprised he had so few questions about how the accident happened. Paul must have spoken to him before showing him to her room. When the von Burens wished a matter hushed up, they seemed quite effective, she thought. What else might they be repressing?

"The rich have many friends," Solomon had written. She was beginning to understand what he had meant. Some people were so in awe of the possessions or power of the wealthy that they sought to cooperate with them.

As she lay there in bed looking toward the window with the drapes drawn back, she realized what had awakened her. Music—there it was again. Viennese or German marching music being piped throughout the rooms via a sound system located downstairs in Wilhelm von Buren's library. She had heard it many times while staying here in Zurich, but she preferred the older Vienna music of Johann Strauss. She tried to dismiss from her memory the pictures she had seen of World War II Germany with egotistical Nazis goose-stepping down the street in polished black boots. It was as if she could hear the crowds of Berliners shouting adulation to Hitler. She envisioned the old black and white photographs of Elsa with Hermann Goering and a young, pretty Elsa with blond hair and a proud, smiling face. Her eyes began to close. The martial music seemed to grow louder in her mind. How could Elsa sleep through this?

At once she tensed. Her eyelids fluttered open again as a strange awareness came over her. There was someone else in her room. Someone who had opened the drapes, who was still there listening to the music. It must have been the opening of the drapes that awakened her from the deep slumber enhanced by the injection the doctor gave her...

She slowly turned her head on the pillow toward the winged-back overstuffed chair in front of the window. Yes, there was someone there who was not a product of her imagination. She could see the cigarette burning a dull red as whoever sat there drew on it, the tobacco smoke curling and drifting toward her.

Krista didn't move. Who was it? Not Paul—she was sure he was gone. He had stayed with her beside the bed until the doctor left, until the injection began working, making her relaxed and drowsy. He had held her hand, toying with the ring on her finger. Then he'd left the room. She assumed he would ask her questions tomorrow, that he'd gone to his Uncle Josef's house down by the lake.

Elsa—could it be she in the chair? The figure appeared to be daydreaming while listening to the marching song. The figure stood unexpectedly, as though lifted with inspiration, and moved closer to the window to look out. It wasn't Elsa, the figure was tall, and with his jacket removed, she could see his outline against the dim night. Wilhelm? How long had he been there? And why? He certainly wasn't disturbed about awakening her. He had opened the drapes and turned on the sound system so he could hear his old music while he sat in the chair looking out. Nor was he concerned that his cigarette smoke would alert her. If he needed to talk to her, why hadn't he turned on a lamp?

Krista lay perfectly still. Her heart beat with the drums of the martial music. He was more of a reclusive figure than Josef, not that Wilhelm was ever unfriendly to her. He was more congenial than Josef, who seemed to think she was a non-entity—unless the loss of her beauty somehow threatened a loss to his company. Unlike Josef, who was away a good deal of the time on business, Wilhelm, since his retirement from the bank, stayed in one of the many rooms here in the mansion. Since he had allowed his son, Ehrlich, to assume his responsibilities, Wilhelm was rarely seen in Zurich. He lived a quiet life, sometimes overly humble and illusive, though he could be efficient and brusque, like Paul. The most frequent mental picture she had of him was leaving the house for early walks to the lake, wearing a long coat and Homburg. Sometimes he went out in his Mercedes with his chauffeur, Willi.

But why was he here in her room? He had seemed troubled tonight after talking with Josef in the drawing room. If he had questions about what happened at Hans Fischer's house, why not wait until tomorrow when Paul returned? Krista did not want to talk to Wilhelm, not now, not this night.

She watched him at the window, his height, his straight back and shoulders almost in a military stance. He had always been a disciplined person, a quiet man who could still lash out in sudden pride, as though furious about the banking scandal.

She closed her eyes tightly and lay there without moving. She knew that what she was hearing was not just music, but part of a belief system. As she clasped her hands tightly together beneath the coverlet, the ring pressed into her fingers.

Once, she thought he walked near the side of her bed. She prayed, asking for God's help and pleading that he would leave her room.

The music played on, then stopped. Suddenly—

The door opened and light shone in from the corridor as he left.

After a minute of silence she became convinced he would not return. Slowly she sat up and stared at the closed door. The moon was now hidden behind dark clouds, throwing the room into deep darkness.

Had Wilhelm thought that either Elsa or Paul would return to her room to ask her questions? Yes, that must be it. He had not wanted to turn the lamp on and awaken her until they arrived. Well, she wouldn't be here tomorrow. If either Wilhelm or Elsa wished to talk to her they would need to come to St. Moritz. When the dawn broke she would go to Uncle Franz's house, then take the train with him to the family lodge.

She shuddered as she lay back down and tried to sleep again. Never again would she be inclined to stay overnight in this house.

11

It was seven o'clock when Jorden crossed the Swiss border into Liechtenstein—a country of only 61 square miles, with a ruling monarchy that was the last remnant of the old Holy Roman Empire. At the tiny capitol of Vaduz he checked into the Hotel Engel under the name of Grell. There was an informal pub downstairs with authentic home cooking. He would have liked to try it, since Liechtenstein had its own unique cuisine, including local crusty, chewy bread, but he couldn't risk being noticed. He may have been followed.

As he went upstairs hearing the haunting music of the synth, zither, and organ, he thought of Krista von Buren. She had looked so innocent and unaware of the philosophy that Gotthard Enterprises supported that he briefly imagined her in a pretty dirndl peasant dress with laced black bodice. But he was only permitting himself to become deceived. She was a spy with old Nazi sympathies, and a grandfather who had been a Gestapo agent responsible for the death of thousands, including Stella's family.

With that, he rejected Krista's haunting memory and went to his room. There would be no relaxing dinner with zithers playing. Flanders had arranged everything. A black ski outfit and equipment waited in the wardrobe, and a box lunch of fruit, cheese, bread, and two chocolate bars—the skier's staple in this part of the world. He wasn't really hungry yet, and so he saved the food for the long mountain hike and the ski journey to the Austrian border where Flanders waited.

Jorden showered and rested until it was time to leave. Carrying his equipment, he left unnoticed during the hotel's busy dinner hour, using the forest footpath.

The path climbed to the base of the ancient family castle of the last living heir to the Holy Roman Empire, His Highness Reigning Prince of Liechtenstein, Duke of Troppau and Jägerndorf.

It didn't take him long to reach Vaduz Castle, a romantic fortress-home with striped medieval shutters and massive ramparts. Standing below it, Jorden gazed out on the majestic view of the wide Rhine Valley. The sun, dipping behind a snow-capped mountain range, weaved a ribbon of scarlet and gold above the darkening peaks.

From the castle he hiked uphill, taking a high mountain road that brought him through Steg, and on to Malbun, over 1,580 meters high—or as Jorden estimated—over 5,000 feet. A pleasant row of resort hotels greeted him, overlooking a broad, verdant mountain bowl. Swarms of local families were here on winter ski vacations and the atmosphere appeared safe and friendly. No one seemed to pay any attention to his arrival, but he had learned that meant little.

He checked in to the eighty-five-year-old chalet, Alpenhotel, run by a smiling family who must have taken him for an Englishman. They informed him that Prince Charles and Princess Anne had once come to Malbun learning to ski while visiting the royal family of Liechtenstein. And that there were varied ski slopes, many of them for beginners. Jorden smiled his thanks, but remained noncommittal about his abilities and his country.

By ten that night he left the chalet carrying his bag and skis. Checking his watch, he told himself he could reach his isolated destination by midnight. Two hours with Flanders, a meal and hot coffee, and he could cross safely into Austria with the information Flanders would give him. In Vienna he would report to Avi Herschel, receive the updates Avi had gotten from Great-Aunt Tirzah Cohen at the hospital, then on to the flat to meet Stella.

On the other side of the bowl ringed with hotels, Jorden stopped in the fir trees to change into the ski outfit. After getting his boots on he stepped to the skis and fastened the bindings. He got his backpack in place and reached for his poles, putting the loops around his wrists before shoving off. He started down the snow-covered path, gaining momentum, his turns skillfully balanced as the path curved and he rounded some tall pine trees.

Accelerating down the slope he swung left and began carving to reduce speed. This was a dangerous area where the snow was thin along the banks and hidden rocks and branches could become a skier's nightmare, especially when attempting the run by moonlight. But Jorden had planned this cross-country journey carefully, and he had hiked here during the summer to meet with Flanders. He knew what to expect.

He maneuvered down the white slope between thick fir trees so tall and dark that the sky, though dense with stars and moonlight, was high above him without a hint of horizon.

As he approached a clearing with the heavy, snow-laden branches on one side of the twisting path, a gust of cold dry air blew the powdery drifts of soft snow, and the moon appeared above the high mountains. Its luminous glow turned the scenery into a wonderland white with trees casting inky shadows.

He was reaching a junction where the trail divided; the left fork circled around and eventually led back to the hotels at Malbun, the other he would take toward the Austrian border. On his right was an incline of fir trees and a steep drop into a rocky ravine, now carpeted with white. He continued as the path began to level out and there were places where he had to use his poles. When the trail turned northeast he paused to check his bearings. He glanced at the towering ridge, then pushed onward again, certain now of his direction.

By midnight he was reaching a white meadow which was softly illuminated by moonlight and starlight. He followed its perimeter for a final quarter mile before coming to a halt beneath a unique cluster of trees. He looked across the meadow. In a half-circle of pine was a lone golden glow from a lantern.

He circled around and came to the back of a log cabin, its roof thick with white crust, the few square windows all black with hangings except for where a small lantern burned, its inside shutters partially drawn. A gust of icy wind struck him, heralding clouds and a chance of more snow by morning.

Unfastening his skis, he left them on the porch against a pile of chopped wood and rapped a coded knock on the rough pine door.

The door unlatched and a man in his thirties of strong Norwegian appearance smiled and thumbed Jorden inside. He shut the door and rebolted it.

Jorden faced a warm room with red coals of aromatic pine sizzling and sputtering on the hearth. A blue and white enameled coffee pot sat on hot bricks. Beside it was a blackened iron kettle of simmering stew.

"It's about time," Flanders joked. "You're all of fifteen minutes late."

Jorden smiled as he pulled off his gloves, then hung his jacket on a wooden hook in the far corner. "I'm not given much time to practice my skiing in either Israel or Dallas."

Flanders cracked a smile and poured two mugs of black coffee. "Well, Jorden, sounds to me like you just didn't have patience to wait for the ski season."

"On the snowy slopes of Texas—you're right." Jorden sank with relief into a chair facing the coals, dropping his head back. Flanders handed him a mug of steaming coffee and Jorden took it gratefully, holding it between his palms, and drank in silence.

Flanders was silent as well, allowing him a five-minute reprieve before speaking: "We'll need to leave tonight. I was spotted today."

"Anything serious or a case of nerves?"

Flanders shrugged. "Maybe a little of both."

Jorden watched him thoughtfully over the rim of his tin mug. Flanders had the courage of a bull and the wits of a lynx. If he sensed danger, they would both be wise to act upon it. "What's bothering you?" he inquired again.

Flanders dished the stew and hauled out a rounded loaf of the chewy Liechtenstein bread. "Just a woodcutter near here today. A little too close, I thought. I watched him through my binoculars. He was playing at cutting. Looked like he was saving his energy for something more important."

"We're on the Austrian border. There's a lot of timber wolves in this area," he said of the woodsman. "Was there anything about him that alerted you?"

"Not sure. I keep thinking I've seen him before—in a business suit."

Jorden set down his coffee. "No wonder you've got a case of nerves." He tried the stew, eating by the light of one large candle and the dying red glow from the hearth. He would need to enjoy the heat while it lasted.

"See anyone on route?" Flanders asked after a minute.

"No. The trail was fresh all the way. With luck it will snow tonight and cover our tracks." He cut a section of bread with a sharp hunter's knife sitting on the low wooden table. The peaceful interlude would not last long.

"Great little place," Jorden said wistfully. "I'd like to hole up here for a year and just sleep."

Flanders smiled. "Sleep is a luxury for normal people." He got up, went to his ski bag, and removed a paper. "This is what I've been worried about. Have a quick look before I burn it, just in case we have unwanted company." He handed it to Jorden, then sat down again by his untouched stew.

Jorden unfolded the sheet. It was a copy of a photograph. The unsmiling man looked to be in his late forties with a full face and a square jaw. His light hair was cropped. A pair of granite eyes stared back unrelentingly.

"He looks nervous, and dangerous."

"He's both. His name is Einer Seitz. Ever heard of him?"

Jorden looked up, sharply. "Yes. You have my undivided attention."

"I thought I would." Flanders leaned back in his chair. "Seitz was a crack spy for the East Germans, cooperating with the KGB until the Berlin wall came down. For years we've thought he also had connections in the Middle East."

"That's right. We suspected him of having an informer among the bomb-laying Hizbullah squads in the Arnoun village, just outside the security zone of Lebanon," Jorden said. "We've been after him for years. After the wall went down we almost had him." He pushed his empty bowl aside. "He disappeared."

Flanders nodded briefly. "We traced his slimy trail to Iran, but he didn't stay there. He seems to have developed an appetite for the Western vices he once decried. He wants money. I have a lead that may help both the United States and Israel. Interested?"

Jorden leaned back in the chair. "You don't need to ask that. What do you expect in return from the Mossad? There's always a condition."

Before answering, Flanders took the photocopy and crumpled it, tossing it to the embers where it shriveled into ash. Only when he was satisfied that nothing remained did he turn to Jorden and answer his question. "I'll get to the conditions later. We've been told that Seitz may be in Zurich."

Zurich!

"Whether von Buren knows this is questionable."

"Even if he does, there's nothing unusual about fleeing to neutral Switzerland. They all do. Why should it matter to von Buren?"

"It wouldn't except we have it on reliable source that Seitz poses a threat to von Buren's past identity as a Nazi Gestapo agent." Flanders added when Jorden stared at him:

"Yes, I thought the news would do something to your adrenaline."

To put it mildly, Jorden thought. He leaned forward intensely. "Are you saying Seitz has something on von Buren?"

"Ironic isn't it. Yes, he has plenty. Enough to corner von Buren into hiring a hit man if he knew. That's what we want to know. Does he know? We want you to find out, if Avi agrees."

Jorden laughed. The things that were expected from him were absurd. "What do you mean, you want me to find out?"

"You may be able to discover something important from Krista. She has inside information. After all, she's engaged to Paul Gotthard."

"And after our last debacle at Fischer's house you think she's anxious to pass secrets to the Texas cowboy?"

It was Flanders who laughed this time. "Whose idea was that anyway?"

"Never mind. I've already been through the mill with Avi. I'm still bruised. And you haven't explained what Einer Seitz has on von Buren."

Flanders took out a piece of spearmint chewing gum and removed the paper. "Seitz's father was an SS officer under von Buren and a cohort at Auschwitz."

Jorden slowly let out a breath and lounged back into the chair. His narrowed dark gaze contemplated Flanders. He looked pleased.

The circle was closing in on his prey, Jorden thought. "All right. Whatever this is about, you have my support. Go on."

"The facts will jell for themselves. Einer's father served in Austria and worked closely with von Buren when he was in Berlin. Near the war's end, like Goering, there may have been a mutual plan between von Buren and Seitz to open a secret bank account at the Bank of Zurich Corporation. All this slimy business may lead back to Stella's grandparents."

Jorden thought of the blood treasure. The gruesome loot—everything from diamonds to wedding rings to gold dental fillings—had been ripped from Jews murdered in the death camps, then carted away by a special train from the region of the gas chambers. Near the war's end, much was brought secretly into Switzerland by trucks and even wagons. It was already established by investigators that Switzerland's National Bank had accepted from the Nazis gold and ingots manufactured from the rings and dental fillings taken from the Jewish victims. In 1945 certain Swiss border guards, as well as others, had been bribed to let the trucks and wagons pass through without inspection. He had reason to believe that many of the goods from the holocaust victims had been stored in caves and underground vaults for years after the war until those involved, or even their grown children, believed it safe to get rid of it on the world market. It was his belief that the jewels sold by Gotthard Enterprises had not all come from South African mines.

Revolted, Jorden stood and refilled his coffee mug. "If they worked together and von Buren came to Zurich, what happened to Reichscaptain Seitz?"

"Berlin, 1945," Flanders said. "Along with the Americans and British, the Russian soldiers came marching and rolling in. Von Buren fled to the Swiss border. Who it was that waited to help him, we don't know. Reichscaptain Seitz, as fortune would have it, got trapped in the Russian sector of Berlin. That left von Buren free to keep everything they had stored. Except for the payments he would have given to those who helped him escape, change his identity, and hide his loot."

Jorden looked at him sharply. A tiny bell just went off in his mind. Naturally he would have needed help. Lots of help.

"You can imagine Seitz's frustration," Flanders said bitterly. "He was caught under Russian rule and there wasn't a thing he could do about it. Both von Buren, and the gold and jewels, slipped like grains of sand from his blood-stained fingers."

But not through von Buren's, Jorden thought. Restlessly, he walked to the hearth, staring at the coals.

"Seitz cooperated with the Russians. We have reason now to think he went on to serve in the East German secret police."

The dreaded Stasi, Jorden thought. It fit him, as well as the other Nazis who had been left trapped behind the new Communist Iron Curtain in the Eastern sector of the city. They had gone from saluting Hitler to groveling before their new master, Joseph Stalin.

"His son, Einer, served in the secret police as well," Flanders went on, "until the Communist Block fell in '89. The 'Evil Empire,' as President Reagan called it, toppled."

"I wonder," Jorden murmured. "I don't think it's dead at all, but the West is as blind to what's really going on as England was to the Nazi threat in 1933."

"You may have something there. As for Einer, when the Berlin Wall came down, he walked free like many others into West Berlin."

Yes, suddenly they were Westerners, freedom lovers, Jorden thought coldly. *All was forgiven, all forgotten. So they thought.*

"And now Einer Seitz is in Zurich," Jorden said thoughtfully, trying to piece together all the far-reaching implications. He could imagine von Buren breaking into a cold sweat when he heard the news. Maybe he already had heard. Von Buren would hire a hit man to kill Seitz if he could find him. For years von Buren had lived as a respectable Swiss banker with a good name. The Nazi years were only a haunting memory. He was like all sinners... believing that a patient God would not call them before the Throne of Judgment to answer for their lives.

What of me? he wondered unexpectedly. The words of the Christian Jewish group who had been witnessing to him in Dallas came to mind suddenly: *Yeshua is our Passover Lamb.*

Jorden turned away from the coals and looked at Flanders.

"Seitz wearied quickly of Iran and its strict Islamic laws," Flanders said. "He has new plans."

"Blackmail is something he would fit into very comfortably."

"Right. He has plans to collect on his father's memory. But von Buren isn't accustomed to playing the victim. Even if he decided to pay Seitz off, he'd never trust him. We want him to live; von Buren wants him dead. And that's our fear."

Fear? Jorden studied his expression, but Flanders gave nothing away yet as he filled his cup. The coals sputtered and the wind moaned around the cabin walls. "Like ghosts from the shameful past they are beginning to march, calling von Buren's name. Perhaps he hears millions of them."

"The security-guards working for Gotthard Enterprises are ex-soldiers, or Skin Heads," Jorden told him. "Most have some of the same old Nazi prejudices and beliefs. If von Buren gives the word, Lars would use them to find and silence Einer Seitz. Not that Einer is an amateur. He too has a pool of thugs to call on from his years as a spy. Von Buren won't find him an easy target."

"Maybe not, but von Buren will want to find Einer as badly as we do. You see how the wind changes and begins to blow a storm in von Buren's direction. For years he's lived as a quiet banker. He has a son, Ehrlich, a wife, Elsa."

And a granddaughter, Jorden thought. *Don't forget that. A beautiful granddaughter with old Nazi sympathies.*

Jorden looked at him. "Along with the banking scandal, and Stella asking questions about her grandfather's dormant account, the arrival of his old cohort's son should have von Buren sweating."

"And in that, Keller, lies the urgency and the difficulty."

"You haven't explained the CIA's interest in Einer."

"I'm getting to that."

He was taking his time, Jorden thought, studying his blank face. Was he laying the unpleasant groundwork first to prepare him for something Flanders knew he would be prone to want to reject?

"The East Germans had one of the tightest and best operated espionage agencies in the Cold War years. Even when the wall was coming down, the Stasi was shredding everything and destroying its computer systems on its international spy network."

"Even so, they made a costly mistake," Flanders said. "They were in such a hurry they forgot about the days of 'antiquity' when information was stored on tapes. Several of these were left behind. We found them locked away in their maze of files."

Jorden was expressionless. He knew all about it. Even Flanders didn't know that a member of the Mossad was there that day too, in East Berlin. The agent retrieved a few important items for Tel Aviv. That was how Jorden knew Einer Seitz had an informer in the Hizbullah in Lebanon. If Seitz could be caught, he could be made to yield information on his father's relationship with von Buren as well. That would spell the end of von Buren. He lifted his cup. "What about Seitz?" he asked.

"Seitz has something we want."

"On von Buren?"

"No, von Buren is your quarry if you can land him. We've already agreed to look the other way while you and Avi do your work." He sat down in the chair. "Seitz has a list of spies who cooperated with East Germany in the Middle East. I don't like admitting this, but we've never been as proficient in getting information in that part of the world as some other countries, like France, for instance. We want that list of names to add to those our NSA deciphered from the tapes. Seitz is important to us both."

"And to von Buren," Jorden said. "If he gives the word, his men will search down and silence Einer Seitz."

"Yes, and that's our worry right now. We want him alive. It would serve both our causes."

"Fine. But you still have me in the dark. What do you want from us?"

"One thing, Keller," Flanders was saying too casually. Jorden knew that tone and turned to look at him. Any time Flanders and the CIA said *Oh, by the way, just one more thing*, it usually meant a bomb was about to go off. And Jorden suspected he would be asked to fall on it. He waited, looking at Flanders with his easy smile. They might just as well have been discussing the latest numbers in a football game.

"We want Avi's promise that no member in his organization will lay a hand on Seitz. It's your turn to look the other way. As far as you're concerned he doesn't exist. Should you come across him while trying to nail von Buren you're to back off."

Jorden's smile froze. He felt the heat boil slowly in his insides.

Flanders behaved as if he didn't notice and went on, looking at the floor as he paced. "You're not going to like this, Jorden. We're going to offer Seitz safe passage to Havana for his cooperation."

"Safe passage!" Jorden walked toward him.

"I don't like it anymore than you do. This is the way things work sometimes. You know that. Sometimes we're forced to let one jackal out of the trap to lure the entire pack."

"Are you trying to convince yourself?"

"Look, I can't justify the way things are. We have our jobs to do."

"And we'll do them. In the meantime Seitz is allowed to make a bargain to save his lying neck!"

"I'm not here to argue, Keller. If allowing Seitz to live a few more years in Cuba means we have that list of names..." he waved a hand.

"Judgment is certain in the end, and that's all that matters now, is that it? Therefore governments are free to reshape truth to fit their agendas? There must be a line drawn in the sand somewhere between good and evil. Compromise truth to the shade of gray and you will soon have a society so demoralized its people won't have the capacity to judge. They'll call light darkness, and darkness light. They'll become apathetic. Everything then becomes relative, just as long as it doesn't interrupt personal agendas."

"You want me to be outraged? All right!" Flanders fumed. "But we still need to make a deal with Seitz!"

"You're letting a terrorist walk free!"

Flanders continued to pace, frowning. "I know, I know. There's nothing I can do to change it." He stopped and looked at him. "We need that list of names. And we need the Mossad to look the other way when it comes to Seitz."

Jorden's cup rattled as he set it down on the table. "Lukewarm," he murmured. "I hate things that are luke-warm. Hot or cold. That's the way everything ought to be. Truth is truth. Lies are lies. A terrorist is a terrorist and ought to hanged."

Flanders turned his head and looked at him. "An eye for an eye. A tooth for a tooth."

The wind picked up in stormy gusts.

"Seitz is equally to blame for the bomb explosions in Tel Aviv," Jorden persisted. "He might as well be a member of the Hizbullah."

Flanders pushed a chair out of his way. "All right, it eats at you that he'll sit comfortably in a Havana coffee house puffing cigars for a few years. But if he talks—and he will— you'll get the names and whereabouts of key terrorists in Gaza, Lebanon, and Syria. Every terrorist you get means one less bus blown up. Isn't that worth letting him listen to castanets?"

Jorden's mouth curved at the corner. "Maybe. But if it were left up to me I'd let the Mossad get that list from Seitz for you. He'd talk all right. You wouldn't need to give him safe passage to Havana. Regardless, I've no authority to agree to your demands. That's in Avi's ballpark, not mine."

"He'll listen to your arguments. I've passed on crucial information about von Buren. If you don't play the game now, Keller, this will be the last Avi ever gets. Nothing must happen to Seitz," he repeated. "We're holding the Mossad responsible."

Jorden's eyes narrowed but he said nothing.

Flanders smiled. "Sorry, but you know how the game works. Perfect justice must wait. We'll leave the final outcome to the One on the Throne. You and I are like doctors. We can't cure cancer, we can only cut out what's possible and keep the patient alive."

"Sure," Jorden said with a faint smile. He heard the wind about the cabin. "We'll agree to disagree, friend. I'll meet with Avi in Vienna and pass on your information. He is likely to go along where Seitz is concerned. We can't risk offending our American friends. And now, I've got a long way to ski tonight and a storm is coming in." Jorden was still angry as he took his coat from the peg.

"One more thing," Flanders told him quietly. "There's something you should know about Krista Grendelmier."

Jorden paused at the name.

No need for me to see her again, he thought. *I'd rather not think about her.* But he turned, just the same, and looked at Flanders.

12

"Her name isn't Grendelmier. It's von Buren," Jorden stated.

Flanders didn't appear to hear him. Again he walked to his ski bag, removed a photograph and brought it to him. Jorden didn't need to be told what it was. He had seen it once too often in the past two months. He knew that beautiful image with his eyes shut, in spite of who and what she was.

Flanders passed him the picture of Krista from *Europa* magazine. There she was, wearing the streamlined black velvet dress, and draped in Gotthard diamonds.

"Krista is not related by blood to either von Buren or Gotthard."

Jorden had been told that before by Krista herself, yet he hadn't believed her.

"She's the daughter of Peter and Anna Grendelmier. They died somewhat mysteriously in a climbing accident about twelve years ago near St. Moritz."

"Yes, she told me. Why do you say mysteriously?"

"They were both excellent mountaineers and skiers. They were said to have become lost in a storm that came up. Anna must have lost her footing and fallen from a ledge. Later, the next morning, Peter located her on his own, but slipped trying to reach her. By the time the search party located them several days later they had frozen to death."

Jorden stared at Krista's photograph. *Not a von Buren? No connection to Wilhelm the Butcher? Then if he wasn't her grandfather, would she be working with Paul Gotthard to protect von Buren from discovery?*

"You see something suspicious in their deaths?"

Flanders shook his head. "Rumors. Someone close to them came to us with his suspicions and suggested foul play. He believes von Buren himself may have been involved in an assassination."

This changed everything. "Why wasn't I told this sooner?" He managed to keep the frustration out of his voice. And he had doubted her completely, treated her rudely.

Flanders shrugged. "Maybe Avi doesn't know. And I had no reason until tonight to mention her." He looked at him thoughtfully, as if seeing through his charade. "Sorry. I didn't realize you and she..."

Jorden laughed unpleasantly. "Don't rush to conclusions. I met her for the first time at the bank in Zurich. That is, it was the first time I'd spoken to her. I've been following her in Rome, as has Hans Fischer."

Flanders nodded, accepting his explanation. "High class, isn't she."

Jorden realized he'd held onto her photograph too long. He handed it back with an attempt at indifference.

"What does Krista believe about Paul?" Jorden asked.

"That Gotthard's cooperation with Interpol is really helping the West crack down on rogue terrorist groups."

Completely false, Jorden thought. And she must have thought he and Stella were against Interpol. No wonder she hadn't trusted him. Nor had he trusted her. They had crossed purposes. "Even if she's not von Buren's granddaughter, she's working with Paul Gotthard. We both know she's contacted enemy agents and passed information, probably for Paul." Jorden wished he hadn't needed to mention this to Flanders. "We know what Gotthard Enterprises stands for."

"Yes, that was an unpleasant turn of events for her. She still doesn't know she passed information to terrorists. We've learned through a friendly Interpol agent that Paul's convinced her he's working for the West. That Gotthard Enterprises is a front. She believes she's a courageous assistant doing duty for her country, and Europe. Our friendly contact tells us she's even willing to risk her life to the enemy. In spirit, she's one of us."

Jorden groaned. Frustrated with himself, believing he had left her in the lurch alone and defenseless, Jorden lapsed into silence. He had scorned a delightful young woman who was not just beautiful, but if Flanders was right, a woman of brave character and explicit morals. Just the kind that could turn his heart into mush.

"Interpol..." Jorden repeated, feeling a mixture of anger toward Gotthard and profound relief where Krista was concerned. She was innocent.

He looked at Flanders. It was too good to be true. "How do you know all this?"

"How do we know anything? Through a confidant I'd personally trust with my life. Unlike Paul Gotthard, he does work with Interpol and with us as well. His situation enables him to know about Krista."

"Who is he? I'd like to talk to him."

Flanders smiled. "Sorry. I can't do that without permission. Take it from one who knows, Keller. She can be trusted."

She could be trusted. The words became a song in his mind, reaching the distance to his cold and sometime hardened heart, defrosting it and enabling it to feel once more. He didn't know why, but it seemed as if he believed in blue birds again and picnics on a summer hill, laughter, and beautiful things. Maybe all wasn't lost in the world after all, not as long as there were still women like Krista and Stella, who could be trusted to do what was principled, who were still virtuous. Women like this actually existed!

Careful, Keller, his emotions warned. *You're much too enthusiastic about Krista, more than you ever were about Stella.* Krista evoked stronger reactions. This could dangerous.

"Something still troubling you?" Flanders asked.

Jorden was thinking of his last meeting with Krista. He had been hard on her, even cynical. He had concealed any outward show of sympathy when the flying glass had cut her. He had deliberately been rough on her, allowing her to escape, and setting up the recording so he could gain information. He had steeled himself against her distraught condition, refusing to allow himself to care. He rubbed his chin, remembering that slap on his face. He had deserved it.

"I see the two of you have hit it off badly," Flanders surmised. "There's always next time. Which brings me to something else."

Jorden hardly heard him. He was no longer in a mood to talk. He walked over to the table and watched Flanders burn the photo of Krista, just as he had of Einer Seitz.

Jorden knew enough about Flanders to understand that he could rely on his judgment. As an undercover CIA agent he had worked in the diamond export business in South Africa and was investigating Gotthard Enterprises.

"We've learned the von Burens own a good portion of Gotthard mines."

Jorden had suspected the jewelry business to be a front, allowing Paul and his security guards to make worldwide contact with important individuals. It was a perfect set-up for exchanging and passing secret information.

Now that he knew the truth about Krista, Jorden was beginning to worry about her being with Paul at the von Buren mansion in Zurich.

"Just what was it that Stella expected to learn from Krista Grendelmier?"

Jorden saw no reason to keep the matter a secret from Flanders. He seemed to know more about Krista than he did.

"Krista is wearing a ring that Stella is certain belonged to her great-aunt."

For the first time Flanders showed his worry.

Jorden paced. He thought he knew why.

"I think it might have come from the von Buren collection of stolen holocaust goods. How Krista may have come to own it is the question disturbing both of us. Until a few minutes ago I was almost certain if it really was a Cohen ring, either Paul or von Buren passed it on to her as a payment. Now," Jorden mused, frowning, "I'm thinking there may be a deeper and nastier secret we haven't unearthed. It could be what Tirzah wants to talk to me about."

"Tirzah?" Flanders asked curiously.

"Stella's great-aunt. She's in Austria. Avi's gone there to see her. Maybe that will be enough. But I'd like to see Krista again, to learn about the ring."

"Who gave her the ring?"

"I don't know. I wish I did. One thing is clear however." He ceased his pacing and looked at him. "Neither von Buren nor Paul recognize it. They'd have destroyed it by now. Only one thing troubles me. Paul knew Stella wanted that meeting with Krista."

"Yes?"

"By now he would have questioned her about what Stella wanted. Even so, she can't tell him very much." Maybe that interruption was the best thing that could have happened. Was she still in Zurich, or had she taken the train to St. Moritz lodge as she had implied she would do?

"They're not likely to guess about the ring," Flanders suggested. "You say Stella didn't have time to question her at the house?"

"No, not as intended." Jorden stood still, recalling what details he could remember of Stella's brief exchange with Krista. After the shooting, Stella had become emotional when she saw the ring on Krista's hand, but he had interrupted her from saying too much at the wrong time. He could only hope that Krista had been so taken up with the gunfire that she didn't recall Stella's behavior. It was a slim chance.

Only a short time ago Jorden had been willing to forget any woman named Krista von Buren. He'd been content to leave her under Paul's sway at the mansion in Zurich. Everything had changed. He now knew she was not one of them and his tension grew. He had left her to face Paul's questioning alone, and maybe von Buren's as well. *She could be in danger,* Jorden thought. *Especially now, with Seitz on the loose.*

"Take it easy, Keller," Flanders said quietly, as though he picked up the troubled mood of his thoughts. "She's been waving that ring under Paul's nose for years. Elsa von Buren has seen it on her hand. So has Wilhelm. As far as we know, none of them have paid any attention. Matters aren't likely to change in just a few days. You can explain your reasons for concern to her when you get back from Austria. By then she'll be at St. Moritz. You should know even more then from Avi's meeting with the older aunt named Tirzah."

Jorden looked at him. How had he guessed he intended to involve himself with Krista? Was he that transparent?

"How did you now I intended to go to St. Moritz?"

"If anyone can explain the ring, it's Krista. Where else would you go?"

Jorden turned away because he didn't want Flanders to see his frown. Flanders wouldn't be the only one to guess that. If Paul and von Buren did learn about Stella's interest in the ring, they would guess the same thing Flanders had. And maybe Lars...

The more he saw her, the more he placed her in danger. Involvement was a doubled-edged sword. If he stayed away she could face danger from another source, yet for him to go to St. Moritz lodge was also exposing her to risk. She had mentioned going there after leaving Zurich. Was she there now?

"If I were you, Keller, I'd see Krista," Flanders said, as though reading his thoughts. "You'll need her help before this is over, and I'd feel a lot better sleeping at night if I knew she had yours. She'll be of more assistance than Stella. Believe me, Krista is cool and smart."

Jorden glanced at him. "You appear to know her well."

Flanders shrugged and smiled. "You know how duty goes."

"Very sacrificial of you."

"I've had her watched in Europe for some time. Including Rome and Venice. Hans Fischer reported back to me."

But not to me, Jorden thought. "She recognized him at the house when he arrived to give me a hand."

"Proves my point about her being cool and smart. She may be able to turn over a whole new spade of information for you and us. After all, she's close to Paul Gotthard, isn't she? Aren't they engaged?"

So that was it. Flanders interest was also in Paul Gotthard. "I could be a risk to her safety," he repeated.

Flanders frowned. "That's the unpleasant side of the coin. It's a possibility that shows up with every toss. In this case, Keller, we think your involvement with her is worth the risk. She could use a friend. Especially one adept with a .38."

Jorden didn't like it. He pulled his gloves on, frowning, looking at them with distaste, but his mind was far away. "What makes you think she'll cooperate?"

"She will," he said with assurance, and when Jorden looked at him, wondering at his confidence, Flanders said: "Someone else will talk to her before you get there. She has reason to trust him. By the time you meet with her, all you'll need do is apologize for your brutish ways and poor Texas accent."

Jorden wished it were that simple. Flanders didn't understand that he had his personal reasons for not wanting to work closely with Krista Grendelmier. Those reasons had nothing to do with von Buren now, but the loveliness of Krista herself.

"I'm on my way to Austria," he told Flanders. By now Avi would be there to see Tirzah and to convince Stella to return to New York. Jorden would need to contact Avi about Seitz. He looked at his watch. 1:15 A.M. He removed his damp ski jacket from the peg. He'd need to contact Meir and Ziv as well. Maybe he could convince Avi to send one of them to St. Moritz to watch Krista. Stella, at least, would be going back to New York.

"I'm at the very border of Austria. Going back to St. Moritz means a loss of time. I'd need to return through Liechtenstein."

"You can be back in Switzerland by morning. I happen to know a train leaves from Sargans toward St. Moritz by seven A.M."

"I'll think about it," was all Jorden said. He walked to the door. "Anything else?" he asked briefly.

Flanders grew serious. "Just watch your step. We have a good relationship with you and Avi. We'd like to keep you around."

That went both ways. "When will you be leaving here?"

Flanders glanced at his watch. "In an hour. There's a small military base a few miles away. Our Austrian friends look the other way when an American helicopter arrives from our base in Germany."

"I'll be in touch."

Jorden opened the cabin door. A gust of wind and a few snowflakes swirled. "An hour may be all you have. Don't wait too long, or you may be snowed in until spring." He smiled and shut the door.

He was physically tired, but his mind was alert. He mulled over the decision on whether to see Krista as he fastened the cold, stiff ski bindings and picked up his poles. He would go to Vienna first and report to Avi.

A few minutes later Jorden was skiing down the snow-covered path toward the Austrian border. He'd only gone a few hundred yards when another skier emerged from the forest. He was aggressive and fast on his trail. Jorden pushed off on the downhill slope knees bent, crouching low, poles straight back, the sound of the wind in his ears. His pursuer followed—the wood-cutter Flanders had noticed. There was bound to be more than one lying in wait. That meant Flanders too would be in danger when he set out to reach the American helicopter. Somehow he would need to turn back to warn him.

At the moment he had more than enough to concern him. With the clouds scattering across the moon he hadn't noticed an unnatural grouping of logs—and what looked like a chain stretched across his path between two trees just a hundred feet ahead of him. Instinctively he veered to the right of the logs. He slid into the snowbank and then tumbled down into a ravine.

A dull pain pulsated at the back of his head. Momentarily stunned, he lay still, then fumbled to remove his right glove, and reached inside his ski jacket for the revolver in his shoulder holster. He rolled over onto his stomach, holding the gun steady with both hands. The skier obviously knew about the chain and came to a stop, snow flying. He released his skis. *He must think I'm unconscious*, Jorden thought. *Will he be satisfied and go on?*

Jordan could see him standing above him looking down into the ravine, a silhouette against a horizon of glittering white. His masked face was scanning the area, searching for him in the blue-black shadows of fallen tree branches. Jorden lay perfectly still, waiting. Apparently having spotted one of Jorden's skis, he began sliding down the bank.

Jorden could see he carried a gun. The man was an easy target in black against the gray-white snowbank. He cautiously approached.

He apparently thought Jorden was buried beside his ski, too injured to move. Jorden saw the man lift his pistol toward the ski and fire a round into the snow. Jorden could see his extended hand against the white hillside. Jorden aimed carefully at the man's forearm...*nice and calm*, he told himself...*just so—fire!*

The man instantly released his gun, dropping to his knees. He tried desperately to retrieve it in the soft snow with his other hand. Jorden fired again. The man flung himself toward safety, crawling off behind some rocks.

Jorden wanted him alive for questioning, and pushed himself onto his knees to go after him. A wave of dizziness sucked at his brain. He must have hit his head harder than he thought. With revolver pointed in front of him, he inched into the darker shadows of the tree branches. There, he would out-wait his equally silent enemy. His opponent had two obvious disadvantages: he'd lost his weapon, and his right arm was rendered useless.

A deepening silence pervaded the night. Could Flanders have heard the shots at this distance from the cabin? Not with silencers. Flanders too was in mortal danger. The man behind the rock would not have come alone. Jorden considered sounding off several shots to try to warn Flanders, but that too, was risky. He would be tipping off more than Flanders to his location. The man in the rocks was no longer his primary worry, but others in the vicinity. He hoped he didn't have a two-way radio.

He waited, listening, hearing nothing but the wind in the trees dropping snow from the overhead branches.

Perhaps five minutes crept by. He heard a sound of snow dislodging from the embankment. Was someone coming down or going up? He couldn't see a thing from where he was concealed. Was it friend or foe? Or the man who tried to kill him, crawling away?

Jorden moved carefully from his position across the snow toward a pine bush. Then he saw the crouching figure climbing the snowbank to reach the top of the ridge. It was his opponent. In a crouching position, the man slipped away into the night.

Had it been Lars? No, he didn't think so. Lars wouldn't have given up so easily. Lars would have come after him—with a knife if necessary. Lars was vicious and fearless. He had nothing to live for but the satisfaction of his hate. And he hated Jorden because of an incident in Lebanon when a woman had been killed—accidentally. Lars believed, and always would, that Jorden had killed her in the attack deliberately. That was the kind of mind Lars had. One that believed Jorden was capable of the atrocities that Lars and his kind of terrorists could perpetrate on the innocent. Lars was the reason he worried about Stella, and now, Krista. Especially if Jorden involved himself with Krista. Lars was the kind of fiend who would kill her just to get at him. If Lars had cared about anyone in all his life, it must have been that Lebanese woman in the village that was attacked by Israeli aircraft and Jorden's squad.

His head was throbbing now. Who was this assassin? Perhaps someone now working for von Buren himself rather than Paul Gotthard.

He crawled to his skis and dug them out of the snow. Using them for support, he was able to stand. He touched the back of his head and found the blood already hardening.

His back and shoulder were bruised and cut, probably on protruding tree branches that had slowed his fall.

He looked up the slope. The height seemed as high as the Matterhorn. He clamped down his frustration and moved forward to conquer or be conquered. By the time he would reach the top and find his way back to the cabin, Flanders would be boarding his American helicopter for the military base in Germany. If he made it. If still another assassin didn't wait for Flanders in the midnight shadows of the forest trees closer to the Austrian border.

Jorden struggled his way up the snowbank, forced by pain to move slowly. He felt in the snow for handholds of buried rocks or branches to help his ascent. As he struggled, his soul found a new path of thought, one he had not asked for, nor explored to its inevitable end. The Old Testament scriptures the Jewish Christian group in Dallas had patiently pointed out to him came to mind as they often did in the silence of the night, when he least expected to be thinking about them: Isaiah 53 and Psalm 22. He had memorized them as a boy in Synagogue school. The rabbi said that it spoke of Israel as the suffering servant of Yahweh, but Jorden knew this did not fit. Israel was not the righteous suffering servant. Israel had rebelled and was in need of a great Day of Atonement for its national sins. The servant Isaiah wrote about was a person. A person rejected by his own and horribly abused, yet cherished by the God of Abraham.

Jorden paused in his struggle upward, resting his face against the cold snow for a moment. The Jewish group insisted the prophecies spoke of Yeshua—Jesus.

Jorden's eyes opened. He saw the moon, pale and silvery now, the clouds flitting by and covering everything with darkness. *Who else could Isaiah and David have been writing about except Jesus?* a thought seemed to suggest. *Why don't you ask Yahweh? Why don't you read the New Testament the Jewish Christians gave to you? Why do you keep it close in your bag, but never open it? What are you afraid of?*

"I'm not afraid of anything!"

He struggled on until he reached the top of the embankment.

He pushed the haunting questions from his mind one more time.

The clouds parted again briefly. In the bright moonlight he saw the assassin's ski poles where he had left them. His wounded arm had rendered them useless to him. He too was on foot and could not have gone far. Though they were shorter than he would have wanted, he was able to use them. He slowly set out on the painful trek.

13

The University lawn was crisp with frost beneath Krista's boots as she hurried toward the graystone building of classrooms. A few lights indicated early risers, or perhaps those who hadn't yet gone to bed. The windows were like square beacons that did not offer the warmth or comfort that she sought. She cut across the lawn toward the faculty apartments in back, skirting thick, rounded privet hedges and trees that were still silhouettes in the silvery dawn.

Would Uncle Franz be awake yet?

She tried to silence her steps on the stone quadrangle until she neared the last apartment on the ground floor. She dug out the key he had given her long ago, and inserting it, turned the lock. She entered the darkened apartment quietly, and locked the door behind her. No use awakening him until his regular hour. He was up by 5:30 anyway. A glance at her watch told her she had made record time from the von Buren mansion. It was 4:45, but early dawn was casting a grayness through the large front window onto the leather divan and chairs. No need to turn on the lamps. She would get a fire going in the hearth, then put the coffee on.

It wasn't quite as light as she had told herself. She bumped her knee into one of the ponderous chairs beside a table that held yesterday's newspaper. She'd better switch on at least the table lamp. As she did, her eyes fell on the newspaper. She noted the date; three days ago on his birthday. Her heart sank. Had he left? He had made no mention of it to her when she was here with Paul.

Then she saw a message written on a sheet of stationary on the coffee table in front of the divan. Quickly she retrieved it and saw her name. *Dear Krista—*

She turned on a second lamp and sank to the divan with the letter in hand. It was brief, dated the morning after his birthday.

I'm leaving this message just in case you come by the apartment. Something came up that needed my attention at St. Moritz. Since you had plans to come to the lodge for a visit anyway, I thought I might as well join you and get an early start before the weekend traffic. This is as good a time as any to get in some exercise skiing and climbing with Trudy. I've called ahead and Henrich is expecting us both. He's all full for the week, however, so Trudy has arranged with her mother to put me up at their forest chateau. Wish you could join us there, but there's not an extra bedroom other than the one I'm using. Since I snore terribly I suggest you don't try it.

Krista smiled for the first time since yesterday.

Henrich says your old room is always vacant and ready for your return. Call me when you get there. We'll have dinner. Take the train. Don't drive.

> *Love, Uncle Franz*

Krista set aside her disappointment over not being able to talk to him now and took immediate action to arrange her travel by train home to the lodge. She wanted to leave at once because Paul might come looking for her as soon as Mrs. Brandt let it be known to the von Buren household that her bed was empty. She dialed the Hauptbahnhoff to learn when the train was leaving Zurich on its run to the Canton of Graubunden. She arranged for tickets. There would be at least one stop at Chur where she would need to switch to the Rhaetian Railway for transportation into St. Moritz.

With that done, she went to the small bedroom she used while staying with him and packed a bag of clothes to take with her. She had not risked packing anything at the von Buren mansion for fear of being discovered before she could leave undetected. She had left a note for Paul telling him she was going home for a rest of a few weeks, and a note for Elsa thanking her for her hospitality and the care of her physician last night. She was feeling much better, she had written her, and was sure going home to family and old friends would help the healing process.

Krista frowned to herself as she caught sight of her image in the dresser mirror. The cuts were less inflamed on her once flawless skin—skin the older generation used to call "peaches and cream." They were still quite noticeable. As soon as they healed over a little more she could began touching them up with concealer. She noticed her facial lines were strained, her eyes appeared worried. In the gray dawn of the room her appearance was far removed from her modeling career.

She packed the items she would need, then went to the telephone to call a taxi. She was tired this morning, and the walk to the Hauptbahnhoff seemed long and dreary. Zurich taxis were expensive, but today she'd splurge. And, there would be less chance of being trailed should anyone be watching her. She hadn't noticed anyone since Hans Fischer had told her who he was. She didn't think she would be seeing him again. As for Jorden Keller, she wondered if he had made it safely to Liechtenstein. Now she wished she had kept silent to Paul and his Uncle Josef.

In Franz's drawing-room the dawn was turning to pale sunlight, showing in through the glass pane. She made the call for the taxi, then stood with her bag at her feet. Her eyes swerved to the bookshelf. She had hardly been able to keep her mind off Elsa's book of photography since rising from bed this morning. She hated to admit it, but she no longer trusted Paul the way she had a few days ago. She was going home to St. Moritz, not only to begin her search into her mother's ring, but she had made up her mind to find out the secret that the family wished to hide about Elsa's out-of-print book.

She glanced about the room as if expecting someone to step out from behind the drapes. The apartment remained in oppressive silence except the sound of her own breathing. She had better hurry. She must keep ahead of Paul. She wanted to avoid any further questions until she talked to her parents' respective families about the ring.

She went to the bookshelf, knelt, and swiftly pulled the bottom books out to the spot where Paul had hidden Elsa's book. What if he knew she would come here? What if he expected her to take the book? No, her fears and suspicions were running wild now. Why should he think that? He and the von Burens had been satisfied last night that she was fully cooperating with them when she told them about Jorden going to Liechtenstein.

She half expected to discover that the book was gone, but there it was, just where Paul had hidden it three days ago. With shaking hands she placed it in her bag and put the other books into place just in time. She heard quick footsteps on the quadrangle. Heart in her throat, she stood and ran to the window. It was only the taxi driver. He saw her and lifted a hand.

Krista grabbed her bag, turned off the lamps, and rushed out, locking Franz's door behind her.

Within fifteen minutes the taxi had dropped her off at the Hauptbahnhoff. She merged with the business throng and collected her tickets, then boarded the Swiss Federal Train, the SBB, that would begin the first section of her journey home.

She didn't think anyone on the train was following her, but she wouldn't make the foolish mistake of taking Elsa's book out now. She kept her bag at her side.

It was an hour from Zurich to Sargans near the regional boundary line with Liechtenstein. Jorden must have come this way, she found herself thinking. Why had he gone there? Whom had he met, and about what?

Soon the train left the Zurich area of eastern Switzerland and entered the Canton of Graubunden, dominated by the world-renowned ski resorts of St. Moritz and Davos. Krista had been born and raised here in Graubunden, with Austria and Liechtenstein on the northern border, and Italy to the east and south. Graubunden had once been the ancient state of Rhaetia, speaking an ancient language called Romansch, a Latin language which some insisted was older than Italian. Rhaetia had been a northern province of the old Roman Empire. Now it was the largest canton in Switzerland, covering one-sixth of the country.

It wasn't long out of Sargans that the train brought her to Bad Ragaz, which paralleled the Austrian border past Liechtenstein. Because of the children's classic *Heidi*, many

Swiss called Bad Ragaz "Heidi Country." Krista remembered that Jorden had called her "Heidi." She smiled, thinking of the children's book by the Zurich author, Johanna Spyri. Little did Jorden know that when a child, the book *Heidi* had been Krista's favorite. She still had an old, worn copy in a trunk in her bedroom at the St. Moritz lodge, along with a Heidi rag doll missing one arm. After her parents died, Krista had read the children's book many times, replacing Heidi's love for her old grandfather with her own love for Uncle Franz. In the children's story, when Heidi's crippled friend, Clara, needed to take a cure, the family had sent her here to Bad Ragaz.

Krista watched the story-book territory slip past the train window where she sat. A passenger came to sit in the empty seat next to her. She glanced at him, and was relieved to see a priest. She smiled politely and he inclined his head in return, then leaned back against the seat to doze, showing no interest in conversation. It was just as well, she thought. His pale eyes had not appeared friendly.

Here at Bad Ragaz there were abundant springs used for over a thousand years for the treatment of rheumatism and other diseases. The springs were now a world famous thermal spa, reaching 97.7 Fahrenheit. In the children's book, the springs had been used for little Clara's paralysis.

Not far away was Maienfield, a graceful little village full of fountains and vineyards and old stuccoed houses. It was in these mountains above Maienfield that the Heidi story had taken place. The little orphaned girl had grown up on her grandfather's isolated Alpine farm, but was taken away to Frankfurt, Germany, to be with Clara. Heidi had languished and grown ill until Clara's family brought Heidi back home to her grandfather again and the mountains she loved. There was a hotel here too, the "Heidihof" Hotel.

Krista had once hiked across the steep open meadows and up the forest switchbacks to what was called "Peter the Goatherd's Hut," and "The Alm-Uncle's Hut" and viewed the majestic Rhine Valley from flowered meadows that would have suited Heidi herself.

Seventeen miles to the south the train brought her to Chur, Graubunden's capitol, the oldest continuously settled site in Switzerland and a busy rail crossroad.

Krista, holding her bag casually, left the stranger, who stepped aside to let her pass, and disembarked from the train. Here at Chur she would need to change trains, taking the local Rhaetian Railroad, the RhB to St. Moritz via the Albula route past the spectacular Bernina peaks.

There was an hour delay before the train left and Krista walked up the Oberegasse, once the main road through Chur between Germany and Italy. Here, she passed small shops, cafes, and open-air theaters. The Romans had founded Curia Raetorium here on the rocky terrace south of the river, where they protected the Alpine routes. But during the Middle Ages it was ruled by Roman bishops and bishop-princes. Like Zurich's Old Town, here too there were narrow streets of stone, mysterious alleys, hidden court-yards, and ancient shuttered buildings wherever she looked. Towering over them all, her eyes looked up to the huge 12th-century cathedral.

She paused outside a huge, luxurious mansion dating from the 1640s with a stone archway. It had been the resi-dence of the strong bishop-princes of Chur, once hosts to Holy Roman emperors who passed through on their way between Italy and Germany, sometimes with massive armies. The bishops were repaid for their hospitality by imperial donations to the people. The thick fortifications of the residence demonstrated to Krista the disputed powers of the bishops. By the 15th-century, irate Swiss inhabitants who rebelled again and again were rebuffed and punished with excommunication. By 1526 the Reformation broke the domination of the Roman Catholic Church.

A German accent interrupted her thoughts. "You are on tour, fräulein?"

She turned her head. It was the priest who had sat next to her on the train from Zurich. The breeze ruffled his black cleric robe. His hair was white, yet his face appeared younger than she would have expected. What caught her attention, however, were the granite-hard eyes.

"Yes," she agreed. "History can teach us so much, and also warn us of repeating many of its errors."

"Ah, but do we ever learn? Do we even want to?"

"I fear sometimes we do not, sir. If you will excuse me, I must go. I have a train to catch." She turned to walk back toward the station. "Auf Wiedersehen."

"Wait," came the low command, all politeness gone from his voice. "Show no alarm. If you are wise you will listen."

Her fingers gripped her bag, but she managed to affect a casual behavior to convince anyone watching that this was nothing more than a brief conversation with an old priest. She could see now that he was not old at all, that there was a ruthless survival in his face, unmasking his religious demeanor as a farce.

"Who are you? Why do you find it necessary to hide behind a cleric's robe?"

"Look up at the stone archway. Gesture, as though discussing it with me. That's right—very good, fräulein. You are cool—and sane. Who I am does not matter at the moment. We cannot talk here. There was a man on the train from Zurich who is my enemy, and yours. He boarded at Sargans, coming from Liechtenstein."

The skin on her arms crawled. She had not noticed this man. Was he telling the truth? "How do you know this?"

"The train for St. Moritz is delayed," he said, ignoring her question. "There was an accident."

How did he know there was a rail accident before the station here in Chur?

"You will find you cannot leave before 3:00 this afternoon. It is important you follow my orders. You will eat lunch at the Hofkellere. You will not appear worried, nor pay attention to anyone who may be sitting near your table. At one P.M. exactly you will leave the inn and begin the walk to the old Cathedral St. Maria. A tour will be underway. Go inside. I will contact you there."

"And if I do not carry out your orders?"

"You will carry them out, Fräulein Grendelmier, because you have no choice. I need your assistance, and you need mine."

"I do not see how I need your ..."

"I must contact Franz Klossner."

Franz! "Why do you wish to see him?"

"That is between Klossner and me. I know he is at St. Moritz."

"Then if you know he is there, why not go now? Why come to me like this?"

"I need you to help arrange it."

Arrange it! As if she would involve dear Franz in anything this strange.

"No. I cannot help you. Please go away."

"That is impossible. I have come too far to turn back. I can offer you in return something no one else can or is willing to give you...information on Anna Klossner."

Stunned, she nevertheless turned slightly and shaded her eyes to look up at the high roof. He pointed to its formidable walls.

"I don't think you have anything to offer me," she murmured. "You are bluffing."

"I do not live a life of bluff. I deal in information, cold and hard. I can tell you about the history of the Klossner family in Davos during World War II. No, do not look at me. You see, fräulein? I already tell you one small thing you never knew; that the Klossners came from Davos, not St. Moritz. Look over there at the door as if I am explaining something that interests you. That's it...I can tell you about Anna. About the ring you are wearing now. I thought so," he said without emotion when she gave a small intake of breath. "One o'clock." He walked on, passing some tourists who were taking a snapshot of the ancient mansion.

Krista just stood there for a moment with her heart beating in her throat. She lifted her hand, pulled back the sleeve of her coat, and looked at the time as if anxious to get back to the train station. She wasn't supposed to know the train was delayed.

The ring and Anna. How could he have known anything about either of them? Who was he? Why did he wish to speak to Uncle Franz? And what was this about Davos! She had been told that the Klossners and Grendelmiers originated from around the St. Moritz area.

That this hard-eyed stranger with a thick German accent knew anything about her and her family was intimidating. Of course that was what he wanted for some reason of his own. Was it a ploy to get her to meet him alone?

Krista walked briskly toward the shops and cafes, still holding her bag casually. She must stay calm. A sense of danger, not just to her but Franz and perhaps to others as well, demanded a cool response. She could not afford even a brief surrender to emotional panic.

In the bright daylight the red depths of the ruby on the ring bled, convicting her that she must understand the reason for its recent strange emotional hold on Stella Cohen and perhaps Jorden Keller as well. She would keep the one o'clock appointment. What could go wrong in a church? There would be others there, and what if he were telling the truth about the man on the train?

She found she was not surprised to discover he had been right about the train accident. It had been a minor delay, the station conductor explained. Just a break in the track. The new departure date for leaving Chur would be sometime around two o'clock.

Krista had a light lunch at the Hofkellere in the Court Entrance Tower, an inn since the 14th century, with Gothic windows and a timbered ceiling from 1522. She hardly tasted her food. She didn't dare look around at the other diners for fear she would see the man who had sat down beside her on the train from Sargans. She kept her expression unreadable during the meal and tried to appreciate the old charm and history of the inn.

At last the minutes slipped by. Twenty minutes before she was due to meet the stranger at the old church, Krista paid her bill, slipped into her warm coat, and began walking in the direction of the strange rendezvous.

14

Krista neared the great cathedral built in 1151 and 1272, but received small satisfaction from its history knowing that the stranger waited inside. The columns displayed Romanesque style carvings of wild and weird evil beasts—a warning? Below them there were humble sheep and the harmless mountain marmot.

Krista stepped into the cathedral, but its beauty and art did not warm her heart. A remote gray dimness, as cold as the stone, encased her with emptiness. Stillness pervaded every nook and cranny, but it was broken by the hushed voice of the guide leading a small group of people, pausing first at a pillar, then a section of a wall, speaking as though he feared to awaken the dead.

"This magnificent three-sided altar, elaborately carved in gilded wood, dates from the 15th century."

Krista's eyes grew accustomed to the dimness. She joined the group, hovering at the back while glancing at the faces of those present to see if her contact was among them. He was not.

"The structure built on this site in prehistoric times was then supplanted by a Roman castle," the guide was explaining. "A bishop's house in 451, and a Carolingian cathedral in the 8th century."

Had something gone wrong? The other man on the train perhaps?

"The marble panels under the altars of St. Laurentius and St. Fidelis have been preserved from the 8th century church," the guide gestured.

Krista caught a movement at the far right of the building where there were stone benches. A priest was kneeling, head in hands as though praying. It was him. Evidently he didn't mind pretending to pray, anymore than it bothered his conscience to pretend to be a priest.

The guide was leading the group into another section of the cathedral. The pretender stood, crossed himself, and left the altar, head bent piously. Krista stood in the cold shadows of a pillar, waiting, her lips thinned with displeasure.

He walked slowly toward her and tilted his head that she was to follow him. She did so a moment later, coming to where he waited in a nave concealed in deeper shadow. There were two benches, one on either side of the small enclosure. There were no windows, the only light came from a candle he lit. She noted the cold hardness of the bench as she sat down, the ring on her finger fading into colorless stone, matching the darkness of the pretender's religious robe. Only his silver hair contrasted, like a halo...

Krista waited in silence, knowing he would speak when he considered it safe.

He came to the bench and sat closely beside her, giving the impression they were huddled together in prayer or confession. Krista closed her eyes, concentrating on his words.

"I cannot risk more than a few minutes with you. Nor can I give you anything in writing for Klossner. You must listen carefully."

She nodded, head bent, staring at her clasped hands.

"He will come to meet me alone at nine o'clock the night of the 14th at the annual Cataract of Flame."

That was the annual festive night when all the holiday skiers moving together and carrying flaming torches wound downhill to St. Moritz from the ski lift.

"He need not look for me. I will look for him."

She stiffened, but kept her startled breath from sounding.

"The American CIA agent who offered me help is dead. He was killed in Liechtenstein. The Israeli secret police will soon be on my trail. My name is Einer Seitz."

He stopped. "Repeat what I have just told you."

She did in a shaky whisper.

Dead! Liechtenstein—Jorden had gone there. He was an American—could he have been a CIA agent? She had been the one to tell Paul and his uncle where Jorden had gone, but they couldn't have been the enemy. And Jorden could not be...the unspeakable word stuck in her throat.

"Fräulein!" he hissed, "are you listening?"

"Yes...the agent killed, was his name Jorden Keller?"

She sensed his relentless gaze. "What do you know of him?"

Krista noticed a sudden change in his behavior. She sensed danger, and saw a slight movement of his hands beneath his cleric robe. What was he reaching for? Her heart seemed to stop.

"I know next to nothing. He is a lawyer from America. Working for…" she hesitated. A cover-up might cost her dearly. "Stella Cohen. She is tracking down her Jewish family killed at Auschwitz. There is something about an account in a Swiss bank belonging to her grandfather."

He was silent, watching her.

"What about Keller?"

"He went to Liechtenstein," she whispered. "I thought he might be the agent killed—but no, that could not be. He is not one of them."

"No, he is not. He is an enemy. A member of the Mossad."

Krista didn't move. Couldn't be. Jorden?

"He will be dead soon. You would be a fool to involve yourself with him."

She could not speak. Mossad! There must be some mistake. But she remembered the cool, almost ruthless manner in which he had taken command at Hans Fischer's house when danger broke. And Stella Cohen was Jewish and his friend, perhaps more than a friend. It was possible that this man was right. Then what had she done in letting Paul know Jorden had gone to Liechtenstein?

But Paul was no enemy!

What this was all about remained in murky confusion.

"You are not to mention me to Keller," he warned. "If you do, you will die, and Franz too. Understood?"

She understood, but had no idea who this horrible man was sitting next to her. Who was Einer Seitz? Why had the CIA agent wanted to help him escape? He must have important information, but what did this have to do with Uncle Franz, and now, Jorden? She should not have mentioned Jorden…

"Understood, fräulein?" he whispered harshly.

"Yes, yes, but you promised me information, Mr. Seitz..."

"Do not speak that name, ever!"

Another mistake. She nodded, fighting against rising fear. "I expect the information you promised me."

"You will get the information when you arrange my meeting with Klossner."

It was dangerous to confront him, but it would be more dangerous if she did not. "No. You will tell me now, or I won't go to Franz."

"Do not be a fool. I could arrange for you to meet with an accident before you ever arrive in St. Moritz."

"Then who will help you? If you did not need me, you wouldn't have risked this meeting. You must be desperate to have risked coming to me."

His pale eyes flashed, and for a moment she thought he might lash out at her, but he remained chill and disciplined. Whoever Einer Seitz was, whatever he had done in the past that set him in so dangerous a predicament, he appeared to be a controlled man, a man who gave orders, but who also knew when he must compromise.

"No, I knew you had courage. I have had you watched for months, just to make certain. You are sometimes clever, but not always smart enough. You think Paul Gotthard works with Interpol?" His hard mouth twisted. "His contacts in Europe are terrorists. When you cooperated with him, delivering messages, you were delivering information to terrorist groups."

"Lies."

"It matters not if you believe. What matters is that you arrange this meeting. So, I will give you one small piece of information that should convince you I know what I am talking about." He lifted her hand so that the ring was visible. "Gotthard is a fool. All these years the danger of their unveiling has been beneath their noses, yet they did not know, they did not recognize this ring. Ask at the convent in Davos about a two-year-old child left in their care when the parents were sent back to the Gestapo. Ask about who took the child away and where she went."

Krista, white, her heart throbbing, stared, into his hard mocking eyes.

"The child was a Jew," he hissed.

Her breath sucked in.

Her shock noticeably pleased him, but his hand gripped hers until she winced. "Pull yourself together, fräulein. When you walk out of here you must be calm, look satisfied about your religious experience," he mocked a whisper. "Now go, and carry out the order I gave you. Franz's life, and yours, depend on it."

Krista, still feeling shaky, managed to stand, looking down at him. His words rang in her mind, sending shock waves through her soul. That child—that Jewish child—had it been her mother, Anna? She must know! She must find out. She would ask Uncle Franz, Anna's brother. He would know. She would ask Cousin Henrich and Veena, and she would go to that Catholic convent in Davos and find someone who was alive in World War II who might tell her about a certain two year old...

His movement shook her awake as he also stood and extinguished the flame on the flickering candle. She turned, drawing her dark coat and hood about her and left the cathedral, hardly aware of the light rain that had begun to fall on the gray pavement as she walked back to the train station. The thoughts circled her mind like restless birds. If he spoke the truth, if Anna had been Jewish, then so was she. The amazing idea settled into her heart like a seed and began to sprout. The holocaust took on new, sharp, painful realities. The Swiss banking scandal, Stella Cohen, the Mossad—was she now related to these wrenching agonies through Anna? Did Uncle Franz know his sister may not have been his blood sister at all but adopted? But! How could this be? Why would her grandparents on the Klossner side take a Jewish orphan as their daughter? Who were her grandparents, really? Again she realized how little she knew about them. All this would soon change. She would dig out the truth no matter what!

Jorden Keller...a member of the Israeli secret police. Why was he here pretending to be a lawyer? What did he really want? More importantly, who did he want?

She shivered. She recalled the documentary she had seen on how members of the Mossad had gone to Argentina and found Adolph Eichmann as a humble worker in a Mercedes car plant. They had arranged to abduct the Nazi fiend and smuggle him back to Israel. They had been successful. He had stood trial for aiding Hitler in masterminding the Final Solution—the murder of six and a half million Jews...Why was the Mossad here in Switzerland?

With a start she recalled Jorden's remark about Jewish gold mingling in the wealth of the von Burens and Gotthards. She had been outraged, but could there be terrible truth to all this?

And Stella. Her interest in the ring was beginning to make sense.

Krista stopped. If Stella believed the Bank of Zurich Corporation had her grandfather's account, and if she somehow connected this with the ring, did it mean that she and Stella were related?

Realizing that passers by were turning their heads to glance at her, Krista hurried on to the station. If this were true, how would it change her life?

She realized that her life had already changed. The winding road led on. What truth would be waiting when she reached its end?

The only trains running in the Graubunden were from the local Rhaetian Railroad with its broad network of narrow-gauge track. The "Bernina Express" from Chur to St. Moritz via the Albula route past the Bernina peaks was the only train available, so she boarded with her mind still on the stranger who had called himself Einer Seitz. Why did he wish to see Uncle Franz? Where had they met, and when? How was it that her uncle would know such a dangerous man? How did Seitz know about Anna and the ring?

A hundred questions rumbled through her mind, keeping pace with the clickity-clack cadence. She tried to lock her concerns away by looking out the window at the massive rocks with jagged peaks and domes smothered in thick white. The glorious mountains, strung in a line along the Swiss-Italian border, were the Bernina group in the Rhaetian Alps, forming Switzerland's third majestic Alpine region. This was "home" to Krista, and to several Alpine resorts that clustered around their peaks, including St. Moritz.

In this area of Graubunden, the word "Piz" simply meant "peak." And the one mighty mountain above 13,000 feet in the entire Alpine chain east of St. Gotthard Pass was the awesome Piz Bernina. Here, the mountains offered more than skiing. There was challenging climbs on rock and ice. Some of the most difficult rock climbs in Europe were found here in the nearby Val Bregaglia. Krista tensed as she thought about it, for it was in this area that her parents had fallen and come to their deaths; it was here too, that Uncle Franz often climbed. Franz, who had been the first on the scene of tragedy to find his sister's and brother-in-law's bodies.

The main river draining the southeast portion of Graubunden was the En, and so the surrounding country was called the "Engadine." It was divided into the upper Engadine, an area of glaciers and lakes, and where St. Moritz was located, and the lower Engadine, beautiful with contrasting meadows.

From the main valley of the Upper Engadine to St. Moritz the area was filled almost entirely by a long series of topaz lakes, each flowing into the next, and forming a grand chain. In the winter when the lakes froze, the villages, including St. Moritz, sponsored a cross-country ski race extending along the entire length of the valley floor over the frozen lakes. When in her teens Krista had always entered and done well. How long ago those days seemed now.

Later that night she arrived in St. Moritz with a mixture of conflicting emotions—everything from relief to sadness, suspicion, and fear. Although anxious to see Uncle Franz, a tiny bubble of doubt had risen in her heart. How was it that a studious professor of history at the Zurich University would know Einer Seitz? What had given Seitz cause to think he could dare turn to Franz for help? She would soon know.

Franz Klossner was seen in the small junction, leaning his shoulder into a porch pillar while smoking a pipe and scanning the passengers leaving the Bernina Express. Krista noted he looked as easygoing in a tweed jacket and turtleneck as a relaxing cup of hot cocoa by a crackling fire. Was he what he appeared? Until meeting Einer Seitz she would not have entertained the thought that he could be anything else.

Franz saw her and lifted his hand in greeting, coming toward her.

"Hello, Krista dear. You were beginning to worry me. I expected you this afternoon."

"Hello, Uncle Franz," she returned his affectionate greeting, looping her arm through his as he took up her bag and they walked toward town. "The first train was delayed. An accident, they said. I had to take the long Albula route. I didn't really mind. I had a lot to think about."

"You look strained. Something wrong?" he asked, his voice lowering.

She glanced up at the side of his face, where the beginning gray touched his brown hair. His light blue eyes were grave as he turned his head to look at her.

"Something is very wrong, Uncle," she whispered. She felt his arm tighten beneath her hand.

"Yes?"

"I've had the unfortunate experience of meeting an unpleasant man."

"With your appearance, dear, you're bound to run into many of them."

She watched his expression carefully, afraid of what she would see. "This man was different. He calls himself Einer Seitz."

Franz stopped. He stared down at her.

"The strange thing is, he told me to bring you a message." The throng was walking around them, their laughter and chatter in the varied languages of German, French, Italian, and English filling the air.

"Not here," he warned in a barely audible voice, his hand tightening on her arm. "Come. We'll talk on the way to Trudy's house."

Then he did know Einer Seitz. Her heart weighed heavily with dread.

15

The evening was lovely with a white moon over the frozen lake. The Alpine resort-town with luxury hotels and private chalets was sprawled across a snow-draped hillside above the lake, surrounded by forested hills and dramatic peaks. Trudy's house was within comfortable walking distance just outside St. Moritz, and Krista went with Uncle Franz along a narrow dirt trail, now covered with new-fallen snow illuminated by the moonlight.

Within a matter of minutes they were away from the tourist attractions among stately Alpine trees. The gaiety of the town was muffled by the sighing of the wind in the pine branches. They passed several private chalets, and saw older Engadine-style houses scattered farther from the lake toward the hills.

When they were still some distance from Trudy's house, Franz slowed to a stroll. "All right, Krista, we can talk here if we keep our voices low."

Amid the still beauty, Krista explained her bizarre meeting with Einer Seitz, from his appearance on the train as a priest to the meeting at the ancient cathedral. Franz grew visibly upset that Seitz had involved her.

"I was told this afternoon he would contact me, but I had no idea he would use you," he murmured angrily. "He must have been watching you for the last week in Zurich, making plans. Unfortunately for our American friends, matters went not only awry, but someone—a personal friend to me and an ally of Switzerland—has been killed. All because of Seitz!"

She had never seen Franz display such passion and it alerted her to the real danger they must be in. She looked at him, trying to shield him from her own fear. A friend, killed? Franz's dislike of Seitz convinced her they were not comrades-in-arms for an honorable cause.

"Uncle Franz, don't be alarmed for me, I managed the ordeal well enough, though he's certainly an unpleasant man. I did get something of value in return. Yes, it's true. Very important personal information to me." She thought of the ring and saw suspicion tighten his usually pleasant features. Did he guess what it might be? How could he, unless he knew Seitz had information about Anna Klossner? She was anxious to delve into the matter of the ring, yet she must move cautiously. Even if Franz did know about Anna, he might not be willing to tell her.

He stopped on the road as they drew near the family lodge, which was within sight of Trudy's house. Lights burned invitingly in the large double-storied pine-and-stucco building. Later tonight she would see Cousin Henrich and Veena, and after a warm welcome with hot chocolate and fondue, she would again have access to her warm and cozy childhood bedroom. She resented Einer Seitz for interjecting his presence into what would have been a pleasant homecoming.

They stood, two dark silhouettes against the brightness of the wintry moon. Franz bit on his pipe, his unreadable eyes shielded in the shadows. "What information did he give you, Krista?"

She knew she shouldn't have hinted of it yet. It wasn't the right time.

"First," she said with more restraint than she thought possible. "Don't you want to know the news Seitz has for you?"

"I'm well aware of what's on his mind. I had a visitor this evening before you came who warned me of what was about to happen."

That surprised her. "A friend of Seitz, or someone more welcome?"

"Our friend."

She breathed easier. It was good to know they were not alone, that there were others in the background.

"I'm sorry you've met Seitz. He's a dangerous man. He grows more so because, like a wounded animal, he finds himself being hunted."

"How is it you know such a man?" she asked in a whisper.

"Ah, a good and fair question, one I promise to answer in due time."

"I thought you might deny it."

His brows shot up, and his face mellowed. He looked like the old Uncle Franz she loved. "There would be no reason for that now, would there, dear," he stated over his pipe. "You're too smart for that."

She smiled. There were times when she felt quite dumb. "How much did he tell you about me?"

"He told me nothing, except that he demands to see you."

"He is comfortable with demanding. What did he tell you about himself?"

"Hardly anything. His name, and what I've learned by observing his actions. He spoke with a thick German accent, and he was wary and suspicious, yet still confident."

"Um. Sounds like him all right. He lived in East Berlin before the wall came down."

She had feared something like this. "Then he's connected with the Communists," she whispered, feeling an icy wind from the Alps.

Franz looked at his pipe for a long moment. "With the Stasi, the secret police."

She believed he watched her carefully to see if she would cringe. She must not fail him now by adding to his worries. Now she believed Einer Seitz had chosen her to deliver his message to intimidate Franz. He had known her uncle would be loathe to involve her.

"No wonder he knew how to act so intimidating," she said with a trace of bitterness. "He's had plenty of practice in terrorizing his subjects."

Franz laid a comforting hand on her shoulder. "What message did he give you?"

"He insists you meet him alone on the 14th at nine o'clock during the ski festival."

She went on to explain Einer Seitz's message in a low voice that was lost on the wind. Franz listened quietly, smoking his pipe and looking out across the frozen lake toward the golden spots of light in the chalets.

Krista took hold of her uncle's arm. "Oh Uncle Franz, don't go, don't meet him," she suddenly pleaded, more afraid now than she had been when meeting with Seitz. The danger of his demands came swirling about her like snowflakes as she realized what it might mean for Franz to cooperate.

"But why you, Uncle Franz? He appears to be in some sort of danger that he wouldn't explain."

"You're right, he is. He poses a threat to some very important people whom he can expose. They want him dead."

"But he's a Communist, or was." Now that the old Soviet Union had collapsed most political scholars claimed the Cold War was over and that Russia supported democracy. But Krista was convinced the hard-liners were still there and that they hadn't truly changed their beliefs.

"Wouldn't Einer Seitz's enemies be our friends? Why help him? Why does he expect such help?" *And why does he think he'll get it from you*, she wanted to ask again, but his hand on her shoulder silenced her. His eyes were grave but held no hint of panic.

"I'm going to tell you the truth, Krista, but not just because Seitz contacted you. Circumstances have changed since we were in Zurich. It is very important for me to retain your trust. Danger now threatens all of us and you must know enough to wisely be on guard."

Krista waited tensely, her gloved hands jammed into her coat pockets. The man she was looking at was a far different Uncle Franz than she was accustomed to, but somehow her heart knew she could trust him still.

"This will hurt you, but you must know. Paul lied to you about working with Interpol. We suspect him of being involved in international espionage and terrorism against the West."

She wanted to gasp, but silently clenched her hands instead.

He watched her, then went on. "It is I who have contact with the agency in Paris. Naturally he doesn't know that, or he wouldn't have made such a mistake."

Krista whispered: "You? With Interpol?"

He nodded.

"But..." her voice trailed off into thoughtful surprise.

He smiled kindly. "Sorry, my dear, but you understand I couldn't take chances and tell you until tonight. I've worked with the agency for the last twelve years since the accident that robbed Anna and Peter of their lives."

She found her voice, and it was low and tight. "Why since my parents' death?"

He searched her eyes quietly. "I can't explain that."

She considered, then nodded. She would let that go for now. "You're sure Paul misled me about Interpol?"

"Lied is the more accurate word. Imagine my dismay when you both dropped that little bombshell on me at the apartment. The information was useful for one thing, however. It proved that neither Paul nor the von Burens suspected me. There were times these last few months when I had begun to worry that Paul might. Especially when he began to get very friendly, dropping by on Wednesday nights to play chess. I thought he might be watching me."

For a moment Krista forgot the danger and smiled her relief. "And I thought you might have gone over to the wrong side. I could have borne anything but that! Oh Uncle, you gave me a terrible scare. But how did Seitz find out about you? And how does your work with the agency benefit him? Surely Interpol isn't interested in helping an old Communist from East Berlin avoid his enemies. And just who are these enemies. What has Paul got to do with this?"

He took her arm and they walked on slowly. "All in good time." The lights in Trudy's house burned warmly through the windows.

"Interpol is known to cooperate with other intelligence-gathering operations in the West like the CIA. They are interested in Seitz for reasons of their own. We can't get into that now."

"They are going to help him?"

"They were, but something has gone badly at their end, leaving Seitz sitting on a powder keg." He shook his head in a demonstration of sadness and regret. "The Americans just lost a top agent here. They can't get a backup in the few days they have left to get Seitz to safer territory. I knew that agent. He was a trusted friend. We worked together a few times in Europe. I've been asked to take his place. I said I would in his memory."

His harsh tone of regret deeply troubled her. That small fear gnawed at her heart again. Jorden Keller had gone to Liechtenstein. *Oh no, it can't be him. It must not be him.* She held Franz's arm tightly. "The American," she whispered, "was he...a lawyer?"

He looked down at her knowingly. "No."

Krista felt a surge of relief. They walked in silence for a moment before her resentment returned. "Neutral Switzerland is not safe enough for Einer?"

He stopped to relight his pipe. "No place is safe. And Zurich is a haven for espionage agents. With the kind of information Seitz has, he could easily be killed. His enemies live here."

In Zurich?

"When I was asked about taking the agent's place I was told Seitz would probably contact me. I expected him to come to me here, at St. Moritz. I had no idea he would meet with you," and his tone tightened.

"Who told you the American agent was killed?"

He looked at her thoughtfully. "Jorden Keller. I've known he was an agent all along. Even when Paul mentioned him at the apartment. We've not met, but will, soon. I've been told he is on his way to St. Moritz from Austria. He wants to see you."

Jorden was coming here. She fought against a surge of unexpected excitement.

"Before Flanders was killed, he contacted me in Zurich asking that I settle things between the two of you. Trust is important, and you'll need to work together on a few matters."

"The agent—his name was Flanders?" she asked quietly.

"Yes, Keller went to Liechtenstein to meet with him. They were both attacked, but Jorden was able to escape. He later found Flanders dead."

"Oh no..." her conscience recoiled. Had her remark to Paul alerted the enemy? Yet, she cringed from that notion as well. Paul would not do such a thing. There must be some mistake about him. Uncle Franz must be wrong...

"Jorden is all right?" she whispered.

"He got off with minor injuries, But Flanders' death complicates matters for us all. Seitz was to have met with him, and the CIA was to arrange for his safe transport out of Europe."

Krista was still struggling with the death of the agent. Did he have a wife and children? What if she had been to blame? And Jorden could have lost his life as well..."But why would Flanders want to help Seitz?"

"For information. I don't think any of us would argue Seitz's worthiness. And if it comes to justice, I think

Flanders should have lived and Seitz should be having the funeral." He sighed. "Matters of injustice do not always have simple answers in this hour in which we live, Krista. We must look to God in faith for ultimate justice. We can know that whatever a man sows, he reaps."

They walked in silence for a moment.

"Your meeting with Seitz has complicated things for us. Keller won't like this anymore than I do. I worry about you."

"You mustn't. Just do what is right, no matter what it costs us."

He smiled at her sadly. "That's what makes me worry, dear. You're too good of a girl to get tangled in all this."

She smiled for the first time. "I doubt Jorden Keller would agree." What would he do when he learned she had been the one to tell Paul he had gone to Liechtenstein?

"We must have your trust, and you must know you can fully rely on us. Paul called me today." His voice suggested trouble. "He told me he was coming up. You had left the von Buren place before he'd arrived there this morning, and he was behaving the worried, concerned man in your life."

She remained silent about Paul. Her emotions were pulled in two directions."

"When he arrives," Franz warned, "he's likely to try and convince you he's on the right side and needs your help. You've got to be sure in your own mind just who it is you are siding with, Krista."

She said nothing, her heart troubled. Surely the Lord would give her wisdom if she prayed for it. He would want her to behave wisely in such a dangerous situation as appeared to confront her. As for Paul personally, she was still uncertain, wanting to believe he was somehow free of anything so clandestine.

"I know I trust you," she said. "And Paul has misled us about Interpol. I'll be careful what I tell him. Much of this is my fault, Uncle. I've been working secretly with him for several years and I should have told you about it. Had I done so, you would have known at once that he wasn't working with the Paris agency. About trusting Jorden Keller..." her voice trailed off deliberately. She found she wanted to trust him. And if Franz did, then it must be safe. She remembered what Seitz had said about the Israeli secret police.

"We must be careful now," Franz told her. "I don't want Trudy involved in any of this."

She nodded. They walked through the pine trees toward the front porch. The two-story house belonged to Trudy's mother, who was the widow of the pastor of a small Protestant church. It was a charming renovated 350-year-old Engadine house setting back from the narrow road. Its many windows faced the lake and the golden lights from the hotels and chalets.

They stopped several hundred feet away, and Franz faced her.

"Jorden was wary of you as well."

She lifted a brow, remembering their last meeting.

"He was nearly convinced you were working with Paul wittingly in support of terrorism."

"Of all the..."

He interrupted with a smile. "Flanders intended to convince him otherwise. I'm sure he succeeded, or he wouldn't be coming here. He'll continue the role of an amiable lawyer, so be prepared."

She was slightly mollified. "He was the one who worked deceitfully. Pretending to be a Hollywood agent for Ava St. John."

"Yes. He had no choice there, I'm afraid."

"When all the time he worked for the Israeli secret police, the Mossad," she said.

"Who told you that?" he whispered sharply.

"Einer Seitz. He was very much against Jorden. He was adamant we say nothing to Jorden about his being here."

"Keller already knows about Seitz. Flanders told him, as well as requesting that the Mossad leave him alone. That, of course, was before Flanders was killed in Liechtenstein." He looked at his pipe as if it held the answer to his concerns. "I'll need to talk this out with Keller myself." He took hold of her hand. "Dear, you must not speak of the Mossad."

"You need not worry. I'll say nothing." But she knew she had already told Paul too much.

"That Seitz knows who he is worries me." He looked off toward the thick forest trees, thoughtfully. "If he has found out, then there may be others who know as well. Perhaps that explains the attack in Liechtenstein, and the reason why Flanders is dead. The opposition may know more than we think." Franz looked at her. "They may also know Seitz contacted us and is willing to talk."

What was it Seitz knew that posed the enemy such a threat? she wondered. Who was the enemy?

Her mind grappled with the obvious, but it was too painful. She remembered what Seitz had told her about the ring and Anna. She must talk to Franz about it, but the moment was robbed from her once again as the front door of the house opened and Trudy came out on the porch. She looked down toward them on the pathway.

"Is that you, Franz? Did you locate Krista?"

"Yes, Trudy, we're coming now."

"Good, dinner is getting cold."

Franz turned to her. "We will talk again in the morning. I think it best that you stay the night here with Trudy. I'll let Henrich and Veena know. I'll sleep on the sofa. You can walk down to the lodge in the morning. We'll all have breakfast together. By then I should know when Jorden will arrive."

"All right, but there's so much more I need to talk to you about."

"I'm aware of that, my dear, and we'll get to it. But not here, nor at the lodge. If we can arrange it, we'll take the ski lift up to Piz Nair tomorrow. We'll talk then."

She was weary and satisfied for the night.

"And now," he said, taking her arm. "Let's not keep Trudy waiting. Are you ready?"

She smiled, and he nodded his approval. "That's my girl," he said. "You can tell us about those cuts on your face. You've seen a doctor? They won't leave scars?"

"No. He promised they would not."

She walked with her uncle up the porch steps and into the warm, glowing room where Trudy waited to welcome them.

16

Ask at the Convent in Davos...about a two-year-old child left behind...her parents were sent back to the Gestapo. Ask where the child went...the child was a Jew," came the slurring voice in Krista's subconscious, startling her.

The jarring words of Einer Seitz awakened her suddenly to the reality of her quiet room in Trudy's house. Bless Uncle Franz for giving it up for her. She sat up and reached for her wristwatch from the bed stand; 10:00 in the morning! She threw the eiderdown lace quilt aside and jumped out of bed, grabbing her blue cotton terry robe, then opening the drapes and lattice shutters. The sunlight warmed the room as it streamed in onto the pine wood floor. Oh no! She had overslept and missed breakfast with Franz and Henrich at the lodge.

As she rushed past the dressing-table she caught sight of a written message. It was from Trudy, who had already left for the Swiss Ski School where she worked as a private instructor.

"Franz asked me to leave you this message saying he would miss breakfast at the lodge, and he didn't want to awaken you. He will meet you for lunch instead, at the Piz Nair ski lift."

In two hours, she thought, glancing at the time again. If she hurried, she might catch Cousin Henrich at the lodge before he went off to keep his guests pleased with the service. What could Henrich Klossner tell her about Davos and his cousin Anna? He must know something, and Franz as well.

Her mouth tightened as she looked at herself in the mirror. The East German Communist, Einer Seitz, might also know something. She recalled his hard, mocking eyes. "Pull yourself together, fräulein," he had said. Well, she intended to do just that, by going to Davos and searching until she knew the answer. She would not allow herself to be intimidated.

Her hand shook as she applied the antibiotic ointment to her face. Despite her determination she wondered if she could have been so brave had she lived in Austria during the time the Nazis came to power. What could she have done? What could anyone do when their government was dedicated to the extinction of a people? There was information now that suggested that some leaders in England and the United States knew about mass extermination of the Jews and yet had done little to stop it. They knew about the railway line bringing Jews to the gas chambers yet allied planes had not bombed the rail lines to keep the trains from running. Instead they had excuses—they couldn't afford to waste the bombs or risk pilots that were needed to fight German troops elsewhere, but Krista had a difficult time accepting this. After the war, when the death camps were open to public scrutiny and the world saw what had been done, the governments had pretended shock. But they had known about it as early as 1940-41.

She tossed the ointment back into her bag and snapped it shut decisively.

She made sure her hair was right and her lipstick hardly noticeable. Her wool slacks and sweater were fashionable and appropriate, but her complexion remained a source of embarrassment with red discolorations. She ran her finger along the healing spots, recoiling at the numerous small but loathsome scabs. She shuddered. Yes, she might as well admit it. Her pride flinched at the sight, realizing Jorden Keller would see her looking this way. She hated the thought!

"You look a far cry from the face in *Europa* magazine," she said to her image.

Maybe she could do something to cover them. Concealer? Talcum powder? There must be something!

She stopped, wondering that it should bother her so much. After all, Paul too was coming to the lodge and his opinion mattered more when it came to her profession. *So why should I care so much about the effect I have upon Jorden Keller?*

She knew why. She wanted to impress him. The secret knowledge that he was a Mossad agent intrigued her, and she might as well admit something else to herself since she was doing some "confessing." She wasn't supposed to put too much confidence in the physical, but she'd need to lose her sight to not notice that he was good looking, his hair and eyes dark and rich. Quickly she shut the idea out of her mind. "I won't think about it. I won't!"

She laid her hairbrush down and frowned. She had always relied on her own looks to feed her self-confidence, though she would be the first to deny it if asked. She considered now the Scripture that emphasized a woman's true beauty. Remembering her decision to begin reading the

Bible again, she went to her small traveling bag and brought out the one Uncle Franz had given her for Christmas. Where was that verse? Yes, that was it, it's in 1 Peter.

She turned there, and after searching for a minute, found the section she remembered. *I want the time to come when I won't need to search and search for the verses I want, but will be familiar with their locations.*

She read chapter 3, verse 3. "Do not let your adornment be merely outward—arranging the hair, wearing gold, or putting on fine apparel—" Krista stopped. Those words couldn't mean she wasn't supposed to look feminine and attractive, or that neglecting her hair and clothing to becoming plain and unattractive meant a woman was more spiritual? She thought of all the beauty that God had designed into His creation that expressed a part of His character and brought honor to Him.

She read on at verse 4. "Rather let it be the hidden person of the heart, with the incorruptible beauty of a gentle and quiet spirit, which is very precious in the site of God. For in this manner, in former times, the holy women who trusted in God also adorned themselves...."

It was clear that a woman certainly couldn't use her appearance as the basis for approaching God, and she also remembered Trudy once telling her that a woman would be doomed to failure if she attempted to win an unsaved man to Christ on the basis on sex appeal. It is the "gentle and quiet spirit" that is the adorning with a greater value than just outward appearance. God looks at the heart. *Paul doesn't look at my heart,* she thought, *neither does Elsa or my clients.*

She thought again of the words: "the incorruptible adornment...which is very precious" in God's sight. *If I want to please God, then I will need this trusting, quiet spirit that rests in Him.*

Oh Father, I've trusted so much in my outward appearance. I've held on tightly to my job at Paul's firm, afraid I'd lose my top position and with it, my identity, my value to Paul and to others. I know I should be more concerned about my relationship with You. I've held on so tightly to the outside that I've neglected the inside. But what I am on the inside is very precious to You and to Uncle Franz too. Maybe I shouldn't worry so much about pleasing Paul and Gotthard Enterprises if doing so would not please You. Maybe there's something else I could do. If they love me only for my appearance their friendship will wither at the first sign of summer drought. Oh Father, it is You who have given me outward beauty, my picture is in all the fashion magazines, but that isn't enough to make my life meaningful. I want the true loveliness of Your character reflected in me. My strength and confidence will fail if Your spirit is not with me! I don't know how to begin, except I realize I need to come to know You and Your word in a more personal way.

Minutes later, as Krista left the room carrying her bag to walk to the lodge, she passed the mirror. Once again she looked at herself—no, not herself, her body. A body that would eventually grow old and die, no matter how many expensive beauty creams she used.

She no longer felt insecure. Her worth was not based on the transient, but on an eternal, loving relationship through Jesus Christ with her Heavenly Father. Nothing could destroy that.

With a lighter step to her gait, she walked the pine-needled path toward the family lodge. Maybe Veena would still have some Swiss pancakes on the big warm stove. She would smother them in creamery butter and pour on cinnamon syrup! A delicious cup of hot coffee to go with them would make her new morning perfect. Well...almost.

17

Cousin Henrich and Veena greeted her warmly when she arrived at the lodge but almost at once she sensed something was troubling them. She didn't think it was her arrival. Did they know about Einer Seitz? No, how could they? Surely Franz wouldn't have told them.

Henrich asked about her face, but Veena made no comment. Krista was prepared with an answer. She made light of it by telling them she needed some time away from her modeling career anyway. "I'm anxious for the quiet life here at the lodge. It might even be mentally restful to go back to waiting on tables on the weekends."

"You would not do that," Veena said, surprising Krista by her show of scorn. Even Henrich appeared a little surprised by his wife's remark. Veena smiled briefly. "You are much too dainty for that, Krista. You were made for better things." She waved a square hand. "Sit and eat. I will bring it to you. It is good you are home again," she added.

Krista felt somewhat embarrassed, and even guilty. Had she been mistaken, or was Veena glossing over some sort of mild resentment? If so, it was surprising. Veena had always been kind to her, and if not the motherly sort, she had at least been accepting.

"Well, if you're sure I can't help…"

"Ja, I am sure. Sit, sit. You too, Henrich. I will get you coffee while you talk to little Krista."

Krista sat down at the kitchen table as Veena walked over to the stove. So the cuts on her face had been dismissed as simply as that. Krista breathed a secret sigh of relief. It was much easier to avoid the uncomfortable details of that night in Hans Fischer's house in Zurich; neither Henrich nor Veena were good conversationalists. Veena, especially, was a silent personality. A woman hard to know, even after the twelve years Krista had spent with her and Henrich in the lodge after her parents died. Veena worked hard, expected little from life in return, and carried on with soldierly duty. She was tall and large-boned, not heavy but solid, with graying-blond hair. She brushed her hair back from her face and braided it so tightly that Krista worried about root damage. But she had always worn it that way in one long braid from the crown of her head down her back like a horse's tail. Her pink face was scrubbed clean and wore few smiles, and her gray eyes were unobtrusive. Though she had always been kind to Krista, the two of them had never been emotionally close. In fact, Veena had not expressed her thoughts about Krista leaving the lodge and going to fashion school in Paris. The frowns had come from Henrich and Franz.

Veena brought her breakfast, and perhaps that said volumes more of her feelings than any cozy conversation.

Krista poured the thick, warm syrup from a pitcher with cinnamon sticks onto the waffles and smiled at Veena, who watched in silent approval.

"Oh Veena, this is scrumptious. You don't know how I've missed your cooking. I loathe caviar," she jested. "I'll take all the calories I can get."

Veena smiled and nodded. "You look well," was her only remark. "You can use the fat and sugar."

Krista laughed and looked at Cousin Henrich. He smiled and drew up a chair, turning it around backward, resting his big arms over its back. "It's good you are home again," he said after a long contemplation. "You should stay," and he nodded his gray head with satisfaction. "The Burgermeister is interested in you. It's not every girl in this area of Graubunden who turns the head of the Burgermeister. That is so, is it not, Veena?"

He looked pleased that the mayor was still determined to make headway with Krista, but she was not. She didn't like the Burgermeister. The older man had been eying her since she was sixteen. His wife had died. He owned one of the nicest private resorts farther north in the Engadine Valley. He often sat in a Bavarian beer garden and drank two and three foamy pitchers at a time, smoked, and tapped his foot to polkas.

Veena looked at him, then at Krista. "The Burgermeister is too old. He would die and leave Krista a widow before she is thirty."

"Then Krista would own everything," Henrich said with a sage nod and wink. "And she would not need to put up with his foolish ways for long."

"Shame on you, Henrich," Veena said, and walked back to the stove.

Krista smothered a smile. "I don't want his lands or his attention, Cousin Henrich. I'd just as soon stay single. When my modeling days are over I'll come and help Veena bake strudel. I can bake apple strudel as good as hers. Isn't that

LINDA CHAIKIN

so, Veena?" Krista's blue eyes twinkled as she looked across the bright kitchen at her.

Veena pursed her lips and thought about it. "Almost," she agreed.

"Only because you have taught me the family secret," Krista said good naturedly. "Perhaps I could open a Swiss bakery in St. Moritz. Think of all the British, Italian, French, and American tourists who will come to buy my goods."

Henrich chuckled and held out his over-sized coffee mug that Veena had bought him at the ceramic shop for Christmas. She refilled it. Henrich looked at Krista. "The Burgermeister would make you rich and politically powerful."

"No one is as rich as the Gotthards," Veena said. "When his Uncle Josef dies, young Paul will own everything. The fashion house, Josef's mansion in Zurich, and the mines in South Africa."

Krista smiled at her, a little surprised Veena knew so much.

Henrich appeared to consider as he drank his coffee. "Maybe Paul will not be Herr Josef's heir. Maybe it is not Josef Gotthard who owns so much, but Wilhelm von Buren. Maybe he only uses Josef's name to conceal his own."

Krista glanced toward him, covering her caution. How much did Henrich really know?

Veena turned toward him. "Why would Herr von Buren wish to conceal his name?"

He shrugged his heavy shoulders. "Why do you think? All the dark talk recently about old Jewish accounts in Swiss Banks. It's in all the newspapers."

Veena made an unpleasant sound in Swiss German and went back to her work wiping down the counters. "Talk,

talk, what is that? There is no proof we Swiss collaborated with Hitler in World War II."

"No? Even the Burgermeister has skeletons in his closet. Old Nazi skeletons, I'm told."

Veena cast him a scolding glance. "You must not say such things, Henrich."

"Where do you think his father got his money after the war? Remember what his father was selling on the black market in the 1950s? The Gestapo knew how to get the Swiss bank account numbers," Henrich said darkly. "They would haul Jews out of Auschwitz and..."

"Henrich! Your talk will get back to him."

"Then what? Will he no longer come to the lodge to eat? Will he tell the others in town not to come, forcing me out?"

"He can do whatever he wants. Men with power always do," Veena said wearily.

"And good people stand back and do nothing because we fear."

Krista took another bite of her waffle, hardly tasting it. The silence grew. She refused to say anything and reached for her glass of milk. *Caution,* she told herself again. *Why do I feel they are trying to get a response from me? Maybe I've been growing too suspicious recently. I must be willing to take risks to learn about the ring and Davos.*

"I do not want to hear," Veena interrupted. "That was a long time ago. Let us forget the horror tales of the past."

Krista wanted to say we must never forget. The future loomed with dark clouds of judgment. A world dictator was coming, the Church had been warned. He would deal falsely with Israel and great persecution would flood the earth. Forget? The past was often a harbinger of worse things to come! We must remember, not forget!

Veena went on with her kitchen cleanup.

Henrich stood up from the chair and limped to the door that connected the kitchen to the lodge parlor with its massive fireplace, hardwood floor, and beamed ceiling.

Veena, as if on cue, left the kitchen for the back porch to fill a bucket with water to rinse her mop.

"How is your leg since your fall?" Krista asked, deliberately changing the subject. Her heart felt heavy. This was home, and yet she believed she needed to watch her words, though she could not explain why she felt this way.

"It has been a year now and it is still not strong. My skiing days are over."

"I'm sorry."

"Where did Franz go?" he asked her, sitting back down, and resting his cup on the edge of the white enameled chair.

"I thought you could tell me," she said with a casual smile. "He thought we could all get together for breakfast this morning for a change, but Trudy said something came up."

"Something always comes up with Cousin Franz. I wonder what he is up to. Why did he come back to St. Moritz? The University year is not over yet, is it?"

"Not until June. He has a leave of absence."

"Why does the University put up with him? He spends more time away then he does lecturing in the classrooms."

She was nettled by the subtle attack on Franz, but shrugged easily, refusing to be embroiled in their disagreement. Cousin Henrich and Uncle Franz always seemed to clash. Their personalities were so different.

"So he went somewhere again. I thought I saw Trudy walking alone to the slopes this morning."

"You don't know where he went?" she asked innocently.

"He never tells me anything," came the slightly caustic tone. "He doesn't think I share his lofty intellectual abilities.

He is a University don, and I am but a simple lodge manager—an ox. Our minds do not run on the same tracks."

"Oh Cousin Henrich, you shouldn't feel that way. Franz always has something good to say about you. He was anxious to see you," she insisted. "He thinks highly of you."

"Anxious to see me!" he stated skeptically.

Krista was careful. "I'm meeting him at the Piz Nair lift for lunch." She pushed the plate of half-eaten waffles away, wondering how she would be able to eat with Franz. "It would be good if you and Veena could join us. We could go to the ski slopes. You could watch us even if you can't ski. Then we could make it a foursome for dinner tonight at one of the dining houses. Veena wouldn't need to fix supper and..."

"No, no, it is nice you ask, but it is no good. I've too much work to do. Veena, too. We cannot leave. Weekend guests will begin arriving this afternoon."

"Oh, I'd forgotten it was Friday."

"Even more guests than usual are coming. I got a phone call this morning from Zurich."

She looked at him, catching the wariness in his voice. Henrich wore a distasteful smile.

"All the von Burens and Gotthards are coming here for a holiday."

Her heart sank. That left her little time to delve into matters on her own. "They're coming this afternoon?"

"No, they will be late, arriving on Sunday to spend the entire week. Paul, Elsa, even Wilhelm. Veena will need to hire a girl to help cook and serve, and I will need to pay Johann more to play waiter. Old Wilhelm is a very precise man who expects to be treated like a prince of Bavaria. I will even need to hire Gert to play his zither. Wilhelm likes to sit and listen by the hour. He dreams of the old glory days of the Third Reich," he mocked in a low voice.

Her heart began to pound. "I'm surprised Elsa and Wilhelm would come with Paul. How long has it been since they've been here on holiday, five years?"

"More like twelve. Not since Anna and Peter died in the fall."

"I didn't realize it was that long ago." Next week! The week of the 14th? The week of the festival. Then they would be here the night Einer Seitz was supposed to meet Uncle Franz. Was that a coincidence? What else could it be, she insisted to herself. There was no evidence that the von Burens were involved in espionage, even if Uncle Franz said that Paul was.

"Next week will be difficult for me," he admitted, rubbing his knee.

She knew he had never truly liked his Cousin Elsa. Perhaps fiscal jealousy had something to do with the dislike. Elsa had done well by marrying Wilhelm, even the lodge actually belonged to the von Burens. Her parents had managed it until their death, then Elsa had permitted Henrich to run the business. There had even been a time when Henrich had talked hopefully of buying the lodge from Elsa, but that idea had fallen through several years ago. Either Elsa had changed her mind, or Cousin Henrich could not afford it. She felt love and sympathy for them both, but facing Paul would be challenge enough, as Uncle Franz had already warned her last night. Now there would be Elsa and Wilhelm too. She thought back to the night before last which had been spent in the mansion in Zurich. Their presence had very much intimidated her.

He looked at her. "What do you suppose their motive is?"

"Motive?" she asked too quickly.

He looked at her plate with the waffles now cold and uneaten. Had he guessed their coming was upsetting her, as it had him? She thought so, yet she dare not tell him about Einer Seitz or about Uncle Franz working for Interpol.

"You don't think either Elsa or Wilhelm would show up here at the lodge if they didn't have some purpose?" he said. "We both know this is not the best lodge in St. Moritz, even if they do own it. They have done little through the years to renovate it to draw finer guests. Normally they would not even come here, but go to Badrutt's Palace," he said of the ritzy and famous hotel in St. Moritz. A room for one night could cost more than a transatlantic flight. Guests arrived in Rolls Royces and Learjets, and the guest list was filled with the names of royalty.

"They were never skiers, even when they were younger," he continued. "So why are they coming now? Wilhelm hates snow. He complains everything is cold and wet. He talks about the war and his years in the Arabian desert. He likes dry heat."

This was the first she had heard of Wilhelm serving in the Arabian desert. "I thought he was a member of the Swiss Army during the war, traversing mountains and keeping the passes open—just in case Germany invaded neutral Switzerland."

His emptied his cup and set it down on the table without comment. He stood. "Maybe Franz knows why they're coming. Maybe he's checking into it and that's why he didn't show for breakfast."

What if Paul discovered that Elsa's book was missing from Franz's library at the University apartment? What could she tell him? *I should have given the book to Franz last night,* she thought worriedly.

She caught sight of Anna's ruby ring on her finger and remembered her main reason for wanting to talk to Henrich this morning before she saw Franz at the lift. She looked up.

"I didn't realize it was so long since Elsa was here. You say she was at my parents' funeral. I guess I was grieving too much to at the time to notice. I recall her visit when I was fifteen."

"Yes, the modeling school in Paris. Franz was not pleased about it any more than I was. I should have stood up to Elsa. She's always been a bully."

Coming from a man with thick, muscled arms, Henrich's remark about Elsa being a bully might have brought Krista a smile, except that the morning was no longer a pleasant one. Elsa usually got her way by using her emotional hold on people, but that didn't explain Henrich's need to feel intimidated. He stood up to everyone else, why not to Elsa? Maybe he feared losing control of the lodge. Unless there was something more sinister. She would rather not consider that because she must discuss the ring with him. She could ask Franz about Anna.

He stood to leave, and before she lost courage to follow through, Krista said in a low voice…"I didn't know Uncle Franz's parents once lived in Davos."

"Davos?" he repeated.

Veena came into the kitchen from the porch, mop in hand, and was looking at them.

"Yes," Krista said. "Franz must have spent a few of his childhood years there. Anna, too. Neither of them ever mentioned it to me."

Henrich looked at Veena. "You know anything about Davos?"

"Nein," she breathed.

"What makes you think your grandparents came from Davos?" Henrich asked, his voice quiet.

Krista had not yet mentioned her matriarchal grandparents, nor could she explain that it had been Einer Seitz that told her. She avoided an answer. "You mean Franz and Anna weren't born in Davos?"

He sat down again slowly, watching her. "I've no reason to say that." He shrugged. "I do not know, actually. They may have been born there." He turned to Veena who stood in silence. "Do you know?"

"I have always lived in the Upper Engadine. I have never been in Davos. Why do you ask, Krista?"

She was almost certain they weren't telling her all they knew.

"I want to know more about my grandparents on the Klossner side. All I have ever heard about is the Grendelmiers," she said of her father's parents.

"Ask Franz."

"I intend to, but I thought you and Veena might also know something about them."

"Franz will tell you. He was always so proud of his father, the doctor."

"A physician?"

"Henrich," Veena interrupted. She was holding the mop handle tightly. "Johann is here. He waits out front to talk about working here next week."

"Why are you asking now?" he asked Krista. "You have never asked us before."

"Oh but I have, Cousin Henrich, many times. I suppose I had the impression my grandparents had, well, founded this lodge and ran it until they passed on, leaving it to my mother to run after she'd married Peter Grendelmier."

"The lodge belongs to the von Burens," Henrich reminded her quietly. "You should know that."

"She must have forgotten," Veena interrupted again. "Henrich, please talk to Johann. Tell him I will need to hire his sister to help too."

"Doctor Klossner never managed this lodge," he said stiffly. "He would not know how to manage it. He could treat a sick baby, but what did he know about keeping complaining tourists happy?"

"Baby?" Krista asked, picking up on the light remark.

Henrich waved a careless hand. "There were many babies in the war. Many left in the concentration camp in Switzerland."

"Switzerland did not have concentration camps," Veena corrected.

"Very well, Veena, 'detention' camps. The Jews were still there, weren't they?"

"They were fed. They were clothed."

"Not always that well."

"I remember. My mother brought things there sometimes," Veena said.

He stood again with new rigor. "Don't you have some shopping to do in town? I ordered the butcher to cut up and package that deer I landed last week. Better have Johann drive you. Here—" he took the keys down from a peg on the wall above a calendar. "He better take the truck."

Veena was untying her apron, her eyes searching his. "Yes, I'll go now," was all she said, and taking the keys from him, she went out onto the back porch. Krista watched her find her purse and coat in the small closet where she kept her snow boots. She glanced back at Krista, then went out the door.

Krista saw the top of her head pass by the bottom window. Henrich stood looking down at Krista thoughtfully.

"Henrich, I..."

"I've work I must do now. If you have questions about Davos you had better ask Franz. I will see you tonight at supper if you get back in time."

He turned and left the kitchen, but she was on her feet, hurrying after him. Not this time! She must have an answer, at least about the ring—

"Henrich, wait."

He did, reluctantly, turning on his boots to look back.

Krista came up. She removed the ruby ring from her finger. "This was Anna's," she said very quietly. "I found it among her things after she died."

"She liked jewelry. Most of it was costume pieces, not expensive. She used to send for necklaces and earrings from America. She had a catalog someone left here on a holiday."

Krista had never heard this about her mother before. Her mother dressed in practical clothing and rarely used makeup. "But this is a real ruby," she told him. "Do you know where she got it? The ring looks rather old, even antique."

Henrich's face remained blank. "Peter must have arranged it with the Grendelmiers. His mother died before Anna, and the family had given him some items."

She hadn't thought of that. "I wish that could be, but I don't think so."

"You haven't said why. Perhaps that crazy American woman has been troubling you with questions?"

Her gaze darted to his. He was frowning again, looking upset. Did he mean Stella? He must. Who else was there from America asking questions about the ring, and herself?

"When did you see Stella Cohen?" she asked, surprised.

He snatched his loden hat with its feather from the peg, and his jacket. "When she came here," he said gruffly, as if the memory of her visit provoked him.

"Stella came here?"

"She made a fool of herself. Most American women do, chasing around on their own, demanding to be treated like men. She pretended to be a journalist, and was poking about asking questions that were none of her business."

"When! When was she here?" Krista asked hurriedly.

"Maybe three weeks ago. I made a mistake and rented her a room. I found her nosing about."

Three weeks ago...that could have occurred before Krista met her and Jorden at Hans Fischer's house.

"What kinds of questions did she ask you?"

His faded eyes came to hers. "Same kind of questions you are asking me," he said in a tone that told her he also found her questions unpleasant. "Then you have spoken to her," he said. "You know her."

She explained about the meeting Paul arranged in Zurich. "Only then, we thought she was Ava St. John."

"Yes, that was the name she used here. You confused me when you called her Stella. A lawyer showed up and they left together."

Jorden Keller. How would Jorden explain himself to Henrich when he arrived to see Franz? Maybe Jorden could avoid the lodge altogether.

"I found out they went to Zurich." He watched her, frowning. "Paul asked about them soon after they left. I wondered how he knew they were even here, but he did know. And that's what troubles me, all these questions from family and strangers. And now Paul's coming back, with Elsa and Wilhelm von Buren. I don't like it. That American woman is trying to track down gold belonging to Jewish relatives killed in Germany. I don't want any of that past evil washing up on my doorstep. Neither does Veena."

He looked so troubled that Krista laid a hand on his arm. "You don't need to worry, Cousin Henrich, nor Veena. Stella didn't come here because she thought either of you were involved in anything dark. It's me she wanted to know about."

He studied her. "What does she want from you?"

Krista wasn't exactly sure, but she knew it had something to do with the ring. She guessed Henrich thought so too, but wouldn't say. With Paul and the von Burens coming to the lodge next week, perhaps it was best that he and Veena behave as if they didn't know. Remembering Einer Seitz she said nothing more.

So Stella had come here. She must not have learned anything from him. If she had, she wouldn't have needed to arrange that meeting with Krista in Zurich.

The best recourse was to make that trip into Davos, this time with even more resolve. Perhaps tomorrow.

Henrich stopped at the front door and looked back, his face relaxing. "By the way, about the Burgermeister. You are sure you won't have supper with him? He saw you arrive last night."

She hadn't thought anyone noticed her arrival. That proved she must be careful. The Burgermeister would have been harmless, but anyone else may also have seen her, even had her followed from Chur where she'd met with Seitz.

"I'll be seeing him this afternoon." He waited.

"No, I'd rather not." The Burgermeister insisted on misunderstanding her motives. He had asked her to dinner before and she had refused. He refused to believe she was not interested in political power.

Henrich shrugged. "He doesn't want to give up."

She smiled briefly. "Then I'll need to discourage him once for all."

He thought about it, nodded, and went out.

Krista sighed. She stood for a moment, thinking, then opened her hand and looked at the ring before replacing it on her finger. From Grandmother Grendelmier instead of Klossner? Was it possible? Yes, but not probable.

Uncle Franz would be the next one to ask. She had to be careful with Henrich, perhaps she had already said too much. *I haven't handled matters well*, she thought wearily. *I need lessons in espionage.* She had better tell Franz what Einer Seitz said to her in the cathedral. That would almost force Franz to tell her what he knew about his sister, Anna.

The clock told her she had an hour before meeting him in town. There was just enough time to go up to her room and look through Elsa's photography book before walking to the Piz Nair ski lift. With Veena gone shopping and Henrich off to do his work, she would have the time to herself.

She stood in the large den aware of the silence. She looked up at the beamed ceiling, hearing some creaks and groans from the rooms above. Not every guest was out on the slopes.

A vague fear, undefined, began to spin a soft thread about her. The absence of Henrich and Veena, the pervading silence, the memory of having been followed in Rome, and again at Chur, began to weave a web of uncertainties.

She turned toward the stairway that hugged the right wall and curved upward to the second-floor bedrooms. Rejecting her run-away emotions she walked across the hardwood floor with oriental runners toward the stairs, giving her fears no more opportunity. Uncle Franz had warned of danger, but there was such a thing as allowing her imagination to run wild.

She climbed the steps toward her bedroom thinking about Elsa's old, out-of-print book. At last, she would learn what Paul feared would be revealed. Her steps slowed. That last night in the von Buren mansion came to mind, bringing some of the same feelings she had experienced when Wilhelm had been in her room. In her memory she could hear the German martial music adopted by the Third Reich.

Hurry, she told herself. *Do you want to miss Uncle Franz at the ski lift?* She rushed up the stairs. Her bedroom was nearly as she had left it several months ago on her last visit to the St. Moritz lodge. Veena had drawn back the white eyelet curtains, and the inside shutters, folded back into the wall, were hardly noticeable. Sunlight welcomed her. The bed with its soft eiderdown cover was—Krista stopped in her tracks, staring. Her overnight bag, which she had carefully placed out of sight in the wardrobe before descending to the kitchen for breakfast, had been opened and its contents dumped on the bed. She took several quick steps and searched through the items, tossing aside her dressing gown. Elsa's book! It was gone—No, she saw with relief that it was still there, concealed within the scarf she had wrapped about it at Franz's apartment. Veena must have begun to put her things in the dresser drawer then gotten called downstairs to the kitchen.

No, that couldn't be. Veena was already in the kitchen cooking waffles and talking to Henrich when I arrived. Anyway, Veena never unpacks for me. . .

Realization dawned on her. Someone had *recently* been in the room, searching. For what? There was only one item that seemed to interest both friend and foe—the book. But how could anyone know she had brought it with her? She must be wrong. Anyone deliberately searching would have found it inside the scarf at once. So why hadn't they? Either her imagination was running wild, or else Veena had actually begun to put away her things before she went to the grocery mart and changed her mind. Either Veena, or someone else, because it was plain her bag had been searched. No, not searched, but had been in the process of being searched when—

Her spine went rigid. Someone hadn't found the book yet because she had interrupted the search as she came up the stairs. She whirled around to confront the intruder and met a dark blanket or rug. Its smothering mass came down upon her like an avalanche, burying her in a dark, airless cocoon. She fought back viciously trying to kick and claw herself free from the grasping hands that dragged her across the room. She tripped on the blanket, landing on her knees. A heavy wallop struck her head—

18

Krista's eyes blinked opened as she became aware of a throbbing, dull pain in her head. She moved slowly, discovering that she was lying on the hard floor wrapped in something dark and warm. Her struggle with the intruder came back to her consciousness. Was he still in the room? She listened and heard nothing. She managed to roll over and with some effort, freed herself from the entangling blanket.

She pushed herself up onto her knees, then grasped the back of a chair and slowly pulled herself to her feet. She felt dizzy. Blood pounded in her head and sent pulsating waves before her eyes. She reached a hand to the back of her head and felt a bump, but no dried blood. How long had she been unconscious? She looked at her wristwatch, squinting to read it. Only five minutes?

She eased her way to the bath and splashed her face with water and found some aspirin in the medicine cabinet. After five minutes of resting on the bed she begin to feel stronger. Had he stolen Elsa's book? Naturally, what else could he have been searching for?

She got up from the side of the bed, determined to keep the noon appointment with Franz. He would be upset, and she couldn't blame him. Depression set in as she imagined herself trying to explain why she hadn't told him about the book sooner.

She managed to smooth her hair into place, added concealer to her skin, and applied some powder and lipstick to add color to her paleness. Nauseous, head throbbing, she slipped into her coat, caught up her shoulder-strap handbag, and made her way slowly down the steep flight of stairs into the shadowy room below. She was sure the man had left, but she would still be careful. Could it have been someone working for Einer Seitz? How would he have known she had the book? And what reason would he have to want it?

Veena was still out doing her grocery shopping, and Henrich, too, was gone. Whoever had entered her room had left in the same way he had arrived—unseen. The lodge front door was shut but unbolted. Anyone could have slipped through unnoticed. The sight of guests coming and going was normal even during the weekdays.

She went out the front door, squinting against the bright morning light that added to her aching head. She fumbled in her bag for her sunglasses and slipped them on, then began to walk toward the ski lift. She could only imagine what Uncle Franz would say.

St. Moritz was the oldest ski resort in Switzerland, its thermal springs known as long as 3,000 years ago. It was also the most chic and haughty. As such, St. Moritz could not be content with just one ski area. Piz Corviglia, Piz Nair, and Grisch on the northwest slopes of St. Moritz boasted 80 kilometers of wide and well-groomed runs dotted with fine restaurants.

When Krista arrived at the lift, there were skiers in all their equipment waiting to ride up, but a careful glance about told her that Franz had not yet arrived. Had anyone trailed her from the lodge, or were they content now to have escaped with the book? Even if she were under surveillance, a meeting with Franz should appear normal. Where had he gone earlier that morning? She suspected it was to meet with someone and report what she'd told him last night.

Skiing was now out of the question for her, but they could take the chair up to the top and talk in private. She had her boots on and they could walk to one of the rocks and view the breathtaking scenery while she explained about Elsa's book. She wasn't looking forward to admitting she had cooperated with Paul in hiding the book in his apartment in Zurich.

She looked at her watch. Noon. Franz should be here. She tensed, wondering if something may have happened to him as well. She told herself sternly not to automatically assume the worse scenario. He was only five minutes late.

There was a lodge at the base of the lift with low benches along one wall where people could sit and put on their skis. She walked there as casually as she could, trying not to draw attention, and sat down, glancing at a group of merry-makers who were just coming out of the lounge. There were four college-age girls and five young men in stylish ski suits and sunglasses. One of them looked her way. Jorden? Definitely, she thought. Dark hair glinting in the sun, maybe six feet, solid, well-proportioned, and wearing a black ski suit and sunglasses. The girls were laughing as they walked along with their skis calling something to him over their shoulders in German. He hoisted a green rucksack over his shoulder and walked toward the bench.

He sees me, Krista thought, *no need to draw his attention.*

He dropped the bag on the bench between them and sat down, removing a tour book from his bag as if studying the possibilities. He glanced at her and smiled. "Guten Tag, fräulein," he said in a friendly voice that carried: "Are you a local? My friends and I are hoping to ski the slopes at Champferer See?" he tapped the book. "How far, do you know?"

Krista leaned over to explain the route by automobile. "It's not far from St. Moritz...you take this road here, and make a right. The slopes should be very good today."

"Franz couldn't make it," he murmured. "Wait a few minutes for the man with the newspaper to go inside, but don't let him see you watching him. Then walk promptly to the See Promenade. A white Audi is parked on the left under some trees. The door's unlocked. Get in and wait for me."

He stood, thanking her. Replacing the tour booklet inside his jacket, he snatched up his rucksack and walked away to where his friends had gone, as though expecting to rejoin them.

Pretty smooth, she thought as he disappeared. Her eyes scanned the area to see if she could notice anyone who might be trailing either Jorden or herself. She felt her skin tighten. A fair-haired young man was leaning his shoulder against the wall of the lounge while studying a newspaper. She was sure he wasn't reading.

She remained seated on the bench, painfully counting the minutes. A waiter stuck his head out the lounge door and said something to the man with the paper. He seemed annoyed, then tossed it onto a bench and, after glancing about the area of the lift, which she was sure included her, he followed the waiter inside to the telephone. Krista stood and walked away from where Jorden had gone, toward the See Promenade.

Once out of sight she quickened her steps, ignoring her throbbing head. She was still a little dizzy as she headed toward St. Moritz lake. She thought of the man lured away by an unexpected telephone call. By the time he got back out to the lift area, she would be gone and he wouldn't know which direction to follow her. She could imagine his anger when he realized he'd been duped.

The town sprawled along the lower slopes and was surrounded by forested hills, with the frozen aquamarine lake below. The majestic Piz Rosatsch dominated the view, encrusted with white, followed by Languard on the east, and Guglia in the west. The See Promenade was a popular walk around the lake, especially at dusk as the lake in the summer reflected the darkening peaks and moonlight. Even in the winter when the lake was frozen there was beauty to behold. Today the owners of race horses were practicing for Saturday's run on the frozen water, as tourists would begin to arrive from all across Europe. As she walked along the Promenade, she saw steam rising from the horses' nostrils as the grooms led them out for a practice run. The horses were fitted with a special type of shoe that kept them from slipping on the ice. There would be dog races as well, and a skaters' ball on the 14th.

The 14th! The night Einer Seitz expected to meet Uncle Franz during the skiers' torch parade. Were it not for Seitz, she would have enjoyed the grand, festive night, culminating in the ice ball. She had hoped to go with Paul, but now...

Her mind turned toward Jorden Keller. She saw the white Audi parked across the street and walked there, leisurely, as though she didn't have a care in the world. Her head was aching and she couldn't wait to sink down into the bucket seat. So...now she would need to tell Jorden about the book instead of Franz. That made her blunder even worse. She wanted him to think she was as cool and clever as he.

The passenger side was unlocked, as he had said, and she slid inside and locked the door. She lowered the visor and looked in the small mirror, powdering her nose and applying color to her lips. Her light hair was coiled in a braid at the back, nothing fancy, but it would do.

The door opened on the driver's side and Jorden slipped behind the wheel, dropping his rucksack behind him with one hand, closing the door with the other. Within seconds, the Audi was moving smoothly away from the lake.

"How did you manage the phone call?" she asked.

"I called the waiter from another phone and described the man I needed to speak with. The hard part was keeping him confused long enough to give you time to get out of sight."

He was looking through the rearview mirror.

"Anyone following?" she asked, trying to sound as casual as he.

"I don't think we'll be bothered." He looked at her for the first time and their eyes locked briefly. Krista sensed an emotional connection. She looked out the window, aware of the heat rising in her cheeks. *Foolish of me*, she thought firmly. *He'll be guessing any moment now, and I'll feel like a girl with her first crush.*

"Why didn't you wear a ski suit? You would have been less noticeable."

First mistake. "I intended to, but after what happened a short while ago I didn't have the energy to put one on." She relaxed into the seat and massaged the back of her neck. "I almost didn't keep the appointment."

"Something happened? Suppose you clue me in for a change."

For a change—meaning?—that she hadn't been doing so. She thought of the book and sighed. *It would have to come to this, just when I wanted to appear cool and capable.*

"Somebody was searching my overnight bag at the lodge. I entered at the wrong moment and was knocked unconscious."

His jaw went rigid. There followed a long silence. "You're all right?"

"Yes, just a bump. I'm a little light-headed. And your driving is making me dizzy, Mr. Keller." She glanced around at the expensive interior. "No Fiat this time?" She smiled.

He slowed down. "What happened? All the details, please."

"All?"

"All."

She shrugged. She had hoped to gloss over the incident and tone down the loss of Elsa's book. He didn't know about the book, she hadn't even told Uncle Franz yet.

"All right..." she paused, and couldn't resist. "But you're missing your gold watch, and large-rimmed sunglasses. No recording this time?"

He looked at her, his smile lingering.

She drew in a deep breath and began with her sleeping past breakfast and getting Trudy's note about Franz meeting her later. He didn't interrupt until she had concluded her saga with crawling out of the blanket.

"Did you notice any guests when you arrived? The man reading the newspaper, for instance?"

"No. The lodge was deserted except for Henrich and Veena. He may have come in later, when I was eating, or arrived beforehand and waited upstairs."

"I don't think so, though it was made to appear that way."

"Why do you say that?" She looked at him curiously. His rich dark eyes met hers briefly before turning back to the road.

"You told me you left your traveling bag up in your room before meeting the Klossners in the kitchen. Is that right?"

"Yes...I see what you mean." She lapsed into thoughtful silence. If he had been there all along, or even followed her from Trudy's house, he would have had plenty of time to rummage through her bag, find what he was looking for, and leave without any encounter.

"Go on, please. What was he looking for?"

She didn't answer at once. "He must have come in during the time I was talking to Henrich about the ring."

His dark head turned sharply. "Are you known for taking that ring off and storing it in your purse or bag?"

Krista raised her hand and gazed at the winking ruby, diamonds, and gold. "No, I always wear it unless I'm modeling Gotthard jewels. He wasn't after the ring..."

She could feel the intensity of his gaze as he waited for an explanation. How much was she going to tell him? Her eyes swerved to glance at him and was surprised by the shadow of amusement.

"Still don't trust me, Miss Grendelmier?"

She did, but if he learned about Davos he might try to keep her from going there. She would allow nothing to stop her now. Not even uncle Franz.

"I can wait until you're ready to tell me," he said glibly, glancing at his watch. "We have all day to pry secrets from one another."

All day? "Is that what this is about, 'prying' secrets from me, Mr. Keller?"

The cold mountain road twisted through forested slopes.

"I'd prefer cooperation. Franz told me he explained to you who I am, as well as my occupation. So naturally I thought you'd be convinced as to what side I'm on. Enough to tell me everything. In return I'll tell you what we know about the ring."

She raised a delicate brow. "Oh, I'm convinced of who you are and have been of your skillful occupation ever since you produced that gun. And if I appear reluctant it's because I have some plans of my own and I don't want anybody stepping in and shutting the door."

"Plans of your own? Now we're in for trouble."

She smiled pleasantly. "Yes, and I intend to carry them through to the end."

He repressed a smile. "I'm on your side, Miss Grendelmier. What more may I do to reassure you? I've even dropped my Texas accent."

"Yes, and you've been able to suppress your many fears. And I've noticed your German accent is even better. How do you manage?"

"With difficulty. Are you going to trust me or not?"

"I'm thinking about it. What information will you give me in return—should I cooperate."

He affected thoughtfulness. "I'll tell you about Stella and what she hopes to accomplish."

"About why you two arranged that fashion showing at Hans Fischer's house?"

"All about it. I'll even escort you on these plans you say you have. After being knocked unconscious this morning, you need me to keep ex-Nazis and Commies off your trail."

She remembered Einer Seitz and concealed a shudder. Did Franz have anything to do with Jorden's sudden willingness?

"Had you arrived this morning when I was being encased in a blanket, it certainly would have been appreciated," she said lightly. "I'd even have forgiven you for mistrusting me at Hans Fischer's house."

"Yes, too bad I wasn't there to clobber him. I would have enjoyed it. I have a special dislike for thugs who beat up on women."

Krista touched the bump on the back of her head and winced. "So Uncle Franz wants us working together?"

"He approves."

But for how long would he approve? Franz didn't know about Davos yet.

He took a moment to look away from the curved road, thick with pine trees on either side. "I've been wondering how I could apologize about Zurich. Our first meeting was unfortunate. It wasn't what I would normally have in mind for *Europa's* most famous model. I was rude. I guess you already know that."

She was mollified. It was always sweetly satisfying when a man like Jorden felt badly about his manners. She had to admit the real Jorden Keller had conduct as smooth as polished medals. She supposed he had a few from his military service in Israel. She smiled at him. "Well...if you're *really* sorry..."

"More than you realize."

She tore her eyes away from his. "What I'd like to know is why you absolutely loathe the von Burens."

"That will be included in our exchange, if you agree to cooperate."

"But you acted as if you despised me at the house in Zurich. Did you really think I was Wilhelm von Buren's granddaughter?"

He moved both hands to the steering wheel, musing as he negotiated the mountainous road.

"You did, didn't you?" she asked quietly.

"I believed you might be and was pleased to learn from a friend in the CIA that you are not. Whatever Wilhelm's actual name is, we don't think it's von Buren. Have you any ideas on that?"

She looked at him quickly. Not von Buren! That astounded her. "You think it is Gotthard?"

He looked curiously intrigued. "Why do you say that?"

She shrugged and played with her purse strap, watching his various reactions, and weighing them. "I don't know...I thought you might. I can see you suspect Wilhelm." She thought of Elsa's book. She would have to tell him about it now, and how it had been taken from her room.

"I think I know why you suspect him and Elsa," she said quietly.

He took his time before answering. "Suppose you tell me."

"Are we going to be honest with each other?"

"In light of the circumstances, I think that would be wise. You are in a risky situation and Einer Seitz has just turned up the heat. You saw what could happen this morning. You're dealing with enemies who are professionals and they won't let anyone stand in their way."

And neither will you, she thought. She twisted her purse strap, growing more uncomfortable by the moment. "All right. I'll tell you everything. First, my bag wasn't just rummaged through this morning. Something was stolen. Something that Paul thought was rather important. Franz doesn't know about it yet."

Jordan slowed down and drove into a densely forested turn-out. He switched off the ignition, then turned and looked at her. She met his gaze, feeling warmth ebb into her cheeks.

"I thought you must have had something they wanted." He caught up her hand touching the ruby with his thumb. "Something, that is, besides this. They don't know about it yet. When they do, you'd be better off having it in a secure place. A safety deposit box would do. Who knows about the ring beside you and Stella?"

He surprised her. Yes, Stella certainly must know something. At the meeting in Zurich she had conspicuously asked about the ring.

"The family has seen it of course, but you're right. No one has paid much attention, not even Uncle Franz. Until this morning I hadn't discussed it much."

"This morning?"

"I asked Henrich about it."

"He's a Klossner?"

"Yes, and his wife Veena. Henrich is Franz's cousin. He's been running the lodge since my parents died. I can trust them...mostly."

"A strange way of putting it. Mostly?"

"I've never been close to them. I suppose Henrich approves of me, but well, I've always thought Veena didn't actually like me." It was dreadful admitting things like this.

"Jealousy, you think?"

She was discreetly silent.

"Some women cannot accept another female's presence if she's beautiful."

She flushed, and he released her hand and drew back. "Tell me about them."

"I was twelve when my parents died. Franz became my 'adopted' parent, but he was a bachelor and gone much of the time. So I lived with Henrich and Veena. Don't misunderstand, they were always good to me."

"Then at fifteen you went to school in Paris for four years."

How would he know that? "Yes, Elsa sent me to the fashion school."

"And after that, Gotthard Enterprises?"

She nodded. "What was Henrich and his wife's reaction when you asked them about the ring?"

"Veena wasn't there, but Henrich said he didn't know anything about where Anna got it. He suggested my father may have given it to her, that it came from the Grendelmiers."

"Wait a minute. Veena wasn't there?"

"No, he sent her shopping. They both seemed tense over Paul's arrival this weekend."

"Paul and von Buren's arrival?"

"Yes, and Elsa."

He lapsed into silence, leaning back against the door. She could see his mind working, that he was disturbed by the news. Did he fear she may cooperate with Paul, giving him information about Einer Seitz, or even Jorden's own background? She thought of how she had unwisely given information to Paul about Jorden's trip into Liechtenstein. A horrible mistake that she'd never make again.

Jorden continued his questioning. She was aware he watched her intently, judging her responses as well as her answers. "Why should their arrival trouble them?"

She shrugged. "Just that Elsa and Wilhelm are so fussy and very rich. I don't know if you've seen the lodge yet, but it isn't Badrutt's Palace, or even the Carlton. It's country. We only have fifteen rooms and Veena does the cooking. I used to help her before I went to Paris."

"But they've come to the lodge before. No surprises there."

"True." So why should this visit make them worry so?

"By the way. Franz and I would like to keep you clear of Paul and the von Burens when they arrive. I think Wilhelm would have preferred to keep you directly out of all this, but Paul got you involved. That's likely to be a tension between them."

"Paul? Oh, but I don't think he has anything to do with…"

"Excuse me, but he has plenty to do with all this, even if he didn't order that attack on you this morning. I'm sorry it turned out this way. Everything has changed recently."

"Because of Einer Seitz?" She remembered what Franz had told her about the CIA helping him escape to South America.

"Yes, because of the information he has. It could mean the end of von Buren."

"Von Buren? But Franz didn't mention that. He said Seitz had information of great interest to America."

"Yes, and Israel as well."

She tensed. "Are you going to tell me? At least some of it?"

"I'll do what I can, but that must wait. Right now Von Buren knows Seitz is a threat to his security. He knows better than we do. Seitz knows who he is, as well as his life in East Germany—even his father's work before him. Von Buren is playing for keeps, but so are we. And you're right in the middle of it. No wonder Franz was worried. Meeting Seitz like that…" he shook his head.

"I had little choice. He forced the issue," she said in a low voice, thinking of his approach on the steps of the ancient building in Chur.

"I know that," he soothed. "Franz told me about Chur. Von Buren will want to know how much you've learned from him."

"But they can't know about Einer Seitz yet?"

"Gotthard Enterprises runs an espionage network. They'll find out Seitz has come to Switzerland even if he hadn't contacted von Buren to blackmail him."

She was shocked into silence. Espionage and blackmail!

He must have seen her alarm. "We'll let that go for now. I need to know what was taken from your bag."

She brought her thoughts back to the theft. "A book was taken," she said in a low voice. Now the dreadful explanation of her failure would be next.

"A book?" he lifted a brow.

"An important book of photography. Taken in 1938 and '39 by Elsa Klossner, who is now Mrs. von Buren. The book is out of print now. She secretly admitted to me that she once worked for the propaganda agency of the Nazis."

His breath released. He looked at her for a long moment as if visualizing something precious slipping through his fingers. Her heart sank. She waited for the emotional avalanche to come crushing down upon her—it didn't. His voice remained restrained and efficient.

"Pictures taken in Vienna and Berlin?"

"Yes, I think so. Unfortunately I didn't have the right moment to look at it. When I was on the train from Zurich, Seitz was sitting beside me dressed as a priest. And when I arrived last night, Uncle Franz and I had so much to discuss that..." her voice trailed. Her eyes searched his for anger. "Believe me, I intended to turn it over to Uncle Franz, but I wanted to look at it first for myself. Waiting as I did was a mistake..." She concluded weakly: "I'm sorry."

He leaned his shoulder into the door, fingers drumming the leather seat, the first signs of a swelling torrent of frustration that she knew he must be feeling. There was a long silence. He looked out the window at a rare, statuesque fallow deer standing in a shaft of sunlight in an Alpine cathedral of calm.

"Where did you get the book?"

"Rhinefelden's book shop on Bergstrasse 19. He sells rare books."

He turned toward her. "How did you know the book was there?"

Here it comes, she thought. "Paul arranged for me to pick it up."

His tone at last revealed restrained anger. "For a man who wishes to marry you he doesn't mind tossing you right into the fire does he?"

As she had feared, that particular book must have been important. She wanted to sink through the seat and crawl away. She had failed.

"What was his excuse for asking you to pick it up for him? Or did he need one?"

"The Swiss banking scandal. He said the von Burens were very upset and wanted no publicity. They had thought all of Elsa's early published work linking her with the Third

Reich had been confiscated and destroyed. But Rhinefelden had discovered a very rare book. He was asking a great amount of Swiss francs for it, and the family had agreed to his price. All I needed to do was go there and pick it up."

"And you did."

She flushed. "At the time I thought Paul worked for Interpol. I was troubled by the banking scandal, but I didn't think Elsa's book had anything to do with it."

He seemed to believe her. "What was in the book, did he give you any hints? Mention of names or places?"

"No. Just that it contained her early work when she was eighteen in Berlin...just old black and white photos, much like the ones she has in her collection at the house in Zurich. You asked me about her work that day at Hans Fischer's, remember?"

"Yes. I remember also that you mentioned a museum showing in Vienna."

"She was preparing for the showing when I left for the bank the day I met you."

"What I'd like to know now is who this so-called museum representative was that met with Elsa."

"One of Einer Seitz's men you think?"

"Could be. But if so, he probably came to deliver a blackmail message from Seitz. I doubt if he walked back out alive."

Her breath paused. He was serious. She told him about Willi, the chauffeur, and Mrs. Brandt, the housekeeper. "Do you think they could be more than mere servants?"

"That's interesting. Willi may work in other capacities for von Buren. We'll check. Good work," he said, and smiled as if encouraging her. "What about Elsa's work in Zurich?"

"She still has most of it, but she claims that photos embarrassing to her and the family were destroyed by Wilhelm. They had many arguments over her pictures disappearing."

"Yes, that makes sense. The out-of-print book must have had something interesting, something that Paul was asked to get for Wilhelm. What about Rhinefelden's? Anything happen there we should consider?"

"Nothing, really. Except, well," she told him about the man in the non-descript gray raincoat and Homburg hat. Something about his presence there had troubled her, but she couldn't decide what.

"Now I know what it was. He looked more like a skier or climber. And I don't think Professor Zimmer was much for the physical sports." He had removed his hat and she remembered him adjusting a pair of tortoiseshell-rimmed glasses. "Red hair and dull gray eyes. They looked like glass." She looked at him. "Contact lenses and a wig."

There was amusement in his eyes. "You're learning. He may have been the newspaper reader we left behind at the ski lift. At least he won't be worried about your identifying him. He may work for Seitz. Rule one, Krista. Never take chances by provoking an agent into disclosing his face. Not every agent uses contact lenses and red wigs."

She glanced at him briefly as he turned thoughtfully to the window, looking again at the majestic white stag with its heavy antlers. *Neither did every agent come off as good looking as Jorden Keller...just what was his relationship to Stella?*

"Then you brought the book to Paul?"

"Yes," she admitted wearily. "Paul was at Franz's place. I had a birthday present for him. When he left the room, Paul concealed Elsa's book on a bookshelf behind several volumes. Franz never knew," she said, avoiding Jorden's eyes. "I didn't approve of the deceit, but Paul convinced me it was important. He made the deception easy for me by informing Franz that he was helping Interpol. I believed him and thought Franz did too. It turns out Franz knew he was lying. I wish he had told me then."

"He feared to involve you further. That same morning Franz got in touch with Flanders, a friend both to Franz and me. Unfortunately Flanders is dead. He was killed in Liechtenstein."

She saw a hint of grief, though he tried to mask it. Her heart was smitten. What if she were responsible?

"How did you get Elsa's book here to St. Moritz?"

"Before I left Zurich I went to Franz's apartment expecting him to be there, but he'd already left, so I brought the book with me."

"Why, Krista?"

She saw that he watched her alertly. She had better be honest. Their trust in each another was yet on a thin foundation.

"After the shooting, Paul questioned me at the von Buren house. I began to doubt him."

He seemed satisfied, but curious. "Why?"

It was difficult to explain. "My relationship with Paul has been unusual from the start."

"I gathered that much."

"On that night I'd just been through an emotional ordeal. I didn't know if you were a friend or an enemy. I didn't know whom to trust, except Franz. Yet Paul insisted I go to Elsa's. Her physician would see to my cuts. Yet, once at the house his entire mood changed. He became an interrogator. He wouldn't let me rest or even go upstairs until he was satisfied with my answers to his questions. Later he apologized. Said he had to please his uncle to find out the truth, but a man doesn't treat a woman he loves the way he treated me. It's just as well I found out when I did."

"I hope you're not in love with him," he said, and when she turned her head to meet his gaze, he went on: "I'd hate to think I sent your man to prison for twenty years."

She stared at him. He looked less perturbed than she did.

"Did von Buren question you as well?"

"No. He came to my room, though, after Elsa's physician left and everyone had retired. Why, I don't know. He just sat in a chair by the window and smoked and listened to German martial music. It was intimidating. I thought it was important to leave Zurich at once, and bring Elsa's book with me."

He didn't interrupt her, just listened, keeping whatever thoughts he had about Wilhelm to himself. That he was disturbed was evident.

"I knew they'd ask you questions about me," he said quietly. "I watched you leave with Paul in the Fiat."

"Then it was you I saw."

He looked at her. "Since we're confessing...I let you escape."

"You what?" she breathed.

He smiled faintly. "I knew you'd go out the terrace. One of our men sent word that Paul and two of his men were on their way. I had planted a small recorder in the Fiat that went on with the ignition. We got your conversation with Paul on the way to von Buren's."

Her breath stopped. She looked at him. She didn't know whether to be irked or in awe of his cleverness. "You must have expected a juicy confessional and got little for all your work."

He smiled, his eyes keeping hers a moment too long. "I wasn't disappointed. But later, I did worry about you, still thinking you were Wilhelm's granddaughter."

"I saw the way you were watching me that time I turned quickly and caught your gaze of disapproval."

"I know you did, and it bothered me that you guessed. I believed you and Paul were working together to conceal Wilhelm's past identity." He looked at her, and his eyes softened. "Knowing I was wrong is a great relief. Later, when Flanders told me the truth about you, I became worried. I realized you were left to their interrogation, but by then it was too late to do anything. I was in Liechtenstein meeting with Flanders. Nor could I risk coming back into Zurich. It was imperative I make a quick trip into Vienna to see a friend and Stella."

It was nice to know he had worried about her after all. Krista concealed her approval, keeping her expression vague.

"So Wilhelm came to your room." He frowned, thinking to himself.

"Yes, at least I think it was Wilhelm."

He looked at her, alert. "Why do you say that? Don't you know?"

"It was dark. He thought I was asleep."

"Then he simply left without waking you?"

"Yes. It was after that I decided to leave the house at dawn. I couldn't wait to reach Uncle Franz."

"Wilhelm may have planned to question you. When he saw you were asleep, he may have decided to let it go. Did a physician come to look at those cuts?"

She was grateful that his eyes did not search her face.

"Yes, Elsa's doctor. He said there would be no scars."

"Then von Buren must have thought you'd been given a sedative and wouldn't wake until morning. You were fortunate."

Yes, but now they were coming to St. Moritz. And there was even more to question her about.

"Why didn't you give Elsa's book to Franz last night," Jorden asked in a tight voice.

She knew it would finally come to that. She sighed. "I thought there might be something in one of the photos that might help me with my own personal quest. Something that would connect me with this ring Stella was so curious about."

There was a long pause.

"Yes, I know," she murmured. "I should have given it to Uncle Franz or just left it on his bookshelf. But there was a good reason to take the book. Paul knew it was hidden in Uncle Franz's apartment. I no longer trusted him. He would have taken it if I hadn't."

"It's also true that Paul would suspect you first, just as soon as he realized it was missing."

She frowned, rubbing her sore head and neck. "I'll get it back," she stated.

"Don't try that," he said evenly.

"I've got to, Jorden. I'm the one who failed."

He shook his head as if amazed. "You didn't fail. I see Flanders was right about you," he said gently.

"Flanders? What did he know about me?" Again, she remembered Liechtenstein and what she had told Paul. Another reason why she must make good. One more reason why she couldn't tell Jorden.

That loitering smile came back. "He advised me to work with you closely on von Buren. He said you were smart. So did Franz."

Her cheeks warmed. "I guess that settles it then, doesn't it?"

"We can't disappoint Franz."

"And do you," she asked, "also think it wise?"

His gaze flicked over her face, her hair. "Very unwise—for you to be seen in my company. It places you at even more risk. Yet, I admit your cooperation would be of great benefit. And in return I think I can offer you some help about the ring."

So he was willing to cooperate with her even after the book was stolen. She wouldn't let him or Uncle Franz down again.

"Franz said you were dedicated. Paul knew it as well and took advantage of that fact. I don't want to play that game, Krista, not without you fully knowing my intentions. My cause is different than your uncle's."

She knew it must have something to do with Israel. She believed he would tell her in time. She wouldn't pry now.

"If it's Paul that concerns you, don't worry. When he comes here I know I can handle him."

"Can you?" he asked too smoothly. "He may have given the order to someone to get that book back—at any cost. He'll know why you removed it from its hiding place and brought it here. If you thought the interrogation at Zurich was uncomfortable, you haven't heard anything yet. And I don't want you to fall victim to his or von Buren's tactics."

"I understand Paul very well. I've known him for years, worked closely with him for the last five, and we were even going to..." She didn't go on. No use mentioning that. But he seemed to have guessed.

"Marry?"

She didn't reply. "I'll have some excuse for having brought the book here when I see him. I'm sure I can get around what happened and even learn if he has it. Maybe I can find out what he did with it. We can get it back."

He leaned over and laid a hand on her arm. "No. An order. From dear Uncle Franz. And from me. It's too dangerous." He watched her for a long moment, as though he were making his own plans about how to handle Paul and the book.

"Let's forget about Elsa von Buren's book for now, shall we?" He turned on the ignition. "Franz won't be back in St. Moritz yet. Not until tonight."

"Where is he? Do you know?"

He delayed only for a moment. "He's meeting someone from the organization. Don't worry. Franz knows what he's doing. He can handle himself. We're to meet him at Trudy's house tonight." He looked at his watch. "It's only one o'clock." He smiled at her. "I can bring you there and you can lie down and rest until Franz arrives. I'll stay on guard. You won't need to worry. Or..."

She smiled. "Or?"

"We'll have lunch and continue our discussion. There's a house around here. I'm welcome to use it. It's the right place to continue our talk without fear of being bugged."

"A pleasant lunch in the mountains might help."

"My pleasure."

19

Krista settled back, her emotions soothed by the pine trees flitting past and the distant mountains glistening with white frosting against a backdrop of clear sky.

"The turn-off is around here somewhere," Jorden said. He left the road and entered a narrow, tree-lined lane that ran for another hundred meters. He drove through a gate into a drive that circled behind the house. There was a small, one-car garage, and he opened it and parked there. "Room enough to get out?"

"Yes, I think so...I'll try not to scratch your door," she teased.

"If you do you'll have the owner issuing a vendetta against you—she's very particular."

She?

He opened the door and got out, reaching behind the seat for his rucksack.

Krista walked out and looked around, drawing her hood up against the cold mountain wind. Tall fir trees guarded the curve of the drive, and behind, Piz Languard in the east dominated the early afternoon view, pristine white. Their presence intruded the deep forest silence. Squirrels stopped chattering and birds flew deeper into the woods. The wind in the high fir branches moaned softly.

She watched as he closed the garage door. She thought about how cautious he was. She hadn't said anything in the car, and he thought she hadn't noticed, but he had back-tracked on the road before taking the turn-off that led to the driveway. She wondered what his life was like as an agent; was there ever a time when he could let his guard down and live normally?

"That headache is bothering you. I'll soon have you warm before a fire," he said easily. "There should be something to help in the medicine cabinet. It's usually well-stocked."

"For emergencies?" she asked.

"Astute, aren't you?" He smiled. He took her elbow, leading her in the opposite direction from where she was headed. "This way to the back door. It's the only key I have that works—watch your step." He steadied her as her boot caught on an exposed root.

"Sorry, guess that bump on the head is finally getting to me. Do you think we were followed?" she asked quietly. "There could have been someone beside the man with the paper? Is that why you put the car in the garage?"

"Just good practice, especially since you're with me."

Krista looked at the small white house with blue-green trim and slanted roof with wide eaves.

"Cute and cozy. Yours?"

"No, a friend's. She won't mind. She's in Berlin."

She, again. "Berlin?" she inquired, and waited, expecting information.

He went up the porch steps, removed a key from his pocket. "Berlin," he acknowledged, and turned the key in the lock.

"Her car too?"

"All hers." He ushered her inside the cold, damp room, closing the door behind them. He tried the light switch. A lamp came on in the corner.

Krista watched as he walked over to the fireplace and stacked pine onto the grate.

"Maybe she wouldn't want us barging in like this."

He struck a match to some wads of paper. "She won't mind."

Krista removed her coat, watching him, as she hung it on a peg by the door.

The fire started to crackle, but her head ached terribly and she felt suddenly tired.

Jorden stood, and turned with an encouraging smile. "Better come and sit by the fire. Doctor's orders. How's that nasty headache?"

"Sorry to whine, but rather miserable." She eased herself into the loden chair feeling warmth from the hearth. Then he wasn't going to tell her about the "she." She watched as he removed his jacket. She noticed he kept his rucksack close at hand. What was inside, weapons?

"It's a little late for an ice pack on the swelling, but we'll give it a try anyway. There should be some jell packs in refrigeration in that room. Medicine is kept there as well." He smiled. "Our host is a generous provider. And just to prove my sympathy I'll make lunch," he said. "Coffee or tea, madam?"

She smiled, enjoying his fussing over her.

"Coffee, please."

"There's also something for pain in the cabinet. Check the next room." He started toward the small kitchen.

"Your lady friend is indeed generous."

Jorden paused and turned, watching her. His dark eyes grew serious as if weighing the consequence of a decision. He seemed to come to one reluctantly.

"The lady is a Gentile friend of Israel. Throughout her life she's worked for Jewish causes at personal risk. She was married to a Jewish doctor who survived Birkenau. She led him into Christianity and later he went to theology school and became a missionary to Jews in Switzerland. She's one of a secret group of volunteers our agency has throughout the world who provide us with safehouses. Our agents have a tendency to find themselves in tough situations," he said wryly. "Whether it's a bullet that needs removing, a room to hole up in for a few days, or a place to have an emergency meeting, these friends are available night and day. You can see how this service on behalf of Israel places them at risk. This particular lady is quite precious to us, but especially to me. She's been praying for me for five years, which makes me worry about her and guard her privacy diligently."

Krista's conscience was smitten, realizing he had shown his trust in her by what he had shared. How could she even think of withholding information from him now?

She rose to her feet and walked quickly toward him, hand outstretched.

"Jorden, I'm sorry. I shouldn't have pried. I'm behaving badly today."

He clasped her hand between his, smiling briefly. "Today we'll make excuses for you."

"You've risked much even to be seen with me."

He frowned. "No, it's the other way around. Even if I weren't involved in this job in Switzerland, I have a particular enemy—a man named Lars. He'd find special enjoyment in harming anyone I cared about. That's why I risked coming to meet Stella in Zurich. I thought she might be in trouble."

She remembered he had mentioned Lars before. "But I know him. He works for Paul. He's polite and friendly."

"Lars is a cold-blooded terrorist. We have evidence he's blown scores of women and children to bits through his bombs. He trained members of the Hizbullah in Lebanon, and he visited Bosrah during the war with Iraq."

She searched his face, wondering. "But why does he hate you so much?"

He hesitated again. "A Lebanese woman was killed accidentally in a punitive raid we made on a border village. They were housing terrorists who were shelling an Israeli kibbutz. The house we entered, expecting to find Lars, was empty except for the woman. Lars thinks I killed her to get back at him."

"He's the reason you worry about Stella and the chain of friends who run safehouses," she said.

"And about you. That's why I'm here. It was either distance myself from you completely, or make certain you are as safe as I can guarantee, especially after your meeting with Seitz and the attack this morning."

That Jorden believed Lars the kind of fiend who would kill her just to get at him sent a terrifying shiver down her back. She remembered him: blond, muscular, cool, always smiling, always so very polite. And underneath that facade—

"He must have loved that Lebanese woman," she said.

"It's hard to think he's capable of loving anyone." He squeezed her hand tightly. "If that isn't enough to convince you to pack your bag and head for New York with Stella, I don't know what will."

She managed a smile. "All I want is a cup of coffee and two aspirin."

"That I can provide." He brought her to the door of the other room, opened it and glanced around. "All in order."

Krista found the medicine cabinet well stocked as he had said. There was even severe pain medication and some medical equipment. All provided freely as a safehouse for Mossad agents! She settled for a pain tablet and one aspirin and swallowed them with water from the dispenser. *Jorden is being especially pleasant to be around*, she thought. She glanced at herself in the mirror and saw her frown. *Yes, you better worry*, she murmured in self-mockery. *Look at you, already falling for him. He could be very charming when he cared to, that was for sure.*

Once again seated before the fire, Krista rested while listening to him fix lunch in the kitchen. What did he really think of her, or did he? He was certainly making up for his arrogant behavior in Zurich. He was polite and—maybe just slightly attracted to her? She suspected he was an expert at keeping himself unentangled. As a Mossad agent he must have conditioned himself to placing other priorities above his personal life. Yet he hadn't walked away from his friends, nor Stella.

What about Stella? she wondered again. Was there something more than friendship?

She closed her eyes wearily. Just for a minute, she thought—but when she opened them again the sun was lower, the fire had turned into a bed of glowing coals, and she heard Jorden in the next room talking to someone on the phone. His voice was abrupt. Now and then he protested. Once he even laughed unpleasantly. She sat up quickly, wincing as the sudden move caused her head to throb. She glanced toward the other room and saw it was a bedroom with the door partially open.

"All right, Avi," she heard him say. "Vienna."

Who was Avi?

Another contact, maybe.

In the kitchen she found he had kept the coffee hot and there were sandwiches on the counter. Hearing the wind blowing around the eaves she went to the small window to look up at the sky. Yes, clouds were gathering in the south. The backyard, if it could be called that, sloped downhill. There was a flight of steps going below to what may have been a stream bed in the summer. In the distance there was forest and a view of more snow-capped hills and mountains.

"Feel any better? You've slept for three hours."

She turned and saw him leaning against the counter.

Three hours! She looked at her watch. "You're right. I'm sorry. It must have been the pain pill." How embarrassing. "We had so much to discuss." She thought of her planned secret trip to Davos. "You should have awakened me."

"You needed the rest. I had to make a few calls anyway."

She tried to keep a lid on her curiosity. "Anything important?"

"The usual emergencies. Better eat something first," he suggested, pouring coffee into two blue cups.

While she ate and enjoyed the coffee, his mood became reflective and his thoughts must have been far away. He had changed considerably in the three hours she'd been in dreamland. He didn't talk, but walked about looking out the windows, and she sensed his restlessness. Yes, she was beginning to know him. Something had happened. What? Her tension grew and she didn't finish the sandwich. She went to the stove and refilled her cup. She could look across the counter into the sitting room where he moved about. "We'll need to discuss a few things about your last modeling job before we head back," he said.

She lifted a brow. "How did that suddenly become an issue? I thought we were going to discuss Einer Seitz? And you promised to explain why you are after Wilhelm von Buren."

"All in good time," he said lightly, setting his cup in front of her.

Her mind trailed backward to her last modeling job in Rome and Venice. Nothing out of the ordinary had happened. She'd been followed, quite a scare in itself, but she'd since found out the man was Hans Fischer, an agent for the West.

"What about my last job?" she asked warily, trying to glean understanding from his dark eyes, but they were masked.

"Just a few questions about Paul and your business relationship with him."

Was his change of interest from Einer Seitz to Rome a coincidence or connected with his phone call?

"What do you want to know? And why?"

"One at a time. You were smart not to board Prince Ahmed's luxury yacht for that glass of vintage wine he promised you. I was afraid you'd take him up on it."

She stared at him in open surprise. How did he know about the Saudi prince?

He lifted his cup. "Hans wasn't the only one keeping tabs on you in Rome. I followed you from Rome to Venice to Monaco."

His matter-of-fact tone amazed her. She leaned back in the chair, arms folded. "Did you? You must have gotten very bored."

He looked at his cup. "I've learned a lot about you, actually, though I never understood what you saw in Gotthard or why he had you under his thumb."

"Until recently I believed in him, remember?"

"Ah yes, misplaced faith, quite tragic."

What was he getting at? They'd already discussed Paul on the way up to the house and she admitted she was no longer emotionally under his sway.

"For instance," he said, "while your lights were dutifully out by ten o'clock every night, Paul was rubbing shoulders with the glitz and glamour at Monte Carlo, gambling away the profits you'd just made him by selling his stolen jewelry."

This news surprised her. Paul had never seemed that sort. He'd even gone to church with her in Zurich. "Why do you say stolen? The diamonds are from South Africa."

"Some of the diamonds, perhaps, but there are other jewels and gold. The gold was melted down and used to buy the Gotthard mine and the fashion business. And some of the jewelry pieces are being sold on the black market. Looted is the correct term. Looted from an entire generation of Jews murdered under the Nazi regime."

She leaned forward, horrified, her hand going to her throat as though tainted jewelry hung there in gaudy display. She had heard about the death camp train that ran from the extermination camps and seen photos of stacks of goods taken from the dead. It was hideous! Profane! She looked at the ring again. *No, please Lord, not 'this' ring! It must have belonged to my mother. Have I worn a ring all these years that was taken from a woman who had suffered a horrible death?*

"What are you saying?" she whispered.

292 LINDA CHAIKIN

"I'm sorry," he said more gently. "But we think the von Burens brought a lot of gold and jewels from the concentration camps into Switzerland after the war. We've reason to think it's being distributed in just the last ten years, laundered through Gotthard Enterprises under the guise of new output from the family mines in South Africa."

"That's absolutely grotesque," she said, "if it's true."

"Yes," he said matter-of-factly. "So much for confiscated loot from Berlin. Now, about Ahmed. You and Paul met him in Rome and Venice before you saw him again in Monte Carlo, is that correct?"

She tensed. The memory of Monte Carlo brought unease. "Monte Carlo?" she asked quickly, blinking. "Um, well yes, I guess we did."

"You're not sure?" he asked quietly.

"It's not that. We met Ahmed in Monte Carlo. But Paul and I were only there for one showing before we flew home to Zurich."

"Was Paul ever alone with him in his suite after the diamond showing?"

She walked to the kitchen window and looked out. "No—I don't think so. He may have met him again after the jewelry showing down in the Casino. I never went down to find out."

"I know you didn't."

She turned. He watched her. How did he know that?

"I thought Paul might have mentioned something to you on the flight home about having seen Ahmed again after the showing."

"No, he didn't." However, she had unfortunately seen Prince Ahmed after the showing. Did Jorden know? She glanced at him under her lashes, uneasily. A brow lifted calmly.

"You saw Ahmed after the showing?" he asked.

She leaned back, arms crossed. *Oh no, not that! Lord, help me do what's right.* The wind rattled the kitchen door. "Is this an interrogation?" she asked with an attempt at avoidance.

"If it is, it's a relatively nice one."

How much did Jorden really know about that embarrassing visit she had made to Ahmed's suite? It appeared that she was getting herself into one too many dangerous situations recently, especially after having believed that Paul was working for Interpol. *So much for trusting certain kinds of men*, she thought. The modeling business could prove dangerous. Traps and pitfalls were everywhere.

She scanned Jorden. Somehow she didn't think he would let her down. He had even helped Stella Cohen when he knew doing so would endanger him. *Always look for a man committed to truth and honor at any price*, she thought. *He won't let you down easily—and he'll be more likely to yield to God's truth than his own natural desires. Yet I must be cautious even of him, and his questions. Where will they lead me?*

"You said you followed me," she began evasively. "You should know whether I saw the Saudi prince or not after the diamond showing."

"I do know, but I'm giving you the chance to confess." He smiled. "Better to me than to some others I know."

"How long did you follow me?" she asked stiffly.

"Oh, about a month." He lifted his cup and drank.

A month. She could imagine the file he must have on her. That he had one at all was embarrassing and irksome. She was innocent, yet felt like Paul's willing accomplice.

"It ought to be against the law to keep files on private citizens," she said testily.

"Nothing unusual really, just a list of background information and observations."

"And after all of that cowboy pretense in Zurich," she accused. "You knew all about me, but I didn't know anything about you."

"Clever of me, wasn't it?"

"You don't play very fair, do you?"

He lifted a brow. "No, actually not."

She smiled at him ruefully. "What did you do with my file, Mr. Keller?"

"Sorry. Top secret. Very provocative."

"It is not!"

He smiled. "I don't have it with me, Krista. It's not something I would carry around. But if you must know, I actually wrote some very nice things about you."

"I wonder…"

"Doesn't drink, doesn't smoke, lights out early, even in Venice. Jogs at six in the morning when everyone else is nursing swollen heads and empty purses. A woman with beauty and brains, I told myself. And spiritual qualities as well. She reads the Bible and goes to church every Sunday. Models black velvet and diamonds gracefully. She could lure any man she wanted, but rejects offers to socialize with oil-rich Saudi princes—most of the time."

She straightened abruptly. "I don't want to hear any more. And I think it's time we left."

"Not quite. Can she be real? I asked myself, as I laboriously recorded observations into my voluminous and sinister black book. What in the world is she doing teamed up with a man like Gotthard? She's a babe in the woods and he's the sly wolf." He walked toward her. "But then after you passed something to Ahmed, I decided it must all be an act. And quite an act it was."

Her eyes rushed to his. Act? Passed something to the Saudi prince? In Monte Carlo?

"Yes, I thought you must know exactly what you were doing."

She sank into the chair. "And just what did I pass to Prince Ahmed?"

"That's what I want to find out."

"My, but you have changed since we arrived. You were being sweet and thoughtful."

"That's just what I like to be, 'sweet.'"

"I have nothing to confess, Mr. Keller." She lifted her cup and drank the now-cold coffee. When he said nothing she glanced at him. He merely smiled. "More?" he said lifting the coffee pot. "We'll have to keep you alert."

"So you can accuse me of all sorts of insulting things, passing information to Ahmed, even of being Wilhelm's granddaughter, a man you apparently have no liking for."

"To say the least."

"And you won't tell me why you dislike Wilhelm so much."

"It can wait. Right now, I'd like you to answer some questions. As for being von Buren's granddaughter, I no longer believe that."

She was relieved for more reasons than one. "And what do you think now?"

"Three hours ago I could have told you. After a few phone calls, I've been forced to reconsider."

Startled, she looked at him and saw the gravity in his eyes. "Reconsider? What is there to reconsider?" she asked quietly.

"I'm afraid your work with Gotthard Enterprises will cause you a few awkward moments in the future."

Although his tone was casual, her heart thudded. She knew that of course, but preferred not to think about it. "That's a nice way of implying I'm in trouble about something." She searched his face but it didn't reveal his thoughts.

"I want to ask you a few questions off the record about Ahmed. Will you cooperate?"

"The questions are for you?" she asked thoughtfully.

"Yes. Your answers are important to me personally. After all, if you expect my help, I'll need to trust you."

She was leery. "And if my answers don't convince you I'm innocent of passing information to Ahmed?"

He was silent a moment too long, and now his gaze was thoughtful. "I will need to do what I feel is wise."

She smiled ruefully. "That doesn't make me feel any better. You're like a nurse just before she pokes you with a needle. What happens if you become convinced I'm guilty of espionage? Thirty years in Siberia?"

"Tell all, and I'll have your sentence reduced."

Why did she think there was a note of seriousness behind his light remark?

"What are you going to ask me— 'where were you the night of the murder?'"

There was no amusement in his eyes. "Maybe."

Startled, she searched his face again. Murder?

"I didn't pass him anything," she said truthfully.

"No? I hope not, at least not willingly. Perhaps we should start at the beginning. Tell me about the Saudi Prince."

Krista sighed. She thought back to the unpleasant incident.

"Very well. Prince Ahmed contacted me through his emissary after a diamond showing. He told me that a number of people would be there, including Paul."

Jorden folded his arms. "This was at Monte Carlo, right?"

"Yes."

"When you say: 'There' do you mean his suite?"

"Yes, his suite of rooms at the Royal Palms Hotel. When I arrived, however, Paul wasn't there yet. I begin to have a terrible feeling he might not be coming at all."

"Neither was anyone else there," he said dryly.

"No, just a guard." She skimmed his face with surprise. "How did you know no one else showed up?"

"Remember the waiter?" he asked with a brief smile.

She scowled, then her eyes widened. "You! You had blond hair—well. Very clever, Mr. Keller," she said with a lifted brow. "Would you mind telling me how you convinced the real waiter to let you deliver Ahmed's caviar?"

"Secrets of the trade, my dear."

"I felt so sorry for you—the way the prince insisted you would be fired after you dropped his tray."

"I hope you've learned your lesson about accepting invitations from scoundrels. Even more importantly, that you've learned the hard lesson about allowing yourself to be a courier for Paul."

She saw the seriousness in his dark eyes. "I've already explained about Rhinefelden's bookshop."

"Rhinefelden's wasn't the only time you helped Paul. But that can wait. We're not through discussing the meeting with Ahmed, are we? Aren't you grateful I made such a mess of his champagne and fish eggs? It gave you a chance to get away, but it cost me the opportunity to lift your purse from the counter where you'd laid it so invitingly for Ahmed."

"What are you saying?" she asked indignantly. "What about my purse? You don't think I left it there deliberately do you?"

"What did you bring Ahmed from Paul?"

"In my handbag…?" For a moment she was at a loss to follow what he was getting at. Then she remembered, she'd forgotten her bag, but so what? Paul had returned it later, everything intact.

"Yes, I left it there by mistake. I was so anxious to get away."

"Understandable, especially when you realized that Ahmed had wine and roses on his mind. Then I saw him take your bag and turn his back. He slipped something inside his shirt pocket. Do you know what it was, Krista?"

She was shocked. She had delivered messages before for Paul, but he had always informed her beforehand. "You're asking me?"

"We might ask Ahmed, except he's dead. And I didn't have a chance to encounter him again that night before I was tossed out on my ear. Perhaps it was better for me that I didn't get the chance to take the object. It might have been me instead of Ahmed."

Dead. Her fingers gripped the side of the chair.

"Poor fellow died of a sudden heart attack."

She stared at him, watching the muscle in his jaw flex. She thought back to her handbag. Did he think Paul had something to do with Ahmed's death? Herself, perhaps? "I tell you there was nothing important in my handbag, Jorden. I vow there wasn't."

He hesitated. "You didn't think you were helping Interpol again?"

"No!" *What could have been in my handbag?*

His gaze softened. He looked at her for a long moment, studying her face. "I think you're telling me the truth."

"Yes, of course I am."

"Then Paul used you to deliver something without your knowing it. Unfortunately the gadget was loaded with a poison spray."

She gasped.

"And Ahmed had an unpleasant surprise waiting for him as soon as he tried to open it. Naturally, the poison was chosen to make it look as if his 'sudden demise' was a natural death. Not that our side is grieving for Ahmed. He supported terrorism in the Middle East. He must have had some quarrel with Gotthard Enterprises, or someone high up in the organization decided Ahmed was too much trouble to keep around. We didn't expect them to kill him. I thought you were delivering a message about terrorist activity."

Krista stood abruptly and paced. Paul had dared use her like this! She felt sickened, then angry. She turned quickly and met Jorden's alert gaze.

He said: "I'm sorry but there wasn't any easy way to tell you."

"Yes," she breathed, "I remember now. Paul did hold my bag for a short time when I was picking up my wrap. It happened just after the diamond showing for Ahmed and his group. He could have placed something inside and I just didn't notice."

"And you didn't look inside again after that?"

"No. A short time later I was asked up to the prince's suite to join Paul and others for a friendly gathering after the showing. Paul wanted me to go. He whispered that Ahmed was sure to buy the South African diamonds, and that we needed to be friendly with him. They were the same diamonds that Stella pretended to be interested in at Zurich."

"Then if Paul held your handbag for a moment while you were getting your wrap, that accounts for it," Jorden said.

Was he satisfied? "Do you believe me?"

"Yes, personally I do. We can forget Monte Carlo now. Unfortunately, there is one thing more we need to discuss. This is not for me, or my agency, but the CIA. For this, I'll need to record your statements."

"What! Oh Jorden, you can't be serious?"

"I'm afraid I am."

What did he mean—for the CIA?

"The recording will be turned over to my superior," Jorden explained. "He'll see to it that it's sent to Flanders' director."

When she sat looking at him, he added, turning grave, "I can't refuse them, Krista. I've already tried."

Was this what he'd been arguing over the phone with Avi about when she awoke? At least Jorden had protested. That made her feel a little better.

"I'm under the gun if I don't," he said. "I must bring this with me when I return to Vienna. I'll be leaving tomorrow."

So much for their working together. He wouldn't be around after all. Well, then, Davos and her own quest waited after all. Perhaps it was better this way, but she didn't see how. She watched him walk to his rucksack and remove a small square object and return to the kitchen table where she sat. She stared at it. It was a recorder.

20

This is a recording device," he explained calmly, as if she didn't suspect it. "I haven't turned it on yet."

"Why do you need to record at all?" she asked warily.

"I'm under orders. Just answer the questions truthfully."

"Who's the recording for? Avi?"

"How did you know that name?" he asked firmly.

"From you. I heard you say it on the telephone a short while ago."

He looked relieved. Had he thought Ahmed had given it to her?

"Am I not supposed to know it?" she asked.

"You're not supposed to speak it. It's unwise to mention names. The same goes for Flanders' superior. Please forget that you heard."

"I've forgotten. But Einer Seitz won't forget you. He told me who you were in Chur."

He scowled. "Did he mention my director's name?"

"No, but he did tell me you worked for the Mossad."

"Franz informed me of that. Never mind Seitz for now. I don't think he'll pass information about me on to Paul, or von Buren. Not if he wants to arrive in one piece in Havana. He knows the Mossad would find him. We take the death of one of our own very seriously. Our enemies know that. That may cause them some hesitation."

Avi is a Jewish name, she thought, *probably Jorden's superior. Have they been debating over me?*

"The CIA isn't accusing me of selling jewelry from Holocaust victims, are they?"

"No. They're not into Jewish justice," he stated flatly. "That's left to Israel and her unrelenting secret police."

Of which he was one.

"The man who will receive this recording is a stickler for duty and detail, so we want to get this right. It's important you answer the questions clearly and accurately."

"Why is the CIA interested in me?"

"Because of Agent Flanders. He was well-liked and respected. He was a top agent, due for a promotion. Now he's dead."

Her stomach tightened and her hands turned clammy.

"I went to Liechtenstein to meet him and someone tried to assassinate us both. We both walked straight into a trap. I was able to make it out with a minor injury, but when I got back to the cabin Flanders had been blown to bits."

Krista covered her face with her hands.

"Sorry," he said. "Flanders was due to meet a helicopter at the Austrian border," he went on quietly. "When he didn't show, one of the American soldiers came to the cabin to find out what had gone wrong. He found me instead, half way between the cabin and the rendezvous. We got his body out, and I flew back with his remains to Berlin, where I gave my report."

Krista sat clutching the blue cup, watching him in perfect stillness. Liechtenstein...

I did this to Jorden and the American agent. I'm to blame. Ahmed's death is dreadful enough, how can I tell Jorden about Liechtenstein? Flanders was his friend.

"I've just learned in my phone conversations that the CIA is certain Paul Gotthard was involved. Maybe von Buren as well. Paul was tipped off about our meeting in Liechtenstein and was able to set up a trap." He set his cup down firmly, his eyes glinting with anger. "Flanders' director is almost certain someone in Gotthard Enterprises gave an order to carry out the assassination."

Her eyes rushed to his. *Oh Lord Jesus, help me.*

"The agent wants everything you have on Paul. We have men watching him and von Buren now. I'm told the von Burens left Zurich and will be in St. Moritz tomorrow. Paul will want to see you and find out what you know. It's my guess he's going to ask some tough questions about why you took Elsa's book from Franz's apartment."

She hardly heard his warning. Her mind had stopped at the name of Liechtenstein. How that word had come to carve ugly letters of betrayal across her heart. A good man, an honorable man, had died for his country because of her slip of the tongue to Paul. She had no choice but to confess the truth to Jorden.

Fear gripped her. But what if the CIA arrested her for collaboration? She could hear them now putting their scenario together. After all, hadn't she worked for Gotthard Enterprises for five years and traveled with Paul throughout Europe? Hadn't she met secretly with this terrorist Ahmed and others? And she had thought he was simply a rich oil sheik! Just as she had foolishly thought

Paul worked for Interpol. Would they believe her? Why should they?

There was more evidence stacked against her. Hadn't she picked up Elsa von Buren's book on photography? Even Uncle Franz had told her last night that Gotthard was a front for a terrorist operation. She had helped Paul hide the book in Franz's apartment and deceive her uncle. Even the attack on her in the room that morning could be construed as having being staged to try to make her look innocent.

Then there was her new cooperation with Jorden Keller. They could say she was trying to use him to protect herself—a beautiful model, without scruples, trying to woo him to her side but all the while working hand in hand with Paul, the future owner of a jewelry fashion business worth millions—millions from bogus mines in South Africa, and a business built on the blood from Nazi war crimes.

For the first time she saw how the evidence could be interpreted far differently than the actual truth. And what evidence did she have to prove her innocence? None. Just her word. Who could believe she was so gullible?

Her eyes sought Jorden's. No one. Even Jorden's behavior had changed this afternoon. Flanders had been his friend, a co-equal in duty and honor. And Flanders' director was determined to get those who had killed him.

"Are you going to tell Flanders' director that Paul may have put something in my handbag before I went to Ahmed?"

He shoved his hands in his pockets and watched her for a long moment. "No."

Their eyes held. Krista's gaze faltered. She looked at the recorder as though it were a coiled serpent. Anything she said about Liechtenstein must be the truth, but the truth would sound like a confession of guilt. Once it was recorded it would convince some that she was a willing accomplice. *"Lord, I must tell the truth, and yet—"*

"Both my director and the CIA agent know you're cooperating with me now," Jorden encouraged quietly. "Just tell the truth."

"How do they know I'm cooperating? Because you had to go out on a limb to get your director to trust me? That's what you and he were debating wasn't it? And he isn't sure! Because he must convince Flanders' superior to give you time to deal with me."

Jorden frowned, convincing her that it was so. Avi didn't completely trust her.

"And you're not as sure about me now either," she said.

"Isn't that a little overdone?" he asked quietly.

"No, not overdone at all. You're having trouble convincing them I'm not an enemy agent working with Paul! If they knew about Ahmed and…" she stopped, fearing she might say that dreaded word.

"As long as I've convinced my director, that's all that matters. I'm not sworn to tell the CIA everything I know. I work for Israel and I intend to keep it that way. At my word he's willing to give you the benefit of the doubt."

"Even you thought I might be an enemy until Flanders and Uncle Franz convinced you otherwise."

"I have come to know the person you are. They will too. I can explain to Flanders' director what he said about you when I met with him near the border of Austria."

"I'm not so sure either director will listen to you. You'd be surprised how people misjudge me because of my appearance," she stood and began pacing the small kitchen floor again. "They'll see what they want to see. A vain European model who never got to keep the diamonds she modeled. Perhaps now, she will. Payment for cooperating with a shady and corrupt fashion enterprise." She stopped and looked at him.

"Come on, Krista, my report on you is convincing. A couple of hundred pages about an innocent walking straight into the wolves' den."

"It isn't as simple as you think. I'm in trouble. You know it."

"All right. I admit," he said wryly, "being Paul's courier is incriminating. So was picking up Elsa von Buren's book glorifying the Nazis at Rhinefelden's bookshop. Somehow we'll get around that. Franz can help me explain that one."

"I haven't even told you everything yet. When I do it will be the end of it all." She paced, massaging the bump on the back of her head.

Jorden's eyes narrowed. He straightened from the counter and took firm hold of her arms. "Will you stop pacing and sit down? What do you mean, you haven't told me 'everything?' You mean there's more?"

"I'm calling Franz..." she started around the table for the bedroom telephone.

Jorden cut off her escape, holding her still against the counter. "Krista," he said soothingly. "Trust me. This isn't a trap I've set for you. I didn't plan this recording session. I made a few phone calls out of necessity and learned of the CIA's anger over Flanders' death. I'm angry too. While men like von Buren and Seitz live someone like Flanders is brutally gunned down. Try to understand their position. Two men were killed in the last month. We've spread ourselves too thin throughout sensitive areas. Most of us are doing double duty. Flanders' superior wants to nail Gotthard. And you may be able to help."

"Two men?" she asked tensely. "In Liechtenstein? You mentioned only Flanders."

"We lost one of our own recently. Not in Liechtenstein, but elsewhere. Before this is over we may lose more. You are in danger as well. We must move quickly." His jaw hardened. "I must have your cooperation, Krista."

"In giving the truth, I fear I will incriminate myself."

"No, I won't let it happen."

She drew away and walked to the table. "Very well. You shall have all the truth." She lowered herself to the chair, avoiding his eyes.

Jorden was thoughtful for a moment, as though uncertain about something, then he walked over and looked down at her.

The cold wind sighed about the eaves of the house as the afternoon light was ebbing.

"We'll make this as simple and fast as we can."

She nodded.

He flipped on the record switch.

"What is your working relationship with Paul Gotthard of Gotthard Enterprises?"

"I model jewelry taken from the Gotthard mines in South Africa." She hesitated. "I'm also a courier for some of Paul's Middle Eastern clients, including Prince Ahmed. On two occasions I've worn a secret recording device at a state dinner in Rome. Once I was seated at Ambassador Valenti's table when Prince Ahmed was his guest."

Jorden looked at her sharply—a look of surprise, turning to restrained consternation. He abruptly pushed the Stop button on the recorder.

"Are you out of your mind?"

She looked up at him, tears wetting her eyes.

He leaned his palms on the table. "You never told me that," he gritted.

"You never asked me until now," she said quietly. "I thought Interpol wanted me to keep those meetings."

He turned away, running his fingers through his hair in frustration. "Interpol! You know what your admission sounds like don't you?"

"Yes, I do now."

"Then *don't* word your answers to make yourself look guilty."

"I told you my answers would appear to incriminate me, didn't I?"

A moment of silence lingered before he snapped the record button, looking at her evenly. "Did Paul Gotthard ever tell you he worked for Interpol?"

"Yes, when I was a courier for him in Europe."

"Did you ever look at the information you passed?"

"No!"

"Would you remember the faces of those you made contact with or recorded if you saw them again?"

"I suppose I would. I would certainly know Prince Ahmed."

"If we can arrange for you to look at a photo file would you cooperate?"

"Yes."

His questions went on and Krista answered as best she could, taking more time to answer. Sometimes he would stop, erase what was there, and start over. It was taking longer than either of them had expected. It was becoming obvious that her story raised more doubts about her cooperation than answers. Neither the CIA, Interpol, nor the Mossad would be easily convinced. And there was little Jorden could do, despite his efforts to word his questions in her favor. What was worse, she could see that he knew it now as well. She could see it in his face and eyes, and hear it in the tone of his voice.

Krista waited for the final blow. If she hadn't known better she might think she had been deliberately framed by Paul.

"Did Paul Gotthard ever discuss Liechtenstein and a man named Flanders with you?" Jorden asked.

She knew he expected a no answer. It was now, or never. If she lied to save herself and keep Jorden's respect, she would end up losing anyway. In the end the truth would be revealed and her lies would grow into a web of deceit. "Whatsoever a man sows, that shall he also reap." How could she lie to the CIA?

Her head lowered. "Yes, only it was I who discussed it with Paul Gotthard."

Jorden's gaze shot to hers in disbelief. As though she didn't understand his question he erased and repeated. Krista looked at the recorder. "Yes, I discussed Liechtenstein with Mr. Gotthard the night I left Hans Fischer's house. While there, soon after the shooting, which left a man dead, I overheard two men talking in the hallway. They were Jorden Keller and Hans Fischer. Mr. Keller remarked that he must go to Liechtenstein, that it was important. Later that night when Paul Gotthard brought me to the von Buren mansion in Zurich, I told him what I had overheard. He was very pleased."

The silence lengthened. The recorder continued recording nothing but the sound of the wind. Krista stood, tears in her eyes, looking at Jorden. He didn't move. She turned, and opening the kitchen door, she went out into the wind, taking the narrow steps down to the backyard to be alone with her pain.

The sun was setting behind Piz Languard in the east, turning the sky above the peak into a flame, impressing her with the appearance of a volcano. The mountain was dark, except where the white snow turned rose in the sunset. There were clouds blowing in too, and it would soon be snowing. *I'm responsible for Flanders' death*, she told herself again. *The CIA will conclude I've been aiding Paul willingly. How can I blame them? Now Jorden knows it as well.*

Her troubled mind grew too weary to think on. Darkness pervaded her pathway. Had Paul planned it this way? Perhaps he had he wanted her to appear a willing accomplice—to share the guilt with him when things went wrong.

The icy wind blew. Where had she gone wrong? How had she come to such a miserable end? Maybe she hadn't prayed enough or allowed the Lord to guide her decisions. Maybe she had ignored the warning signs and plunged ahead with her plans, unwilling to give up what meant so much to her. Or maybe it was none of these things but part of a plan God had for her life. What good could come of it all? Were there lessons to be learned, new truths to be discovered about trusting Him more in the future? Yet her eyes of faith could see nothing before her path but obstacles. The Lord must remove the obstacles or make a way around them. Whatever route she took tomorrow she must keep walking and trusting.

Oh Father, she prayed with a sob, and no other words would come.

Inside the kitchen Jorden kept his emotions under tight wrap. He hit the rewind switch on the recorder. He remembered now. He had come in from the corridor where he'd been talking to Hans. Krista was sitting on the edge of the bed. Even then he had suspected she may have been standing near the door listening. He'd told Stella to keep an eye on Krista, but she had left her alone in the bedroom.

His faith in her did not waver. Krista must have told Paul about Liechtenstein out of uncertainty. At the time she still believed he was working for Interpol. Jorden would never believe she had deliberately worked with him to unveil the cover of two Western agents. At the time she hadn't even known they were agents.

But he was under no illusion that Avi or Flanders' superior would see it that way. They would, however, come to see the truth eventually. They would have to. But by then Krista would have been detained for questioning. If she had thought his behavior was intimidating she hadn't seen anything yet. Even after detaining her they might not let her go for days, and there was the possibility that they might believe she was guilty.

He stood looking at the recorder. Then, fully knowing the consequences of his choice, he held down the erase button. The Mossad had always told him that in the end he was on his own. Well, he had just made up his mind; he would do what he must. As the tape came to the end he rewound about half way and hit play…nothing. He wasn't satisfied. What if the tape maintained a detectable residual? He replaced the cassette with a new one, then pocketed the first. He returned the recorder to his rucksack.

A ring from the phone startled the chill silence. He knew it would either be Avi calling back to check on how the recording went, or Meir, or Ziv. It might even be Flanders' superior, a man named Kurt Branden.

Jorden let it ring. He would need to talk to Avi, but only when he had what he needed to land von Buren and, now, Paul Gotthard. In the meantime he would work on his own. It would mean looking after Krista as well. He couldn't allow her to see von Buren tomorrow. He didn't trust him alone with her—not now. By now Wilhelm might have learned that Einer Seitz had met her in Chur.

The phone went silent. Avi wouldn't give up. He was right. A moment later it rang again. He could easily pick it up and make an excuse, but he didn't want to mislead him. Avi would know that. The silence was a message that he had sided with Krista.

And now, he thought dourly, *after this, and the Stella debacle, I'll be placed on the dead duck list.*

Jorden left the bedroom and slipped into his jacket. He would need to work quickly to get information before Avi or Branden could get on his trail to stop him. He had what Krista told him about Seitz. He knew it must have something to do with her ring. Perhaps in that lay a path that could bring him out of this maze.

He took Krista's coat from the peg and went out the kitchen door to find her. He came down the porch steps, his boots crunching on snow. She stood by the slope facing the black and purple mountain. Above, in the rose-colored horizon an early star faintly gleamed. The smell of pine was on the wind as it sighed and moaned.

He walked up behind her and placed her coat over her shoulders. She turned and looked at him. As she did her moist, wide blue eyes softened his frayed emotions and brought them sliding down in an avalanche. Careful...He told himself that this was no time to get singed. He clamped the lid even tighter on his defenses. He'd already walked too close to the edge of disaster tonight by deciding to scrap the recording. He wasn't about to jump off the slippery slope by taking her into his arms.

He reached into his pocket and removed the cassette. His gaze lifted toward the horizon as he tossed it far out over the edge of the cliff. She watched its flight in bewilderment as it descended to the deep valley below. "Let's go," he said simply. "We need to talk to Franz. And you still need to tell me about Seitz."

Surprise widened her eyes. "I don't understand," she whispered. "You're not going to report to Vienna?"

"Not yet. I'm taking a chance on you, a big one. I know Flanders' superior. He's as hard as iron. He moves quickly and asks questions later. I might almost rest easier knowing he'd detained you. Right now, we need to cooperate if we expect to outwit the enemy."

Krista blinked hard, as if to keep the tears back. "If I had only known what could happen, I would never have said anything."

"I know that," he said gently. "You're not to blame for Liechtenstein. Flanders would be the first to agree. He'd want us to get this job done. What do you say?"

She reached a hand to his arm. "I'll do whatever I can, Jorden, especially to make up for being so wrong. Thank you for believing in me."

He must have given his desire away, for he saw her cheeks warm and her eyes falter.

Some other time, he thought, *neither of us is ready*. Yes, she was very desirable, and a woman's trust and devotion was a treasure he sought—especially this woman's. The realization surprised even him. With firm resolve he bolted the door on his desires. Wait. Everything must wait.

He walked to the slope and looked down. "Meir and Ziv will soon be on my trail, and von Buren will be watching you. We'll need to come up with right answers to justify the action I've taken." Neither Avi nor the CIA would be easy to convince.

"Who are Meir and Ziv, colleagues in the..." she stopped as if catching herself.

"Yes. And we don't mention their names in public. After tonight, the St. Moritz ski lodges will be the wrong place for either of us to be lolling about. If Gotthard and von Buren come there, count on it, they'll be heavily equipped."

"Agents?" Her voice was steady, though she was pale.

"Agents, not a few," he said dryly.

"And there's also Seitz and his allies."

"Quite right." He didn't mention Lars, but he was sure he would be there, somewhere out of sight and with a personal vendetta of his own.

"But, Jorden," she whispered incredulously. "Why would Seitz dare show up to see Franz if he knows von Buren is here?"

"Seitz would be taking a big chance were it not for the CIA. Normally, he'd just as soon put a bullet hole through Wilhelm as look at him. But he won't, not with the false hope of wealth dangling before his nose. But von Buren should still fear. If he doesn't appease Seitz, he has much to lose. And Seitz has safe passage to Havana, courtesy of the CIA."

"That infuriates me."

He too had been riled when Flanders told him. "Don't let it. Perfect justice doesn't exist apart from God. But don't worry, the CIA knows what it's doing. They're getting a chest of crucial information in return for Seitz's safe passage out of Switzerland. If von Buren knows Seitz is here, he'll want to eliminate him fast. That's another problem, one for the CIA to worry about. It's von Buren we want."

He walked along the slope watching the rose hues of the horizon darken. The stars were out now, peeping from beneath a caravan of clouds. The wind was cold, but he liked it. It helped him stay alert and think. He must come up with answers in the next few days. The clock was ticking and when the alarm sounded it would all be over. Either things would work out, or they'd be buried in an avalanche. Avi might be angry now, just as he had been over Stella, but if Jorden could produce von Buren, Avi could be appeased. He might storm and protest, or become icy-silent, but he also respected reasonable initiative among his agents, especially, Jorden thought, when the agent produced the quarry bound for trial in Israel.

Krista had walked up to him, the wind tossing her fair hair like the strands of spun gold. "We can go to Franz and Trudy. Naturally she would never say anything about Franz, but I now think she knows more about him than I do. We can trust her."

He could see she was trying to appear calm, but he knew she was afraid, not only for herself, but for her uncle and his girlfriend. He had met Trudy and liked her. He believed she could be trusted because Franz appeared to believe in her.

"No need to put others at risk unnecessarily. The less she knows, the safer she'll be. We don't want Einer's or Wilhelm's thugs calling on her with questions. We'll see them briefly tonight." Franz's cover with Interpol must be safeguarded. After tonight he would arrange to contact Franz some other way.

"Do you have some place outside St. Moritz you can stay for the next few days? Some friend neither Paul nor von Buren knows about?"

"No." She shoved her hands into her coat pockets. The gesture told him a lot. He wondered that she didn't. He would have expected someone with her looks and talents to have numerous friends, but perhaps her assets also alienated as much as they attracted, and she was particular about involvement. He liked that. He also had to be careful. His line of work automatically excluded many types of relationships that otherwise would be acceptable. That was one of the reasons he hadn't thought seriously about marriage. His occupation would leave too much for his wife to have to explain. And there was little that was more frightening to an agent than the thought of his home address falling into the wrong hands.

"There's Franz's apartment in Zurich," she said. "They wouldn't look for me there."

He remained silent. He turned toward the safehouse. The perfect place, now useless since Avi knew he was here. By now he may have ordered Meir or Ziv to start in this direction. Krista must be brought somewhere else.

"Your friend, the lady living in Berlin?" she asked quietly.

"Avi would check there as well, first place he'd look for me."

"Is he a bloodhound, this head of your secret police?" she asked, somewhat frustrated.

"Worse," Jorden said with a slight smile. "I may yet need to bring you to her, though. I think she'd conceal you if I asked her."

"If only it hadn't turned out like this. Oh Jorden I've got to visit Davos! I must take the risk. I can't go into hiding."

He turned and looked at her. "Davos?" he said thoughtfully. "Yes, perhaps…"

"What?" she looked bewildered by his acceptance.

"I know a place in Davos. In fact, it's a good idea. I'm beginning to think you might fit into this kind of life. Davos, that's it."

She was looking at him. "But I haven't even explained why I want to go…"

"You can explain in the car. Let's grab our things and leave. Now I think we'll foil the bloodhound." Jorden smiled, somewhat relieved, as he slipped an arm through her elbow and propelled her toward the house. *Beauty*, and *brains*, he thought in amazement. *Can it be? What a perfect combination. I can look into those big blue eyes and know that there is something more behind them than mountain mist and acorns.*

He hoped Franz would be at Trudy's house. Without Meir and Ziv to depend on in a tough spot, as well as his friendly acquaintances in the CIA, Franz would be his one trusted contact.

21

Night had fallen rapidly, dropping a black curtain across the narrow mountain road as Jorden took the sharp turns smoothly. Clouds now veiled the stars. Krista tried to relax, but her adrenaline was elevated. Jorden continued his questioning, asking about her meeting with Seitz and details regarding Davos. She explained everything, including Seitz's apparent knowledge of the ring.

"Davos," he repeated with keen interest. "It fits the scenario perfectly. A military hospital..." he mused, "and a convent. I may have a break into Wilhelm von Buren at last."

Krista's interest almost ignited. "A hospital?"

"An important military asylum during World War II. The Swiss were neutral, or thought to be. Because of it, there was also a recuperation center in Davos for war-weary soldiers, not just Germans but Americans and Brits."

"Yes," she agreed, but still saw no real connection. "I read that Davos' citizens worried about the Allied soldiers meeting the Germans on the street when they received liberty from the hospital and getting into fights, but they never did. What has that to do with what Seitz told me?"

"Elsa was a photographer at the time, wasn't she?"

"Yes."

"That was the period when she worked in Nazi propaganda. She was there taking pictures of brave German soldiers."

"Yes, but Seitz mentioned the convent. 'Ask at the convent in Davos about a two-year-old child left there when her Jewish parents were sent back across the border into Austria,' " Krista repeated tensely. She would never forget those words, the rasping voice, the slur in his meaningful tone. "'The child was a Jew.'"

She turned her head and saw only the handsome contour of the side of his face. "We'll leave for Davos tonight," he told her. "As soon as I meet with Franz."

Her excitement escalated. Was the truth finally going to be learned? "I'll need to pack some things from my room at the lodge," she said, and seeing his frown, hastened: "It won't take me long. I'll need to give some explanation to Cousin Henrich and Veena."

"No, tell them nothing. Let Franz come up with an explanation when he sees them tomorrow."

"You don't trust them?" she asked surprised.

"I don't know. We're not going to trust anyone we're not certain of right now. By tomorrow Paul and von Buren will be there as well. Franz will need to have a story to explain your absence to all of them."

Krista glanced at her slacks and boots. "You don't expect me to eat, sleep, and walk about Davos in these clothes for the next week do you?"

He smiled. "You look all right to me."

She looked away as if she hadn't noticed the slight warm tone in his voice. "At least I need a comb and toothbrush."

"We'll splurge and buy them on the way."

Why didn't he trust Henrich and Veena? They wished her no harm, and surely the man who had stolen Elsa's book wouldn't be waiting the second time behind the door of her room. Precaution, she decided. He must know what he's doing.

"You and Stella also know something more about this ring. Why did you arrange to bring me to Hans Fischer's house? What was it Stella was going to ask me? It had to do with this ring."

"I know only what Stella told me. I can't vouch for the truth of her convictions."

"And what's that?"

"Stella believes it belonged to her great-aunt in Vienna."

"Her great-aunt," she whispered, stunned.

They were entering St. Moritz with the lights from the resort hotels and chalets reflecting like golden pearls along the lake. Krista was perfectly still, gazing at the ruby ring.

Jorden parked the Audi out of sight behind some trees a distance away from Trudy's house. Was Franz there? Krista opened the door, and stepped out, looking up toward the Engadine-style house. The scent of pine wafted on the breeze with wood smoke. The silent night was cool and crisp, and a seemingly endless slope of white, glittering snow stretched off toward the upper forest. Only in the far distance did jagged peaks wall them in, mere silhouettes reaching toward the heavens.

Jorden waited for her, and they walked in silence toward the house. When they were near enough to the porch steps he took her arm and turned toward her. "Better go ahead of me."

She knew why. Should something go wrong and she walked into a trap, it was wiser to have Jorden free to maneuver.

"Where does that door on the side of the house lead to?"

"A pantry."

"I'll enter that way."

She left him in the shadows of the pine trees near the drive and took the steps up to the porch.

Jorden waited out of sight in the dark trees near the edge of the drive. It was a risk to have come here, but the meeting with Franz was important. He was taking too many risks, he thought with a frown. He looked back toward the Audi. He didn't think anyone in St. Moritz had seen him driving it this morning. Not even Franz knew about it.

His gaze came back to the front window. He saw Franz walk up and draw the drapes. Not a good sign. A man rarely worried about closing curtains like a woman did. Where was Krista?

Jorden moved quietly toward the side of the house where the pantry door faced the drive. Krista was already there unlocking it, inching it open slowly, leaving the room dark. He entered the pantry silently, seeing a light from the sitting room ahead.

Her blue eyes were anxious as they met his, her hand on his arm. "Franz is here," she whispered, "and so is Seitz."

Franz's silhouette appeared in the sitting room doorway.

His response was automatic as he drew her aside to safety. Franz didn't move and neither did he, but his hand was already holding his .38 in his pocket and aimed straight ahead.

"You had me worried, Keller. Come in, quickly. We've unwanted company."

His tension ebbed like the tide. Jorden walked toward him, looking past Franz Klossner into the lighted sitting room.

"Seitz! Here?" Jorden gritted. "He was to come on the 14th. Whose slip was this?" He looked at Krista.

"I got the date right, didn't I, Uncle Franz!"

"Yes, she did," Franz said.

"Where is he?" Jorden asked quickly.

"Upstairs waiting." Franz said with a frown. "Seitz has put us at risk. I notified our contact this morning that Seitz would be here on the 14th. Now I've got to get through to him some way. I'm not sure I can arrange it so quickly."

"What's he doing here now?" Jorden asked, cautious, still sizing Franz up. He liked him, he had from the moment they met, but that didn't guarantee he wasn't a double agent. He glanced at Krista and hated to even think about betrayal. She doted on her uncle.

"He's a frightened man."

"A frightened man is a danger to everyone trying to help him."

"My thoughts exactly. We need to get him out of here to a safehouse. You've heard? Paul and Wilhelm are on their way here."

"Yes. And Krista and I need to disappear. But not with Seitz."

If Franz was concerned about him disappearing with his niece he didn't show it.

"What about the safehouse you've just come from?"

"How did you know about it?"

Franz smiled easily. "You're careful and suspicious. Good. I feel better already with Krista in your care. Come into the next room. It's secure. I've a message for you."

Franz reached over and took Krista's hand, letting her pass in front of them into the sitting room. "Trudy and her mother are spending the night with friends," he told her calmly, giving her a kiss on the forehead. "Don't worry, dear."

Krista seemed to know he wanted to talk to Jorden alone. "I'll make some sandwiches and tea," she told them, and left.

Franz brought him into the sitting room and closed the doors to the other rooms in the house. "Avi called here with a warning," he said in a low voice. "Kurt Branden is determined to track you down."

Branden had been Flanders' director. If Avi had taken the risk to call here to Franz, who would warn him, then Avi wasn't breathing the fire and brimstone Jorden had thought. Sometimes he pretended hot displeasure, yet secretly supported his independent initiatives. Was it that way now?

"What did the dragon breathe on me, fire?" Jorden asked.

"A warning. If you don't want to hang by your thumbs you'd better come up with the proof you need on von Buren. I may be able to help you there. I realize you're helping Krista. I have a recording you can play in her defense."

Franz walked to his tobacco tin, removed the lid from the bottom, and ejected a cassette. "My secret little recorder," he said smoothly. "I've suspected Paul for months. Even before this last diamond showing in Rome, Venice, and Monte Carlo. For weeks he'd been coming to my apartment at the University to play chess. We had some interesting conversations, all recorded, including his last one with me when he brought Krista a few days ago to a birthday gathering." Franz dropped the cassette onto Jorden's palm. "You'll find Paul lying about working with Interpol."

Jorden looked from the cassette to Franz, and broke into a smile. "Very astute of you, Franz."

Franz's blue eyes twinkled. "I thought so. I may be able to help you with Wilhelm. What do you know about Elsa?"

Jorden thought of the book on photography but remained cautious. "Not as much as I'd like to know. She is your cousin, isn't she?"

"Mine?" Franz's sandy brows lifted. "No. My father's. They lived in Davos before the war. My father, Gerhart, was a physician, my mother Inger, an International Red Cross nurse. They were both devout Christians with love for the Jewish people. Unfortunately, there wasn't much they could do to save them in those days. My father never got along with Elsa. Her political beliefs upset him, as they well should have."

"Did Doctor Klossner work at the military hospital at Davos during the war?"

"Yes, as did my mother until she decided to join the Red Cross. She was one of the workers who tried to warn the United States and England of Hitler's extermination camps, but her secret messages apparently were either undetected or ignored."

Jorden refused to waste his anger. He could do nothing about the past, but he could invest his energies now into standing for what was right and just. He found that he liked Franz more and more. He saw much of Krista in him.

"Elsa Klossner was a bright and pretty photographer in those days," Franz went on. "I'm told she arrived in Davos in 1939 totally enamored with Adolf Hitler and Hermann Goering." He shook his head sadly and paced, one hand in his trouser pocket, the other holding his old pipe. "She told my father she was now employed in the propaganda machine. She wore my parents out, talking of the glories of the Third Reich well into the night. She went with him once to the hospital. There was an officer there who was injured."

"But the war hadn't begun yet."

Franz looked at him. "Exactly right. But you forget the Nazis' first take-over of another country."

"Austria."

"Yes, and this officer had been thickly involved in the plot to assassinate Prime Minister Englebert Dollfuss. The conspiracy had the full approval of Hitler. One of those involved in the brutal murder of Dollfuss was the man we know as von Buren. He had an old wound that often troubled him from those earlier days. Elsa was mesmerized by him right off. She visited von Buren in the hospital every day thereafter, taking photographs and praising his "gallantry." Later she went off with him to Berlin and they were married there."

Jorden's excitement grew. "I had thought it was something like that. Franz, von Buren's name—what is it? You must know."

"Good heavens, Jorden, if I did, do you think I'd keep it from you? I've been searching on my own for years! Ever since Krista's parents were murdered in a fall at Piz Nair."

"Is that why you started working with Interpol?"

"Yes. I was certain von Buren had something to do with their deaths. He may have considered them a risk to his identity. Peter may have discovered something and gone to him about it. A mistake. For years I worried about Krista. I came close to sending her to America on several occasions after that, but I relaxed my guard when Elsa seemed to take a special liking to her. Elsa had always wanted a daughter. But after Ehrlich they could have no more children. There were many times afterward when I regretted ever allowing Krista to work as a model for Gotthard Enterprises."

Jorden proceeded carefully. He didn't want to be the one to inform Franz that Krista had helped Paul deceive him in Zurich. There would be time enough later for Krista to explain. He approached the matter from a different direction: "Elsa worked for Hitler's propaganda team in Berlin as a photographer. Do you know anything about her work or an out-of-print book first published around 1938?"

"Wilhelm has been destroying any works that might endanger him or Elsa. He would never be so careless as to leave evidence lying around."

Yes, Jorden agreed. And one book had been stolen this morning. No use telling Franz about it, or that Krista had been knocked unconscious. After tonight, he was going to make sure she was nowhere about St. Moritz.

"You might like to know I've already tried to get hold of von Buren's military records at the Davos hospital," Franz said. "They don't exist."

Jorden wasn't surprised. For a man like Wilhelm to have assumed another identity he would have seen to the destructions of those records years ago.

"Wouldn't that be almost impossible to do without inside help?" he asked.

Franz looked at him for a long moment. "If you're asking me if my father, Doctor Klossner, may have assisted him, the answer could be yes. Wilhelm may have black-mailed him and Inger."

They looked at each other with quiet understanding and allowed the subject to drop. He must discover von Buren's identity some other way. Franz's parents were dead, and Jorden would find no records in Davos, either at the hospital or the convent. Wilhelm would have made certain of that. Einer Seitz was wrong when he had told Krista to go there if she wanted the truth. The truth could only be found through individuals who may remember. He thought of the Cohen flat in Vienna. Avi had visited there with Stella, and neither of them had found anything. Still, he must go there himself and search. There was also Tirzah, though he doubted the elderly lady could remember much.

"Do you think Wilhelm was a Gestapo agent?" Franz asked quietly but bluntly.

Jorden respected his honest question enough to answer forthrightly. "Yes. I'm sure that's what he's trying to hide. We also think he made his millions of Swiss francs through holocaust victims—both jewelry and Swiss bank accounts." Now was the time to get the matter straight. "What do you know about the ring Krista wears? It was her mother's, wasn't it? Do you know where she got it? Your Cousin Henrich seemed to think you might."

Franz sighed. "It was Anna's. My mother left it to her when she died."

"You know it once belonged to the Cohen family in Vienna?"

"I suspected it might, but I knew it meant nothing to the von Burens. It was safe for Krista to have it. I didn't have the heart to take it away. It means a great deal to her. It's a connection with her mother."

And more, thought Jorden, and was sure Franz knew it as well. Franz walked over to the fireplace, his shoulder toward him, and Jorden willingly said no more.

Jorden looked at his watch, then toward the ceiling. He heard stealthy steps. Einer Seitz moving nervously about in his room.

"Any other message from Avi?"

Franz turned, looking vaguely amused. "Avi's giving you forty-eight hours before he sends Meir and Ziv on your trail. Meantime he's given Kurt Branden a false lead. Have you met Kurt yet?"

"No. I've heard about him," Jorden said wryly. "A real wall to run into. Takes the safety of his men seriously. Flanders' death must have hit him like a sledge hammer."

"Yes, I'm afraid so."

So good old Avi had given him a break after all. For that, he wouldn't let him down.

"We haven't much time where Seitz is concerned. How about filling me in?"

Franz told him that Einer Seitz had arrived just after dark at the back door, coming undetected from the forest. He couldn't wait until the 14th, he said. The news of his presence in the area had somehow leaked out; there'd been one attempt on his life already at Chur.

"He is convinced Wilhelm knows he's here."

Bad news, thought Jorden. "Branden will arrive soon."

"I hope so," Franz murmured. "He's illusive. Unless he contacts me, I'm stuck. In the meantime, I have the East German agent upstairs. I must get him out of here before Trudy and her mother learn about it. Luckily they went to a friend's house tonight before he showed up. I don't want to have to explain all this to them. The less they know of my work, the safer they will be."

Jorden thought of Krista. She was right in the middle of it, surrounded by danger. He must get her out of St. Moritz. He glanced toward the stairway. So Seitz was up in one of those rooms. "Having him here is about as pleasant as having to hide a barrel of rotting squid."

Franz covered a smile by reaching for his pipe and his tobacco tin. "We'll need to move Seitz tonight before our company from Zurich arrives."

If von Buren had given an order in Chur to kill Seitz, then there was a good chance von Buren's agents would pick up his trail here to St. Moritz. Von Buren wasn't likely to suspect Franz of harboring him until the CIA could snatch him away, but Trudy's house was much too open. Trudy herself might let something slip if Franz was forced to explain Seitz's presence.

"We can't leave him here. Was he alone?"

"He has a bodyguard he trusts. The man is somewhere close at hand, probably in the forest off the drive."

Then he must have seen him and Krista arrive. As long as he thought they were protecting Seitz he would keep his distance.

"The bodyguard would like to kill von Buren."

Jorden worried as he moved restlessly about the sitting room. Franz stood smoking his pipe, frowning to himself.

"Avi suggested we take him to a certain house about an hour into the forest. He said you could arrange it."

"Yes, I just came from there."

The sooner the CIA got their prize, the less he would need to worry about Seitz suddenly turning upon von Buren like a shark smelling blood.

Krista entered from the kitchen, looking tense. "Ziv is here," she whispered.

Ziv! He was supposed to keep an eye on von Buren. He and Paul couldn't have arrived yet. If they were here, he and Franz were short-handed to guard Seitz. Had Avi sent

Ziv to stop him? Maybe Avi's message to Franz had been a deliberate ruse.

He turned to Franz. "Keep an eye on Seitz. If his guard saw Ziv arrive he may think we're trying to pull something."

Franz headed for the stairs, his hand in his tweed jacket pocket, no doubt holding his gun. Jorden walked to the kitchen. He noted that Krista had already pulled the blinds, and the back door was locked. He took her arm. "Wait for us in the next room, will you?"

She left without question, looking pale. When she'd gone, Jorden reached over and closed the kitchen door, all the while watching Ziv.

"If Avi's sent you to detain Krista until Branden arrives from the CIA to hassle her with questions, I'll need to stop you. We're leaving tonight."

Ziv, instead of responding as Jorden expected, laughed softly and leaned against the kitchen door, hands in his coat pockets.

"Well, well. That was fast. What Stella couldn't do in a couple of years, Krista has accomplished in days. Wait till Meir finds out. He'll stand on his head. He's been mooning over Stella for a year."

"Wise guy. Did Avi send you just to cheer up our day with your sunshine and humor?"

"He sent me, but not for the reason you think. If I didn't have news would I be here?"

"Good question," Jorden said dryly. "Would you?"

Ziv wandered over to the counter where Krista had been making sandwiches. He picked the biggest one up, opened it to see if there was any ham in it, then satisfied, took a chomp. "You're going to be as disappointed as Avi and I about the news."

"So what is it?"

"Maybe you'd better sit down," Ziv jested.

"I promise not to faint. Why aren't you tailing von Buren? By now he and Gotthard should be half way here from Zurich."

"Where von Buren has gone, I don't want to follow," Ziv quipped, waving his sandwich. "Von Buren blew his brains out in his library last night. I found him still clutching his Luger." He looked at Jorden, shook his head, and took another bite. "Disappointing, isn't it? After all we've been through to get the buzzard. You, me, and Meir. Then he goes and kills himself."

Jorden felt as if he'd been rocked by an explosion. "He can't be dead," he gritted.

"Sure, that's what I said. It's not fair. I heard the shot just as the German martial music hit the crescendo"—WHAM!—Ziv slammed his palm down on the counter. "He played that marching music all the time. Drove me wacky. Get this—he was wearing his old uniform, the jacket, that is. And—I found this on him." He reached inside his pocket and handed Jorden a small photograph. His eyes were grave as he watched Jorden's sudden frown. "What do you make of it?"

Jorden studied the picture of himself and Avi sitting at an outdoor cafe in Vienna. The photo looked to have been taken from long range. Even so, the face of Avi was clear, as was his own. He could clearly see the two coffee cups on the outdoor table and the Viennese eclairs that Avi had a special liking for.

"I don't like this at all. This was on Wilhelm?"

"In his shirt pocket. Naturally I took it before I called the Zurich police."

Jorden didn't need to ask how Ziv got inside, or whether he had stayed to report his findings to the police. He wouldn't have been caught within a mile of the von Buren mansion.

"Suicide," Jorden gritted. "The typical Nazi response. "Hitler, Goering—all of them. The moment you close in on them, they pop a cyanide pill. Cowards."

"All except Eichmann. We hung him," Ziv stated calmly.

"Maybe Paul pulled the trigger and put the gun in his hand."

"First thing I thought," Ziv said. "Not a chance, for two reasons. Von Buren was alone in the house. I know. I had that place staked all day. Secondly, Paul Gotthard wasn't there. Nor was Mrs. von Buren. He was alone. Even the housekeeper and her husband were gone. They're all on their way to Vienna."

Vienna? Jorden didn't like the sound of it. "Is Meir watching them?"

"On the same flight."

"Avi is aware?"

"Perfectly."

Everything had changed. His plans had been ripped apart and tossed to the wind. Had he killed himself? Could Ziv be wrong? Could someone have gotten inside the mansion undetected? Lars? No, what reason would he have to kill the man he admired and who paid his bills?

Who, then? One of Seitz's East German friends? But nothing would have been gained by killing Wilhelm now. Seitz had first of all wanted money, not revenge. Only when he feared for his own life had Seitz sought help from the American CIA.

"You're certain Paul and Elsa were nowhere around?"

"Positive. I saw them all pile into the Mercedes and take off for Kloten airport. Meir was right behind them."

"Any note? A confession?"

"Nothing." Ziv helped himself to coffee. "I searched him and there was nothing except that photograph. That's what worries me. That picture of you and Avi."

"Lars knows what I look like," Jorden said. "No secret there. So do the East Germans." His worry increased. It was Avi whom the Mossad tried to keep under wraps. He looked at Ziv soberly. "Whoever took this photograph did it secretly in Vienna. I think I remember when. It was soon after I'd met with Stella over the banking scandal. Somebody wanted Avi's picture, not mine."

Ziv set his cup down quietly. For a moment, they said nothing more.

"Where is Avi now?"

"At a safehouse in Vienna. I don't know where, neither does Meir. Avi is to contact Meir soon after the plane lands in Vienna."

"But does he know about this picture?" Jorden asked.

"He knows."

Someone wants to assassinate Avi the way they did Flanders, Jorden thought. *I've got to get to Vienna to protect him as well as bring Seitz to the safehouse in the mountains.*

"Avi wants to see you as soon as we get Seitz packed away. Is the bird here?"

"He's here. Upstairs. Franz is watching him. There's also a guard somewhere in the forest."

Jorden's fingers tapped thoughtfully on the counter. Von Buren was dead. "Well, that changes things, doesn't it," he said, still trying to accept the idea that his trap had been sprung and his quarry had flown the coop. An entire year of his life spent tracking von Buren, only to have him end it all before he could close him in.

Why would Elsa and the Gotthards go to Vienna? They must have known Seitz was here. Paul did, at any rate. And von Buren too.

"Maybe Wilhelm did himself in because he knew Seitz was too close," said Ziv. "He was afraid Seitz would reveal who he was to the newspapers. It would destroy everything he had worked for in the banking world."

"What about Ehrlich, his son? He wasn't in the house either?

"No. He was staying in town at the Savoy, preparing for another meeting today with the Jewish organization from London on the banking scandal. The police already checked. Everything rings solid for him. He's taking it hard. If anyone is innocent in all this mess, it's probably Ehrlich von Buren. His whole life has been the bank. Now it's crumbling around him."

Jorden walked restlessly about the kitchen. "It doesn't make sense for Wilhelm to put a Luger to his head. He would naturally be afraid that Seitz would unmask him, but committing suicide in his library during the money scandal would also bring much negative attention to Ehrlich and Elsa. No, if he killed himself, he did it because he was tired of it all and wanted out. But that doesn't fit the kind of man that Wilhelm was. He covered his slimy tracks all these years. He would have played the deadly game of chess to the very end, expecting to win one way or another."

Ziv considered, then nodded. "I have to admit it doesn't make sense. Then did he really kill himself?"

"Maybe not."

"If someone got in, he had to get past me and..." and a slow frown brought his brows together. Jorden saw it and stopped prowling about the kitchen.

"Yes?"

Ziv shrugged. "Maybe there was one small opportunity for someone to have gotten past me unnoticed. Hans Fischer called me from Berlin. I was taken up with that call for perhaps five minutes."

"In five minutes most anything can happen. That's it," Jorden said. "That's time enough for someone to have entered after the others left for the airport."

Ziv looked at his watch. "They should be arriving about now in Vienna."

Jorden thought of Einer Seitz. He could breathe a little easier, but there were others from Gotthard Enterprises he would need to avoid. The CIA would still want that list of espionage agents from Seitz in exchange for his freedom, but Jorden's own plans had exploded with the bullet through Wilhelm's temple.

"It's best if Seitz doesn't know von Buren is dead until Branden meets with him." The CIA agent would want that list of names at any cost. "If Seitz thinks he's relatively safe, he may no longer think he needs Branden to arrange his safe passage to Cuba."

"You're right. Have you talked to Seitz yet?"

"No, but now's as good a time as any. I still want the real name of Wilhelm von Buren. If we can twist it out of anyone, it's Seitz. His father must have told him."

"You know," Ziv said quietly, "there's something about all this that bothers me."

"Yes," said Jorden cryptically. "The big fish got away." He touched Ziv's shoulder and headed for the door. "Come on, let's get this over. I want to get to Vienna to see Avi."

Ziv followed. "If someone did silence Wilhelm and make it look like he killed himself, who? And what was to be gained?"

Jorden wondered. He glanced at the photo of Avi again before sliding it into his pocket. Why had Wilhelm been carrying it just before he died? Maybe Avi would have some ideas.

He was still deep in thought when he came out of the kitchen with Ziv. He saw Krista in the sitting room. She stood from the sofa when they entered. She looked tense and worried and he hated to inform her about Wilhelm. He would have to, otherwise she might think Ziv had come to St. Moritz about Liechtenstein.

He walked up to her and managed a smile. "Still holding firm? We'll need to award you a medal when this is all over. You look tired, Krista. Why not go up to your room and get some sleep? It will be several hours before we can leave. I've got to question Seitz and then see he's brought to the safehouse."

"I'm all right," she said quietly, her blue eyes searching his. "Is there—news?" she glanced toward Ziv waiting on the stairs.

"Wilhelm is dead," Jorden said quietly. "He killed himself in his library late last night."

A small gasp escaped her lips, and Jorden took hold of her arm.

"Killed himself? You mean suicide?" she whispered.

"That's what the Zurich police are saying."

"You don't think so."

She was quick, he thought. "I'm not sure, no. Do you have any thoughts on why Paul, Elsa, and the servants would go to Vienna instead of coming here as planned?"

She looked as bewildered as he felt, then she came alert. "Yes, that is, maybe I do. Remember the museum showing I told you about? The arrangements did come through. Elsa was excited about it. If the museum decided to show her work, nothing would keep her away. She'd cancel the trip here to St. Moritz in a minute."

Jorden nodded. "And Paul? He must know Seitz is here somewhere in the area. Was he close to Elsa?"

Her brow wrinkled. "Close?"

"You know, grandmother-son type of situation. He lost his parents early like you, didn't he?"

"Yes. His uncle raised him. And I suppose he thinks well of Elsa too. She may have needed him. If they've gone to Vienna to the museum, they must not yet know about Wilhelm."

He tapped his chin, musing, but made no comment. A piece of the puzzle was missing, but which piece? How would it change things if he knew?

He glanced up at the ceiling, hearing light footsteps moving about. Seitz, and maybe Franz. Then he walked to the stairway where Ziv waited to get the information he wanted from Einer Seitz.

22

An hour crept by while Krista waited below the stairs in the sitting room hearing low staccato voices coming from one of the rooms upstairs. She could only imagine what Einer Seitz must be going through under interrogation. She was standing on the bottom landing, her hand gripping the carved banister when a door opened above her and there were footsteps. Jorden and Franz appeared. One glance told her they were not pleased.

"His father was a subordinate officer to Wilhelm in Berlin during the war. He must be telling us the truth, Jorden, though it's as much a shock to me as it is to you."

"It doesn't make sense."

"Yet Seitz insists Wilhelm's the wrong man."

Wrong man? Krista thought, astounded.

"He must be lying. Unless..." Jorden lifted a photograph and stared at it.

Krista hung on his every word, tension mounting. She gathered from the little she had just heard that Seitz must have said the picture was not the real Wilhelm von Buren. Amazed, she looked from Jorden to her uncle.

"Unless," Jorden repeated, "I've been a fool. We all have. We've been deceived into chasing phantoms while the real SS officer, whatever his name, has been standing in the shadows."

"Clever indeed, if it's true," Uncle Franz said, scowling. "The question is, who is the real Wilhelm von Buren?"

Jorden replaced the photograph inside his jacket.

"One thing's certain," Franz said. "Wilhelm won't be around to tell us. It comes as a shock and disappointment. Suicide."

Jorden remained silent for a thoughtful moment, looking at the time. "We'd better get Seitz into the car. He won't budge without his bodyguard. Signal him, will you? Ziv and I will be there in fifteen minutes."

Franz came down the stairs putting an encouraging arm about Krista's shoulders. They walked toward the front door. "This will soon be over. Wrap up those sandwiches you made for us, will you? We'll take them with us. And put some coffee in a thermos. Jorden looks dead on his feet. When was the last time you got some sleep?" he called over his shoulder.

Jorden remained on the stairs. "Thirty-six hours ago."

"I'll do the driving on the mountain road," Franz said, but his eyes twinkled.

Krista smiled in spite of herself and went back into Trudy's neat and bright little kitchen. Her mind remained on the conversation between her uncle and Jorden. What did it mean?

She found Trudy's food wrap and began to fold the roast beef sandwiches in it. She gathered apples and cut some cheese and squares of gingerbread. All the while she was thinking of the exchange on the stairs between her uncle and Jorden over Wilhelm. She was filling the large thermos with steaming coffee when she heard Jorden come up behind her. He reached to help lift the heavy urn. They were standing close enough to cause her heart to skip a beat. Her cheeks warmed. "I can get it," she murmured.

"Your wrists are small for that heavy pot."

"Would you...um...hand me those napkins on the counter please?"

He did so, and she knew he was watching her. She avoided his gaze, as if her task demanded profound concentration. At last she glanced at him.

"Sorry if I make you nervous," he said silkily.

"After my interrogation at the safehouse?" she quipped to sidetrack his thoughts.

"Then there must be some other reason why my presence appears to bother you."

She looked at him with what she hoped was innocence, and saw his lurking smile. "Bother me? Why—I don't know what you mean." She turned away, snapping the big lunch bucket closed.

He came up beside her and took her hand. The ruby ring shimmered. She pulled away too quickly as if his touch burned. "What are you doing?" she asked, and her tone came off stiffly.

"Relax," he said softly. "I just want to tell you good-bye, that's all."

"I think—Franz has come back," she said softly, afraid her voice would give her away.

"That's just the wind. He's gone to signal our watchdog. It should take him about—" he looked at his watch "ten minutes." He smiled.

A lot could develop in ten minutes standing this close to a man she found extremely attractive.

Quickly she stepped behind an emotional barrier by asking: "How did the interrogation with Seitz go?"

The mention of Seitz brought the chill she had expected from him. Even though he gave no immediate reply, she persisted, now interested in the meaning behind the discussion on the stairs.

"What did you mean when you said Wilhelm was the wrong man?"

"We believe he took the name from a soldier at the military hospital in Davos. When the soldier died he assumed his identity. We've just had the tables turned on us. Seitz took a look at a picture we had of Wilhelm and swears it's not the man that his father served in Berlin."

"You—you mean Elsa's husband isn't Wilhelm?"

"No, and neither was he the Gestapo agent we're trying to track down."

"Then who was he?"

"That's what I need to discover."

"So the real von Buren died at Davos," she said thoughtfully. "Then that's why you were interested in the hospital."

"Partly. Von Buren died there around 1940. Franz told me tonight that Elsa had gone to the hospital with Doctor Klossner to take pictures of the German soldiers for Hitler's propaganda machine in '39. We think that's where she met the Gestapo agent we're looking for. He may have known the real von Buren while both men were receiving treatment. If we had his name we could check the records. Not that I expect them to still be there."

"He couldn't have done all that on his own," she said worriedly.

Jorden looked at her soberly. "No. Frans told me his father, Doctor Klossner, must have helped. We think they were blackmailed into it. Perhaps they had a secret they didn't want revealed."

Krista could only guess what it was. She was surprised that Uncle Franz knew about Davos.

"He never told me."

"He wanted to shield you from anything that might hurt you."

"Yes...but Jorden, if Elsa's husband isn't the man you thought he was, does that mean the real Auschwitz SS officer is alive and related to the family?"

"Yes. That's why the book by Elsa was important. We might have learned something we couldn't otherwise discover. It may have had a photograph."

Again, she felt as if she'd let them down.

"How long will you be gone?" she asked, troubled.

"A few hours."

He slipped into his coat, watching her.

"Be careful, Jorden. Don't take any chances. Especially now. You don't know whom you're looking for. It could be anyone."

"Not anyone. He must fit the uniform. Right age, right temperament. I'll find him," he said evenly.

"Nevertheless, please be careful."

He lifted a brow and asked softly, but forthrightly, "Why?"

"What a question!" But she avoided an answer.

"Yes, and one I'd like an answer to just the same."

"I don't want to see you injured," she said in a small voice, glancing toward the sitting room as if expecting Franz or Ziv to appear.

"No one is going to walk in on us," he said. "It's you I'm worried about. Don't go near the lodge. I should hate to come back and find I'd lost you."

She turned her head quickly to look at him, and her glance must have betrayed her heart.

She liked the way he had said that, and the way his eyes warmed as he gazed down at her. They wandered to her lips and lingered.

"You want to know what I'm thinking?" he asked.

"I'm not sure…"

"After questioning Seitz upstairs tonight, and wasting a year of my life tracking von Buren only to have him commit suicide, I'm thinking how delightful it is just to look at you. Your eyes are clean and pure, as blue as cornflowers…and innocent. Your lashes make delicate shadows on your skin. Your lips look sweet and inviting. I'm sure they'd blot everything unpleasant from my mind."

Her heart lurched as he slipped both arms around her waist and drew her toward him. Paul had held her in his arms, but his closeness had never made her feel like this.

Jorden gently smoothed her hair away from her throat, then he bent toward her lips. She never wanted to let him go, but a still small voice within warned that she must be careful. He must know where she stood in her Christian faith, and how it affected the relationship between a man and a woman. He wasn't a Christian. Who knew what he expected from her?

"We mustn't," she whispered, turning her head away, though she wanted his kiss as badly as he wanted hers.

"What do you mean we 'mustn't,'" he breathed with a slight irritation to his voice.

"I can't kiss you," she murmured, not daring to look at him, afraid she would succumb. She pushed gently away.

"What is this?" he murmured wryly. "'Can't.' You're not in love with Paul. You owe him nothing after the way he's treated you."

"No, I don't love him…" I think I'm falling in love with you, she could have said, but restrained herself.

"Then there's no reason to put me off."

"You…don't share my faith."

"I believe in God and the Old Testament Scriptures. Doesn't that count?"

"Yes. Oh, Jorden, don't you see?"

"No," he stated quietly.

"We're playing with fire…"

"I agree with that."

"What if we fell in love?"

He smiled.

"No matter how honorable and courageous you are, or how much I care…how would we resolve the issue of marriage, of children, of everything? Would you let me send our children to a Christian Sunday School?"

His eyes narrowed. He looked as if he were about to say something, but as she looked at him, tears coming to her eyes, he stopped. Silence held them, and she worried that he might think she was being coy or too religious. The tenderness that came to his eyes surprised her.

Slowly he released her. "I'll not insist you kiss me goodbye, no matter how much I'd like you to. You're very wise, Krista. The Lord has blessed you with spiritual qualities and outward beauty."

The compliment only made her want him more. She stood there, her heart longing and yet hurting, wanting to tell him how strongly she felt about him while knowing she must wait.

She turned away and blinked hard, feeling somewhat foolish as she picked up the lunch bucket. She swallowed the lump in her throat, turned, and handed it to him, avoiding his gaze.

He smiled. "Don't forget the thermos."

"Oh—yes, of course." She handed it to him and their eyes met. Seeing the smile in his gaze and realizing he did not think badly of her, that he wasn't angry at her refusal, she smiled, but even that soon faded. "Come back," she whispered.

His now-serious gaze held hers. "I intend to." He turned and walked out of the kitchen.

She heard his footsteps fading, going up the stairs to where Ziv waited, guarding Einer Seitz.

Krista was still standing there a few minutes later as he went out the front door with Ziv and Seitz.

When they had gone, she walked quickly into the sitting room, feeling dull and cold. She went to the door and pushed the heavy bolt through its lock as she had promised she would. She leaned her arm against the door, resting her forehead, closing her tired eyes. She heard nothing now except the beating of her heart. *Please Lord, help Jorden come to know you as Messiah, Israel's Redeemer whom the Old Testament Scriptures foretold.*

The minutes passed in silence. Krista listened and heard nothing, not even the distant sound of an engine starting. They were being extremely careful.

She began to pace the sitting room floor in her stocking feet. The Black Forest cuckoo clock startled her with its seven o'clock chimes. By now the car would be twenty minutes out of St. Moritz on the mountain road toward the safehouse. If everything went as planned, he would be back with Franz by nine.

On the final chime she stopped and looked up the stairs. It seemed days since she had risen to find the note from Trudy and went to have breakfast at the family lodge. Her head was aching again and her eyes smarted from weariness. Now would be a good time to bathe, lay an ice pack on her head, and rest her eyes. The more she thought about resting beneath the soft eiderdown coverlet, the more she longed for the reprieve. She walked to turn the lights down and tensed. A quiet knock sounded on the front door. She stood still, her heart leaping to her throat. Then she realized she was only afraid because she knew the truth of what was going on. No one else did, not Henrich or Veena, not even Paul. And he wasn't even in St. Moritz yet. By now Paul and Elsa would be in Vienna. She must answer. It could be a neighbor, or maybe a friend sent from Interpol. Then again, it could be an enemy. If it was, there was little she could do about it anyway. She had no gun and wouldn't know how to use one if she did. If they wanted to get in badly enough, they would know how to go about it.

Gathering courage, she walked across the room to the front door and turned on the porch light. She looked out the window. Veena! Veena saw her looking out and gestured desperately to let her inside. Quickly Krista unbolted the latch and opened the door.

"Veena, what on earth?"

Veena rushed in. Her face was pink from the cold wind and her long blond-gray braid swung over her shoulder.

"Dear Heaven, you had me so worried, Krista! I come home from the grocery mart and find you are gone all the day, all the evening. Henrich is out looking for you, and I told him I would come to Trudy's, that you must be here with Cousin Franz." Her eyes darted about anxiously looking for him.

"Franz isn't here," Krista explained. "He went out with friends for a little while."

"Where is Trudy?"

"She's out too."

"I am getting everything ready for tomorrow when the von Burens arrive. Supper was late tonight and you still did not show."

How was she going to tell her the news about Wilhelm's death? She decided to let Franz do it tomorrow. Veena would begin to ask too many questions.

"Oh Veena, I feel badly about missing dinner, but, well, one thing led to another and before I realized it the day was over and I thought I might as well stay here and wait for Uncle Franz to come home."

Krista was relieved when Veena nodded without protest or further questions. "I will tell Henrich. He will understand. He is so busy now, he hardly knows the difference anyway, except he was worried when it got dark and you had not returned from the slopes." She scanned her curiously. "You look so tired. You are all right? You are not getting a fever?" Her eyes studied her hair. Krista imagined the bump on her head sticking out as noticeably as a young horn on a deer. She smiled. "I'm all right."

"Then I will go back to the lodge. I have some mending of the curtain in the bedroom to do before bed. Frau Elsa will stay there tomorrow."

"I'm sorry I can't help you, Veena. If I were you I wouldn't worry too much about Elsa's arrival." Veena looked so frazzled and worried that she felt sorry for her.

"That is all right. The work I do is not meant for hands like yours. Oh! I almost forgot the other reason I walked so far." She dug into her brown coat pocket and pulled out a sealed envelope. "I found this when I came back from the grocery mart. It is for you. There is no sender's name on it."

Krista accepted the envelope, hoping her face did not give anything away.

Veena watched her. "I noticed your things were scattered across the bed. So I hung them in the wardrobe for you. I was afraid they would get wrinkled. Your brush and pretty things like makeup and perfume were scattered too."

"Oh. Yes…" Krista fingered the envelope, feeling her cheeks burning. Veena must think she had grown lazy and spoiled.

"You do not need them for tonight?"

"No, I shall get along fine. Thank you. I'm sorry you had to…straighten up my mess. I was in a hurry to get to the slopes."

Veena looked momentarily disapproving, then putting her scarf back on she tied it firmly beneath her chin. "Then good night. Come for breakfast. Tell Franz he is welcome. The others will be there by two o'clock."

"I'll tell him. Good night, Veena, and thank you for bringing the letter."

At the door Veena looked back. "There was a telephone call for you too. She did not give her name. When I said you were not in she disconnected the phone. She was rude."

Krista gave no explanation—she had none. She wished Veena would go so she could open the envelope. Was she delaying, hoping to find out what was inside? Krista laid it on the table beside a chair as if it were of no importance. Veena finally gave up and opened the door.

Krista stood in the cold on the porch until Veena had gone down the steps and walked across the rock pathway toward the lodge. When her tall figure faded into the night, Krista hurried inside, locked the door, and snatched the envelope from the table. Her name was scrawled with flaring black letters across the front. Had it been delivered by hand? Maybe the person who had taken the book had left it!

She opened the seal and removed a single sheet of paper folded in half.

> *Must see you tonight. Urgent. Will meet you at the Veltlinerkeller cafe at 8:30 P.M.*
> *Stella*

Stella in St. Moritz? Jorden couldn't possibly know that, Krista worried. She glanced at her wristwatch. 7:15. That left a little over an hour. Maybe Jorden would be back in time to accompany her. She hoped so. Stella was a friend of his and must be warned of danger.

Urgent, she had written. Something had happened, what? Trouble, no doubt. Maybe it had to do with Wilhelm's death, but how would Stella know about that? Krista burned the note and hurried up the stairs to the guest room where she bathed and changed into fresh clothing, borrowed from Trudy, a berry-colored woolen dress with belt and white accessories at cuffs and collar. She unbraided her hair and winced as she brushed it out and left it loose. Rebraiding pulled her scalp too much. The thug! She felt tired and grumpy. What a day, and it wasn't over yet, not by a long shot.

She added some light makeup and a berry-colored lipstick, then checked the time. If she left now she should get there with five minutes to spare.

As she came downstairs the house was perfectly quiet. Should she leave a note? Jorden had asked her not to go to the lodge...but...the Veltlinerkeller wasn't the lodge...and

Stella, surely, was important enough to meet. And one had to make allowances for emergencies, she consoled herself. Anyway, she had already made up her mind!

She wrote quickly—

> *8 P.M.*
> *Gone to meet Stella at the Veltlinerkeller.*
> *K*

She grabbed her coat and handbag and went out the door into the frosty glittering night.

23

Krista entered the Veltlinerkeller, which was styled with an abundance of wood and moldings of grape clusters. A few oversized game trophies decorated the walls. It was popular with the tourists and locals alike, who were drawn by the regional food. Meat was roasting over an open fire, attended by the owner and within view of the diners.

Krista scanned the restaurant and saw Stella entering from the lounge. Stella's dark eyes met hers as she walked to the back where a secluded table was located away from the windows.

The waiter came forward with a smile. "Your friend waits. This way, please."

A minute later Krista was seated opposite the woman she had briefly met at the Hans Fischer house in Zurich. For a moment they considered one another. Stella's gaze lowered to the ruby ring and some inner excitement caused her smooth olive skin to glow. Her dark hair was loose about her shoulders and she wore a stylish black suit. She was quite pretty. Krista again wondered about the relationship between Stella and Jorden. He hadn't mentioned her, but there had been so much to discuss that it wasn't surprising.

"I was afraid you wouldn't come," Stella said.

Krista smiled. She rather liked the young woman who may have been five years her senior. Now, she had information of her own to pass on to Stella. She would be shocked about Davos.

"You have my curiosity piqued," Krista said in a low voice. "Why wouldn't I come?"

"After our last meeting?" Stella grimaced. "Ghastly, wasn't it? Bodies all over the place, and that flying glass...say, it's healing nicely."

"Do you think so? I wasn't sure..." she touched her face gingerly, but was distracted by discomfort from the back of her head. "I have to admit I've taken more bruises recently than I ever did skiing on Corviglia."

Stella rested her elbows on the edge of the table, chin on folded hands, studying her.

Am I right, wondered Krista, *or has her acceptance of me somehow mellowed? She looks positively friendly.*

"What would you do if it left scars so you couldn't model?"

Krista shrugged with more indifference than she felt. She continued to pray for new guidance with her life, but she felt anything but confident about the future.

"I'd be disappointed...and afraid."

"Afraid?" Stella frowned with surprise.

"Insecurity," Krista confessed.

"You? If I had your looks I'd never feel insecure," Stella said with a small, hard laugh. "You should have my problems."

"You look fine to me," Krista said with a smile.

"I wished Jorden thought so."

Krista felt the tension. "Without my 'appearance' as you call it, I wouldn't have a job."

"And you'd miss all the excitement."

Krista toyed with the edge of the white linen napkin. "I'd miss the traveling, yes." But not Paul. How dare he use her to deliver lethal devices! She smiled ruefully. "But I've had more excitement recently since meeting you and Jorden than from all my fashion showings combined."

Stella watched her. "Be careful about Jorden. He'll never settle down. His job means as much to him as your modeling does to you. He's afraid of marriage. There'd be too much risk for his wife and children. He told me so. He has so many enemies."

Krista concentrated on the sparkling silverware. The slight resentment in Stella's voice over Jorden's attitude toward marriage told her a great deal. She could envision now what may have happened between them in the past. A good relationship must have developed. When Stella wanted to take it a step further, Jorden must have backed off.

"If you did lose your modeling position, with your looks you could find another easily enough."

"I know you didn't come all the way from Vienna to discuss my work. Your note said it was urgent."

"For Jorden, yes. I have important information from Tirzah. She's still in the Vienna hospital, poor dear, and wants to see him badly."

Krista wondered what Tirzah had revealed but didn't ask, knowing Stella wasn't likely to trust her enough to share it.

"He should return soon. If he doesn't walk here from Trudy's house, we can go back and wait for him there. When does your train leave for Austria?"

"Not for another hour. I've been here all day."

Krista didn't mention her visit to the safehouse. She suspected the Mossad would not want that floating about.

"After everything that's happened, I imagine you'll be leaving Gotthard Enterprises anyway."

She is right about that, Krista thought angrily. *And just what will happen to the family fashion and jewelry business if Paul goes to prison?*

"Did Jorden explain about the gold and jewelry taken from Auschwitz victims?"

Krista looked across the table at her grave face. "Yes. The idea is revolting, but we need to be fair. So far, there's no proof Gotthard Enterprises is involved."

"No, not yet," came Stella's abrupt tone. "There will be before all this has run its course. I'm not giving up on my great-grandfather's account either. That number is loitering somewhere in the back of Aunt Tirzah's memory. I'm sure of it. So is the name of the Gestapo agent who's responsible for extracting it from him by ruthless interrogation. We're almost sure it was Wilhelm von Buren."

If it wasn't Elsa's husband, then who was it? His age could be hidden. Nowadays, cosmetic surgery and face lifts could take twenty years off a person if they were in good health. The Gestapo agent who had carried out Eichmann's devilish work at Auschwitz might look only in his fifties!

Krista may have suspected something as dark and sinister all along, but she had left it buried in the back of her mind because it was so ugly. Stella's accusation shook her to the core. She drew in a breath, searching her gleaming brown eyes.

"It is too late about—Wilhelm. He's dead. He committed suicide," Krista said in a low voice. "They found him last night in his library. He shot himself with a German Luger."

Stella was visibly shocked. "Suicide?"

Krista nodded. "Horrible, isn't it? I hate to think where he is now—having rejected God's provision for forgiveness."

Stella looked offended. "Do you think it even matters after what he did? Are you trying to tell me that a just God could forgive a man like Wilhelm? A Gestapo agent? A murderer of thousands?"

Krista knew she must be careful in her answer. "I like to remember what Isaiah wrote before predicting the sufferings of Christ: 'Come now, and let us reason together,' says the Lord, 'Though your sins are like scarlet, they shall be as white as snow…' "

"But the prophet wrote that to Israel. And since then many Jews have suffered. What do the sufferings of Christ have to do with forgiving wicked men like Wilhelm?"

"Because ultimately, all sin is against God. He is the only one who can forgive it. And you are right, because God is just, He can't just dismiss it. That is where the suffering Messiah comes in. Only the Creator of all men was great enough to make possible the forgiveness of all men's sins."

Stella toyed with her glass. "It sounds like you're saying Jesus is like the Passover Lamb. I'll need to think about that. I've heard Jorden say much the same thing."

"Jorden!"

"Yes, he knows about it, but he hasn't decided yet." Stella glanced at her watch. "Look—that's not why I came. My train leaves in an hour. I've so much to tell you. I'm wondering how you'll take the news. I thought it would be shocking to a blue-eyed blond with Nordic looks, but..."

Krista found that she was squeezing her napkin tightly. "You don't need to worry about me. You see, I already know. At least I think I do." Krista surprised her by saying: "I also, have news, though I can't promise it's all true yet, not until I do some research at Davos. It concerns this ring and my mother, Anna Klossner."

Stella leaned forward, keeping her tone low, but her brown eyes were shining. "This is amazing. How did you find out about Davos?"

"I'd better not say now, not here." The name of Einer Seitz might reach someone's hearing. "Jorden can explain later. What of you, how did you know?"

"Aunt Tirzah explained things to me. She wanted both of us to know. Shall we get right to the point? We both have too much to say."

"Yes, no beating around the bush, as you Americans like to put it."

Stella's brown eyes gleamed and there was a faint rosy color to her pretty face. "No beating around the bush, then I'll say it—we're cousins. We have the same great-grand-parents from Vienna, Austria. They owned a tailor shop below their little flat in the Jewish sector. I'm living there now, researching our roots and tracing our history from Auschwitz to Switzerland to New York. Your mother, Anna Klossner, was once a two-year-old baby named Anna Cohen Harman."

"Then it's true!" A gush of emotion broke free from her heart and filled her eyes with tears. She had thought she was ready for this, but hearing it aloud, all doubts removed, she felt vulnerable and terribly shaken. The part that hurt so painfully was Auschwitz. All these years she had been hotly against anything hinting of anti-Semitism, but she had done so as a Gentile. Now she was suddenly Jewish. She could almost feel the past diabolical hatred of the Nazis as she envisioned all the documentary films of millions killed in gas chambers, left starving behind barbed wire—men, women, children, even babies—

Her eyes met Stella's. They stared at each other. Stella blinked hard too, but she must have understood the emotion Krista felt because Stella's eyes rimmed, and tears trickled down her cheeks. They hesitated, then reached at the same moment across the table, clasping hands, their cold fingers squeezing.

Cousins. Then the elderly lady in the hospital is my aunt too.

"Krista Harman Grendelmier. What a name! They won't want me modeling with a name that sounds like that!" She wanted to laugh, then cry. "Elsa and Wilhelm didn't even like Grendelmier. Elsa's going to positively flinch at Harman."

"They already knew who Anna was."

Krista's gaze swerved to hers. Could it be? And if they had known, why had they never said anything? What reason would there be for hiding her mother's identity?

"Tirzah is your grandmother's younger sister. When orders from the Gestapo came for the family to report at the station for Auschwitz, our great-grandparents had made plans for the family's escape into Switzerland. But Benjamin was called in for questioning a last time, and he never made it out of Vienna. Afterward he was too weak to reach the border. Their children left without them at his insistence. Judith was the eldest. She was your grandmother. Tirzah was fifteen, and Fritz was twelve. They traveled with another group who was under the guidance of a German minister, whose name I don't know. They reached the border of Switzerland near the Inn River, but were caught by Swiss guards and refused passage. They were sent back into Austria. Your grandparents, Judith and Reuben Harman, were caught by German soldiers and eventually sent to Auschwitz. As far as we know they never met up again with the others in the Cohen family."

Krista tried to hold down her emotions. "And Tirzah and Fritz?"

"They hid when the German soldiers arrested your grandparents. Eventually they crossed into Italy. They were caught again, but the Italians put them in separate slave labor camps and somehow, by God's grace, they both survived. In 1945 they met again in New York."

"How are we related, through Fritz?"

"Yes, he was my grandfather. He died two years ago. And he never talked about this! Like Aunt Tirzah, he lived with these repressed truths."

"What about Davos? How was it my mother was left as a two-year-old at the convent? And what about this ring?"

"Aunt Tirzah saw your grandmother plead with an International Red Cross nurse to take the baby. That was 1942. The nurse was Swiss."

"And her name?" Krista whispered.

"Inger Klossner. She was married to Doctor Gerhart Klossner who worked at the military hospital in Davos."

They actually kept my mother. They must have adopted her and managed to keep it a secret.

She looked quickly at Stella. "Elsa von Buren was Doctor Klossner's cousin. You say Elsa knew about my mother?"

"We fear she may have."

"Fear? Why?"

"Because Dr. Klossner and his wife could have been arrested or blackmailed for having a Jewish child. We think

Mrs. Klossner may have lost a child, and Anna's tragic situation touched her heart. Like Pharaoh's daughter with baby Moses, nurse Klossner was someone that God had prepared to take your mother."

"If she hadn't taken her, then I might not be here," Krista said, awed. "Because even the Red Cross followed the rigid Swiss laws about Jews and would have returned my mother to the brutal Nazis in Austria. She would never have married my father, Peter. Ah! The sovereignty of God! And the ring?" Krista asked.

"Tirzah says she saw her sister pin the ring inside Anna's diaper before turning her over to Nurse Klossner. She thought that even if the Swiss nurse didn't keep the baby someone else might, and have the ruby ring to help pay for milk."

Tears wet Krista's eyes again as she touched the ruby gently, remembering a young Jewish girl of twenty who had given up her child before returning to be taken captive by the Gestapo.

A tear splotched the napkin on the table and Krista absently used it to polish the ruby.

"How does the convent fit in?"

"I visited the Mother Superior. There are no records, but she remembers that a Red Cross nurse brought in a small child, a girl, and left her, promising to be back. She left the ring with her. True to her word, she returned, this time bringing her husband, Doctor Klossner. They said the child was of Swiss nationality. That there'd been some misunderstanding when Inger left her there, and they wanted her back. Doctor Klossner signed a form and the Sisters went along with the request. At the time, a concentration camp for Jews was being opened in Switzerland and all Jews who had crossed the borders were being rounded up. The Sisters probably knew the truth and were relieved to go along with the ruse. They must have returned the ring as well."

They sat for a long time, their food untouched and cold.

"We know some of the truth," Stella said. "There is more to learn at Davos."

"You'll go back?"

"Yes, eventually."

"I intend to go also. And Stella, I must visit you in Vienna and see our grandparents' home."

"I want you to come. Come with Jorden," she urged. "He has work to do there. Has he told you?"

"No, but I want to know about that too." She looked at her watch. "He and my Uncle Franz might be back by now. I had hoped Jorden would come and join us." She looked over her shoulder toward the door and saw only strangers.

Turning back to Stella, she whispered, "But why would Tirzah tell the story now?"

"Because of the Swiss Banking scandals, the U.S. Senate hearings initiated by Senator Alfonse D'Amato, and the tragic stories of other Holocaust survivors trying to claim Jewish assets. Jorden had begged her for the truth when he saw her last year in Queens. So did Avi. Tirzah knew I was writing a book about the family and decided to come and see me. All of it together, I suppose, stirred her conscience so that at seventy-six she wanted to preserve the memory of her loved ones whom the Nazis had murdered."

"Yes," Krista said tensely. "It's not the genocide alone that grieves me, but the grizzly, diabolical ways in which the Nazis went about killing us. Satan hates the Jews because God used them as a depository for His truth. He used them to write the Scriptures and to fulfill His promise to send the Messiah through the tribe of Judah."

Stella's eyes faltered. She started to say something more, then stopped.

Krista looked at her and saw her eyes dart away from someone behind them at one of the tables. Her face looked strained in the low lamplight.

"What is it?" Krista whispered.

"Nothing. Look, I've taken longer then I intended." She glanced again at her watch. "I've got to make a telephone call. I'll be in the lounge. Wait for me, will you?" She stood and left casually.

Had she seen someone that frightened her?

Krista's concerns mounted when Stella didn't return for five minutes. She looked subdued. Something had happened in that interval.

"I was beginning to worry."

"It's hard to get through the phone lines."

"To Vienna?"

"No, another friend…someone named Meir. I couldn't get him."

"Meir is in Vienna."

"Are you sure? How do you know?"

Krista told her about Ziv and how Paul and Elsa had gone there, probably to a museum to arrange a showing of her photography. "They didn't know about Wilhelm, but Ehrlich may have called them at their hotel by now. It's going to be hard on Elsa. She depended on Wilhelm for everything."

"I also called the hospital. Tirzah is asking for me. I'll need to go straight there instead of returning to Davos for more research. I'll leave the rest for you."

Krista worried about Stella's phone call. "You don't think the phone lines could be tapped, do you?"

"I don't know. I was very careful. I once worked with Meir and Jorden. But if Meir is in Vienna, that's good news for me. He's been a friend."

Krista was surprised. Stella worked with Mossad agents?

"Anyway, I won't risk trying to call him again until I get back. I'm not certain, but I think I'm being followed."

"I was afraid of that. What information do you have for Jorden?"

"A letter from Aunt Tirzah."

They looked at each other.

"I may need to break one of Jorden's own rules and trust you implicitly. You're one of us now, Krista. We have the same great-grandparents."

"Yes," she whispered, "don't worry so. I'm committed to our cause now. We'll work together to discover grandfather's account number. And we'll keep the old flat, too. You can give me the letter for Jorden."

Stella smiled. "Now you really sound like my cousin."

Krista reached for her bag, laying it on the table between her and Stella. A model could be expected to worry about her makeup. She took out her compact, opened the small mirror, powdered her nose and looked behind her at the table but couldn't see anyone out of the ordinary. Stella casually slid the letter beneath Krista's bag. When she drew her purse back, Aunt Tirzah's letter came with it.

A noisy group of skiers entered the restaurant and ordered food and drinks.

"This is the perfect exit," Stella murmured.

"See you in Vienna."

"Auf Wiedersehen."

"Shalom," murmured Krista.

Stella left through the side door. Krista remained at the table as if she wished to finish her tea. A few minutes later, with the letter safely inside her handbag, she left the Veltlinerkeller.

She walked briskly through the darkness toward Trudy's house. Within a few minutes St. Moritz proper was behind her as the trees thickened along the path. Wait. Someone was following her. She could hear footsteps in the snow, stopping when she stopped, then hurrying on as Krista quickened her pace. A novice. Someone of Jorden's caliber would never allow himself to be noticed until the moment he intended to act. She saw a chance and darted off behind some trees and stood silently, hardly daring to breathe as she heard the cautious footsteps rush to catch up.

Krista waited, pressing herself flat against the trunk of the tree, and peering over her left shoulder at the dark path. Whoever it was walked along the path, stopped undecidedly, then turned, glancing right and left. As he did, Krista saw the face. It was…a woman.

Ahead on the path, Cousin Henrich pushed through the tree branches and confronted the woman who had followed her.

"What are you doing?" came his low voice. "You followed me."

"Nein, I followed Krista…" Veena stood on the path, hands shoved in her coat pockets, looking glum.

"Krista! You risked showing yourself to her!" Henrich rebuked.

"She met with that American woman tonight in the Veltlinerkeller. I told you she was involved with the two Americans. I was right. We must talk to her. We must stop her before Herr Wilhelm arrives and discovers this."

"Leave Krista out of this. The American girl is gone now. She just boarded the train. You were a fool to come. Krista might have seen you. If she finds out the foolish thing you did this morning…"

"She will not. She does not suspect me. I had to do it, Henrich, I had to. Frau Elsa said she would take away everything we've worked for if I didn't get the book back."

"An evil woman. She always was. How did she know of the book?"

"Herr Paul did not find it in Franz's apartment. He said only Krista knew where it was. He was right. It was in her bag, but she came in sooner than I thought."

Henrich muttered something and grabbing her shoulders shook her fiercely. "You might have killed her."

"No, no, I did not hit her hard…"

"Quiet!"

Veena was sobbing softly into her hands. "She did not see me. She does not know. She thought I went to the grocery mart.

"Lower your voice."

"She's gone back to Trudy's house. She has something else—I know she does. We've got to get it before they arrive." She pounded his wide chest with her fist. "I have worked too hard to lose the lodge now!"

He shook her again. "Control yourself, Veena. It will be all right. If Krista has something from the American woman, it is probably meant for Keller. I will take care of it. Leave it to me. There is no need for anyone to be hurt. What did you do with the book?"

"It's in our room, under the mattress."

"Good, leave it there until they all arrive tomorrow. Go to your brother's house. I will handle all this."

"What are you going to do?" she hissed.

"Never mind. Just do as I say. I do not want Krista hurt, is that clear?"

Veena said something else, but her voice dropped into a sob. Henrich held her for a moment, patting her back as though consoling her, then directed her back to the path. "Go spend the night with Claude. I will handle Paul and the von Burens when they come."

Veena left slowly, her boots slushing through the snow.

Henrich stood there on the path then turned and walked back toward town. Krista held back behind the trees, then followed at a safe distance. He mumbled and grumbled to himself all the way, then walked toward the Bavarian-style beer garden.

Krista's heart ached with disappointment. Veena! She touched the back of her head and thought of the struggle with her assailant. Yes, Veena was strong enough, and if she had felt threatened by Paul going to Elsa about the lodge, she would do what she must to appease him. So Jorden was right. Paul had known she had the book.

Krista turned back toward Trudy's house. She had not gotten far when Veena's words repeated in her mind. "I hid it under the mattress." She ran on, her breath forming crystals in the icy air. The house was ahead, the lights still burning. She did not see the Audi hidden anywhere and suspected Jorden and Uncle Franz hadn't arrived yet. She rushed up the steps, opened the front door, and hurried inside, looking about. All was silent except for the tick of the clock.

Now was the opportunity to redeem herself. She would get the book back. Henrich would be in the beer garden trying to drown his woes, and Veena had gone on to her brother Claude's bungalow. Krista turned and left the house for the lodge. Jorden would be astonished when he returned and found out all that she had accomplished while he was away.

24

K rista entered the lodge through the kitchen door, her heart pounding. Voices and laughter came from the skiers gathered in the large front den where a fire burned cheerfully. The boy Johann came into the kitchen carrying a tray of empty glasses and began refilling them while his sister poured fondue into a bowl and arranged bread for dipping. They both looked at her as she entered the kitchen and greeted her.

Krista managed a smile and hurried into the warm den, glancing at the strangers who nodded her way. She greeted them in German, then went up the stairs.

Once in the hall she turned toward Henrich's room, paused tensely once to listen, then tapped lightly to make certain it was empty. Veena could have returned. The bedroom was still. She gripped the door handle, opened it quietly, and slipped inside. *Lord, be with me. You know I'm only taking back what is not Veena's. Don't let them catch me.*

Her trembling fingers found the light switch on the papered wall, and she flicked it on. A flood of golden light filled the pretty room, showing a familiar woven forest-green rug, crispy-white curtains, and a large iron bed that had been in Veena's German family since the 1800s. On the bed was a meticulously stitched white and green quilt. Krista rushed to the mattress and struggled to lift the heavy edge, holding it up while her free hand frantically searched for Elsa's book. It was there. Her spirits surged. Victory! She grabbed it, stuffed it inside the front of her dress, drew her coat tightly about her, straightened the quilt and fled the room, remembering to turn off the light and shut the door.

Down the hall she raced, coming to the flight of wooden steps covered with tweed rug. She slowed sedately and descended. Her face felt warm and she had to force herself to breathe normally. If only Henrich didn't come walking in through the front door, she would be safe. Even if he did, he wouldn't know she had just taken the book.

She crossed the den as the guests were discussing the difficulties of skiing the various slopes. Others anticipated the horse and dog races to begin on Saturday on the frozen lake. Krista nodded and smiled and passed through to the front door, closing it quietly. The cold night air felt good. Down the stone walkway she rushed, cut across the yard she had grown up playing in, and toward the distant road that ran between the lodge and Trudy's house on the wooded slope.

Once across the road among the Alpine trees, Krista ran toward the house, taking a different route to avoid Henrich or Veena.

She was glimpsing light glowing from the windows, when a shadowy form emerged from the trees, coming from the opposite direction. They nearly collided.

"Krista!" came the frustrated whisper.

She gasped with relief and fell into Jorden's arms, surrendering to his confident strength. For a brief moment he held her close, and she laid her cheek against his woolen jacket. "Is someone coming?" he asked quietly.

"No...I've come from the lodge..."

He drew her aside. She sensed the emotion stirring beneath his calm surface. "I asked you not to go the lodge. It might have been dangerous."

"I'm sorry, I had to go there."

"Where is Stella?"

"Gone—Jorden, listen, I overheard Henrich and Veena on the path a short while ago—Veena took Elsa's book—but I've gotten it back," she whispered jubilantly.

"What! You're serious?"

"Look!" She reached under her coat and pulled it out victoriously.

He plucked it from her hand and read the title in the dim starlight. She saw him smile in spite of himself. "All right, Beautiful. Brilliant work, even I must admit it."

Beautiful?! Hmm...She smiled. "Are you going to hire me to work as your partner from now on? After tonight, Gotthard Enterprises will be through with me. I'll be unemployed."

"Interesting. With a tempting offer like that I'd better do some serious consideration—about a lot of things. Especially after your noble performance earlier tonight."

Was he serious? Did he think she was noble? Her heart felt a warm, happy glow.

"Where was the book hidden?"

"Under their mattress."

"A unique hiding spot," he said with a wry smile in his voice. "Then it was Veena who attacked you this morning. I thought so."

"Did you? Well I didn't," she murmured with a frown. "She struck me terribly hard. I could almost think she enjoyed doing it."

"Unfortunately, she probably did. Jealousy and greed are nasty vices. They often eventually lead to anything, including murder. Did Stella come to Trudy's house?"

"No, Veena did, with Stella's message. I met Stella at the Veltlinerkeller. She had a letter for you from Aunt Tirzah. I have it safe in my handbag. She's gone now, back to Vienna. She thought someone might be following her."

"Following her and she left without telling me?"

She could see his worried frown. "I couldn't stop her. She behaved strangely."

She explained about Stella's reactions at the table and how she had tried to make a telephone call but couldn't get through.

"Did she say who she tried to contact?"

"Yes," she whispered, "Meir."

"I don't like this. Where's the letter?"

She opened her bag, fished it out, and handed it to him. "Stella also called the Vienna hospital and they told her Aunt Tirzah wasn't doing well, that she was asking for you and Stella, so she rushed back."

"I can't read this here." He slipped it inside his jacket pocket. "Let's go." He took her arm and they walked quickly to the house.

"Stella's already been to Davos," she told him.

"How did she know about it?"

"She said Tirzah told her much the same thing Seitz told me at the cathedral in Chur."

"We'll discuss that in the car. It's time we got out of here."

When they reached the front porch, Uncle Franz came from the shadows. "Everything all right, Krista dear?"

"Yes, Uncle Franz." She bounded up the steps and threw her arms around him. Did he know about Anna? That she hadn't been his blood sister and that her daughter was not his real niece? That idea was the one sorrow connected with her discovery. Her eyes searched his. One day soon they would need to have a long talk. She suspected he knew the truth already, that he may have known about Anna from his childhood, but now was not the time to bring it up.

She began to ask about Einer Seitz, but Franz gestured for silence. "It's not safe. Too many trees. Let's go inside."

Jorden shut the door behind them and leaned there reading Stella's letter while she and Uncle Franz said their good byes.

"Our bird is packed away with his guard," Franz told her. "We'll take it from here. The CIA agent will arrive soon. This is no longer your worry, Krista. I want you to go with Jorden. I assure you he can be fully trusted." He lowered his voice. "We had a long discussion in the car tonight on the way back from the safehouse. I feel he's very close to believing in Christ as the promised Messiah. You must be patient. Don't push him, but pray. Let the Spirit of God do the convicting. Jorden already knows the Scriptures. I was amazed at how much."

Krista also lowered her voice: "There's been a Christian lady who has been praying for him for five years."

"He's close to a decision. Rest the matter with the Lord. And now, I want you with Jorden. He'll protect you. I won't worry as much knowing the two of you are together."

"What of you, Uncle? Do you really think you should stay?"

"Neither Paul nor Wilhelm suspect me and I've a man from Interpol coming from Geneva by way of France. He'll be here tomorrow. The American agent will also come. He'll handle the matter of getting Seitz to South America." He smiled. "There, you see? Not a thing to worry about."

Krista shook her head sadly. "You can't fool me that easily. There is plenty to worry about, but our God is great."

He looked pleased, and she kissed his cheek.

Jorden had struck a match to burn Stella's letter and was watching it disintegrate when Franz turned to him. "All set?"

A glance passed between him and Franz. "Yes. Ready, Krista?" Jorden asked.

She wasn't happy about leaving Franz behind, but both men seemed anxious for her to be off. Things had taken longer than expected.

Jorden walked up and was quietly explaining to Franz about Henrich and Veena. Krista was afraid that Franz would be overly grieved, but he didn't look surprised.

"I've thought Paul could be using them. He's been threatening to have Elsa take away the lodge. Naturally they would react to this fear. Henrich has not succeeded in life as he once expected, and Veena is the kind of woman that will never let him forget it. She resents so many things, the need for her to work, her appearance, that she never had children. She's bitter. Trials can have one of two effects upon us: they can melt or harden hearts. Veena has hardened."

Jorden watched him, and Krista saw respect in his face for Franz. "I think you're right," he said. "Isn't there a verse in Hebrews that says, "Today, if you will hear His voice, do not harden your hearts?"

"Yes. So you've also been reading the New Testament?"

"I've worked my way through it once and am now reading Matthew for the second time."

Krista looked at him, and her heart felt a new confidence.

"About Veena," Franz was saying, "I never thought she could be dangerous. After attacking Krista, I am no longer sure."

"She panicked," Krista hastened, hoping Veena would not be punished. "Can't we just let this ugly matter go?" She looked from Uncle Franz to Jorden and saw the two men exchange glances, but they did not reveal their thoughts on the matter.

"I'll handle her and Henrich," Franz soothed. "He's actually a decent man," he told Jorden. "He cares about Krista, but he's been intimidated by Paul and frightened by someone in the von Buren family."

"Just be careful anyway."

"I'll be alert."

"You know how to reach me if you need a backup," Jorden said.

"I have the number memorized. Take care." He touched his shoulder. "Let's make a date for the three of us to meet together again in Zurich. My apartment. We'll celebrate."

"I'll be there."

Krista hugged Franz again, then turned away as Jorden opened the door for her to pass through.

Outside on the porch she heard Franz slide the bolt lock. Jorden's confident look encouraged her. They came down the steps and walked across the yard toward St. Moritz proper.

Lord, please protect Uncle Franz. And may it be as he suggested, that we all meet again together in a happier time. And You know the desire of my heart. If possible, please bring it to pass. That we may honor You all the more with our lives.

They walked in silence through the trees until they came out onto the road toward town. Once they were in the open and away from being overheard, she whispered: "What if we're followed? Or are we safe now because Wilhelm is dead?"

He slipped an arm about her and drew her toward his side for safety. She knew he was armed and that he was especially alert as they walked along. "I wish it were so easy."

Krista lapsed into silence. She was surprised when their walk brought them to the train station rather than the car. She was even more surprised when Jorden told her in a barely audible voice they would not be going to Davos.

"But I thought…" Krista began, until a gentle squeeze of her arm silenced her. "Voices carry. We'll talk later."

Krista waited a few feet away as he bought their passage. When he turned to her, he opened his hand to show her the ticket destination. Back to Zurich, and from Zurich to Vienna. She looked at him, wondering, but remained silent as they walked briskly toward the train.

She had thought they would go first to Davos, but Wilhelm's death and new suspicions must have altered his immediate plans. He would naturally wish to talk things over with Avi, and there was still the message Aunt Tirzah had written him in the letter he'd burned at Trudy's house.

They boarded a few minutes later and Jorden ushered her through the minor confusion of the corridors into a cramped, overheated sitting compartment with soiled glass windows and short curtains drawn wide open. He drew them shut at once and surprised her by making a quick but through search as if he expected to find something unsavory.

"Safe?" she asked when he turned toward her.

"For the moment." He smiled briefly, as he took her bag and put it up on the rack.

"It's horribly stuffy in here, can't we open a window?"

"Sorry, no. Voices carry here as well. Anyone could walk by." He helped her slip out of her coat, hanging it on the peg as he scanned her. "Nice dress," he commented. She smiled to herself, wondering that in such a moment he would even notice. He removed his coat, but kept on his dark suit jacket. She thought she knew why—his leather shoulder holster. She pushed her long hair back from her shoulder and sank with relief into the leather seat next to the window. Jorden stood at the compartment door glancing out the windows.

"Excuse me a moment." He stepped out, closing the rattling door behind him. Krista craned her head to see what he was doing. He was leaning there, silently discouraging passengers who might wish to join them by refusing to budge. He had opened a large map of Austria, giving the impression to anyone walking by that he was a rude tourist on holiday.

He behaves as though he hasn't a care in the world, Krista thought, *yet he's been without sleep and feels he's back to square one in his search for his Gestapo agent. No wonder I've fallen in love with him.*

The train began to move slowly at first. Soon the wheels were clacking over the track and the cars were rumbling. A delightful but mournful whistle echoed through the mountains as Jorden opened the compartment door and joined her on the leather seat. St. Moritz was left behind, its distant lights turning into pinpricks of gold in the snow-chilled darkness. The moon was still beautiful, quietly shedding its white light. As the track started a gradual climb, she could look out the window and see dramatic mountain peaks, white-blanketed valleys with little hamlets, and a scattering of weathered wood-and-stucco chalets.

The train chugged up the curving forest track over scores of bridges with deep drops, the rivers beneath partly frozen and looking like silver ribbons. The sound of the train echoed as they passed through many dark tunnels, coming out on the mountainous ridges, met by still more snowy peaks rimmed with Alpine trees.

Jorden casually reached into his jacket and slid out Elsa von Buren's out-of-print book of photography. Krista glanced at it, then toward the windows with drawn curtains. Unfortunately they had no locks.

"This should occupy us for the next hour or two," he commented, his voice dropping naturally. There was enough background noise to keep anyone in the corridor from hearing, and anyone who didn't know better would think he was talking about the scenery. "This is the only thing I have left that may lead me back on the path."

Krista felt a small sense of pride that she'd been able to recover it from Veena.

"What if it doesn't give us any direction?"

"Then the bump on your pretty head was all for nothing," he said heartlessly. "My guess is, Paul thinks it was very much worth the risk of scaring Veena into getting it back."

Jorden looked up at the small light. "If nothing else we'll get eye strain."

He studied the book jacket first. Krista saw nothing but Elsa's name written in small block letters at the bottom. The title was sprawled in fading black letters against a dull gray background. *Glories of the Fatherland.*

376 LINDA CHAIKIN

"Doesn't look very glorious to me," Krista commented.

Jorden opened the book. "Looks like an all-night ordeal. Can you stay awake? You may notice something about a member of your Swiss clan whom I don't."

Swiss clan? "I know who I am. I think you do too."

"Stella told you?"

"Yes. She and I are cousins all right. My mother was Jewish. Her given name was Anna Cohen."

Jorden reached over and lifted a strand of pale, shimmering hair. "Your papa's hair and eyes. You're like my aunt. My family came from France. Her looks saved her from being turned over to the Nazis."

Krista moved closer beside him and looked at the book in his hands. She stifled a yawn as though bored. "Page one," she murmured.

"Too cozy," he said. "This is the wrong time to lose my concentration. You'd better scoot back where you came from."

She turned her head slowly and looked at him. All hope of serious study was lost this time. He stared back. She leaned toward him. His arms went around her tightly and their lips met.

The compartment door opened. Krista stared, shocked at the dour-faced elderly woman who had poked her head in.

Jorden had stood, hand inside the front of his jacket, but left it there. He and the startled woman looked at each other.

"Entschuldigen Sie!" the woman breathed and shut the door firmly behind her.

"You're excused," he said dryly.

Krista giggled with a release of emotion.

Jorden looked at her, his brow lifted. She sobered quickly and stood, smoothing her hair. She picked up her handbag. "While you study the photographs I'm going to powder my nose," she said with a tone of dignity.

He didn't look pleased about her going off alone, but didn't stop her as she opened the compartment door. "I'll bring you back some tea. Cream and sugar?"

"Coffee," he corrected with a smile. "Black."

Their eyes lingered as she stepped into the corridor, and closed the door behind her, releasing a deep breath. *Krista Harman Grendelmier, you are in love.*

Wearing a dreamy smile, she walked down the passageway past numerous small compartments. Krista Keller, how did that sound? She liked it very much.

25

The wind rushed past the train window. Jorden opened Elsa's book to the first page and read:

> *Our task is to give the dictator, when he comes, a people ready for him!*
>
> Adolf Hitler,
> 4 May Speech

Jorden thought it fitting quote for her book of propaganda. He turned the next page and saw her faded autograph, "Elsa Klossner." Below, sprawled in smudged ink: "For you, beloved Karl. Always, Elsa."

"Karl." He came alert. The Gestapo agent he was searching for? He thought back, trying to place the name among the hundreds he had researched in connection with von Buren but came up against a brick wall. He'd begin a new search as soon as he arrived in Vienna. At least he now had a name he could offer Avi. But Karl *who?*

Next, he studied the index page listing places and events in Vienna and Berlin where the photographs had been taken. Nothing of interest. Nothing on Karl. He leafed through the fading black and white pictures showing parades of goose-stepping German soldiers saluting a prideful Hitler. More pictures of Hitler making early speeches at Nazi gatherings. There were the typical elaborate militaristic poses of the dictator with his willing henchmen, Hermann Goering and Adolf Eichmann. Yet Jorden found little that was new. Nothing but the name Karl. What he needed was something definite that connected Karl to the Geheime Staatspolizei, the Reich Main Security Office in Vienna, the Nazi ministry that had been set up by the Gestapo to register Jewish property. If he could find an officer with the name of Karl who had worked there in Vienna, he might have the man who had interrogated Benjamin Cohen for the number of his Swiss Bank account.

Except for the mysterious name Karl, Jorden was beginning to think he had run into another dead end. His instincts, however, insisted there was something he was overlooking. Paul wouldn't have gone to such trouble to threaten Veena into getting Elsa's book away from Krista if it did not pose a threat to him.

For a second time he went over each black and white photo with a magnifier. The time-worn pictures were deteriorating, some were blurred beyond recognition. He studied one of the better photos. It was a picture of an elderly Jew in a long black coat with a white beard being taken into custody by police as early as 1934 when there was a boycott of Jewish doctors. He studied the faces of the soldiers. Wilhelm? There was a sign nailed to a physician's door: "Take Note: Jew. Visiting Forbidden."

He glanced at another photo of the Fuhrer as animal-lover, a 1934 postcard showing him feeding two small deer. How touching.

Jorden slowly continued turning pages, noting the smiling faces of Goering, Himmler, and Eichmann. He felt angry. He wondered if they were smiling now. What was it Eichmann had said in '45 as the war ended? Something like: "Even though we had lost the war I can jump into my grave laughing, knowing I killed six million Jews."

Jorden felt his hatred boil up. He began to hope there was a hell after all. He remembered what he had read in the book called Revelation. The unbelieving dead, great and small, stood before a great white throne. The unbelieving were judged out of the things written in the books. And every person whose name was not written in the Lamb's Book of Life was cast into the Lake of Fire. While on Earth, Eichmann had been an atheist, but he knew better now.

I'd hate to be in Eichmann's shoes, explaining the "final solution" to Jesus—the King of the Jews—at the great white throne.

Jorden stopped suddenly. Like a flash of light a voice seemed to say, "True, but what about you? What about your sins?"

Mine!?

"In the sight of a holy God you too are guilty of breaking the Mosaic Law. Have you kept all Ten Commandments perfectly, twenty-four hours a day, seven days a week, three hundred and sixty-five days a year, year in and year out?"

No.

"Then you let me take care of men like Eichmann. You make certain of your own soul, otherwise you too will stand before the throne and be judged by what is written in the books. But if you turn to Me, and accept My substitutionary death for you on the cross, I will wash away your sins. Like Jacob, your name will be changed to a prince with God. You will be a true son of Israel, and I, your true Father."

Jorden heard the train wheels clicking, the wind whistling. The words echoed in his mind. He almost looked around the compartment to see who had entered the door without his realizing.

My conscience, he thought.

He knew it was more than that.

What had Saul of Tarsus said on the Damascus Road on his route to persecute Christians? "Who are you, Lord?" Jorden already knew His name; it was Jesus, Yeshua in Hebrew.

He had just called Jesus "Lord." He knew enough about the Scriptures to realize that to own Jesus as Lord meant that he also acknowledged Jesus as the true Passover Lamb, the one true offering to atone for sin. Why else would Jesus have died on the cross at Passover time?

He could hear Lydia's voice praying for him as she often did. The elderly Christian lady whose husband had survived Birkenau was talking with the Lord she knew so well, saying: "Now, dear Lord Jesus, You know my adopted boy, Jorden. I want him to know and serve You, to come to understand just how wonderful You are. Show him that You're the Lamb of God who takes away the sin of the world, just as John the Baptist declared at the Jordan River. And just as the angel said to Mary, 'You shall call his name Jesus, for he shall save his people from their sins.' "

Savior and Lord, Lamb of God, King of Israel, Head of the true Church made up of both Jews and Gentiles. What else had Saul said on the Damascus road? "Lord, what will You have me to do?"

"This is the work of God, that you believe in Him whom He has sent...whoever lives and believes in me shall never die. Do you believe this?"

Yes, Lord, I believe that You are the Christ that should come into the world.

Hope filtered through the train window like the rays of the moonlight. In the midst of assassins, death, and the ravages of sin, which swept like tumultuous waves over the earth, if Jesus Christ was alive at the right hand of God, if Jesus had conquered sin, the grave, and hell, if He had a future for Israel and a plan for the world, then all was not lost.

Jorden felt no tidal wave of emotion, only conviction. He must act on the truth.

Lord Jesus, I believe You are the promised Messiah, and I accept You as my Savior and King.

Peace filled his mind and spirit, along with a joy he had not previously known. Peace with the holy God—through His beloved Son! Peace with God—at last.

26

Jorden went through the photographs a final time, examining each page. Nothing. He snapped the book shut and sat looking at the front of the dust jacket. For an out-of-print book the jacket was in excellent condition. Wait a minute—the jacket was a more recent addition! He sat up. He should have noticed at once, but his mind had been set upon the inside photographs, perhaps a wrong assumption.

He took out a pocket knife and loosened the heavy clear tape that held the jacket to the hardcover. A moment later he had his answer.

Jorden removed a small photo taped to the inside back cover. He drew out his magnifier again. A young, smiling Elsa Klossner was standing to the side of a group of SS officers with Goering in the center. On the back was written in Elsa's hand: "Elsa with Field Marshal Hermann Goering, Karl, and Conrad. June, '39, Berlin."

An unsmiling man, possibly Conrad, but known as Wilhelm von Buren stood a little off to the right of Elsa, but his uniform was not like the infamous SS. He appeared to be an unassuming aide, holding what might have been a brief-case, perhaps serving on the staff of one of the other SS offi-cers.

The man whom Krista had always known as Wilhelm von Buren had assumed that identity at Davos hospital but was previously known as Conrad.

What was strange about this photo? Jorden squinted at it thoughtfully. Conrad was Wilhelm he decided, but he looked unobtrusive. Unimportant was the better word. Although Elsa had been married to him all these years in Zurich, she was not standing beside him in the snapshot. She stood beside an SS officer whose face was in shadow beneath a duck-billed hat. It had to be Karl.

Jorden's excitement grew. He focused the magnifier on the man's face but to no avail. He checked every centimeter of his uniform, down to his boots, his hands, hoping for something that would dispel the shadows surrounding his identity.

Lack of sleep had caused a dull headache that nagged between his eyes. *Relax*, he told himself. *You've got a name now. You've got a photo to go by, poor as it is. Patience. Turn it over to the Mossad when you see Avi in Vienna. Just a few short hours now. Our colleagues in the Mossad can occasionally bring out contrast in a weak photograph. Somehow Karl's identity will eventually be revealed.*

Finally he closed the book and leaned his head back against the leather seat and listened to sounds that echoed through the mountain peaks. Soon they would be nearing the Austrian border.

Suddenly he came awake. *Krista!* He sat up. He looked at his watch. Forty-five minutes had lapsed! He was on his feet, slipping the small book back beneath his shirt and reaching for the compartment door. As he did so, she opened it and came in carrying two cups of coffee and a paper bag. "Sorry it took so long."

She smiled as she set the coffee and paper bag down on the small table. "I met an old German minister who had insomnia. We talked and he even prayed for us, speaking our names before the throne of grace." Her eyes reflected an inner confidence and she said, "He asked that your soul would belong to God forever."

"Your prayers and his have been answered," Jorden said quietly.

She looked at him curiously, with growing anticipation, then excitement.

"Jorden, you mean…?"

"Yes. I told you tonight I believed in God and the Old Testament Scriptures."

"Yes," she said softly, almost breathlessly, her eyes searching his.

"I'm now convinced Isaiah 53 and Psalm 22 speak clearly and uniquely of Jesus as the suffering Messiah, Israel's redeemer for all mankind. I have tonight acknowledged and trusted Him as my savior and Lord."

Krista stood without moving, then the glow in her eyes turned to a smile that reached out and touched his heart.

"Jorden!" She came toward him, tears wetting her eyes. He held her, kissing her lightly on the forehead, then for a long, sweet minute on her lips, convincing her he had made another decision as well…that their relationship had just begun.

A minute later, their gaze met longingly. "I'm in love with you, Krista," he said softly. "But my work would be a danger to our relationship, constantly troubling you wherever we went, wherever we lived. We would never be safe from terrorists. You would never be safe. Not in Israel, not in Dallas, not in Zurich."

"We will be as safe as God intends us to be. I am not afraid." She drew his head down toward hers and kissed him again. "You are worth the risk."

He held her closely in silence, then: "I'd better turn you loose…"

She drew away, smiling happily, and sank to the leather seat. She lifted the sack from the small table, still breathless.

"We celebrate finding each other on the bumpy road of life! Look, sandwiches and coffee. What would you prefer, sausage and egg or cheese and bacon?"

"I can see this is a real celebration," he said. "I'll give you first choice."

She took the sausage and egg, lifted her paper cup, and they toasted with a smile.

"To our happy beginning," she said.

"To Monday's Child," he said softly. "Fair of face, and still fairer of heart, she has won mine!"

Jorden had forgotten about sleep and his head no longer ached. What he needed now were answers about Karl. His voice dropped, "Ever heard of this name?" He turned to the dedication page where Elsa had written her inscription to her beloved Karl. Jorden watched her puzzled expression until she whispered "No, who is he?"

Jorden handed her the photograph. "This was taped to the back inside cover. If Elsa hadn't changed the dust jacket to conceal it, I may not have discovered the picture."

He waited to see what her reaction would be without his suggestions. "Recognize anyone?" he asked briefly.

"Elsa, of course."

Jorden remained silent.

She frowned, then caught her breath.

"Why that's Paul's uncle, Josef Gotthard."

Jorden frowned. He thought she'd misidentified Wilhelm. "That's the man who was known as Wilhelm von Buren. His real name was Conrad."

"I recognize Wilhelm," she whispered. "But that's Paul's uncle, Josef Gotthard, beside Elsa."

"Gotthard?"

She looked at him anxiously. "Though I can't see his face, look at the way he holds his arm. It's always been a little stiff. Paul told me he injured it in a skiing accident many years ago."

Krista pondered anew, looking uneasy. "Jorden, I don't know…maybe I'm wrong. I wouldn't want you to rush to any conclusion."

Jorden leaned against the door, frowning to himself. He tried to recall everything he knew about Gotthard, and realized that the Mossad had all but ignored Josef while centering their research on von Buren. No wonder they had not come up with anything solid. Conrad, in the guise of von Buren, had not been in the SS. His front had succeeded in protecting Karl—now Josef Gotthard.

"Flanders was looking into more than Gotthard Enterprises. He'd just returned from researching the diamond mine in South Africa. He may have gotten close to discovering Josef's identity. That could be the reason for the assassination in Liechtenstein."

"Yes! I remember now. I didn't pay much attention at the time, but Josef was standing with Paul when I mentioned Liechtenstein. I remember the way Paul turned and looked at Josef. The exchange between them was demeaning to me. 'You see?' he seemed to say, 'Contrary to what you thought, she is useful.'"

Jorden restrained his anger. "Josef's attitude doesn't surprise me. I doubt if his anti-Semitism has waned since the war. People's bigotries rarely change unless they undergo a spiritual change. Gotthard's had none. He's still masterminding new terror, now in the Middle East instead of Vienna and Berlin. Don't forget he knows who you really are. It was probably Gotthard who forced Doctor Klossner to help him at Davos by threatening to betray his secret about keeping a Jewish child."

He walked over to her and held her in his arms. "I'm just sorry you were there that night. Gotthard already knew about Flanders, so learning we were to meet in Liechtenstein gave him the opportunity to move against us. It's not your fault, darling. If not Liechtenstein, Gotthard would have used another time and place to strike."

"When Josef arrived that night Paul looked surprised and afraid. Come to think of it, Paul always seemed a little afraid of his uncle."

"Paul was afraid that night with good reason. He had failed in the attack at Hans Fischer's house. I don't think Josef was ready to move yet. He wanted Lars to watch me for a while to discover my intentions. But Paul moved too quickly and without Josef's knowledge. One of his agents was dead. I was alerted to the fact they knew about me, and the Zurich police would begin poking about. It turned out badly for them.

"I'm thinking Elsa, Wilhelm, and Josef were in this deception together after the war. That Elsa may not even have been married to Wilhelm but to Josef. It certainly fooled their enemies. Misinformation is the foundation of espionage. The ruse kept us searching in the wrong files. What better masquerade than to have Elsa apparently married to Wilhelm?"

"What about Ehrlich?"

"I think he is Wilhelm's son from some affair in Berlin. If anyone is innocent, it's likely to be Ehrlich."

"There were times when I thought Elsa behaved strangely around Josef. That night when he arrived unexpectedly, Josef was caustic with her and Wilhelm. He caught them together in Wilhelm's library listening to music. He said he hoped he wasn't interrupting their pleasant evening together."

"I imagine the triangle had its difficult times through the years. If this proves true, then Paul is most likely Josef's grandson, not his nephew. It's too bad I don't have a picture of Josef when he was young. We may discover a marked resemblance between grandfather and grandson."

"And Paul's parents?"

"There's no reason why their deaths couldn't be just as he told you, but his father or mother was Josef and Elsa's child."

Krista was thoughtful. "That would also account for Paul's dedication to Elsa. She's his grandmother." She looked at him. "You said Paul's with her now in Vienna."

"Yes, it all begins to fit. I wondered why he would run off to Vienna to help Elsa with the museum showing instead of coming as planned to St. Moritz. Paul knew you had his grandmother's book and ordered Veena to get it or lose the lodge. He also must have suspected that Seitz had come to St. Moritz, especially if he or Josef had wanted to assassinate Seitz at Chur. Yet he's gone off with Elsa to Vienna to show her World War II photography."

"Josef," she murmured in a tone of amazement. "The Gestapo agent who cruelly interrogated my great-grandfather and multitudes of others. I can hardly fathom it. And all these years I've been right among them. It's frightening. I knew so little about Paul's so-called 'uncle.' "

"He was illusive, that fits. He was gone much of the time, wasn't he?"

"Yes, trips to South Africa, Europe, everywhere."

"Or so they wanted everyone to believe. More than likely he was in his own mansion in Zurich, working on his schemes. Ziv found a snapshot of my director on Wilhelm's body. There may be a plan for Lars to assassinate him."

"Oh no, you don't think...and Paul is in Vienna, with Elsa."

"Yes, I do think so. Ziv has warned Meir, who is there by now. But where is 'dear' Uncle Josef?"

Krista sank back to the seat, grimacing. "That night when I thought Wilhelm came to my room? Maybe it was Josef."

Sitting there smoking, listening to German martial music. Who could know what he may have had on his mind. He might have considered a "final solution" for Krista. Elsa might have intervened, or even Paul. Jorden believed Paul had ordered Veena to get the book from her, but probably hadn't realized what Veena would do.

He checked the time. They would arrive in Austria by dawn. He kept worrying about Stella, alone in the Cohen flat, and the old woman, Tirzah, also alone in the Vienna hospital.

It may have been Josef who had ordered Wilhelm's murder. Had he turned on him at this late date for some reason? Over the banking scandal maybe. Something may have developed that threatened the reputation of his son, Ehrlich.

"That would explain almost everything, wouldn't it," Krista said into the silence. "He used Wilhelm as a front, but all the time he was the one who was really in control. The von Buren wealth, the mines, the fashion and jewelry business—all sponsored by money stolen from death camp victims."

Jorden replaced the book's dust jacket. Why had she placed the photograph here? How had the book fallen into the hands of Rhinefelden? And why had Paul not tried to remove the picture before hiding the book at Franz's place? Perhaps he hadn't known about it. Krista had said that Elsa had been trying to hide her photos to keep them from disappearing. She may not have told anyone why she was worried about the book. Or perhaps Paul feared the dark nature of his Nazi grandfather and intended to use the photo as a leverage, just to make certain everything was left to him in the end?

Jorden took out the snapshot taken within the last few weeks showing him and Avi at the Viennese cafe. Disturbing. Who had taken this picture, Lars?

He looked at Krista, her head back and her eyes closed. Asleep. He was troubled. Lars would give anything to know how he felt about her. He probably had already seen them together.

He hoped Kurt Branden had met with Franz by now. The sooner the CIA had Seitz, the sooner Ziv would start for Vienna. He was going to need both him and Meir, and maybe even Hans Fischer.

Jorden made up his mind. He couldn't leave Krista unguarded in Vienna even for a short time. Somehow he knew that Lars was just out of sight. *If I didn't have so much on my mind to think about. If I just had Lars, but there was Avi to worry about, Karl and Paul. And to be at my best I need some sleep.*

Jorden sat down facing the door, his head back against the seat and his feet resting on the table. With his hand near his revolver he closed his eyes and listened to the sounds of the train rushing toward Zurich.

27

The train arrived in Zurich at the Hauptbahnhoff. Jorden surprised Krista by ushering her into a waiting taxi instead of boarding another train for Vienna.

"But I thought..." she began.

Seated in the taxi, he put an arm around her and leaned closer as if he were going to kiss her. He dropped his voice. "We're being followed."

"You saw him on the train?" she whispered.

"He passed our compartment just before we arrived here."

"Lars?"

"No. I'm sure he's already in Vienna, but this guy works with him. I noticed him yesterday at the ski lift."

She remembered now. "The man with the newspaper?"

"He's probably reporting our whereabouts now."

She was worrying about it when he kissed her gently, then abruptly directed the taxi driver to the side of the street. He handed the stunned driver some money and scrambled out of the back seat, pulling Krista with him.

"We're on the run again," he said, flipping the door shut. "How are those shoes for sprinting?"

"They'll do."

"Good. Let's go."

The next few minutes were hectic as he rushed her through a maze of differing directions until at last he hailed another taxi. He asked to be brought to the University, but stopped the driver a block away. Within fifteen minutes they arrived at Franz's apartment.

They walked briskly across the quadrangle toward the familiar two-story lodge where the graystone apartment waited on the ground floor. Jorden used a key Franz had given him in St. Moritz.

"I need to make a few phone calls. By now the phone in my room at the Savoy could be tapped. Franz has a second phone line that's relatively safe. It's checked frequently by Interpol."

They entered the apartment, and Jorden switched on the lamps. "Lock the door, Krista," and wasting no time he headed for an office in the back.

Despite danger, the familiar apartment made her feel easier. It seemed as if nothing could go wrong here. She could almost see Franz walking out of the study to greet her.

Krista followed Jorden into her uncle's study, keeping her long coat on. The rooms were cold. Jorden rolled the top back on the large old-fashioned secretary desk. He used a small key in a second lock on a smaller wooden drawer. She watched, curiously, as he lifted out a small white telephone and began to punch in numbers.

To think that Uncle Franz had worked for Interpol for years, cooperating with the CIA and sometimes even the Mossad, and she hadn't known it!

Krista sat down on the arm of a ponderous chair, trying to relax. Jorden was waiting for his call to Vienna to go through. He was removing his tie and gesturing for her to open his one small suitcase he had left on the opposite chair. She found a white shirt still in its package and new dark trousers. Was this why he always looked so neat? When in a hurry, he apparently didn't take time packing and instead just purchased what he needed at his destinations.

"Extravagant."

He smiled. "I'm ready for a hot shower. While you're putting my things out will you be a doll and make some coffee?"

She curtsied. "Yes, anything I can do to help."

His dark eyes flickered. "You'll make the perfect wife."

She looked at him. His call came through.

"It's Keller."

She lingered at the doorway, listening. Avi said something.

"Zurich," Jorden replied. "At Klossner's place...yes, she's with me. You're going to love her. You may have a husband and wife team before long."

Krista blew him a kiss.

"What?" he asked Avi. "Yes, Seitz is stashed away, waiting for Branden to arrive at the safehouse. He should be there by now." Jorden looked surprised by something. "Seitz did what? Contacted the von Buren's chauffeur? When? Before he came to St. Moritz? About what? Interesting...no, I haven't any idea and Seitz didn't mention it. We'd better tell Franz. He can pass that on to Branden. Yes, Ziv stayed to guard Seitz, but I don't expect any trouble there. It's Vienna I'm worried about. Lars may be there. Did Meir explain about the snapshot of you at the cafe? I'm afraid Lars is planning an assassination."

Avi said something else and Jorden frowned. "Ziv found the picture on von Buren's body. Lars must have taken that snapshot. Who's there with you? By yourself! Avi, I know Lars—look, get someone there with you, will you? There must be someone in Vienna the CIA can spare. What! You trust the Austrian police to protect you! Are you kidding!"

Jorden's frown deepened. "I should know where you're at—just in case." He listened, writing it down. "Got it. I'm on my way."

Avi must have joked about something because Jorden smiled. "Dead duck or not, I've got news on our Gestapo agent. No, it wasn't von Buren, Josef Gotthard. His real name is Karl. Yes, I'd almost stake my life on it. I thought that would change your mind. Do us a favor will you? Don't leave the safehouse."

He hung up. Krista saw him memorize the address Avi had given him, then burn the scrap of paper. Krista, her anxiety growing, went to lay out towels in her uncle's bathroom, then she went to the kitchen to make the coffee. If Avi wasn't safe, what about Stella? Had Meir arrived to be with her at the flat?

She was deep in thought when Jorden returned. In less than ten minutes he had showered, shaved, and changed into fresh clothes.

"That was fast."

"Survival techniques," he said with a smile as he took the cup of coffee she handed him. "There's a flight to Vienna in forty minutes."

"Were you able to call Stella?" she asked, searching his eyes.

"No, she hasn't arrived yet."

"But she should have arrived in Zurich before us."

He finished his coffee. "She may have taken the train to Vienna. It's ten hours."

He didn't believe that. Jorden was trying to keep her from worrying, but she could see he was as anxious about Stella as she was.

"She was anxious to get back to see Aunt Tirzah. I would have expected her to fly."

"We can't do a thing about it now. When we can't change things, honey, we don't waste emotional energy fretting. It won't help. Let's wait until we get there. Our concerns may be for nothing." He glanced about. "Where's your coat?"

"On the chair," she said dully.

He helped her into it and walked with her toward the door. Before they went out, he drew her into his arms and kissed her with deep satisfaction.

Soon they arrived at Kloten airport and boarded the flight for Vienna, Austria.

The old city was just as Krista remembered, cool and gray, with an overcast sky that wet everything with a mizzling rain. Yet Vienna would never be the same now that she knew the truth about her Jewish roots. Her mother had been born here, her grandparents and great-grandparents had been rounded up and sent to Auschwitz-Birkenau. The Vienna that had lived in her imagination when she had listened to the beautiful music of Johann Strauss had become a sad and mournful refrain. Perhaps one day she would no longer feel this strain in her heart, but only Christ could help her forgive and let go of the past.

Now, as she walked with Jorden along the Negerlegasse in the Second District, her tensions grew like a brewing storm. After Hitler's army had marched into Austria, the

Nazis forced the Jews throughout the city into the Second District, turning it into a ghetto. Hitler had wanted the Jews rounded up and confined to one area so that when the orders came to deport them to the death camps they would be trapped. Every child of Abraham, Isaac, and Jacob had to register, sign over their property and businesses, and display a yellow star in public. Naturally this made them easy targets for the Nazi Brown Shirts to persecute on the streets when they had to go out in public.

Krista's tensions grew taut as the sound of their footsteps echoed on the narrow cobblestone street, small and crowded with its 19th-century tenement buildings packed closely together.

They passed old shops with small flats above. The faces of the owners were different, so were the names on the shops. She noticed that none of the names were Jewish anymore.

"This is it," Jorden told her, stopping outside a small Viennese cafe that had once been her great-grandfather's tailor shop. The cafe was closed, but above it, in the small flat, a light burned in the window.

"Ready?" he asked quietly.

Krista nodded, emotion welling up inside her heart.

Jorden drew her to a side door that opened into a small vestibule with two flights of narrow stairs. He went ahead of her protectively, his right hand in his jacket pocket. Once outside the door, he motioned her to the side. He knocked three sharp raps. A minute must have passed before it opened a few inches, then swung wide. Meir stood there, replacing his revolver. Krista noted his strained expression as she entered the flat, Jorden following. Meir closed and locked the door again.

Krista stood in silence looking around the small drab rooms. The furniture was old and worn, and the curtains on the window facing Negerlegasse looked as if they might have hung there for thirty years. Her first reaction was a hollow sensation in her stomach. Her grandmother had been a girl here, just twenty when she and her husband had fled with Tirzah and Fritz to the Swiss border. Krista could imagine the despair that night as she gathered a small bundle of baby things that would need to last for so many days and nights of hardship while the Nazis, like hounds of hatred, were everywhere. She imagined her trying to keep her small child silent so that fussing and crying would not be noticed. Finally they reached the border to neutral Switzerland—only to be turned back.

How could Stella stand it? How could she live here with the frightening past hovering over and around her like a smothering blanket?

Jorden's voice interrupted: "Stella still hasn't arrived?"

"No. I'm worried," but Meir's voice remained steady.

Krista turned swiftly, looking from one man to the other. "Isn't there any way to check the train stations and the airport?"

"I have," Meir told her. "They haven't anything on Stella Cohen."

"Would she have used another name?" Krista asked hopefully.

"Perhaps," Meir said.

Jorden walked to the phone. "I'll call Franz. She may have decided to stay at St. Moritz after all and wait for me, unaware that I left with Krista."

"She called me from St. Moritz yesterday," Meir said with a trace of doubt in his voice.

Jorden was making the call to Franz. "When was that?"

Krista remembered how Stella tried to call Meir at the Veltlinerkeller.

"Last night around nine o'clock," Meir said.

"She told me she couldn't get through," Krista protested.

"She didn't," Meir said patiently. "But she left a message with Avi. She told him she was being followed. She asked that I meet her in Zurich. I couldn't. Avi wanted me here. That's what has me upset."

Krista turned to Jorden. "Zurich. Then maybe she did plan to take the train here to Vienna. In which case she won't arrive until morning."

Neither Jorden nor Meir appeared satisfied.

"But she hasn't called from Zurich," Meir said. "It seems like she would. She knew I'd be here at the flat."

"You're sure of that?" Jorden asked, still waiting for the call to Franz to go through.

Meir scowled. "I'm sure Avi told her."

"We'd better check with Avi," Jorden said. He stopped. "Franz? Keller here. We're in Vienna at the flat. Stella hasn't arrived. Any news from that end?"

Krista walked over to Jorden.

"You're sure?" Jorden asked Franz. "All right, then. We've lost her somewhere between boarding the train at St. Moritz and Vienna. See what Interpol can come up with, will you? Something may have happened."

Krista felt her hands turn cold with fear. She avoided looking at Meir. She suspected he was in love with Stella. Jorden, she noted, showed nothing, yet she knew he was as anxious as they were. He had risked everything to help Stella in the beginning. Remembering that long mountainous journey from the Engadine to Zurich, with Stella alone and someone following her, left Krista's nerves on edge.

"What of Branden?" Jorden was asking Franz. "He hasn't arrived! I'll let Avi know." He hung up, turned and faced Meir.

"No one has seen Stella since she boarded the train last night. Either she decided to take the train into Austria, or she remained in Zurich for some reason."

"Why would she remain in Zurich?" Krista asked.

"She may have been on to something," Meir hastened. "She's a journalist too, remember."

"Possibly, you have something there," Jorden concluded. He looked at Krista. "She's in the middle of researching her book on the Swiss banking scandal. And Morgenthau, her lawyer, was due to be back in Zurich to meet with Ehrlich von Buren."

"I've checked everything in her office," Meir told Jorden quietly. "I can't see anything amiss. Even the book she's working on is all here."

Jorden walked into the small dining room, and Krista followed. She saw that Stella had turned the table into a workplace. Her computer was there and a stack of messy, pencil-written papers full of hurried notes. Books were everywhere, piled beside her computer, on a side table, on the floor. A half-eaten box of Viennese chocolates sat on her desk along with a coffee mug imprinted with her name. There were photographs, too. She saw one of Stella with Jorden in New York, another of Meir. There was also a snapshot of a bright-eyed Doberman with its pink tongue to one side, looking as if it were smiling.

"Maybe she's at the hospital," Krista said, suddenly hopeful. "She was anxious to get back to see Aunt Tirzah."

Meir looked at her. "I checked an hour ago. She hasn't been there in three days. But she did speak with Tirzah yesterday from St. Moritz."

Jorden looked at Meir. "Has Avi called here?"

"No. Not since I arrived yesterday and he told me about Stella's call."

"What about Elsa von Buren and Paul Gotthard?"

"They're staying at the Vienna Hotel with the housekeeper and her husband. It looks as if that museum showing is on the up and up. Mrs. von Buren is consumed with preparations and Paul has been helping with the arrangements."

"Do they know about Wilhelm's death?"

"Her son has been in touch with her, but if she's grieving over her husband's death she's not letting it interfere with the showing."

Krista looked at Jorden. Elsa's seeming indifference added weight to their earlier conclusions that it was the Gestapo agent named Karl she really loved.

"Anything on Lars?" Jorden asked.

"Nothing. Maybe we're wrong. Maybe he isn't here in Vienna."

Jorden was thoughtful and tense. "Maybe he's in Zurich for some reason." He exchanged a careful glance with Meir. "What about Josef Gotthard. Have you seen him here in Vienna? With Elsa or Paul, for instance?"

Meir took a moment to recall the name. "No. I thought Josef was in Zurich with Ehrlich, taking care of funeral arrangements. Ehrlich is pretty broken up about his father's suicide."

Krista could see that Jorden wasn't satisfied. "You 'thought' he was in Zurich or you know?"

Meir's silence was answer enough. Jorden's jaw tightened. "Call Zurich police," he told Meir. "See what you can find out from our friendly policeman about Josef Gotthard's whereabouts. Ask him to check with Morgenthau as well. See if he's heard from Stella. Morgenthau is staying at the Savoy."

Jorden handed Meir the picture he'd found inside the book jacket. "Who comes to mind when you look at the SS officer beside Elsa von Buren?"

Krista watched Meir alertly. Meir brought the snapshot over to a lamp for a better view. He studied it for a long moment, then shook his head. "Can't be sure. The face is faded. Wait—isn't this other one Wilhelm von Buren?"

"Yes. His real name is Conrad. The Gestapo agent standing beside her is a man named Karl. We think it's really Josef Gotthard."

Meir took a careful second look. "Eichmann's butcher, you think? Well, that's something. Gotthard! I wouldn't have guessed it. He's always stayed in the background."

"Right. Just where he wanted to be, blending in the murky shadows. But Seitz's arrival changed things. Josef is feeling the pressure of a crack in his identity. He may have even killed Conrad—the man we know as Wilhelm. What has me worried now is that he may also try to move on the rest of us, using Lars and some of his East German agents."

"If this is Josef Gotthard," Meir said, "we'll have a hard time proving it without a clear picture of his face."

"I'll show the picture to Avi. He's already ordered the Mossad to begin a new search on Josef. If he is the Gestapo agent named Karl, all we need is his last name and we'll have our Nazi war criminal after all."

"Good work," Meir said with a nod of his head. "Avi will be forgiving."

"Better call Hans Fischer in Berlin as well. We're going to need help. Ziv will be on his way here as soon as he turns Seitz over to Branden, but Kurt Branden hasn't arrived in St. Moritz yet. Something has gone wrong."

Krista stood listening intently, saying nothing. Why hadn't CIA Agent Branden arrived to help Uncle Franz and Ziv? Her mind raced back to something Jorden had just told Meir. She watched thoughtfully as Meir handed Jorden the snapshot. Jorden placed it back in a folder. Her breath caught and she looked at him alertly.

"Wait, Jorden. I just remembered Elsa's photography!"

While Meir went to the telephone, Jorden walked over to her. "Elsa's museum showing, yes. What about it?"

She was so excited she couldn't get the words out fast enough and just stood looking at him.

Jorden looked amused. "Your blue eyes are glittering like a Siamese cat's. What momentous discovery loiters at the back of your mind?"

"Photos," she whispered eagerly. "Two very special pictures that Elsa hid at the von Buren mansion in Zurich."

A brow arched. "What pictures?"

Krista told him about the morning in Zurich when Paul had called her to meet him at the Hauptbahnhoff. "When I was leaving the house I met Elsa. She was in her study with boxes and boxes of her photography work spread out across the floor. She'd just been contacted by the museum to show her work on the war. But she was quite upset because someone, presumably Wilhelm, had been in her study earlier and removed several pictures. At least she couldn't find them and she was angry."

Krista had Jorden's full attention. "Elsa insisted someone had removed two boxes from her storage room. At first she blamed Mrs. Brandt, the housekeeper, and her husband, Willi, but she switched to Wilhelm. When I complimented her work she was pleased. 'Here are my two favorites,' she told me. She brought me to a nearby table filled with stacks of pictures she'd been sorting through. She removed two that she'd apparently hidden behind a large photograph of the Deutsches Reich building. She handed me one of them. 'A friend took this one,' she told me. 'I can't bring myself to destroy it.' I saw Elsa standing with some German SS officers."

Jorden quickly removed the snapshot from the folder he carried. "Anything like this one?"

"Similar, but I don't remember seeing either Wilhelm or Josef. But, Jorden, there was a second photo she didn't show me. She changed her mind. It could be a snapshot of Josef Gotthard."

"What did she do with it, do you remember?" he asked intently.

"Yes, she slipped both pictures back in their hiding place. 'I should not have showed you,' she said. She looked like a guilty child. I'm almost certain she wouldn't have destroyed them or brought them to Vienna for fear someone in the family would have seen them."

"Perhaps they could still be there. What was her reason for hiding them?"

"She was afraid Wilhelm would burn them."

"Or maybe Josef, though she wouldn't have mentioned him at the time."

"Yes. She said something about the two boxes of pictures that were missing. She implied there wasn't anything left in them to destroy. I don't whether she meant she had hidden more pictures from him or if he'd already burned them. She seemed sullen."

"You can be sure Josef and Wilhelm both destroyed anything that might incriminate them. But she may have concealed important evidence. Those two pictures you mentioned, for example. This is one time we can be glad her work means so much to her."

"I don't think Paul knew about them," she said.

"I'm inclined to agree. About those two boxes you say Elsa feared was stolen, did she think Wilhelm took them away?"

"I don't know. She accused Mrs. Brandt. She insisted she call Willi up to her room."

"Ah—now we're getting somewhere. And their response?"

"Mrs. Brandt looked afraid. Willi seemed nervous, but he was in better control."

Jorden was thoughtful. "Yes, it just might be..."

"What might be?" she whispered.

He looked at her. "Avi learned someone from Seitz's camp contacted Willi."

Krista remembered Jorden's conversation with Avi at Franz's apartment in Zurich. There had been something about the chauffeur and Einer Seitz.

"Seitz may have promised Brandt money if he could deliver certain kinds of pictures. Presumably, anything with Josef Gotthard in a Gestapo uniform. That would give weight to Seitz later on if he chose to blackmail Josef. If it's true, it would also account for Elsa's book being at Rhinefelden's and why Paul may have been so anxious to get it back. I doubt if Josef or Wilhelm even knew about that book or the picture she had hidden inside the cover. They would have destroyed it long ago."

"Yes! That makes sense," Krista said. "Elsa could have hidden it in one of those two boxes that Willi took. That's why the housekeeper was so nervous that morning. She must have known what Willi did. Mrs. Brandt was so nervous she tripped, so preoccupied that she didn't notice where she was going. You think Willi sold the boxes of pictures to Seitz?"

Yes. However, I don't think he knew the book was in there."

"But Elsa did."

"Right. And that's why she was upset. She must have told Paul the boxes were missing and that she suspected Willi. Paul must have worked the chauffeur over into confessing. Paul must have contacted Rhinefelden."

"But what about Rhinefelden?" she asked. "He doesn't work for Seitz does he?"

"Seitz informed us that Rhinefelden has had connections with East Germany for years. In other words, the bookshop is a pick-up station. Paul knew it as well as Seitz. Gotthard Enterprises has also used Rhinefelden. I'm beginning to think the man you saw there in the red wig was one of Seitz's men."

"That's why Rhinefelden was afraid?"

"Probably. We haven't asked him because he's useful right now. We're watching him."

"And Seitz used the bookshop to pick up the material from von Buren's chauffeur?"

"Paul must have contacted Rhinefelden about the book when the chauffeur confessed. Seitz didn't even know it was there."

Her eyes narrowed. "And Paul asked *me* to pick it up."

Jorden mused, "Who was in that second picture Elsa decided not to show you?"

"Josef Gotthard?" she breathed. "A clear picture of Karl in an SS uniform standing beside Goering!"

"If it is, we have him. He may not know about it and Elsa isn't about to tell him."

"I know where it is," Krista said excitedly. "No one would suspect me if I went home to the mansion. After all, there's to be a funeral. It's natural for me to show up."

Jorden took firm hold of her. "Oh no, darling, you're not going anywhere. I'll do the searching."

"But you don't know where it's hidden," she protested.

"I can find it easily enough if you draw me small diagram of the room."

"But, Jorden! It's so much easier for me…"

"No, Krista." His fingers tightened on her arms. "Lars is around somewhere. Until he's taken care of you're in danger simply because he hates me."

"But you can't get into the mansion."

"I would remind you, dear heart, that even Ziv paid a secret call inside the house."

"Yes, the picture of Avi and you on Wilhelm, I'd forgotten. But…"

Jorden laid a finger to her lips. "No. Let me handle it." She frowned.

He drew her toward him, enclosing her in his embrace. "I can risk some things that are important, but not you. I just found you. I can't lose you so quickly. You've brought something precious into my life. Something I've never had before. If anything happened to you…"

Krista locked her arms about his neck, looking deeply into warm brown eyes. He kissed her tenderly. "Stay here with Meir. I'll need to decide about Zurich later. First, it's important to call on Tirzah at the hospital. Then I need to meet with Avi. When all that is behind me, I'll come back here. By then Stella may have shown up. Franz will call here also. He seems to think Kurt Branden is in Vienna. Why, we

408 LINDA CHAIKIN

don't know. He should have been in St. Moritz handling Seitz."

She yielded to his arms and sighed. "All right, but I expected to meet Tirzah at the hospital."

"You'll meet her soon enough," and he smiled. "One look at her great-niece and she'll be hoping to bring you back to Queens."

Her eyes clung to his. "I'm more interested in where Jorden Keller wants to bring me when all this is over."

"Anywhere that makes you happy. Just as long as you become Mrs. Keller."

Her heart was full and at peace, at least where their relationship was concerned. "Dallas, Israel, Switzerland— anywhere, as long as I'm with you."

He kissed her again and Meir cleared his throat.

Jorden slowly released her and turned. Meir stood leaning against the door smiling. "Hans is on his way. Zurich police is checking into Stella's whereabouts. And Josef Gotthard booked a flight to Vienna this morning. We think he's on his way to join Elsa and Paul at the hotel. The museum showing begins this weekend."

Krista tensed and looked at Jorden. She thought she knew what he was thinking, that Josef would be meeting with Lars, perhaps prepared to give an order to eliminate Avi.

Jorden looked at his watch. "I've just time to see Tirzah and get over to Avi's apartment. Meir?"

"Yes?"

"Expect Kurt Branden. Something is up with the CIA but no one has explained. Franz will call Branden here."

"And Stella?" Meir asked tonelessly, his eyes reflecting inner worry.

"Let's wait until Zurich gets back with us on what they've found out. Her absence may be something simple. You know Stella as well as I do. Did you contact Morgenthau?" he asked of the lawyer from Tel Aviv.

"He's out. I left a message at the Savoy Hotel."

"Then all we can do is wait."

"The hardest thing of all," Meir complained.

When Jorden had left the flat, Krista watched him catch a taxi from the parlor window. It was drizzling out and the gray street was wet and bleak.

28

Jorden checked at the front desk and asked the unsmiling nurse for Tirzah Cohen's room number. He was told she was on the third floor, room 14.

When he entered, a gray-haired little lady with alert brown eyes stretched a wrinkled hand toward him. "Thank God! I've been wondering where you were."

"Sorry, Tirzah," he said gently, taking her hand between his as he sat down beside the bed. "I've been detained. You have news for me?"

"Yes, but first, did you find my sister's granddaughter, Krista?"

"I found her." Jorden smiled.

"Is she as pretty as those pictures in the magazines?"

"Prettier."

"Why didn't you bring her? We have so much to say to each other."

"You'll have plenty of time to get to know one another. I'm pressed for time, Tirzah. It's crucial you tell me anything about Benjamin Cohen that might help us locate the account number and the Nazi agent who dealt with your father."

She nodded, her hand tightening on his as if she were afraid. She glanced toward the door. "They won't come in will they?"

"No. We have a friend in the CIA watching this room." That was the reason she was still alive, but he didn't tell her that.

He removed the picture from his pocket and handed it to her, bringing a lamp closer. "Ever see this man before?"

Tirzah squinted. "I can't see his face very good, Jorden, do you have a magnifying glass?"

Jorden handed it to her, watching.

"I'm sorry, I can't see him. Is he important?"

Jorden concealed his emotions. "Ever hear your father mention the Gestapo agent?"

Tirzah sighed as she handed the picture and magnifier back. "Our father never talked about the Nazis. He pretended they didn't exist until they came banging on the flat door one Sabbath. They entered, and they struck him with their fists. Judith and I had just enough time to hide under the bed as they came through the door. I remember we were frightened to death that baby Anna would cry and they'd find us."

"Yes, I can imagine. So you don't recall?"

Her eyes brightened. "I do remember something. It's what I wanted to tell you about. I've been lying here for days trying to think of things. Well, there was something strange you should know."

"Suppose you tell me?"

Jorden felt sympathy as he watched the old lady struggle to bring her emotions under control. "Take your time," he soothed. "It's all over now. You're just thinking back. There's nothing to be afraid of."

"Yes…my father received an order to report to the Reich Main Security Office to register Jewish property. The Gestapo made him clean all the latrines belonging to the SS officers with boiling water and acid, using a toothbrush. Then they beat him up because they found a star of David in his pocket—when he came home he was so sick." Tears filled her eyes and ran down her wrinkled cheeks. "He was afraid for me and Judith and the baby…"

Jorden found a tissue and wiped her cheeks, then handed it to her. She blew her nose.

He waited until she could go on.

"He told Judith he hadn't given the Gestapo—" she stopped, her eyes widening as if a memory came flooding back. She tried to lift her gray head from the pillow. Jorden bent over her. "Easy, Tirzah, what do you remember?"

"The Gestapo—yes, father was so pleased he fooled the Nazi beast. That's what he called him," she spoke as if in shock. "And he said his name was Karl Becker."

"Becker," he whispered. "Karl Becker." He paused. "Did he tell the Swiss account number to Judith?"

"Yes, he did. And she told me at the Swiss border but I didn't remember. She wasn't even sure she had it right. Our minds were so full of fear and worry, who cared at that time? We were hunted by mad dogs and it was survival. But—there was something else he did. That's what I remembered and wanted to tell you. That night after Father returned from the Security Office I heard him get out of bed. He could hardly move, but he drug the step-stool inside the closet. Then he did a strange thing. He managed to climb to the top and he had a writing pen in his hand. He wrote something there."

Jorden tried to stay calm. "Where did he write, Tirzah?

"I heard him tell Judith no one ever painted on the top of a closet door. And when it was closed it was invisible. You had to climb up on a step-stool to see it."

Jorden smiled. The top edge.

"He was right, wasn't he?" Tirzah whispered. "The Nazis never looked there."

"No, I'm sure they didn't. And it's my guess no one has since the night Benjamin wrote it. I'll find out. In the meantime you rest, and don't worry. We'll have you out of here in a few days and flying home in style to Queens."

Tirzah looked satisfied and proud of her decision to come to Vienna.

"I did the right thing, didn't I, Jorden? I faced all my nightmares and returned to Negerlegasse."

"You did right, Tirzah." He bent over and kissed her forehead.

He looked down at her as she smiled wearily and closed her eyes to rest. *You did wonderfully*, he thought. *Benjamin and Judith would be proud if they knew. You defied age and fear and returned to face Goliath. And this time, you won. The diabolical Gestapo agent was Karl Becker!*

He left the room to report his findings to Avi and the Israeli director of the Mossad in Tel Aviv.

The telephone rang in the flat and Meir answered it. Krista rose from the chair by the window and hung on his every word. Was it Jorden calling from the hospital or Avi's apartment?

"Stella," Meir said with frustration, "Thank God. Where are you?" he looked over at Krista and gave a high sign of victory. Krista's hand went to her heart. Her cousin was alive.

"Vienna airport? What? You're with *whom*?" Meir asked with a note of displeasure in his voice.

Krista walked toward him, wondering.

"Kurt Branden? Let me talk to him."

But Kurt Branden is the CIA agent, Krista thought. *Why is Meir displeased? Jealousy? What is Kurt Branden like?*

"Yeah? Branden? Meir here." His eyes glittered. "What the thunder is going on, pal? You're supposed to be in St. Moritz handling Seitz. What do you mean 'can't Ziv and Klossner handle him.' Sure they can, but Seitz is your prized turkey. Yeah, sure, so you want to come and lend us a hand, huh? Well, the door's wide open. We're short-handed. Avi's in the cross hairs and we're out-gunned. What do you mean you knew it. Wiseguy."

Krista smiled. So Kurt Branden was another tease. At least Stella was safe.

"Keller is here. Yeah, Hans Fischer is on his way. He should be here by dawn, if not sooner. You're coming here?" He looked at his watch. "How's Stella? What do you mean, you're getting along good? Take it easy, Pal. Yeah, the coffee's on."

He hung up and looked at Krista. He smiled. "They're on their way. Branden says he'll explain when he gets here."

Twenty minutes later Krista heard a car and looked out the window. It was only a delivery truck. She turned away. Jorden must have gone to see Avi after leaving the hospital. There was a rap on the door. Meir opened it. Two repair men walked in. Meir shut the door. One of them was Stella. She smiled as she pulled off her cap and shook out her dark hair, walking quickly to Krista and putting her arms around her.

"Krista, this is Kurt Branden."

"Miss Grendelmier."

Yes, Krista could see why Meir was frowning. Kurt could have passed for Jorden's brother, except his hair was the color of wheat and his eyes were a cobalt blue. He was deeply tanned, muscular, and unsmiling. He scanned her, nodded politely, then walked to the phone. He punched in the numbers, then waited for the call to go through. Meir scowled at him, hands on hips, as if measuring an opponent. Stella headed for the kitchen. "I'll get some coffee, Kurt," she smiled.

"Thanks. Is this Avi?" he said into the receiver. "Branden here. I was told from Berlin you could use a little help in Vienna. Yes, I'm at the flat with Meir. By the way," Kurt glanced at Krista, "where's that recording you owe me?"

Krista felt her face began to flush. She turned her shoulder toward Stella. Now what!

"Now, now, good friend, none of that. A deal's a deal. We'll hash it out later. I just thought I'd let you know you're about to have unwanted company. Someone who has a special interest in Jorden. That's right. Lars himself. He's not alone. Meir and I are on our way." He hung up, turned toward Meir and nodded his head. They both started toward the door. "Sorry about that coffee, Stella. I'll take a rain check." Kurt turned to Krista. He smiled for the first time and his eyes softened. "Lock the door after us, Miss Grendelmier."

She followed them to the door, and slipped the bolt through the lock. She heard their footsteps rushing down the stairs. Krista let out a breath.

"Did they go already?" Stella asked from behind her.

Krista turned worriedly. "Jorden and Avi need help."

Stella's smile faded. "Yes, I thought that was the reason Branden came back with me. Someone must have contacted him."

"Where did you meet up with Kurt Branden?" Krista asked curiously.

"On the train, about an hour after I left St. Moritz. I knew someone was following me, but I never guessed there were two men—one from the CIA."

"Was it Kurt you saw when we were in the Veltlin-erkeller?"

"Yes. I had seen him one other time here in Vienna and he had me worried. He was so handsome too."

"Better not say that in front of Meir. He's been so worried about you. I think he likes you."

Stella looked surprised. "Meir? That's interesting... Anyway, Branden showed up at my compartment on the train. He told me as calmly as if asking to borrow a match that there was someone on the train following me back to Vienna. The man didn't have my best interest in mind, was the way Kurt put it. He guarded me all the way to Zurich, then on the flight here to Vienna."

"What about Einer Seitz? Did Kurt say why he hadn't kept the appointment with Franz and Ziv?"

Stella shook her head. "He was very careful about sharing information."

Krista worried about Kurt showing up because Jorden had balked on the recording. He had implied so on the phone. And yet, he had looked at her kindly when he left with Meir. Maybe he wasn't as hard as everyone thought.

They both jumped when the phone rang. Stella's hands were full with cups of coffee, so Krista went to pick it up. "Hello?"

"Krista?"

"Jorden..."

"Look, darling, I haven't time to explain. I'm still at the hospital. But I want you and Stella to have the Swiss account number. Don't worry, it's just a precaution. Get a step-stool and look on the top edge of the closet door. You should find the number your great-grandfather wrote there. Krista?" he added, his voice calm but tense. "I love you."

"Oh Jorden, I love you too. Please be careful."

"Don't worry. I'll arrive later. Keep that door locked." He hung up quietly.

Her eyes closed and she was praying for his safety, still gripping the receiver when she became aware that Stella stood beside her. They looked at each other. *She heard me say I love him. What will her response be?* But Stella took the receiver from her clenched hand and placed it back in the cradle, showing nothing.

"Better sit down," Stella said.

Krista shook her head. With difficulty she turned to the task at hand. "Jorden learned where Benjamin wrote the account number. You were right, it's here in the flat."

Stella's eyes narrowed with excitement. "Then dear Tirzah must have remembered. Bless her heart. Where!"

"I'll show you. You'll never guess, and I'll wager no one else ever did either. Is there a step-stool here?"

"Yes, in the kitchen."

"Bring it! And a flashlight if you have one."

"In the drawer beside the bed."

Krista sped into the bedroom and looked toward the top of the closet door with wonder. What a clever place to write it.

Stella brought the step-stool. Krista, with flashlight in hand, climbed up until she could look down on the unpainted top edge of the door. She switched on the light and flashed it across the wood. "I'll wipe the dust off—it's here! The number and something else. A name wait, it's in German. Gestapo Karl Becker of the Vermogensverkehstelle."

"That was the Reich Main Security Office here in Vienna," Stella said. She rushed to the drawer and pulled out a sheet of paper and pencil. "Go ahead," she called, "give me the name and number again."

A few minutes later they both stood staring at the sheet of paper where Stella had written the information. "We did it," Stella said. "By George, we did it. And I had almost given up on Tirzah. Bless the memory of Grandfather Benjamin, and God bless Aunt Tirzah. We've got both the account number and the name of the Nazi who helped carry out Eichmann's cruel edicts. Just like wicked Haman in the Book of Esther, events have turned swiftly against Karl Becker."

"Josef Gotthard," Krista informed her.

"What?"

Krista's eyes were grave. "Josef Gotthard is Gestapo agent Karl Becker."

Stella stared at her.

29

Jorden left the Vienna hospital and came down the steps on the narrow path leading to the square. Passing the garden he came toward the main street. Seemingly from nowhere, a dark sedan intercepted his path as the door flung open.

"Inside."

Jorden's hand resting in his jacket pocket gripped his revolver but it was Avi's broad face that greeted him. Jorden slipped into the back seat and barely closed the door before the driver had stepped on the accelerator.

"Branden is here," Avi explained.

"Why isn't he taking care of his own business with Seitz?"

"Seitz is in capable hands. Another CIA agent out of Berlin is ferrying Seitz to safe ground. Ziv is on his way here, and Franz is wrapping up loose ends at St. Moritz."

Jorden watched him. "The CIA got what they wanted?"

"They got it. And we're about to get what we want if you're right about Josef Gotthard. He's under surveillance now. He's on to us. He's made arrangements for a sudden trip to Moscow."

"And we haven't moved to stop him? Once he boards the plane we've lost him!"

Avi tapped his large fingers on his chest, his brown eyes calm. He picked up his cell phone. "One call is all it will take. We must be certain."

"I'm certain! Proof waits at the von Buren mansion. All I need to do is get there."

"Patience. You need to realize the international hue and cry should we nab Josef and bring him to Israel if he is not the war criminal we are looking for."

"It's Gotthard," Jorden insisted. "I'll stake everything on it."

"You may have to. You are in enough trouble already. Branden is here for two reasons. One of which is your refusal to turn over the recording of Krista von Buren."

"Krista Harman Grendelmier," Jorden gritted.

"And soon to be Mrs. Keller no doubt." Avi smiled. "Ah well, a husband and wife team I have always wanted."

"Look, Avi, there's no chance Branden can get anything on her now."

"He's not trying to get anything on her. He just wants answers."

"He can have as many as he wants as long as the CIA doesn't interfere with the Mossad," Jorden said stubbornly. "I've got proof she helped unmask Josef Gotthard as Karl Becker of the SS. I've also got a recording from Franz that nails Paul. What about Josef now? He may be boarding that plane to Moscow."

"The flight doesn't leave for an hour," Avi said calmly. "Let's see that picture."

"This is only one of them." He handed it to him.

"Where's the other one?"

"Krista knows where it is," he said, thinking it would be better for her reputation.

"You think this man in the Gestapo uniform is Karl Becker, alias Josef Gotthard?"

"Yes," Jorden said firmly. "And Conrad was Wilhelm von Buren."

Avi was silent for a minute. "I'm inclined to agree. I'm going to stick my neck out with you and Krista." He reached for the phone and pushed some numbers. "Put a call through to Zurich," he told the other end. "It's Josef Gotthard. Take him alive for a trial in Israel." He hung up.

Jorden relaxed a little.

Avi settled back into the seat. "You owe Branden."

The suggestion surprised Jorden. He looked at him. "For what?"

"He's been following Lars from St. Moritz to Zurich and then here to Vienna. He intervened to safeguard Stella on the train, rather than go on to the safehouse to collect Seitz."

Jorden was silent. So that was part of the reason why Kurt was here.

"It isn't me Lars wanted so badly, even though the snapshot Ziv got from von Buren's body was taken by Lars' camera. He appears to have switched plans. He has another prey. Branden came to Vienna to warn us, to avert a tragedy."

Jorden tensed. His mind surged ahead and he believed he knew what Avi was going to say.

"I've just gotten word that Lars is on his way to the flat on Negerlegasse."

Jorden stared at him, feeling helpless and angry.

Avi laid a restraining hand on his arm as if he expected him to lean forward and shout at the Interpol agent to drive faster. "Nice and easy. We've got Lars under surveillance. Kurt and Meir parked the repair truck a block away and doubled back."

All that was fine, but Jorden knew he had to assume that Lars wasn't that easily fooled. And when Lars grew suspicious, he would usually retreat, then wait for another opportunity to strike.

Krista and Stella are unguarded in the flat. Lars has it just the way he wants it. But Krista isn't alone. The thought crossed his mind that she would never be truly alone. Not as long as the Spirit of Christ was with her.

Jorden thought that this was where his new faith would surely be tested. If anything happened to her, he didn't think he could emerge unscathed from the scars it would leave in his heart. Though he believed that Christ would be sufficient for any loss, he quickly prayed that the Lord would not need to show that sufficiency now.

As the sedan neared Negerlegasse street, Jorden was thinking that even if they survived this moment, there would be other times like this in the future, just as long as he worked for the Mossad. Krista would always be in danger of men like Lars. And he would be needing to face them.

The sedan stopped on the corner, and Jorden climbed out quickly and merged among the cramped buildings.

A few minutes later he entered the building through narrow porch steps up to the first floor tenement laundry. He took the hall to a vacant room that Avi had told him about. When he slipped through the door, he saw Meir at the window facing the street.

"Where's Branden?"

"In the building across the street. He'll let us know if Lars approaches."

"I'm surprised he's with us. He hasn't assisted before."
But then the problem with the Swiss Banks, Nazis, espionage, and Seitz was complicated enough to get help, even if he was CIA. There was also cooperation from the Swiss police and Interpol.

"Good thing he is," Meir said.

Jorden agreed. He saw the two-way radio on the scarred stand by the window. He picked it up and called Branden.

"Keller, here. All set. Anything at your end?"

"Too quiet. Hope he didn't smell a trap and inch off."

"By the way, thanks for the warning. I owe you."

"I'll remember that, keep you on call...There's some movement now. Your man's on the way. Can you handle it?"

At a time like this, he wants to joke. "Just keep your watch. Out."

Jorden set the transceiver on the table, glanced out the window but saw nothing yet, then moved to the door. He opened it and glanced out, getting his bearings. There were stairs down to the main entrance from the street. A second stairway led to the flat where Krista and Stella waited, unaware.

Lars smiled to himself as he watched two men leave the tenement building, get into the delivery truck and drive away. Fools, he thought. But that is the way he had wanted it. While Keller, the CIA agent, and their Jewish friend rushed across Vienna to protect the Mossad director, he was free to enter the Cohen flat undetected. When Keller got back to the flat he would have a bloody surprise. Lars smiled grimly. Such luck! He hadn't expected to have both women together at one time. He would kill the Jewish woman as well as the model—double revenge. His eyes narrowed as his thoughts raced unchecked. Yes, Keller would pay a heavy price.

Lars stepped from the building across the narrow cobbled street and glanced up at the window in the Negerlegasse flat. It was dusk and one of the women was drawing the curtains. With his hands in his jacket pockets, Lars walked across the shiny, wet cobbles toward the building housing the flat.

"Here he comes," Meir told Jorden in a low voice. "He's stepped out from the building. He's glancing around and lighting a cigarette. He's looked up at Stella's window. He knows where he's going all right. The swine. Let me get him, Jorden. He planned to kill Stella on the train from St. Moritz. I'll blow his..."

"Take it easy! You're angry."

Meir seemed to snap out of it. He drew in a breath and slowly nodded. "I'll be all right," he said flatly.

Jorden watched him, his eyes narrowing. "Take your place upstairs," he said quietly.

Meir left the window, passed through the door and silently went up the steps. He disappeared into the corridor's shadows, waiting, crouching near the balustrade where he could just see the bend in the second floor stairway before the second floor landing. If Lars somehow got past Jorden, Meir would get his chance before Lars could reach Stella's door. Jorden intended to stop him first.

Jorden waited just inside the open door, the powerful .38 with its silencer in hand. The terrorist he had first encountered in Lebanon would take the stairs from the street level and pass by here to reach the stairway to the second floor.

He stopped. Someone had entered. Cautious footsteps sounded, then paused below the steps.

Jorden waited, counting Lars' footsteps, listening, envisioning each of Lars' movements.

Lars started up the steps, but stopped again.

Something made him hesitate. Had Meir given his position away? It was dangerous to work with an angry man. Jorden reminded himself to keep a lid on his own emotions. The day he could no longer do so was the day he must quit the Mossad.

But there was no sound from the corridor above where Meir waited. Lars was uncanny, as though sensing danger on the breeze.

Only silence. For a moment Jorden thought he had backed off. He was about to go after him, but the footsteps sounded again, inching up the stairs.

In Jorden's mind there flashed a moment when, like Meir, he could envision Nazi soldiers stomping up the steps to terrorize the Jews living in this same tenement. The old building had witnessed a great deal of anguish.

It was time. Jorden stood with his door open and stepped partially out, pistol aimed steady with both hands. "Halt!" he shouted in German, his ruthless voice startling Lars, setting him off guard.

Lars was just a few steps below the landing, gun in hand. He momentarily froze, then dropped into a crouch, firing wildly, his blue eyes startled to see the one man he hadn't expected. Jorden fired one accurate shot and moved behind his doorjamb as old plaster shattered around him. Lars crumpled backwards from the impact and toppled. His body came to rest on the bottom steps, his eyes staring fiercely at nothing.

Meir came running, clambering down the steps past Jorden and stood over Lars. His lips compressed. "Dead." His arm lowered to his side.

Jorden heard doors opening and feet rushing. A woman in a bathrobe, her hair rolled in curlers, stared down toward Meir with a scowl, but she evidently had forgotten her glasses for she didn't appear to see Lars at first.

"What was that noise?" she cried in German.

"What noise?" Jorden called up calmly.

She looked puzzled as her eyes came to the body. "The man fainted?"

"Yes, he fainted," Meir called up, and stooped beside him. He took off his jacket and dropped it over his face and chest. "Come along, pal, we'd better get you out of here."

Others rushed to the stairway. "Jorden…"

Jorden saw Krista coming down from the second floor with a surprised expression on her face. Stella joined her. "I thought you two…" she began, then stopped when she saw Meir lifting the body. She reacted at once, coming down the stairs. "Poor man fainted? Better put him in the laundry room. Here, I'll show you…"

Jorden went up the steps to Krista, and she came toward him, her eyes searching his. "Lars?" she whispered knowingly.

He nodded.

Her eyes closed and she relaxed into his arms as though it dawned on her what might have been, but had not. He held her tightly. "It's over now."

The von Buren mansion was empty and still when Krista arrived with Jorden from Vienna. He followed her up the stairs and down the hallway to the room that Elsa had turned into her studio. Jorden switched on the lights and a golden glow added warmth. For a moment Krista stood facing old World War II photos on the walls. Distaste filled her heart. She walked swiftly to the display.

Were the photographs still there? At this very hour Josef Gotthard was secretly being abducted by the Mossad for a flight to Israel, while the CIA and the Swiss secret police looked the other way. If the pictures weren't there—

Her eyes met Jorden's, then Krista held her breath and removed two pictures from behind a large photograph of the building for the Deutsches Reich. She handed them to Jorden and watched his face for the answer. She saw him study the first, showing nothing. Then he looked at the second picture and his dark eyes flickered. "We've got him—Karl Becker." He handed her the picture. A young Josef Gotthard stared back in full Gestapo regalia. Beside him stood a smiling Elsa looking up at him with adoring eyes.

Epilogue

U ncle Franz's apartment at the University lodge was warm and safe, with a comfortable fire sputtering in the hearth. Lamps glowed their welcome, and Trudy, visiting Zurich, had brought in a fresh, warm ginger cake with applesauce. Outside, through the large front window facing the college green, the April moon gleamed full and silvery in a clear black sky. On Krista's left hand a diamond engagement ring glittered. She stood with Jorden in front of the window while Trudy laughed with Uncle Franz, who insisted on cutting the cake. Trudy poured tea and coffee, and as she did her own engagement ring from Franz shimmered. There was a glow to her eyes and her golden hair was brushed softly into a chignon, which added a new prettiness to her face.

Krista, looking at Trudy, thought that hers was a beauty that transcended outward appearance. Trudy would be lovely at seventy! And what's more, Franz would always think so since he had fallen in love with who she was, not with what she looked like.

But the conversation soon turned to serious matters again as the evening wore on.

"They arrested Paul today," Franz announced.

Krista felt Jorden's glance, as if he wondered how she would take the news.

"Good," she said heartlessly. "I hope they lock him up for twenty years."

"They'll keep him longer than that," Jorden said. "He shot an Interpol agent in Paris trying to get away."

Paul had managed to escape Vienna back in February with two of the agents who had worked with him and Josef. He got through Austria undetected into France. Uncle Franz had been working with Interpol for two months trying to track him down, and his perseverance had finally paid off. He had not forgiven Paul for risking Krista to carry out his espionage and to deliver cyanide to Ahmed.

"What will happen to Elsa?" asked Trudy.

"She's likely to get light handling," Jorden said. "Apart from helping to conceal Josef's identity she wasn't involved in the espionage or killings through Gotthard Enterprises. At any rate, she doesn't need to testify against her husband."

"She's a broken woman now anyway," Franz said with a trace of pity in his voice. "She's left all alone with her prized pictures of Nazis. I suspect they'll be little comfort in the dark of night. She's lost the only other things in life she cared about, Karl, and her grandson, Paul."

"The harvest is bitter when it comes at last," Trudy said sadly. "It's not that I feel sorry for her, but it's sad when anyone goes on in life ignoring God and building a life on wood, hay, and stubble. One day they will go up in flames, then what will she have left? What will anyone have left without a relationship with the One who made and loves them?"

"Well said," Krista agreed. "There is nothing in the end, when everything in our lives is built upon the perishable."

"Einer Seitz will learn that too," Jorden said, taking the cup of coffee Krista brought him with a plate of cake. "I doubt if he's enjoying Havana all that much."

Krista wasn't thinking of Seitz but of Cousin Stella, feeling thankful that matters had turned out well for her and Meir. Stella had written from Vienna telling her that she and Meir were seeing each other and getting serious. She had finished her book on the Cohen family and was making plans to return to Queens. Great-Aunt Tirzah had recovered and had already left Europe for home. Krista had visited her in February in Vienna and was looking forward to seeing her again in New York.

Ehrlich von Buren had located Benjamin's bank account and Jorden said the money would be divided between the different members of the Cohen family that lived in America. Krista had refused her share, turning it over to the Jewish Holocaust Fund. It was enough that she had her grandmother's ring and a Mossad agent who was starting on his second piece of ginger cake. She smiled to herself. They would be married on May 1st and, except for plans to honeymoon in Paris, the future remained open. They had been praying recently about what the Lord might want them to do. So far, Jorden hadn't felt the need to leave the Mossad, but he was willing. Krista wasn't certain either. Her own career remained undecided. The cuts on her face had healed nicely, but her interest in modeling was ebbing. Avi teased her about working for him, and while Krista toyed with the idea, finding it intriguing, she knew Jorden hadn't been won over. Where they would live after their

Paris honeymoon was still undecided. Naturally, Uncle Franz wheedled and teased Jorden to settle in Zurich. Jorden hadn't said yes or no. If he did stay in the secret police, Krista believed he would want her safely within reach of Franz and Trudy.

As for Cousin Henrich and Veena, they both had been so upset over Veena's failure that Krista had forgiven her. She had written and even joked about the bump on her head finally going flat. Then she had given her the verse in Ephesians. "And be kind to one another, tenderhearted, forgiving one another, just as God in Christ forgave you." Krista hoped and prayed the words would soften Veena's heart to turn to Jesus.

"I never did learn who killed Wilhelm," Trudy said unexpectedly, and the mood swerved back to one of sobriety.

"Mrs. Brandt confessed that it was Josef Gotthard. Wilhelm was panicking over the Swiss Banking scandal and threatening to tell the truth to safeguard his son, Ehrlich."

"Whatever happened to Mrs. Brandt and Willi?" Krista asked.

"They'll go to trial soon. Seitz has passed on enough information about their cooperation in espionage to send them both behind bars."

"Then it was the housekeeper and chauffeur who were trying to sell the pictures and book to Agent Seitz?" Trudy asked.

"It was," Jorden said. "The pictures were worthless, however. Josef and Wilhelm had managed to destroy any evidence linking them to Eichmann years ago. All except for the photo in the book, and the ones Krista discovered for us in Elsa's studio."

"But why did Paul hide the book here in Franz's apartment?" Krista asked. "I would have expected him to bring the book with the picture to Elsa."

"He would have, but something unexpected came up that altered his course," Franz said quietly.

She saw Jorden exchange glances with Franz. Obviously they were deciding how much more they could tell her and Trudy. As if on cue, Trudy stood from the sofa, gathered the dessert plates and made a polite excuse about getting them out of the way. It would have been easy for Krista to offer to help Trudy, but curiosity wouldn't release her.

"Then I'm not supposed to ask," she told them, "even though I know so much already."

"Yes, too much," Jorden said dryly. "And still wanting to know more—it's dangerous."

"Now, Jorden, I don't see why I shouldn't ask, unless it's so secret that you're both committed to silence."

Franz smiled and looked at Jorden. Jorden walked over to the window. "The answer to why he hid it here rests with Hans Fischer," Jorden said.

Hans Fischer? Confused, she walked over to Jorden.

"He's a double agent," he admitted darkly.

Her heart went cold. The tone of his voice appeared to imply that Hans must have escaped arrest in Vienna, or perhaps that he hadn't even come in response to Meir's phone call from Stella's apartment. A double agent...She was remembering how Hans had lent his house to Jorden in Zurich, and he had supposedly aided Jorden when they were attacked. It was all a ruse.

"Then could Hans have planned to have you killed there?" she whispered.

"Yes, and perhaps Stella as well."

And herself? But Jorden looked away as though he didn't want to add credence to her suspicions.

"Then when I noticed him that morning at the Hauptbahnhoff, he really was working for the other side," she stated, remembering the terror she had felt when meeting those hard gray eyes up close. "But when he showed up at the house after the shooting he appeared to be friendly."

"And clever," Jorden said. "I trusted him because the CIA did. I've known him for two years. Even Avi trusted him. Not to mention Kurt." Jorden frowned. "Hans probably removed something important from the body of one of his own men when he searched him."

"Where is he now?" she asked in a low, tense voice.

"We don't know for certain," Franz admitted, "but he's left Zurich."

Jorden took hold of her hands. His eyes told her not to worry. "He fled Berlin after Meir called him from Stella's apartment. As soon as he knew we were on to Josef Gotthard, Hans realized things were falling apart for him as well. To save his own neck he acted while he had the chance."

"Do they have any idea where he went?"

He hesitated. "The CIA is working on it—that is, Kurt Branden is. They've traced him to Athens and the Isles of Greece.

"You're not going there," she whispered, her hands holding his tightly.

"No, fortunately Hans is Kurt Branden's problem now, I don't envy him."

"The CIA is still questioning Paul," Franz said. They may get more out of him that will help Kurt track him down."

"Let's hope the price is not another safe passage to Havana," Jorden remarked.

Franz scowled. "I don't think it will work as easily for Paul as it did for Seitz."

"Did Paul and Hans Fischer cooperate about Elsa's book?" she asked.

"Paul insists Elsa asked for help when she realized the book was missing. Paul was going to bring it to Elsa but things went badly when Hans Fischer learned about the boxes of Nazi pictures delivered to Seitz. Hans' interest was in protecting Josef and Gotthard Enterprises. Paul claims he was to meet Hans the morning you brought the book here from Rhinefelden's, but Hans' arrival in Zurich was late."

"So Paul concealed it here," she said, looking over at her uncle's library shelf, reliving the moment when he had hid it among Franz's books.

"Yes, he left it in a secure, and most unlikely, spot."

"Under my very nose," Franz grumbled, lighting his pipe.

Krista blushed. "I'm sorry, Uncle."

His eyes twinkled. "But in the long run it was better he did leave it here. Had he brought it to the von Buren mansion, it would have been turned over to Hans soon after his arrival. Though we might still have the two pictures Elsa hid at the house, the book set us on the path that revealed the true identity of Wilhelm."

"Paul always used you as his courier," Jorden said coldly. "Remember when he left you early the morning of Franz's birthday?"

"Yes," she mused, "I assumed he had to keep an appointment with Wilhelm or Ehrlich at the bank."

"That was an alibi he had already arranged should anyone inquire later about his schedule of events that morning," Jorden said. "His plan had been to meet Hans and turn over the book, but he received word shortly before he arrived that Hans was detained in Vienna. He might have called it all off for another day, but by then you were already on your way to the bookshop."

"Then Hans didn't arrive until the morning I noticed him at the train station?"

"Yes."

And since Paul didn't want to get caught with evidence, concealing it here at the last moment was safer than carrying it around with him or bringing it to the von Buren mansion.

The unexpected debacle at Hans Fischer's house had followed, along with her sudden return to the apartment before going to St. Moritz. The events had foiled Paul from coming back and turning the book over to Hans.

She thought back to Paul's strange response when she had reminded him here in the apartment that morning that someone had been following her as clear back as their visit to Rome and Venice. Paul had frowned, behaving as though the information was new. He had claimed he didn't recall her telling him, but she had. The man must have been Hans, and Paul was privy to it all along.

"Then Paul's concern when I called him from the station was also false," she said shortly. "He pretended to be worried, but he knew it was Hans."

"He'd been cooperating with Hans Fischer all along," Jorden said. "I'm beginning to think Hans was the source of information for Lars in the Middle East. He has friends there. Kurt has his work cut out for him in Greece."

She thought of the man she had met briefly in Stella's apartment in Vienna. Kurt hadn't appeared as cold and unfeeling as she had imagined him to be. She wondered what he was really like behind that hard CIA veneer. She was relieved that Kurt had changed his mind about the recording after becoming convinced of her allegiance. The last she had seen of Kurt had been in Vienna. He would be taking a vacation, Jorden had told her, preparing for his next assignment. And one thing was for sure, if Jorden was right about Kurt's difficulties in tracking down Hans Fischer, she was thankful that Jorden wouldn't be working with him this time.

"One thing more," he told her. "We now think it was Hans who arranged for Flanders' death in Liechtenstein." He held her close. "It was I who told him where I was going when we talked out in the hall."

The feeling of relief that washed over Krista was immense. As she hugged Jorden tightly she could only feel gratitude that Flanders' death was not her fault. It was the last thing she needed to know.

As the evening wore on, Jorden took Krista's coat from the peg and helped her into it. "I feel like a walk," he said.

Although the April night was chill, the breeze was pleasant and the sky clear. As they walked downhill toward the lake and the Uto Quai, they slipped their arms around each other in comfortable silence.

Lights from the houses and hotels that overlooked the lake were shining brightly on the black water. In the distance the ice-rimmed peaks of Switzerland rose tall and rugged.

They came to the Uto Quai and stood in silence looking out at the little boats. Jorden lifted her hand where the engagement ring sparkled and kissed it. He smiled and drew her into his arms. "You're the best thing about Switzerland. Sometimes I think you belong here: to the snow, the ski slopes, the apple strudel."

She laughed. "Just as long as I belong to you, and we both belong to the Messiah."

His eyes reflected pleasure and joy as he held her in his arms with the back drop of the stars, the lake, and the snowy mountains. "Those are two decisions you can be sure I've made—the first for the rest of my life, the second for all eternity."

She smiled and took his hand. He grasped it warmly, tightly, and they walked on in the moonlight together.

Harvest House Publishers

For the Best in Inspirational Fiction

Linda Chaikin

TRADE WINDS

Captive Heart
Silver Dreams
Island Bride

A DAY TO REMEMBER

Monday's Child

Virginia Gaffney

THE RICHMOND CHRONICLES

Under the Southern Moon
Magnolia Dreams

Maryann Minatra

THE ALCOTT LEGACY

The Masterpiece

LEGACY OF HONOR

Before Night Falls

Lisa Samson

THE HIGHLANDERS

The Highlander and His Lady
The Legend of Robin Brodie

G. Roger Corey

In A Mirror Dimly
Eden Springs

Melody Carlson

A Place to Come Home to

Lori Wick

A PLACE CALLED HOME

A Place Called Home
A Song for Silas
The Long Road Home
A Gathering of Memories

THE CALIFORNIANS

Whatever Tomorrow Brings
As Time Goes By
Sean Donovan
Donovan's Daughter

KENSINGTON CHRONICLES

The Hawk and the Jewel
Wings of the Morning
Who Brings Forth the Wind
The Knight and the Dove

ROCKY MOUNTAIN MEMORIES

Where the Wild Rose Blooms
Whispers of Moonlight
To Know Her by Name
Promise Me Tomorrow

THE YELLOW ROSE TRILOGY

Every Little Thing About You

CONTEMPORARY FICTION

Sophie's Heart
Beyond the Picket Fence
The Princess

	DATE DUE		
MAR 0 4 1991			
Jan 17			